P9-CMO-212

M Grimes
Grimes, Martha
Rainbow's end /
Alfred A. Knopf,
c1995.

DATE DUE

MYNDERSE LIBRARY

Seneca Falls, N.Y.

ALSO BY MARTHA GRIMES

The Horse You Came In On
The End of the Pier
The Old Contemptibles
The Old Silent
The Five Bells & Bladebone
I Am the Only Running Footman
Help the Poor Struggler
The Deer Leap
Jerusalem Inn
The Dirty Duck
The Anodyne Necklace
The Old Fox Deceiv'd
The Man with a Load of Mischief

POETRY

Send Bygraves

Rainbow's End

Rainbow's End

A RICHARD JURY NOVEL

MARTHA GRIMES

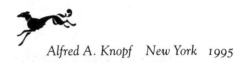

Alfred A. Knopf   New York   1995

THIS IS A BORZOI BOOK
PUBLISHED BY ALFRED A. KNOPF, INC.

Copyright © 1995 by Martha Grimes

All rights reserved under International and Pan-American Copyright Conventions. Published in the United States by Alfred A. Knopf, Inc., New York, and simultaneously in Canada by Random House of Canada Limited, Toronto. Distributed by Random House, Inc., New York.

Library of Congress Cataloging-in-Publication Data

Grimes, Martha.
   Rainbow's end : a Richard Jury novel / Martha Grimes. — 1st ed.
      p.   cm.
   1. Jury, Richard (Fictitious character)—Fiction.   2. British—New Mexico—Santa Fe—Fiction.   3. Police—England—Fiction.   4. Santa Fe (N.M.)—Fiction.   I. Title.
PS3557.R48998R3   1995
813'.54—dc20   94-48876
                             CIP

Manufactured in the United States of America
First Edition

M

MYNDERSE LIBRARY
31 Fall Street
Seneca Falls, New York 13148

Diane's

Acknowledgments

My very deep thanks to Dr. Elizabeth Martin, pathologist at Northern Virginia Doctor's Hospital, for her valuable medical assistance.

Sunrise, Salisbury

He could work out how the men went about it, but how about the women? Made Trevor smile, that did. Great square wells these garderobes were, and no delicate sign directing you to Gents/Ladies. Made Trevor laugh as he walked round the fortress, high up on the ramparts, smoking his first cigarette of the day. He tried to ration himself, no more than ten per. Hard. Helped to have a sense of humor, and he went back to thinking about the privies. It was all for one and one for all, never mind you had to drop your trousers or lift your skirts. It was a bit of a game with Trevor. At every stop, the postern gate and the Bishop's Palace, he'd try to place himself back in Roman times, pretend he was one of them. Imagined himself as a palace guard one time, maybe working in the bakehouse another time—he could really throw himself into these roles, he could. Trevor considered himself a student of history, and if things'd been different when he was young, he could've seen himself at university, reading history, maybe making a name for himself. Oh well. No use crying over spilt milk. Most he could do now was read it on his own. Plenty of time for that, now he'd retired. Selling the tickets here two days a week and having his little tour groups several more days a week, at least in summer, for that's when the tourists came to Salisbury. All that could keep a fellow busy. Out of the house and out from under the wife's feet. Out of the house, that was a blessing.

He was up above Bishop Roger's Palace now, high enough that you really caught that north wind, so he turned up his collar and shoved his mittened hands down in his pockets. February and cold as blazes at this hour. Not that he had to be here at this hour; of course, he didn't. February was a grim old month, wasn't it? Could be depressing if you let yourself sink into it.

There was going to be a storm. Trevor could smell the rain long before he heard the thunder. It was that uneven hour just before first light. He loved to see the first flat seam of gold along the horizon make the distant hills behind Salisbury shine like ice hills. Trev thought of the Ice Age. A hundred thousand years ago most of the earth's surface was ice. He tried to imagine a world locked in ice. He tried to think "a hundred thousand years ago." But his spinning mental globe could not conceive of such distances of time and space. Bloody hell, he could barely get a mental image of the distance between here and Salisbury.

Freddie Lake, who shared the ticket kiosk with him, disliked the job, found it boring, too much sameness day in, day out. Nothing to look at but bloody broken walls and tourists. Well, you needed imagination, too, besides your sense of humor to get on in any job, certainly this one. Just what he'd said to Freddie: It needs imagination, boyo.

Lightning struck far off, ornamental. Rain was still pretty far away. But it would come. Hard to judge distances here. Another streak lit up the spire of Salisbury Cathedral. Beautiful, if you had an eye for the arty stuff, and he did. If not history, he should have gone into the arts, have followed some artistic pursuit. Yes, he could appreciate these sunrises, these sunsets. He watched now as the edge of gold, a false light, diminished, diffused into milkiness and almost disappeared. He was one to appreciate Nature, he was. Always had been.

He doused his cigarette, wishing he'd waited a bit before lighting up, and blew on his hands, making a bellows of them. Fingers would be frostbitten, handing out the tickets. There wouldn't be many tourists today, not in bloody February.

Trevor was coming up on what had struck his funnybone now, one of the garderobes, just fancy Middle Ages language for cesspits. There were several of them around the site; this was the one just inside the wall that was probably for the guards. Never failed to give him a chuckle, the privies. He walked down the hill a few feet, came to the iron balustrade put up around the big square hole to keep people from falling in. Or maybe pissing in it. What a laugh.

He leaned over the iron railing, looked down as far as he could. God, imagine getting out of bed some February morning and having to drag your freezing feet along stone highways and byways until you got to this lot. Trev wondered why it'd taken so long to invent plumbing. Not that plumbing was all that great, either, having to yank on the bloody chain. When it came to the toilet in his house, that meant yanking more than once.

He squinted and leaned over the garderobe a bit farther. Eyes not what they used to be, so he could be wrong.

He wasn't wrong: down there in the thick shadows, at the bottom, something lay. He tried to tell himself it couldn't be a body, not down there, only he knew it was.

Trevor reared back so abruptly he nearly fell himself, but backward. He started to shout and knew it would be useless; there was nobody within a mile to hear him. He turned in a circle, turned again, as if a ritual were needed to tell him what to do. *Come on, boyo, a bit of brainpower, a bit of backbone, that's what's needed; don't fall apart like an old woman.* The ticket kiosk, of course. That had a telephone. Get the hospital; no, get the police—whoever's down there doesn't need an ambulance, not now.

He started running, pausing just a second to slip another cigarette into his mouth with shaking hands. *Be the death of me, these things will.*

2

IT WAS limelight time for Trevor Hastings, and after the initial shocks and shakes, he was hoping he was making the most of it. It wasn't until this Detective Chief Inspector Rush of the Wiltshire CID arrived in his black car and his black raincoat that Trevor began to get nervous. The DCI was pulling his raincoat pockets so tight together you might have thought he was a flasher. Only nothing flashed from Chief Inspector Rush, not from his body, not from his face.

And even then, it wasn't until DCI Rush had put a number of tight-lipped questions to Trevor that Trevor finally twigged it: he himself was looking suspicious. *His* presence here suspicious? Bloody hell, *he* had done no more than his civic duty, calling the police. He could have just disappeared, never called anyone, just got in his mini and driven away. *Would* have disappeared, wouldn't he, if he'd pushed whoever it was down there, right?

Nevertheless, Trevor was asked—no, *told*—to stay. As if he was a damned dog. *Stay.* The medical examiner hadn't finished the examination yet; it had taken a bloody long time to winch the body up from that cavernous enclosure. *Privy,* Trevor had told them. This was a

Roman fortress, this was Old Sarum, had they never been here? Lord, the country's fate was in the hands of those who didn't know history. DCI Rush told him to "keep yourself available," one of those ways the coppers had of talking just before they slammed you in the nick. Bloody hell.

Trev had gone off to the ticket kiosk to warm himself. Let those ones out there stomping all over the icy grass get the frostbite. Ordering honest citizens around. And that poor pile of broken bones ought to make them realize she'd been dead awhile, could have been for days, not pushed over the iron balustrade early this morning.

He stamped his feet to shake some warmth into his toes. Trevor was more incensed than scared. The nerve. Bloody great hulks of blue-bottles can't see past their noses. That body could have lain there for days, well, for one or two, easily, as there'd been not but a handful of visitors. It was February, after all, and what tourists there were were over having a deco at Stonehenge, not bothering with Old Sarum, which Trev personally believed was a lot more interesting. Now his ire was rising at the tourists. If they'd been here at Old Sarum instead of gallivanting round Stone-bloody-henge, well, he'd have been spared the stupid insinuations of the Wiltshire constabulary.

Trev blew on his hands, thinking what a tale he'd have to tell, and him at the center of it. Make the wife perk up those cloth ears of hers, it would. "Oh, forgot to tell you. I found a dead body at the site. Must've fallen down one of the latrines." And not even look up from his Daily Mirror when he said it. Casual, as if dead bodies turned up every day at Old Sarum. Maybe then she'd feel she owed him a good listen for a change.

Detective Chief Inspector Rush obviously felt he didn't owe Trevor a damned thing, least of all an apology after the pathologist had made it clear the woman had died twelve hours ago at the very least. Rush told Trevor this while he stood outside the booth, the black coat still pulled tight, drawing his shoulders down; the eyes still flat and dark. Hard as nails, this one, thought Trev, as the chief inspector told him all of this.

"Twelve to fourteen hours would have put her here late yesterday afternoon. Assuming she was a visitor. You remember her?"

"Well, I wouldn't know, would I? Seeing as how I haven't had a look at her." Trev congratulated himself for this retort. Two could play at this game, they could.

Except Chief Inspector Rush didn't look as if he was playing, as he stood there in that coruscating flash of lightning that made ghostly shadows across his face. He seemed to be weighing up the risk of allowing a noncopper to view the body. "Come along, then."

Trevor was sorry he'd opened his mouth.

ODD, he thought, standing with the others in the sullen gray light, looking down at the body of the dead woman. Odd that she didn't look, well, more *dead*. A fall like that? She lay facedown, or, rather, with only the side of her face showing. Except for the bruising on her cheek and the forearm twisted that way, she looked . . . *asleep*. Trevor always hated it when people described a corpse that way. Mavis always did. *"Might've been asleep, ever so natural he looked."* But there it was, that's how the dead woman looked. Even though he knew she must be all broken bones inside those jeans, that jacket. Trevor nodded, cleared his throat, tried to keep his reaction calm as the policeman's. He said, "That's her. Came just before dark."

"It didn't register on you that she never left?" asked Rush.

Defensively, Trev answered, "No reason it should do, is there? We sell them tickets; we don't wipe their bums for 'em."

Rush's eyebrow moved up fractionally, but he said nothing.

Trevor pointed to a short trail of worn grass leading away from the garderobe and up the hill. "See over there? Those rubbed-out places from where people like to cut up to the top. Well, that's dangerous, that is. I'm surprised more haven't slid and lost their balance. Nearly did myself once or twice."

Rush looked at the footprints worn into the grass. After a few moments of concentration, he said, "I don't think so. Either pitched into it or was pitched into it." He didn't elaborate.

Oh, sod off, thought Trev, and how do you work that out? "Should save my breath to cool my porridge," that's what Mavis was always saying. For once, Trev agreed with her. He crossed his arms hard against his chest, defying DCI Rush to ask another question.

Which he did. "Have you any recollection of who else was here and bought a ticket around the same time? Or had one of those National Trust passes?"

"Friends of the Trust, you mean." Trevor looked down again at the prone figure. "Well, I guess there might have been a handful, but off the top, no, I can't say I remember anyone particular. Maybe Freddie remembers." God, but this lot seemed determined to make it out to be "foul play," as they said.

Poor girl. To have her life snuffed out just by taking a wrong step. At least, that's what he supposed had happened, in spite of what this sorry lot thought. It just went to show. You never know when your number's up. Wake up in the morning, right as rain, sun shining, and gone by nightfall.

And here again came the sunrise. He looked down at the city which seemed to smoke in the distance, mist rising from the corrugated rows of pitched rooftops, the stacked chimney pots. The sun wrapped a veil of light round the spire of Salisbury Cathedral, which looked, for a few moments, dipped in silver.

Pretty, that, thought Trev, only half hearing DCI Rush's words. "Sorry. What?"

"She was American."

Trevor thought the copper said it in a brooding sort of way. "Well, seeing an American at Old Sarum isn't exactly like seeing a brontosaurus. We get a lot of them."

Rush thought for a moment and then said, "We won't detain you any longer."

Before Trevor could reply, the policeman had turned away to talk to the medical examiner, who Trev now realized was female. A woman, good Lord.

The sun shone brighter now, furring the outlines of the policemen standing near the edge of the garderobe. Trev thought: like they was taking turns taking a piss. He drew up the collar of his anorak and started down the incline. Well, there'd be no tickets sold today. He had to admit he was almost sad to go, away from the drama, back to his ancient mini, his terraced cottage (two up and two down, the kids were all gone) in Endless Street, and the weak bulb that Mavis kept in his reading lamp what with all of her penny-saved frugalities.

He stopped to light his third cigarette, allowing himself one or two extra today; after all, it'd been a hell of a morning. As he flicked the match away and continued walking he ran through his story to Mavis. And wouldn't she get a kick out of learning the medical examiner was a lady? A lady going down into that pit and messing about with a dead body.

What women got up to these days.

"Janet Leigh never took another shower."

Diane Demorney, purveyor of arcane bits of information, adjusted her cigarette in her mouth as a signal for someone to light it. As she leaned forward, her hair, black as a buzzard, formed a razor-sharp wing across her cheekbone. Diane was good-looking, in a rapacious, raptorlike way. She kept her fashion-model body all planes and angles; her lipstick was blood red; her nails sharp as tiny scythes.

Both Melrose Plant and Marshall Trueblood looked up from the lists of names they were working on, glanced at each other, then, in concert, at Diane.

Melrose Plant had sworn to himself he would no longer encourage Diane to explain herself, but he knew he couldn't have resisted, had Trueblood not asked her himself.

"Janet Leigh?" Marshall Trueblood raised an eyebrow as well designed as the rest of him. He had sparked up his Armani ensemble with a turquoise shirt, a pale-green and turquoise striped tie. Right down to his shocking-pink Sobranie cigarette, he was a carnival of color.

She sighed. Had they not been listening? "Janet Leigh never took another *shower*. Only baths. Isn't *anyone* going to give me a light?"

Trueblood obliged. "The actress Janet Leigh?"

Diane looked at him as if he were simple. "My God. If you'd been knifed to death in a shower, even a film shower, wouldn't you prefer baths, too?"

Said Melrose, "I do anyway. My rubber duck won't float in the shower."

"You mean *Psycho*? That Hitchcock film, *Psycho*? Is that what you're talking about?" Trueblood asked.

"What else?" She looked around the Jack and Hammer for Dick Scroggs and her vodka with the unpronounceable name. He was nowhere to be seen. "Is he out there messing paint around again?"

The Jack and Hammer, ordinarily a traditional cream-washed fake-Tudor sort of building, had been tarted up recently by Dick Scroggs's slapping ultramarine paint on its façade to match the trousers of the mechanical "Jack" perched high up on a bracketed beam. Fortunately, Dick's competitive spirit (or his hatred of work) did not extend to the pub's interior, which had been knocking along for ages now, round deal tables, rickety chairs, a huge fireplace in its saloon bar; in the public bar, narrow benches against the walls and a dartboard. Tourists would have loved it had they ever got to see it. Fortunately for some, Long Piddleton was off the beaten tourist path. As was Northampton. As was the whole of Northamptonshire, it being rather low on the totem of "counties of choice." Long Piddletonians, the rich or retired contingent, were much in favor of this apparent falling off the map; those in trade, however, wouldn't have minded a coach party or two. God knows Dick Scroggs would be happy to turn his back garden into a car park if need be.

"He's out there," said Vivian Rivington, who was sitting next to Melrose on the bay window embrasure, staring through leaded glass panes as if sighs and longing looks would bring on spring. But Melrose knew the real cause of those sighs: she was about to pack up and go to Venice again. My Lord, how long had she been engaged to Count Dracula? Six years? Seven?

Trueblood added "Janet" to his list and fired up another match to light a fresh cigarette, this one deep blue. His fingers, thought Melrose, should surely be rainbow-stained after years of those Sobranie cigarettes. He looked over at Trueblood's notes. " 'Janet'?" he read. "You're kidding. She wouldn't be named Janet."

"Mind your own list, dammit." Trueblood quickly covered the page he'd been writing on.

"She wouldn't be named Janet," Melrose insisted. He pursed his lips. "Wonder how old they are?"

Trueblood scribbled down something else and said, "Same as us." He looked round the table. "Forties."

"I *beg* your pardon!" Diane wasn't having *that*. "All of *you* might be," disposing of her aged company with a flick of her hand. "I'm still in my thirties, *early*ish. Of course, Melrose could be anything. He never changes. He was probably born with all of that tarnished gold hair and those spectacles. Well, it's about time! Yoo-hoo, Dick!"

Dick Scroggs, stout and fiftyish, finally entered with his paintcan and Diane drew the shape of a martini glass in the air. Then she said, "Are you two still working on your lists? I finished mine ages ago." She tapped an envelope lying on the table with a red-painted fingernail. "Deadline's tomorrow morning; you said so yourselves."

"That's right. But I keep changing my mind about the name of the *wife*." Marshall Trueblood went back to chewing on his pencil and staring at the air. He was satisfied with the names he'd chosen for the children of the Chelseaites, but not the names he'd chosen for the mother.

Diane continued, "I *hope* this family moving here doesn't mean London has discovered Long Piddleton, for God's sake. We've been free of that sort of person thus far."

Considering that Diane Demorney had moved to Long Piddleton direct from London with no stopover in a That Sort of Person decompression chamber, it was hard to distinguish her from a London "emigrée," in other words, That Sort of Person. Melrose reminded her of this.

"*Don't* be ridiculous. I was never from Chelsea or Sloane Square or even South Ken. I was way, way down the King's Road, practically in Parson's Green, which is hardly fashionable"—Diane had lately started making a fashion out of being "un-"—"and, anyway, I haven't the energy to be a Week-End Man—or Woman. I thought they were supposed to move into Watermeadows months ago. Where are they?"

"They're probably out Walesing," offered Trueblood.

Melrose wrote a name on his tablet. "They're going to be disappointed. You can't Wales around here."

Vivian Rivington gave up on spring and turned from the casement window. "Don't be silly; you can't Wales *anywhere* anymore." Her naturally rosy complexion was quite pale, and the awful artichoke-colored jumper she was wearing did nothing to heighten either skin or auburn hair.

"The Week-End Man can. 'Walesing' is a state of mind, independent of royal indiscretions, divorces, or geography," Trueblood explained.

Diane Demorney yawned and ran a tiny garlic clove around the edge of her martini glass. Finally, Dick Scroggs had reappeared and was mixing up a fresh Demorney martini. She had to furnish her own garlic cloves—essential, she claimed, for the perfect martini. She had also furnished the perfect glass. The vodka itself was a Demorney find: it had buffalo grass in it, long threadlike things waving about in the bottle that looked as if they'd been harvested from the ocean floor. Trueblood had named it the Captain Nemo martini.

The Week-End Man that Trueblood was describing was actually a Week-End Family, who had presumably taken a lease on the country estate between Long Piddleton and Northampton called Watermeadows. The trouble was, they could get no information out of the estate agent, Mr. Jenks. Mr. Jenks, a thinnish man somewhere in his sixties, had many vices: greed, avarice, a manipulative character masked by a crust of blandness, like a beef Wellington made from gristle, but he had made himself unpopular mainly because he'd upset the balance of shops along the High Street by annexing the building next to Trueblood. He did have one virtue, if refusing to give out information regarding his clients could be called virtuous. Actually, it could well be merely another facet of his vices: acquisitiveness and secretiveness.

Mr. Jenks had set himself up in a shop sporting a double-sided sign, one side advertising his estate agency, the other his travel agency. He was likewise the double-hatted representative of both firms. This Janus-faced shop was a narrow Georgian building with a bowfront window, companion to Trueblood's Antiques. Marshall Trueblood was doubly irritated by this takeover of premises he had himself been thinking of purchasing in order to expand his own business. But he took it with the same soigné grace with which he took most things, and even listened with a fair amount of patience when Mr. Jenks talked about market upheavals, sliding interest rates, mortgage buyouts. Mr. Jenks was always hard on the trail of anyone who couldn't meet his mortgage payments.

This was not, however, the reason the vast estate of Watermeadows had been let—not sold, but let—to the family Marshall Trueblood and Melrose Plant were making up lists about.

"The children will have names like Alistair and Arabella. You said they had two children, didn't you, Viv-viv?" said Trueblood, chewing his pencil.

"No." Her chin in her fisted hands, she had turned once again to the window. A crust of snow ruffled the sill, refusing to melt on this sunny February day. Melrose noted that her awful artichoke twin set was set off by a moldy green skirt. Beautiful as she was, she seemed determined to deglamorize herself.

Trueblood continued. "He'll be wearing a rubber coat with a hood and elbow patches; she'll have razor-cut blond hair and a tweed jacket. Two chocolate Labs, of course. They'll call out 'Cheer-o' and describe everything as 'simply *lovely.*' And a Land Rover. Let's not forget the Land Rover. Or a Range, makes no difference. Labs in back, with, perhaps, a marmalade cat. The cat is Arabella's. She insisted on bringing it though Mummy would have preferred to leave it home with Cook. It sheds so. Its name is—"

Vivian turned from the window. "For heaven's sakes, do stop going on." The request was not rancorous, merely slightly bored. They *had* been going on about these new people for weeks.

Vivian was about to make one more trip to Venice. How many had she made (Melrose wondered) since her engagement to that Italian count? How many times had the wedding been put off, delayed, usually through some subterfuge Plant and Trueblood had cooked up? This last time the respite had been supplied by the death of one of the Giopinno aunts. But that was over, the family having survived the loss remarkably well. Marrying the Count Franco Giopinno, Melrose had told her at tea at Ardry End, seemed to be a sort of hobby for her, something she could take up, like tennis or the *Times* crossword, when she hadn't anything better to do. Vivian had thrown a watercress sandwich at him.

"Well, perhaps I'm wrong about the cat." Trueblood twisted round to call to Dick for another pint of that execrable ale Dick was making to keep up with Trevor Sly, proprietor of the Blue Parrot. "Frankly, I'm just as glad they'll only come at the weekend," said Diane Demorney. "At least that way we don't have to put up with them all year round."

"Honestly," said Vivian, "you both act as if you own Long Pidd. As if you own all of Northants."

"I do," said Melrose. He added, sotto voce, "Hell's bells, here's Agatha."

Lady Agatha Ardry entered, her big black cape swirling about her, talking as she did so: "Well, I can certainly tell you one thing about them," she announced, "them" having been such a hot topic during the past days that it was unnecessary to identify "them."

Marshall Trueblood sat up. "Ah! You've seen them?" He was mildly annoyed. It would be extremely irritating if Agatha were to be the first to see the new tenants of Watermeadows. "How many are they? What do they look like? Their dogs? Cats? Cars?"

Agatha took a vast amount of time settling herself, straightening the collar of a brownish-yellow suit that made her stout, compact form look just like a bale of hay. Her dull gray hair must have been freshly done; curls were shaped and plastered, newly minted, as if the beautician had scrubbed them with silver polish. She called for Dick Scroggs to wait upon her, before saying sententiously, "They're entitled to their privacy, Mr. Trueblood. Some of us don't spend half the day in beer and gossip."

Entitled to their privacy, thought Melrose, simply meant she didn't know anything.

"Did you see them?" asked Diane.

"Not . . . pre*cis*ely."

"Meaning," said Melrose, "not *im*precisely, either."

Dick Scroggs was paying no attention to the queenlike wave of Agatha's hand, palm rocking back and forth. He rolled a toothpick in his mouth and kept on reading the *Bald Eagle*. So she shouted, which was her wont anyway. "Shooting sherry over here!"

"Meaning," continued Melrose, as Scroggs spilled his pint over the paper, "that you haven't really come upon them at all."

Agatha was arranging the folds of the cape with a self-important air. "Hate to disillusion you, Mr. Trueblood—"

Few things she'd rather do, thought Melrose.

"—but your Week-End Family is *not* from Chelsea."

Trueblood looked alarmed. "But they *are* from SW3 or -4, aren't they?"

"Or W1, that might do," said Melrose.

Agatha looked pleased with herself to bursting. "I haven't got my drink yet, I notice. Mr. Scroggs—" she turned towards the bar, where Dick was leaning over the newspaper with the toothpick in his mouth—"is ignoring me, as usual."

Trueblood called to Scroggs. Scroggs looked up, nodded. "So where? Where do they come from?"

As soon as Scroggs plunked down her sherry, she said, "E11."

Trueblood choked. "The East bloody *End*? You've got to be joking."

"Whitehall or Shoreditch," said Diane, exhaling a plume of smoke. "Although Shoreditch might be E13." Diane had once memorized all of the postal district numbers to impress a postal carrier she fancied.

"Good God!" Trueblood clapped his forehead. Then his face lit up. "Wait a tick, you're talking Docklands! Well, that's different. A lot of Chelsea and Sloane Square are moving to there since it's been gentrified."

"They got it for a song," said Agatha. "That's what Jenks told me. They're not just anybody, they're some sort of relation."

Melrose looked at her through narrowed eyes. "Mr. *Jenks* told you that? Mr. Jenks of the zippered lip? Don't make me laugh. You heard something from Mrs. Oilings"—Agatha's weekly char—"so we can discount that because Oilings doesn't know anything either."

"Oh? Oh, *really?*" asked Agatha, working as much sarcasm into her tone as possible. "I'll have you know that Mrs. Oilings *chars for Mr. Jenks!*" She sat back in triumph. Until she realized she'd been trapped.

Melrose smiled. "Saturday afternoons. When nobody's there."

Agatha quickly changed the subject. "I can also tell you they like their drink."

Said Diane, "Who doesn't?"

"How do you know that?" asked Vivian.

"Because one of them spends a great deal of time"—here she raised her voice again, directing her words towards Dick Scroggs—"at the Blue Parrot!"

Scroggs wheeled at the mention of his rival. "What's that, now?" He forgot his newspaper and headed for their table.

Delighted that she had bad news to impart to Dick Scroggs, and *any* news to impart about the new tenants of Watermeadows, Agatha looked pleased as punch.

Scroggs stood, hands on beefy hips. "Since when do you go to the Blue Parrot?"

"I? Don't be ridiculous; I wouldn't be caught dead there. I just happened to notice their car nipping down that dirt road. And the only thing on it is the Blue Parrot."

"And how," asked Melrose, "did you know the car was the Watermeadows car?"

"It came out of their drive, didn't it?"

"Did it?"

"Yes. The one that leads down to the Northampton Road."

"And you followed it." Vivian looked disapproving.

"I didn't *follow* it. It was ahead of me on the Northampton Road, is all." Agatha pursed her lips, considering the next detail. "I was driving to Northampton."

"No, you weren't," said Melrose. "You never drive to Northampton. You make *me* drive to Northampton when you want to go there. What you were doing was lying in wait down at the bottom of the drive in case anyone drove out."

"*Spying?* I have better things to do with my time."

Dick Scroggs said, "Well, I can see how it's going to be, can't I? Them as want can take their business to Trevor Sly, be my guest." Disgusted, he stomped off back to the bar, where he noisily rattled glasses and bottles.

Melrose called over, "Don't worry, Dick. One taste of Cairo Flame and they'll run for the door with fire shooting out of their ears. I'm still tasting the stuff."

That Trevor Sly brewed his own beer was hardly a consolation to Dick Scroggs, who had been trying to do exactly that for some time now and hadn't been very successful. He broke a glass and cursed.

Vivian sighed and let her eyes rest on a row of some half-a-dozen white envelopes. She picked one up. "R. JURY," it read. She dropped it back, shaking her head at Jury's name. "You're even corrupting him. He's getting to be as silly as you."

Trueblood frowned. "You know, he scarcely gave his list a second thought. Did you notice? He just stood right there and scribbled it out without half thinking."

Vivian spoke more to the casement window than to the table. "Why does he keep going to Stratford-upon-Avon? He was just *there*." Her tone was crotchety.

"Friends," said Melrose. He thought it better not to mention it was *one* friend, and of the female variety. Melrose had never really sorted out the relationship between Vivian and his friend Jury. Something (he suspected) had happened a long time ago, when Jury had first come to Long Piddleton. Now *he* felt crotchety.

Taking up his own line, Trueblood went on: "He didn't spend more than two or three minutes on it."

"In a hurry," said Melrose, crossing out "Fiona" and replacing it with "Polly." That was a good Chelsea-sounding name. "He wanted to get to Exeter."

"Exeter? I thought he was going to Stratford," said Vivian.

"Exeter afterward."

With a note of alarm, Trueblood said, "You don't think perhaps he actually *knows*, do you? I mean, after all, he *is* a CID man. It would be no trick at all just to march into Jenks's and demand to see his files."

"Don't be stupid," said Plant. "Jury wouldn't cheat."

But Trueblood looked apprehensively at the R. JURY envelope.

"It would hardly be worth the trouble for only sixty pounds," said Diane. Ten pounds was the contest fee. Six had paid up. "And the next time you go tooting off to Northampton, Agatha, let me know, would you? There's an off-license there where you could pick up some buffalo-grass vodka for me."

Agatha, thought Melrose, would sooner get her a buffalo. Agatha loathed Diane Demorney.

"But you never told us, old sweat," said Trueblood, pencil poised over his list, "what kind of car was it?"

"I didn't notice."

"Uh-uh," said Trueblood, slapping his hand down over Agatha's envelope, the one she was surreptitiously reaching for. "No you don't."

Diane Demorney had apparently been thinking, a task she didn't often engage in. "Exeter. Is it that Exeter Cathedral business? The one he got the phone call about?"

"That's it," said Melrose, folding his sheet of paper into an envelope.

"It's the Stendhal syndrome," said Diane, eyes on the plume of lavender smoke rising from her cigarette. "You remember. I told you about Stendhal fainting when he saw great art?"

"Stendhal," said Melrose, as he rubbed down the flap on his envelope, "never took another shower."

THREE

Richard Jury did not know why, in the short time that had intervened since he last saw her, he thought Elsie would have grown. Perhaps simply because she was a little girl, and children grew magically, grew as beings did in fairy tales, one day small as a pea, and the next, tall as one of those Grecian statues in the garden.

"Hullo, Elsie. Remember me?"

"Oh, yes!" she said, with a great deal of enthusiasm. "You were from Scotland Yard! Are you still?"

It was as if "Scotland Yard" were some summer address, dropped when the season was over. "Am I still? Absolutely. Richard Jury, superintendent, CID."

Elsie smiled up at him, clearly impressed. She was wearing her apron, a large white one unevenly wrapped so that points of the hemline just missed the floor. From the direction of the kitchen came the most deliciously pungent fumes, redolent with onion and wine and herbs he couldn't identify.

Elsie held the door wide. He imagined she remembered what a fine captive audience he had made on his last visit and probably would do again. "I expect you're busy. Have I come at a bad time?" he asked her seriously.

Taking her cue from that, Elsie tempered her enthusiasm with a sigh. "Oh, *that's* all right. I'm just keeping the stock stirred. It's for the cockle vine. Come on in and sit down."

Settled in his chair, Jury tried to identify "cockle vine," but couldn't. Was it some trendy green? Like radicchio? He looked out at the small patio, leaves dripping rain, and thought that, once again, his mind had been drawn to comparisons with Grecian statues because

Jenny Kennington had at one time lived in a huge house with colon-naded walks whose courtyard contained such a statue (though not Grecian), the image of which reclaimed his mind whenever he came into her presence; not her presence, even, but her surroundings.

Smoothing out her apron, Elsie informed him that Lady Ken-nington was "down the pub." Like a rather bored young matron, she drew a magazine from the end table and flipped through it casually. Elsie was ten, and looked ten, but wished to adopt the insouciance of bored society. The image was just a little tainted, though, since the magazine she now tossed aside was neither *Majesty* nor *Country Life* but *Chips and Whizzer*. Rearing up, she said with alarm that she'd for-gotten to chill the shadow child.

Jury was left to turn this over in his mind, but reached no con-clusion, and then she was back. "You went to chill—" He inclined his head to one side, inquisitively.

"The wine. To have with dinner. I had to put it in the chiller."

Wine. She *had* said—

"Yes, that's right. It's a very good year for shadow child." Casu-ally, she reclaimed *Chips and Whizzer*. "Lady Kennington is buying a pub. I expect you might know that."

Jury imagined Elsie suspected he knew nothing of the sort and was pointing out to him that not everyone had the ear of Lady Ken-nington. "No, as a matter of fact, I didn't. I remember her saying something about opening a restaurant, though. Where is this pub?"

"It's a little way outside of town."

"What's its name? I might have seen it."

She pursed her lips and looked at the ceiling. "I expect she'll change the name."

Meaning that Elsie couldn't remember what it was called.

"Will you be working there?"

"Oh, yes. Probably I'll do the teas."

Teas? In a pub?

"See, it's going to be a little bit of everything," said Elsie, spread-ing her arms to encompass this "everything." "A restaurant and tea shop and a pub and maybe books."

"That sounds awfully ambitious."

"It's got a lot of rooms." She thought for a moment. "Maybe a gift shop, too." She thought for another moment. "And a disco. That's my idea." Here she glanced over at Jury to see how he was taking the news of this incredible entrepreneurship on the part of Lady Kennington and, of course, Elsie herself.

"Good Lord, Elsie, but you're going to be busy." The pub venture appeared to be getting out of control, together with Elsie's imagination. All she'd omitted was a supper theatre for the RSC. "Well, if Lady Kennington's trying to see to all of that, I don't expect she'll be back for a year or two." Jury started to rise.

"Oh, she won't be *that* long. She can't, because she's expecting a call from Mr. . . . Someone."

Elsie's face screwed up in an effort to remember—unsuccessful, to judge by the frown. "Anyway, he's giving her money to buy the restaurant. She was away to Lincolnshire to visit him. He's rich."

Jury's heart sank. But that was no concern of Elsie's, who kept on handing out the bad news. "He's to give her heaps of money to buy the pub and a lot more to run it." Ostentatiously, she consulted her round-faced watch. Jury thought he saw the black ears of Mickey Mouse. "I don't know why she's not back. . . ."

Feeling suddenly weary, Jury did rise this time. Elsie did not want him to leave and looked crestfallen. "But I expect she'd want to see you."

He smiled. "Tell her I stopped for a moment. Tell her I'll ring her."

YEARS BEFORE, he had taken this same walk and felt much this same disappointment. He'd left Jenny Kennington's house after they'd shared a cigarette, sitting on packing cases before she'd gone off on that voyage. He'd taken this walk along the banks of the Avon between the theatre and the church where Shakespeare was buried. It had been dark then; today it was a late afternoon and everything looked varnished with light. Colors were so muted and pale they seemed almost transparent, the sky with the sheen of an opal, the Avon flowing like smoke. Then the sun broke through its cloud cover, and as if this were a signal, ducks rowed over to the bank where Jury stood, loitered there expecting food. Farther out, a swan was moving along the sun-drenched surface of the river, as if it were gliding through handfuls of sequins.

He stood there watching the swan, thinking how he had almost been inclined to pump Elsie for information about Mr. Someone. ("Are they very good friends?") He had resisted because he might learn what he didn't want to know. ("Oh, *yes, really,* the best of friends.") Or else he'd have to suffer the consequences of Elsie's imagination and watch this chap emerge from the shadows rich, handsome, smart, and a connoisseur of cockle vines and shadow children. He sighed and told himself he was being ridiculous.

He knew Jenny Kennington to be a very serious person, nothing arch about her, nothing glib or manipulative. If the man were someone important to her, she'd have mentioned him. Surely. And just as surely, Jury should have told her he was coming.

A ray of sunlight smote the river. That archaic word was the only one that properly described it, for he saw it as a violent strike, a sword on armor, light so strong it turned the swan an incandescent white. Watching the swan on the fiery water, he thought of an old poem about a girl walking through a fair, and the narrator watching her move about, and watching her make her way home—

> . . . with one star awake,
> As the swan in the evening glides over the lake.

Jury found this inexpressibly sad, though he did not know why.

From his wallet he drew a snapshot. It showed a girl of eleven or twelve, whose name was Jip and who lived in Baltimore with an aunt. What was her real name? Not just her last, but her first. All he knew was "Jip."

Like the orphan lines of poetry, she was a girl without a context. In this photo she stood in a sober, unsmiling pose, squinting into the light that cast her and everything around her in deep shadow. A shadow child.

He was as parched for a cup of tea as ever Sergeant Wiggins would be.

Jury stopped in the little restaurant directly across from the cathedral and sat down at a table in the window where he could drink his tea and munch a Chelsea bun and gaze across the cathedral yard. There, blue-uniformed schoolchildren, probably students at the cathedral school, were all walking in procession along the pavement that encircled Exeter Cathedral. They were all dressed in navy blue blazers, white shirts, ties. A couple of dozen children of varying heights and ages.

It was a sight Jury had seen often, and was often affected by. He could see them walking, skipping, turning, long hair floating behind some of the girls, and knew they were laughing as they crossed the yard, though he could hear none of it. His job did not allow for much sentimentalism, yet, he could not help seeing himself in that collection of children, for all of their separate personalities, and he could not suppress the nostalgia that threatened to overwhelm him, watching the little band filing double-breasted through the church enclosure.

It had not been a part of his own childhood; probably it would have been had either of his parents survived the war. His father had been a wing leader in the RAF, flying a long-range mission over Munich. In that respite after his father had been shot down and before his mother had been killed, he had not yet been quite of school age.

Still, he had sat and watched them go by, the kids in uniforms, the ones walking down the Fulham Road in dark green, walking past his block of flats. They had seemed so chummy and clubby and ages older than he.

He remembered sitting there on the lower steps outside of his flat where he had lived with his mother, just the two of them now, sitting outside while his mother, inside, sewed.

His mother had done a great deal of sewing and managed to earn their living doing it, and he could still hear the comments of her "ladies" as they bustled down the steps into the Fulham Road, comments that told him she must be a very good seamstress indeed. Some of her clients were rich; most of them were stout—figures that needed the drape and fall of dark materials, cleverly designed. His mother favored black, even for herself, though she was thin, not stout, and young and pretty. And she always seemed to him to be wearing that bracelet of pins, a soft mound with straight pins sticking out of it on a ribbon tied round her wrist. It made him think of a porcupine's back.

He had sat on the steps in the mornings eating his toast, in the afternoons drinking lemonade, watching the schoolchildren troop by, making their way to the Boswell School up on the corner. This world of the Boswell School seemed to him enchanted and its students forming a magic circle he could not enter, not if he didn't have one of those uniforms.

"Mum, when can I go to school? Go on, Mum," he would demand, as if it were his mother's stubbornness and not the educational system which prevented his entrance into the magic circle of the Boswell School.

Then another long holiday, and back again they trooped, the dark green uniforms. The time between holidays seemed like years to his six-year-old mind, and it was hard for him to believe that when the next long holiday was over, it wouldn't be time for him to go to school. Time stretched and stretched like the strand of taffy his mother would loop over the doorknob for him to pull. As thin and narrow as it got, it would never give up, but stretched still farther. That was his Time. Between Whitsun and some time in July he thought surely he must have aged years and grown inches.

"Mum, when can I? Mum, go on!"

It was especially painful to him, having to sit out the day (or so it seemed to him) on the steps watching, since his heart's desire, Elicia Deauville, who lived in the flat next door, at seven and a half had joined the procession in her own new hunter's green uniform. Elicia would fly past him, tumbling down the steps with an almost disdainful toss of her long, thick hair; yet, she would smile slightly, as if even she had a hard time keeping up the pose the green uniform seemed to demand.

Later, he would pick up the pin-quills from the faded turkey carpet upon which his mother kneeled before the dressmaker's dummy, fixing a hem. While he pushed the pins into the porcupine bracelet, he hit on a clever (he thought) notion: his mother could make him a uniform.

And in this uniform he might be able to steal quietly into the procession passing the steps, simply meld with the others, and no one would know.

"Make me a uniform, Mum!"

The trouble was (his mother had said), the headmaster might ask him what twelve times eighty-two is, and what would he say?

To this, he had no answer.

Or the headmaster might ask him, How do you spell "agape"?

He had never even heard the word, much less knew how to spell it. It, or much of anything else.

"What's 'agape,' Mum?"

His mother had turned from the hem, smiling and giving him a peck on the cheek. True love, that's what it is.

It had only been a little while after that that the bomb had fallen late at night and brought the ceiling and walls with it, covering his mother in rubble and beams.

Across the Exeter Cathedral yard, the last of the dark blue uniforms rounded the corner, the last but for the one girl, hair flying, running as fast as she could to catch up, and who looked, to Jury's overtired mind, all the world like Elicia Deauville.

"Go on, Mum!"

"Were you wanting more tea, then, sir?"

Jury blinked several times, blinking up reality, and finding the face of the young waitress. "What? Oh. No, thanks, I'm just leaving. If you could give me my bill . . ." His voice trailed off, as if uncertain of the propriety of this request.

She wrote on her small book, ripped off the ticket, smiled at him.

Jury left the tea rooms.

THERE WERE sixty-four cities in England, which meant there were sixty-four cathedrals. And yet he could name fewer than half a dozen—Exeter, Ely, Salisbury, Lincoln. He stood in the nave of Exeter

Cathedral, gazing up at the clerestory, the elaborate vaulting, the intricate designs of the ceiling bosses, and wondered if any of those sixty-three other cathedrals could be more capacious, more massive.

Jury was early, and so he thought he'd take advantage of the taped tour of the rondels. These tapestry cushions—the rondels—extended for the entire length of the cathedral nave, and it was to hear a bit of the story of their making that Jury had paid his one pound for a tape recorder. He was bending over the cushion depicting the Great Fire of London, started, as the embroidered words read, by "a spark from a baker's oven." He stood marvelling at the intricate stitching. . . .

"Took you long enough, Jury."

Jury nearly dropped the little tape recorder when he heard the voice behind his back. Brian Macalvie stood there, hands in trouser pockets, holding back his mackintosh. Several of the supplicants, seated or praying in their chairs, looked up at him. Something about Macalvie drew people's eyes to him.

As God (Jury assumed) looked down, a slant of sunlight pierced the rose window behind them as if its only purpose were to halo Macalvie's copper hair. Macalvie didn't need the trimmings. "Sorry, Macalvie. I had to make a stop along the way to live my life."

Macalvie was already leafing through a spiral notebook. "That shouldn't have taken long." He thumbed the pages. "The body was found almost exactly at the spot where you're standing, did you know that?"

"Only you are blessed with second sight, Macalvie. No, I didn't."

"The woman, Helen Hawes, but always called Nell by friends, was seventy-two. At first, she appeared to be in some pain and then just keeled over. Very sudden. According to witnesses, she seemed to get very sick, retching, clutching herself, and then—" Macalvie shrugged. "That was a week ago end of January, when you were diddling around in the States."

"Thanks."

"Not many people here, it was just before closing, and not many tourists this time of year anyway."

Macalvie's eyes scanned the jottings in the notebook, but Jury knew he was not reading, he was reciting. He carried all of this information in his head; therefore, he was searching for something else.

He continued: "Nell Hawes lived in Exeter, an unexceptional elderly woman, reported as being quiet and very pleasant, lived by herself and was—as I told you on the phone—one of the tapisters who worked on the rondels."

"We haven't seen each other in two years, Macalvie. Aren't you going to say hello?"

"Hello. According to her friends, Nell Hawes hadn't been ailing, not to their knowledge, they were under the impression she had a bit of trouble with her heart. Nothing severe. Otherwise, her health had always been good for a woman of her age—"

"Which would be even more reason to think she died of natural causes, which she undoubtedly did," said Jury, dryly.

Macalvie paid him no attention. "There were probably half a dozen pilgrims moving down the nave around here, studying the rondels, with those headsets"—he glanced at Jury's earphones—"and when she fell down they said they assumed she'd fainted. Witnesses"—his finger now was acting as a bookmark in the place in the small notebook he'd been searching for—"all said the same thing. Nil. Nobody saw anything, nobody'd noticed her until she dropped on the floor there before these cushions." With his free hand, the one not holding the notebook, Macalvie folded a stick of gum into his mouth and continued: "Nell Hawes lived in a small but mortgage-free cottage over in Lucky Lane. That's near the river. Didn't have friends or family outside of Devon, except for a couple of cousins who live up in the Lake District. Her address book looks newish, has a few phone numbers in New Mexico, and that's all." Here he opened the notebook to the notation he'd been looking for, and read: "Silver Heron, Canyon Road, Santa Fe. And another reference to 'Coyote Village' that I'm getting nowhere with. Anyway, seems Nell Hawes had made a trip there in November. Her fellow tapisters say she would take a trip maybe every two or three years, usually in winter. Not so many tourists."

"You contacted that address?"

"I did. I mean, I tried. Nobody there. According to the cops, who checked it out, the owner was away, they thought maybe out of the country. Come with me." Macalvie moved down the nave toward a long table where three women, all with gray hair and looking much alike, were bent over embroidery frames. These women, Macalvie told him, were tapisters. They made vestments, chasubles, maniples, stoles; they belonged to a guild of needleworkers who together had worked on the rondels. They appeared to be on quite good terms with Commander Macalvie (who could manage to ingratiate himself if it was necessary), for they smiled and nodded as he introduced Jury.

"Look how intricate," said Macalvie, bending himself over the embroidery. "Must be a dozen different patterns of stitches in that background." Macalvie picked up a skein of colored threads, let it fall through his fingers. "Try and see the colors apart from each other and it won't work. Rainbow mechanics."

"Two dozen," said one of the women, whose clear complexion shone even more under this police influence.

They moved away from the table and Jury asked, impatiently, "Didn't you tell me the pathologist put this woman's death down as a coronary?"

"A lot of things can look like a coronary."

"Including a coronary." Jury shook his head. "Macalvie, what are you getting at?"

By way of answer, Macalvie said, "Wiltshire police have a weird case on their hands. Did you read about it? Body of a woman was found at Old Sarum."

"I haven't seen a paper." Actually, that was not accurate. Jury had seen several; he just couldn't concentrate on them. Jenny Kennington's face kept floating in front of the print. "Old Sarum? Strange place to find her."

"Glad you think so."

"What happened?"

"Coronary." Macalvie cut him a look. "Sound familiar?"

Jury looked up toward the vaulted ceiling. "Certainly does. How many cases of death by coronary occlusion or some such heart condition did we have last month alone?"

Macalvie said, "Very funny. The woman was from Santa Fe. New Mexico, in case you've forgotten."

That did give Jury pause. Still . . . "A coincidence."

Macalvie snorted. "Oh, *give* me a break! I was in Salisbury yesterday—"

"That's Wiltshire, Macalvie. Not your turf."

"DCI Rush made that abundantly clear. He's not one of my biggest fans. Never has liked me since he was a detective sergeant here."

Jury said nothing.

Macalvie was exacting, to say the least. Over the ten years Jury had known him, he'd watched Macalvie do battle with medical examiners, scenes-of-crimes people, fingerprint experts, even a forensic anthropologist. Macalvie usually won. He won not only because he was smart but because he was dedicated. Even though he was a divisional commander (roughly equivalent to Jury's own rank of superintendent), no job that related to policing was too small for him. Jury had been with him when he'd chased speeders on the A24 and handed out tickets.

"So I couldn't get anything out of him about the lady," Macalvie went on. "All I know is what I read in the paper. That and I also heard that some family member, a cousin, I think, flew in day before yesterday to identify the body. I'm going back this afternoon. To Old Sarum." Sunlight pouring through the rose window fell in broken patterns of color at their feet and turned Macalvie's copper hair to small tongues of fire. "So, what do you think? Will you go?"

"To Wiltshire? I don't—"

Impatiently, Macalvie cut him off. "To Santa Fe, for God's sakes."

Jury just stared at him.

"*Somebody's* got to go. I can't, too big a caseload."

"You could reduce your caseload by staying out of New Mexico. Stick to Devon and Cornwall. *No*, I'm not going to Santa Fe."

Macalvie said nothing, just stood there in silent contemplation of the rondel depicting the murder of Thomas à Becket. For some reason, Jury felt he had to justify himself. "It's pure coincidence, Macalvie. You've got nothing but an address in Ms. Hawes's book there and the other woman's an American—I assume—happens to live in Santa Fe. What? You think somebody killed her? Druids?"

"Come on, let's go."

Shaking his head as if refusing, Jury still followed him up the nave.

He knew he wasn't going to like this.

FIVE

Macalvie pulled into the little car park on the other side of the short wooden bridge leading to the inner bailey of Old Sarum's medieval castle. Four other cars belonging to the Wiltshire police were already there.

"Old Sarum. A hill fort in the Iron Age," said Macalvie, as they crossed the bridge over the moat. "The original Salisbury. Hard to believe."

"Humbling experience, isn't it?"

"Maybe for you." Across the entrance near the ticket kiosk, crime-scene tape marked off the area, that gaily colored tape the police used, a sunny yellow strand of it undulating in the wind, following a course up and around the stone remains of what had been the Bishop's Palace.

A hard knot of uniformed police stood up on the ramparts, turning as Macalvie approached. He showed them his identification. One of them addressed him as "Commander," and with respect, although he was clearly puzzled, given the county Macalvie was "Commander" in. It wasn't Wiltshire.

"I asked Rush if this was okay," said Macalvie, cheerfully neglecting to elaborate on Chief Inspector Rush's reply. "This is Superintendent Jury, Scotland Yard CID."

That certainly came as a surprise to them. But they merely nodded when Macalvie said he wanted to have a look at this privy where the body was found.

" 'Garderobe,' it's called," one of Rush's men corrected him with a nicety of diction Macalvie couldn't care less about. His eyes were pale as ice and no warmer in expression.

"Down there, Commander," said another, more helpful. He nodded toward a deep stone well some fifteen or twenty feet downhill.

Macalvie and Jury moved carefully down the footworn path. It required a bit of balancing to avoid sliding. They found themselves looking down into a deep well-like enclosure. Macalvie stared down into the privy for some time, and with almost as much concentration and intensity as he would have given it had the body been *in situ*.

Jury had patience with people, but Macalvie had patience with evidence. He could look at something, turn it over for uncommonly long periods of time. Despite his irascibility and what his colleagues took for arrogance, his cut-dead attitude with anyone who got in his way, Jury knew his judgment was unerring, and his tenacity nearly legendary.

But his patience with crime-scene particulars was, at the moment, getting Jury down. Jury did not want to be dragged into this. "Exactly what theory are you constructing?"

"I'm not. I'm merely noting."

"When you start noting, I start getting nervous." When Macalvie didn't answer, just shaved him a look, Jury said, "You don't have enough evidence to construct a theory, Macalvie. And God knows Rush isn't going to share any evidence he might have with you. So what do you have to go on?" The question was rhetorical, since Macalvie had been constructing, deconstructing, *re*constructing theories all during the three-hour drive from Exeter. "You know she's an American, thirty, from New Mexico."

"Santa Fe. Her name is—was—Angela Hope." He looked into a dark blue distance.

"I don't think you're paying attention to me."

"I'm not." Macalvie was looking south, toward the city of Salisbury. The modern Salisbury.

And to the west, where the blue was beginning to fade, was a vat of dark gold.

He squinted into the sun. "All Rush would tell me was her identity. The other bits I got from someone who owed me a favor. According to the ME, Angela Hope was very sick before she died. Vomitus traces. What's that suggest to you?"

"Nothing. For God's sake, her neck was broken, among other things. Reason enough to die."

"You're just like Rush, you know that?" Macalvie sighed. "Well, he wouldn't tell me any more."

"If you were Rush, you wouldn't want some other cop messing around your manor."

"He would do you, though."

Jury's frown was puzzled. "Would do me *what?*"

"Share the information. He talked to Angela's cousin. I'd like to know what transpired, as they say."

The cousin had come from New Mexico to identify the remains. "Wiltshire police haven't asked for any help from Scotland Yard," said Jury.

"No. But Scotland Yard could ask for help from the Wiltshire police." Macalvie was down on one knee, sighting along the footpath to the edge of the garderobe. Jury tried to ignore the thought pushing to the surface. "Help for *what?*"

"Your lady in the Tate."

Astonished, Jury started to move away, turned back. "Macalvie. What reasonable cause is there to connect an American breaking her neck at Old Sarum and a Brit pegging out in a London gallery?"

Macalvie was still inspecting the path. "You left one out, Jury."

Jury stared at him. "Who?"

"Helen Hawes. Of course, you don't want to drag her in when you talk to Rush, or he'll know I'm trying to get information."

"I'm not dragging her in, because I'm not *talking* to Rush."

Macalvie plowed on as if Jury hadn't spoken. "The fact that Nell Hawes and your lady might both have died from the same cause. Probably you shouldn't mention that."

"She's not *my* lady, she's A Division's lady."

"Would you mind filling me in on the details? All I know now is what I scraped together from newspapers and the Yard's information office. She keeled over, sitting on a bench in the Pre-Raphaelite room of the Tate, landed on some citizen sitting beside her."

"Then you know it all."

Macalvie looked truly amazed. "How the hell could I know it *all?* I wasn't there, much less was I first on the scene."

It was Macalvie's firm belief that if anyone got to a crime scene before he did, ninety percent of the usable evidence would blow off into the stratosphere. Jury smiled. "Okay, I'll describe it all in relentless detail. Remember, though, *I* wasn't first on the scene. The gallery was full of people."

"Meaning they tramped all over everything." Macalvie looked disgusted and shoved another stick of gum in his mouth. Why was the world up and about when somebody got killed?

"I was in the Tate's shop, the gift shop, when the commotion started. When I asked the guard, he told me a woman had suddenly died. They called West End Central; I just happened to be there and got there first."

"Stroke of luck."

"Not mine."

"A Division's, I meant."

"Good Lord! Is that a compliment?" As Macalvie looked off noncommittally toward the tower ruins at the other end of the bailey, Jury went on. "The woman—Frances Hamilton was her name—who had been sitting on one of the benches in the Pre-Raphaelite collection suddenly fell to one side. The young lady beside her thought she was either being pushy or had fallen asleep, something like that—unfortunately, the girl was more interested in touching up her boyfriend than in the woman beside her. She wasn't paying any attention to Frances Hamilton. Neither of them was until Mrs. Hamilton fell on her. No one saw anything out of the ordinary, from what I could see and hear. Remember, I wasn't doing the questioning. Only the observing, after A Division and the ambulance got there. Coronary occlusion. Or a stroke."

"Which?"

Oh, hell, thought Jury. "The pathologist wasn't one hundred percent sure which. But she was on nitroglycerin, that was clear."

Macalvie's eyes burned into Jury's. "Coronary occlusion, stroke. Vague, but they're still two different things, Jury."

"No kidding?"

"Go on."

"With what? That's it."

"That's what you call 'relentless detail'? What pictures?"

Jury looked at him.

"What painting or paintings was she looking at?"

It had occurred to Jury, too, how much the painting she had been sitting in front of might have reminded her of her nephew. "*The Death of Chatterton*. The Henry Wallis painting."

"Great picture. But how do you know she was looking at it?"

"I don't. Do you think it's important?"

"Jury, I don't *know* what's important. Nell Hawes dropped over dead in front of some embroidered cushions. That doesn't mean looking at them killed her. And it doesn't mean it *didn't*, either."

"The painting on one side was Holman Hunt. A man and his mistress at a piano. Sad . . ." Jury shook himself free of this memory. "The other side, I don't recall. Fanny Hamilton might not even have been paying any attention to the art when she died. She could have sat down to rest, period."

"Uh-huh."

When Macalvie appeared to be agreeing, Jury knew he wasn't. "I expect the police closed the file on that one. The only reason I was in on it at all was because of a friend. A favor for a friend. Lady Cray. This Frances Hamilton had just lost her nephew. He was murdered in Philadelphia. Outside of Philadelphia."

"You told me. That's what you went over there for."

"Frances Hamilton had gone to the States to see if she could help the police. She'd been back a couple of months when this happened, I mean, when she died."

They stood there in silence and the pale light of late afternoon. The three policemen, ranged about the garderobe, looked, in their dark uniforms, like narrow black monoliths.

"What part of the States?" asked Macalvie.

The question seemed to have no underpinning. "What do you mean?"

"Your—pardon me—" Macalvie clamped his hands to his chest—"I mean, A Division's lady. You said she'd been to the States. What states, exactly? Only Pennsylvania?"

"Pennsylvania. Maryland."

"Nowhere else?" Macalvie had stooped down to pick up a stone or a bit of flint. He was studying it.

An image surfaced in Jury's mind; he let it sink again. "Macalvie, I swear to God you're building this case just like those masons who had to raise the lintels at Stonehenge."

"Did she go anywhere else?"

Another mental nudge. Jury felt uncomfortable. In his mind's eye he watched Lady Cray's hand turn the block of turquoise with the silver band, the silver flautist. *He's called* . . . What? Jury tried to dredge up the name. Lady Cray had been holding it the way one does a talisman, an amulet, an artifact from which one draws strength.

In like manner, Macalvie was turning his bit of flint. "You remembered something." It was not a question.

"Nothing important." *He's called Kokepelli.*

"Something *un*important, then."

"Stop trying to read my mind."

Macalvie smiled. "But you're so transparent, Jury."

Jury walked off a few paces to stand and look down into the garde-robe. The fall had broken her neck. The fall, surely, had killed her.

"The point is, Jury: what do you have to lose? Time, maybe; but we're losing that anyway."

"I hate chasing will-o'-the-wisps."

Behind him, Macalvie laughed. "You do it all the time."

Jury couldn't help but smile, then. "I still have no good reason to break into Rush's investigation. Racer'd have me for breakfast. The commissioner would finish me off at dinner."

"But you wouldn't be breaking into his investigation. You'd just be trying to illuminate *our* investigation. Hell, let Rush do his *own* investigating. Save me the footwork. Anyway, you don't give a flying fuck for Racer. Or the commissioner. Don't try to kid me."

"*Our* investigation?"

"Of course, *our*. You said you wanted to transfer. So we can work this case together. You'd be on probation, naturally."

"I don't think I want a transfer that badly." Jury smiled. "I go much more for the obvious than you do. I'm Rush-ian, you might say."

"The hell you are. But you're damned grumpy. You must be hungry. I know I am. Come on, I know a pub that's got good food a few miles away."

The black monolithic figures that were the Wiltshire policemen were melting away into the shadows down the bank and seemed to have forgotten the two other, alien policemen.

"Where's the pub?"

"Steeple Langford. Rainbow's End."

Jury smiled. "So will it be there, or not?"

"The pub?"

"The pot of gold."

SIX

Rainbow's End was a quiet pub that had once had the advantage of traffic now diverted onto the A36. It backed onto a wide river that flowed through the Langfords, twin hamlets some twenty miles from Salisbury. It must have done a lot of dinner business, for the newish-looking dining room was surprisingly large.

But Macalvie and Jury were in the older, much smaller saloon bar: brick and wood; handsome, upholstered Queen Anne chairs set around small tables; plenty of glass, gilt, and tulip-shaped wall sconces. Jury was reading a framed newspaper article (in which the pub got a mention, hence the framing) about New Agers trekking through the Langfords, leaving their philosophy (if one could call it that) and remnants of belongings along the way. New Agers. Jury felt strange, time-warped, having just come from Old Sarum and with the pub's being so near to Stonehenge.

"Fifteen million pounds to turn the landscape into what it looked like in 2000 B.C.," said Macalvie. "Now, is there anything in that that strikes you as just a little wacky?" He was complaining about the expensive and extensive plans the National Trust and English Heritage had for revamping Stonehenge and putting in a new tourist center.

Jury smiled. "It does, yes."

"I mean, what in hell did the landscape *look* like in 2000 or 3000 B.C.? Neolithic man we're talking about. How do these architects know?" Macalvie brooded, studying his nearly empty pint of lager.

They had moved to the dining room where they ordered the river trout and another pint of lager.

After a moment, Macalvie said, "The hard thing is going to be to get Rush to check for poisons. And get the body in London exhumed."

"What in hell are you talking about?"

"You know what I'm talking about. Give me the bread."

Jury absently handed a wicker basket to him. "Actually, I don't. Poison?"

Macalvie answered obliquely by saying, "You can bet my lady's going to get a going over. At least I control that much."

"And what poison are you looking for?"

Macalvie was examining his empty glass as if he were going to dust it for prints.

"You didn't answer my question. You don't know the answer, that's why. So it shouldn't take more than a millennium or two to identify this suspect poison." Jury's smile wasn't very sincere. "You know how difficult it is if you don't know what poison you're looking for."

"I can eliminate, or the path guy can, obvious poisons. Tox testing can eliminate a lot more. A comprehensive serum and urine analysis will either turn up what it was or else eliminate hundreds of poisons."

Jury was getting impatient. "I don't get it, Macalvie. Here's a tourist who has an accident and ends up at the bottom of a well. The fall killed her. Why're you making something else of it?" But Jury knew why, although to give Macalvie a connection between Angela Hope and Helen Hawes was apparently to grant him an even more tenuous connection to Frances Hamilton. "If you're trying to account for the sickness before this Hope woman died, maybe it was simply food poisoning."

"Possible. But not very likely unless they all took tea together."

This begging the question irritated Jury. "You're already *assuming* the same thing killed all of them."

Almost innocently, Macalvie looked at him. "Of course."

Jury shook his head, turned toward the windows of the pub overlooking the river, becalmed in the evening sun. Jury watched the water, the chequered light coming through the trees. Near the opposite bank, a swan buried its head beneath its wing, drifting. And he thought about Stratford and Jenny.

Macalvie frowned at his own thoughts, his eyes following the direction of Jury's own, out where a smoking mist hung along the riverbank.

Light gathered over the river, still and still gliding, glanced and darted through the dark branches as if the sun, in its slow descent, had fallen suddenly, then caught itself and now fanned out in a golden silt of light. Jury watched the swan, stationary as a paper cutout pasted against the water. Death seemed far away.

"What are you getting at?" Jury asked it again.

"Deep time," said Macalvie.

Jury looked at him as the waitress set down their dinners, told them to be careful of the plates. They were hot. "What's 'deep time'?"

"The kind of time you think of when you see Old Sarum or Stonehenge. That kind of time. Deep time."

"Well, that explains it." Jury separated his fish from the bone.

"Like trying to think in terms of light-years. We can't do it."

Jury watched him over the plate of succulent trout. Macalvie seemed to be tasting his thoughts, his words, and not his dinner. "Think of the king's yard, Jury."

"I would if I knew what it was. Your fish is getting cold."

"The king's yard was the measurement between the end of the king's nose and the tip of his finger. Right?" He raked his fish off the bone.

"If you say so." The trout was delicious.

"If you think of this measurement in terms of 'deep time,' our civilization would disappear in a single fingernail filing." He prodded his fish with his fork.

"Then let's hope the king doesn't get a manicure."

Macalvie gave him a dark look. "I'm serious." Ignoring his plate, he gazed at the river. "Movement in time is deceptive, Jury. Because we're in the wrong time frame. You know how I feel? As if I'm accelerating at a hundred per and holding in my hand one of those time-release photos of . . . I don't know . . . the petals of a flower opening slowly as I watch. It's jarring. Did you ever think there might be two worlds moving along, side by side, but at different times?"

Jury smiled. "Only when I'm with you, Macalvie."

"Very funny. Stonehenge, Sarum, Avebury—they make me feel that. Everything we do now is speeded up so much, the time release working in the opposite way." Macalvie separated the long bone from the fish, looked at it. "I like the patience of science, the way they can repeat experiments ad infinitum. Like Denny Dench." Dench was a forensic anthropologist.

Jury thought it was probably the fishbone that reminded him. The only time Jury had met this brilliant forensics man, Dench had been lining up the bones of a quail he'd been eating.

"What do you think is the most potent motive for murder, Jury? Love? Greed?"

"Revenge." Jury was surprised that his answer was so emphatic. "The Greeks knew that."

The two of them sat now in silence, turned toward the window and the river beyond. The rim of the sun, vapor-orange, showed just at the edge of the trees. The sky was nearly purple. "It's rainbow mechanics," said Macalvie after a time. "There appear to be colors, separate bows of color, but they really just bleed into one another. If they're there at all." He kept looking out of the window, at the sky. "She was only thirty. At least if you live to fifty or sixty you've had a chance to work things out. Not that you've taken advantage of it, but at least you had the chance. You had a proper go."

"A proper go," thought Jury, watching the swan under the dripping boughs on the other side of the river seem to drift, propelled by the motion of the water. " 'Fondly I watched her move here and move there . . .' "

Macalvie raised an eyebrow in question.

Jury hadn't even realized he'd said it aloud. "It's an old poem, or an old song." He turned again to the evening sky, the river.

"And then she went homeward with one star awake,
As the swan in the evening drifts over the lake."

From a state of equanimity, Jury was plunged without warning into a terrible sadness. He tried to counteract it by saying, "I'll talk to Lady Cray again. And A Division."

"I knew you'd see reason, Jury."

SEVEN

Funnels of yellow dust blew out from the rear wheels of the Bentley as Melrose Plant and Marshall Trueblood made their bumpy way across the wasteland that lay between the Northampton Road and the Blue Parrot pub.

"I've wondered who in hell would come here but us. It's a good mile off the main road and nothing but dry fields. Is that wheat? It looks burnt."

"That's the point," said Melrose. "Sly does everything he can to create the illusion you're trekking across hot sands and thinking, 'God, I'm thirsty,' when you really aren't. Sells more beer that way."

The Blue Parrot was an undistinguished-looking square building out in the middle of nowhere that no one would even find had Trevor Sly not had the foresight to put a large and gaudy sign out on the Northampton Road. The pub was painted bright blue, in honor of its name, and over it hung another gaudy sign, a smaller version of the one by the road, this one depicting a veiled lady with bejeweled forehead and a couple of rough turbanned types. They must all have just de-cameled, for their mounts were tethered to a post. One could just make out, through the painted open door, a belly dancer doing her stuff in the sign's den of iniquity.

Since Melrose had last been here, a whole new little desert scene had been enacted to embellish the Moroccan image. There had never been grass around the Blue Parrot, but there had been a brownish stubble enclosing a dry stone fountain. The fountain was, of course, still dry, but was now surrounded by sand, as was the pub itself. And on an iron post-perch above one window swung an anomalous blue-green painted bird with a yellow beak that could have been anything from a blue hawk to a blue vulture. It swung gently in a freshening breeze.

"Rain? Do I smell rain?" asked Marshall, with a dry, parched little cough.

"Not here, you don't."

The orangish yellow light splashed around outside by the setting sun stopped short at the door. Directly inside, it was dark as pitch.

"I can't see! I'm blind!" yelled Trueblood, clutching at Melrose's sleeve.

"Oh, shut up." Melrose pushed aside the beaded curtain (also new) that had been hung here to make a little alcove of the entrance. On the other side of this curtain, gray light filtered through slat-shuttered windows. Ceiling fans whirred softly; the fronds of potted palms drooped; and tendrils of smoke appeared to be swirling around the ceiling, forming, dissipating, re-forming.

"Is something burning?" Trueblood sniffed the air.

"Be careful of the camel."

Trueblood, in his so-called blindness, had nearly toppled the large camel cutout that was used to display the menu for the day. And the menu looked similar to the ones Melrose had seen when he was here with Jury two years ago. How could Trevor Sly keep serving the same food month after month, year after year, given the food was (supposedly) some sort of Middle Eastern stuff, Lebanese, perhaps. Melrose could see how a Happy Eater might serve up the same egg, beans, and chips for a zillion years, but how long could you keep cooking up Kibbi Bi-Saniyyi? And then Melrose remembered that all of the main dishes bore a surprising resemblance to one another and also to minced beef.

"What the hell's Kifta Mishwi?" Trueblood was leaning over, squinting at the blackboard menu.

"Same as Kibbi Bi-Saniyyi."

"That's a help."

Trueblood continued to study the hump of the camel, part of the chalky blackboard, as Melrose looked around the room, eyes having adjusted to a darkness that he didn't remember. There hadn't been shutters before, that was it. Melrose threaded his way between tables and chairs that looked much too delicate for hordes of Riffs and opened one of the shutters to let in more light.

Otherwise, the Blue Parrot was all as he remembered it: little tin camels on each table, with mustard-pot howdahs standing beside Branston pickle and catsup. The green-glowing palm-tree lamps were new, however. So were the slot machines. He wandered over to the three machines and saw that the winning combinations weren't (as was usual) cherries and bells, oranges and lemons; they were sand dunes and turbans, palm trees and (once again) camels. Where on earth had Trevor Sly managed to secure *those* specimens?

Posters of exotic locales—pyramids, burning sands, shadowy courtyards, dusty doorways full of olive-eyed children looking earnest—all lined the walls. Scattered in amongst them were old film posters; there was *Casablanca*, naturally; there was the dark camel train plodding along from *A Passage to India*; and the real train along which strode Lawrence of Arabia—or, rather, Peter O'Toole as Lawrence. Plant wondered what milieu Trevor Sly had in mind for the Blue Parrot: it could have been an outpost in Arabia, Calcutta, L.A., or Las Vegas, from the look of it.

Customers might have got the idea that the owner himself hailed from some far-flung, romantic place, some distant sand dune, and that he would be a swarthy man with a ring in his ear and a knife in his teeth. However, he was none of this.

Trevor Sly (from Todcaster) slipped like a shadow through another beaded curtain, which separated the long, polished bar from the back—the kitchen and his own private rooms. He was tall and thin, *stretched* thin, he looked, as pale as pulled taffy. He carried his thin hands before him, limp appendages that he liked to wash together when he talked, and now he was talking, had started even before the curtain tinkled together behind him.

"*Gentlemen*, gentlemen, gentlemen . . ." The voice ran down like a windup toy and then picked up again. "It's Mr. Plant, isn't it? How lovely to see you again. And your friend?" His peaked eyebrows rose, his liquid brown eye glittered (the other was slightly off-center), and he washed his hands in anticipation.

"Mr. Trueblood." Plant pegged Trevor Sly as a person who would have preferred to get on a first-name basis as quickly as possible.

"A pint of my Cairo Flame? Or the Tangier?" Trevor Sly's smile split his lantern jaw. He brewed his own beer, not because he was a great believer in CAMRA but because it was both cheaper and gave him an outlet for his ingenuity.

"The last time I drank your Cairo Flame, I woke up in Cairo. Just some of the real stuff." Melrose added, when Sly looked puzzled, "You know, the brown stuff with a bit of foam on top. How about an Old Peculier?"

Trevor Sly pursed his lips, shook his head in a no-accounting-for-tastes manner.

Trueblood said, "I'll have a pint of the Tangier."

"Bottled lava," said Melrose. "Draft lava," he corrected himself, when he saw Trevor Sly's fingers touch one of the beer pulls.

"And have something yourself, Mr. Sly."

Trevor Sly smiled broadly, winked, and went into action. His long arms, reaching for glasses, sliding about amongst the optics and beer pulls, the bowls of nuts, packets of crisps, cigarettes, and jars of pickled eggs, appeared to be involved in many more things at once than two arms could possibly be. The same could be said of his two legs, after he'd set the Old Peculier and Trueblood's pint before them, and had settled himself on a high stool behind the bar, twining and twining the spindly legs like ivy round the rungs. Trevor Sly was everywhere, and in constant jittery motion, even when he was seated.

"What's this funny sediment on the bottom?" asked Trueblood, pint raised to the light.

"I told you," said Melrose, cherishing his pleasantly familiar Old Peculier. "They've got the same thing at Vesuvius. Mr. Sly, where did you get the fruit machines?"

"The what?" Trevor raised his eyebrows, followed the direction of Plant's gaze to the back wall and the slot machines.

"Those. They call them 'fruit machines' in the States. Though I expect they'd call yours 'camel machines.' "

"Mate of mine, lives in Liverpool." Sly studied the ceiling fan and the flies lazing round it. "I believe he's in the secondhand furniture business."

"Lorry decor, that it?" said Trueblood, finally taking a drink of his Tangier, and coughing. "My God," he wheezed, "that's strong stuff."

"You were warned," said Melrose. He added, when Trevor pushed a menu toward him, "No, nothing to eat. We had a camel for luncheon."

"You are a treat, Mr. Plant," said Trevor.

Weakly, Melrose smiled, and introduced the subject they had really come calling about. "You know, speaking of lorries, as we were passing Watermeadows, I could have sworn I saw a van. Removal van, it looked like. Is Lady Summerston returning, do you know?"

"Far as I know, yes." Trevor was at the optics, eking out his portion of gin.

This totally unexpected answer left both Plant and Trueblood staring open-mouthed at the dispenser of gin and beer.

"But we—I—thought the property had been let. . . ."

"A family, that's what I heard," said Melrose. "Husband, wife, two children."

"And two Labradors," said Trueblood.

Melrose gave his ankle a kick. They'd invented the Labs themselves, for God's sake. But, then, they'd invented nearly everything, hadn't they?

"Well, I'm sure I don't know where you heard that." Trevor Sly took a puff of his cigarette, laid it, coal end out, on the edge of the bar. And added nothing at all to Melrose's speculations.

"I think it was . . . Mr. Jenks. Yes!" Melrose snapped his fingers as if in sudden recollection. "You know him, that new estate agent in Long Pidd."

Trevor gave a short laugh that was more of a snort. "Oh, don't I ever. I know *him* all right. Him as worked for that Sidbury firm and scarpered with their listings. Right villain, that one."

"Really?" Melrose feigned interest in the villainous estate agent, exaggerated villainy, he was quite sure. All Melrose wanted to know was who in hell was living at Watermeadows.

Trueblood took time out to gag on another swallow of Tangier and asked, "Didn't we see a Land Rover up the drive near the fountain?"

"Can't see the fountain from the Northampton Road, can you?" Trevor rubbed his hands together, twining the fingers in his spidery way. "I seriously doubt you saw a Land Rover, Mr. Trueblood."

Hell's bells, the man doubted and denied but wasn't telling them one damned thing. "Then you say it's Lady Summerston come back?"

"No, I didn't exactly say that, did I?" Trevor Sly rewound himself on his high stool and smiled.

"I can't imagine she'd want to live there alone, with just that butler of hers," said Trueblood. "Not after that murder several years ago." He was more concerned over the role played in it by his own exquisite *secrétaire à abattant*.

"But she's not alone."

"No?" said Melrose, leaning forward.

"She isn't?" Trueblood perked up.

Trevor Sly studied his fingernails, hand flat out in front of him. "Well, you know, they keep themselves to themselves, don't they? And I'm not one to talk."

Oh, but he was, he was, which was why Melrose and Trueblood had come.

"We were told they were from London. Docklands, to be precise. Took the place for a year." At least, that was true enough.

"Ah, yes. I expect so."

Wasn't that just the way with gossips? thought Melrose, with a sigh. When you didn't want to listen to them, you couldn't shut them up.

Trueblood said, "And they've really taken to the Jack and Hammer."

That got a response. "Jack and *Hammer?*" Sly flicked the towel from his shoulder he'd lately been polishing glasses with, swatting at air as if he couldn't breathe for all the flies. "They wouldn't bother themselves. Not when the *Parrot's* here, right close and where they can get *real* beer, and not that yellow swill Dick Scroggs pulls. Why, just the other day, Miss Fludd was saying—"

"*Miss Fludd?*" Plant and Trueblood chorused, leaning across the bar like two shipwrecked sailors over the edge of their lifeboat, so eager at a report of land they'd gladly swim for it.

"That's right. Miss Fludd was just saying—well well *well*, hello hello hello!"

This gibbered greeting trilled past their shoulders and towards the door.

Melrose turned.

The girl who stood stopped in the doorway wore an old black mackintosh and had hair the color of the coat. Light was behind her and he couldn't see her eyes very clearly, their color or expression. When she moved, it was with difficulty, for she had to drag the right leg, which was in a heavy and unwieldy brace. Yet, she moved with a certain smiling energy, as if she were simply carrying a rather heavy package, an inconvenient encumbrance but one that she would soon be able to set down and get rid of. She was, actually, carrying a package, a very small one, under her arm.

"Hullo, Mr. Sly," she said, pulling herself up on one of the high bar stools and smiling from Trevor Sly to the two other customers. She shook herself free of the shapeless black mac to reveal a plain dove-gray dress beneath it. She studied the dress for just a moment (like a child making sure she'd put on what she'd wanted to), then smiled again.

The face was calm and gentle and the smile almost beatific, like something bestowed. She crooked her finger, calling Trevor Sly over. He moved down the bar and she engaged him in a low-voiced colloquy as she opened her package and offered him something. It looked like a thin cookie or cake, and he took a bit, munched it, and nodded. He moved back to the beer pulls to get her drink and she smiled at Plant and Trueblood as if she'd just performed a clever trick.

Melrose stared at her, rather blindly, and feeling a bit as if he'd fallen over the edge of the lifeboat. It was difficult to guess her age. Suffering might make a young face old; forbearance might make an old face young. Melrose guessed she was in her early thirties, and then he thought she could almost as easily have been thirteen. She sat there in her gray dress, looking at the beer pulls, the mirror, the shelves of beer and brandy glasses, and smiling as if the object of her outing were about to be realized.

That was what got Melrose: her smile, her expression. It was the smile of a little kid and the satisfied expression of one whose toils were finally to be rewarded. That she should turn up in a place like this, the Blue Parrot, down this dusty road (*how* had she got here?), struck him as an utter anomaly, like finding a seashell in the Strand.

Trueblood was joshing her about the half-pint Sly was setting before her. "Tangier! My God! Do you also like to crawl around inside active volcanoes?"

Trevor Sly gave his silly, high-pitched giggle. "Oh, now, Mr. Trueblood, you *do* tell tales. I'm sure it's not that strong." Sly minced his way down the bar again to give Melrose and Trueblood refills.

"To tell the truth," said Miss Fludd, "a volcano would make a change." The long sigh she exhaled seemed to release something into the room. "Wouldn't it be nice to see, oh, Mount St. Helens?" Then she slid from her stool, and, carrying her half-pint of strangely orangish beer, made her difficult way across the room, her object being, apparently, to view the posters which lined the walls, as if Sly's collection were paintings in a gallery.

Miss Fludd.

Melrose said the name to himself as he picked up his own drink and moved to stand beside her. "Miss Fludd," he said, then, aloud.

"Hello," she said, scarcely turning her gaze from the poster. It was an advertisement for *The Sheltering Sky*, one of the newer ones in the Sly expo of desert wastes; one dark form more or less superimposed on another in dark and windblown garments. She studied it for a moment, as did Melrose. She moved on to another, Melrose following her in her silent circuit of the film posters. There must have been seven or eight big posters, new and old, most of them pictures of a desert, or at least having the suggestion of being stranded near one.

Miss Fludd said she really liked it here in the Blue Parrot. It was so exotic.

Melrose was astonished. He blushed deeply, and was glad for the dimness of the lighting, which simulated desert nights rather than days. Now they were standing in front of *A Passage to India*. The tiny figure of Peggy Ashcroft stood atop a howdah at the head of a long procession of camels, early evening sun turning the acres of sand amber.

She loved Peggy Ashcroft, she said. Had loved, she corrected herself. Now she was dead.

Beside that poster was the one of Lawrence in his flowing white garments, walking along a procession of dark boxcars. Melrose recalled Jury's speaking of the two posters, hanging side by side, how the camel train in the one and the railway train, with all of its boxcars, in the other, moved toward one another, yet were destined never to meet. Jury had said that. Melrose wondered if he himself had grown cynical or simply lacked imagination, looking at the posters, looking out over the room (trying to see it through her eyes). He told her of Jury's comment.

She said that he must be a romantic man. Sipping her beer, looking from one picture to another, she added, "And a disappointed one."

Melrose thought about that for a moment.

Standing in front of the *Casablanca* poster, she asked him, "Have you ever been to Paris?"

He was, again, astonished. Hadn't *everyone*? But he didn't, of course, say that. Paris, to her, must have been as inaccessible as Algiers. Travelling for her was very difficult. Ruefully, she indicated her leg, hidden by the long skirt of the dove-gray dress.

" 'We'll always have Paris,' " she quoted from the film. She sighed. "Isn't that what they said? 'We'll always have Paris.' "

He realized that one of the disarming qualities about her was her directness—her thoughts, either well- or ill-formed, right away became words, as if there were no time to lose. And Melrose thought with a bit of a shock that rarely did he say what he was thinking. It had nothing to do with honesty or dishonesty; it was that his thoughts (and wasn't it this way with most people?) remained just that—thoughts, inarticulated.

They completed their turn around the room, a shabby old poster of *The Desert Song*, and Rudolph Valentino, and a smoky scene of dancing girls scattering veils. They returned to the bar, where she put down the dregs of her Tangier, said hello to Trueblood (smoking one of his shocking-pink cigarettes), and said she had to go.

Melrose helped her on with her coat and walked outside with her.

Standing by the dry fountain, she opened up the small package. "I just got these from Czechoslovakia. They come from Marienbad. Or what was Marienbad. I wonder if they'll change the name back again. Want a piece?" She held out the big circle of wafer-thin vanilla biscuit.

Melrose broke off a bit, tasted it. "Delicious."

She nodded. "If you live next door, you should come and see us."

Melrose smiled. Sounded like Ardry End and Watermeadows were a couple of terraced houses. "Thank you. I shall."

"Well, goodbye, then."

He looked around. There was no car except for his; he hadn't heard one before, he remembered. "But how did you get here?"

"Walked."

"But—look, I'll be more than happy to give you a lift."

"No, thank you."

Melrose frowned. It must be a good mile from here to Watermeadows. And the dirt road to the highway was hard and rutted. Difficult walking in the best circumstances.

She saw his expression. "It's good for me. I need to walk."

"I see. Well, goodbye, then."

She made her difficult way across the sandy courtyard and onto the road, where she turned and waved.

"Thanks for the biscuit!" Melrose called, and watched her wave again.

Watching her progress on that hard road, he recollected his first sight of her. He couldn't have been more surprised if the goddess Diana had appeared in his door with the moon under her arm.

Miss Fludd.

"Well?" asked Trueblood, excitedly. "Well, *well?*" A stagey whisper: "Who are they? How many? Little brother and sister? Alistair and Arabel—"

"Oh, be *quiet!*" Melrose said, irritated. "Her name is . . . Miss Fludd."

"I bloody well *know* that, old sweat. Sly told us *that.*"

Trevor Sly came from the back room in a tinkling of bead curtain. "Gentlemen, gentlemen, anything?"

Grumpily, Melrose shoved his pint down the bar. "Give me a Tangier."

Marshall Trueblood put his hand on Melrose's shoulder in a comradely and (Melrose thought) even commiserative gesture. Melrose didn't answer. He just sat, feeling inexplicably miserable, with his chin in his hands.

"What about the chocolate Labs?"

EIGHT

The small, shy-looking maid-servant wearing a black uniform and an uncertain look admitted Jury to the Belgravia house.

In a living room full of exquisite pieces, exquisitely upholstered in variations of blue and gray, Lady Cray herself was setting fluted glasses on a silver tray beside a silver wine cooler, when the maid showed Jury in. Lady Cray was wearing one of the silvery-blue outfits she favored, a long dress with a fold of chiffon collar and cuffs encrusted with tiny pearls around the edges. The dress matched the room, that elusive blue-gray of Waterford crystal, when the facets are turned at certain angles. Jury had always thought Lady Cray had the look of old crystal.

Champagne was her favorite drink, the hell with tea for one's elevenses. She said, "If you tell me you're on duty and can only drink Ribena you won't be getting any information out of me during this interview."

He accepted the glass she held out. "Actually, I was going to ask for a tumblerful of gin."

"Ah. I take it the investigation isn't really proceeding. Whatever the investigation is. Cheers." She tipped her glass in his direction, made a sweep of her arm toward the sofa behind him.

Jury sank into its impossibly soft, deep cushions. He thought he could have stayed here for days on this sofa, drinking champagne, listening to Lady Cray.

"It's about Fanny, again?"

Frances Hamilton had been her best friend and, when she died so suddenly in the Tate Gallery, had been living here in the house in Belgravia. Jury wondered if he had told Lady Cray that the last image on the dead woman's eyes had been the portrait of Chatterton. He thought of it now, as he looked around Lady Cray's beautiful living room, and noticed that the furniture had been rearranged, probably to accommodate a large escritoire and a jade and ivory carved Oriental screen that had supplanted the small sofa and Queen Anne chairs. They had been moved to sit before the french windows which led to a patio surrounded by ornamental trees and clay pots and flowerbeds that in spring overflowed with flowers. As the furniture had been changed, so had the ornaments and oddments arranged on the tables and in the glass-enclosed commodes and escritoire. Jury didn't see the turquoise-and-silver piece.

"I don't think you were ever satisfied," Jury said, "with that verdict of cardiac arrest."

"I don't think your medical examiner was, either."

Jury smiled. People had a way of pinning the responsibility for this investigation on him, didn't they. "Well, actually, it wasn't ours, Lady Cray."

She shrugged slightly and looked off through the french windows. "Satisfied or not, her heart still stopped. Which is why I didn't press the matter." Over the top of the tulip-shaped glass, she regarded him. "And you?"

"There's a question."

She said nothing.

Jury set his glass on the silver tray and leaned forward. "You told me Mrs. Hamilton visited the western United States."

"Yes, that's right. Last year, in November, after she went to Pennsylvania."

"Texas, you said. Or Arizona."

"Your memory is better than mine. I'm getting on, I expect." Lady Cray sighed artificially and poured herself another glass of champagne. "Or getting drunk." She set the bottle back in the cooler. "I expect I wasn't paying much attention to Fanny when she went rattling on about her travels."

"Only because you were distracted."

The glass she was setting down hit the tray with a decided click. "I beg your pardon?"

"Well, you told Sergeant Wiggins, I think, you'd just been to Harrods Food Hall and there'd been a bit of a dust-up about a box of Belgian chocolates? Your nephew, Andrew, took care of it and brought you home. Is that right?" Jury gave her a wide-eyed, innocent look.

"How clever. Are you going to blackmail me into total recall of the details of Fanny's trip?"

Jury laughed. "Not exactly. It's where Mrs. Hamilton went when she was away that interests me."

"Why?"

"Do you mind if I don't say, at the moment?"

"Of course I mind."

"It's probably not connected."

"With what is it not connected?"

Jury didn't answer directly. "She brought you a piece of sculpture, turquoise and silver. I remember it was on this table that day Wiggins and I came to see you."

"Yes. It's over there, in the escritoire. Why?"

"Would you mind if I had a look at it again?"

She rose and moved to the glass-fronted chest. She opened the door, brought out the turquoise block, and handed it over to Jury.

He turned it around, looked at the little silver flautist. "Where did she get this?"

"Texas, I think. Albuquerque or Abilene. Or was it Austin? Began with an A, I remember that." Lady Cray took a cigarette from a cloisonné box, sighed, put it back.

"Albuquerque isn't in Texas. The other two are, but not Albuquerque. It's in New Mexico."

"You know that, do you? How clever."

"Did she mention Santa Fe?"

Lady Cray cocked her head. "As a matter of fact, she did. And you're right, it was Albuquerque, or at least that's where the airport was. Superintendent, are you investigating the death of that young woman in the West Country? Salisbury?"

There had been a brief account in the papers, kept brief, no doubt, by Chief Inspector Rush. It didn't look good, foreigners dying on National Trust property. "You know about that?"

Lady Cray's silvery eyes slid him a look. "A body turning up at Old Sarum has a way of getting one's attention, yes."

"It's not my case." Wasn't Macalvie's either, he told himself yet again. "I'm merely helping a divisional commander out there."

"You mean the two are connected? Fanny and that young woman?"

"The divisional commander thinks so." He shrugged. "It's a hunch." *The hell it is*, he could almost hear Macalvie's voice.

There was a silence. They both sipped their champagne. "Well, and are you going to tell me? Hunch-wise, I mean?" Another silence. She picked up the turquoise sculpture. "To do with this?"

"Yes. But I'm not sure what. Was Fanny Hamilton actually *from* Philadelphia?"

Lady Cray nodded. "Remember, we talked about her family when I told you about Philip. You know her background."

"Foreground, then. She'd come back from America about two months before she died. Was she different in any way?"

"Only in respect to grieving over Philip's death. To tell the truth, she didn't really rabbit on about her trip."

"What about postcards? Did she send postcards?"

"Yes." Lady Cray frowned. "She did. But I might have thrown them out."

"All the same, would you have a look?"

She nodded, started to get up, sat back down. "What about the people in the Tate who were there when she died? What about the people around her at the time? Could someone she came in contact there have—?" She made vague gestures with her hands. A large stone, a marquise-cut diamond, Jury thought, slid a fraction back on her thin finger.

Jury thought back to the couple who'd been sitting on the end of the bench where Fanny had died. Bea and Gabe. "Yes. She more or less fell right against a young woman sitting beside her. And her boyfriend." He remembered their names because he'd found it so ironic that two kids would be making out in front of Rossetti's painting *Beata Beatrix*. He'd have to ring Wiggins when he got back to his flat and tell him to find out from C Division the whereabouts of Bea and Gabe, and any other witnesses, too.

"I imagine that if they *had* been questioned, it wouldn't have been with the same bare-knuckles approach reserved for witnesses to a murder." She flashed him a smile.

"That the treatment you get from the cops? Beatings? Strip searches?"

"No. I generally just confess. I noticed you were looking at my ring. Wondering if I'd been to New Bond Street lately?"

Jury smiled, shook his head. Lady Cray had had plenty of trouble with police. She was a kleptomaniac. But improving lately, since her thieving focused only on certain things. Not diamonds, certainly.

"This turquoise, in case you're interested"—she picked up the small block—"is the real thing. Persian, probably, as that's where most of it comes from. Not many turquoise mines left in the States. And one has to be careful not to be fooled by the fake stuff. The kind that's been injected with plastic."

Jury smiled. "You're quite knowledgeable, Lady Cray."

"In my line of work, it's better to be. God knows what sort of rubbish I might pick up otherwise." She bestowed upon him another glittery smile. "Right now, I feel like going out and robbing a newsagent or something. Your 'inquiry' is beginning to tire me." From under the rosewood lid of the desk she took out papers—letters, cards—and sifted through them. "Here's one." She held up a postcard, looked at the message. "Unfortunately, Fanny was of the 'Having wonderful time, wish you were here' category of postcard writers."

"What does she say?"

" 'Having wonderful time, wish you were here.' I just told you."

Jury held out his hand.

"You don't believe me." She sighed. "Oh, all right: 'Truly the Land of Enchantment; one almost dares to hope—' something or other; it's a blur—'burden of the past . . .' Here. I can't read it and it sounds too horribly deep for me anyway." She squinted at the postmark. "New Mexico, but I can't read the rest of it. Down at the bottom's all this squinty little printing. Here." Her silk skirt rustled as she moved over to Jury.

But he looked first at the picture. An almost violent explosion of formations of red stone. High-vaulting formations of it, mountains of red rocks. It looked like something out of Disney, some futuristic Hollywood thing. It was, of course, beautiful and impressive. "Tao—no, Taos," he said.

Looking over his shoulder, she said, "Stupid of me. It's printed right down in the corner."

"May I keep this?"

"Of course you'll want to milk it of all of its secrets."

"Of course."

"But how could Fanny possibly have been murdered, Superintendent? No weapon, no wound—well, it's a mystery still. Fanny was so healthy. How could it have been some heart thing?"

"I don't know. But her death bears looking at just a little closer, I think."

She whisked the turquoise piece from the table, held it out. "And this? Next you're going to tell me a similar piece was found with the dead woman at Old Sarum."

"Not exactly. But the way you describe Fanny Hamilton, she strikes me as flighty. A bit like meringue. Tasty but lightweight. You didn't take her very seriously."

Lady Cray looked sad. "If that's the way I talked of her, I'm sorry. One has a way of speaking slightingly, sometimes, of a thing or a person who means more than one cares to admit. And, yes, Fanny *was*, as you put it—" Lady Cray smiled—"a meringue. But believe me, at my age, I take *everyone* seriously, that is, everyone I have any liking for. When you're young, you can afford to discard or ignore or even abuse your friends and your family. We're very careless when we're young. It's not that we become kinder when we grow old, we simply become more careful. Fanny is the sort of person I would probably have been careless of when I was young. At nearly eighty, I place more importance on holding on to people. I miss her, honestly."

Jury rose to go, slipping the postcard into his pocket. "No, you're right. We are careless of people." He smiled and rose. "I've got to get to the Yard."

"But I wanted you to join me in a glass of champagne. You did such a wonderful thing about Philip. And I was hoping Andrew—you know, my nephew—would be here by now. He was going to come round today. With Adrienne. That's his fiancée." She sighed. "You know, you might want to talk to Andrew. Why don't you stop back later? In the meantime . . ." Lady Cray twisted the bottle of iced champagne.

Jury looked ruefully at the silver wine cooler. "I've been trying to stop smoking—"

"I've never smoked champagne, to be honest."

"I mean, drinking that stuff, and sitting here relaxing, well, it just cries for a smoke, doesn't it?"

She sighed. "How true that is. Fanny smoked like a chimney and it couldn't have done her any good. But there you are, we seldom go for what's good for us."

Jury smiled. "I expect you're right. Goodbye, Lady Cray."

NINE

TO: RJ
FR: JK
MESSAGE: ZILCH

Jury read this aloud to the recumbent figure on his sofa, the one who had written it on his "While You Were Out" pad. Carole-anne Palutski lay with her arms gracefully crossed on her breast, sunk in her "meditations." Jury had once asked her, Why the plural? Because there was more than one. The tone added: *obviously*.

Her eyes, which could shift through a range of semiprecious-stone colors, ranging from turquoise to lapis lazuli, were gently closed, meditatively, or so it would seem.

Jury looked from the message to Carole-anne's placid, pellucid face. "Carole-anne, what does 'zilch' mean, exactly?"

"Exactly nothing."

He glared at her and her pleased-as-punch little smile. "On the other end of a telephone line, it's impossible for a caller to say 'exactly nothing.' Unless heavy breathing's in progress."

"You know what I mean." As if she were flicking away flies, she gestured with her freshly manicured fingernails.

"No, I don't."

Carole-anne yawned, sat up, and reached for her manicure gear—Koral Kiss, Jury saw, was the color of the nail varnish bottle—preparatory to continuing the job. "She just wanted to know were you back in London yet?" Her chin on her updrawn knee, she set about giving her toenail a lick of Koral Kiss.

"And you said . . . ?"

"Didn't know, did I?" The sleeve of her coral-colored silk top slipped from her shoulder when she shrugged.

If Christian had depended on Carole-anne to carry his messages instead of Cyrano, Roxane would have ended up an unwed crone.

" 'Didn't know, did I?' " Jury chirped in mimicry. "Well, now, let me point out clues to my whereabouts, shall I?"

Jury had gone to Belgravia to see Lady Cray after a brief stop at his Islington digs, a stop just long enough to check his mail and his messages—chief of which he had just read off to his beautiful neighbor who occupied the top-floor flat in the terraced house, together with Jury (ground floor) and Mrs. Wassermann (basement). In between his and Carole-anne's was the vacant first-floor flat of which Carole-anne was overseer: meaning, she had convinced the landlord to entrust her with its rental. ("We don't want a lot of riffraff, Mr. Mosh, now, do we? You'll see. I'll get someone superior, like ourselves, with whom you'll have no trouble.")

Poor Mr. Mosh. Mr. Moshegeiian to the rest of the world. Carole-anne had turned down or turned away dozens of applicants, most of whom, according to Mrs. Wassermann, at least, seemed perfectly nice. According to Carole-anne, they had been totally unsatisfactory, squalling babies ("You want that living over you, Super?"), Shepherd Market whores, thieves, cutthroats, or New Agers. Carole-anne really had it in for the New Agers, with their exotic minerals and stones and out-of-body experiences. But given her job at a Covent Garden emporium as fortune-teller and Principal Ornament, where she plied tarot cards in her silken tent, her objection to the mystical and astronomical concerns of New Agers struck Jury as somewhat hypocritical. Granted (Jury had thought), for Carole-anne to have an out-of-body experience verged on the tragic. Why she troubled to paint any part of herself—lips, eyes, toenails—baffled him. It was the ultimate in lily gilding, like dipping stars in sequins.

Acidly, he pointed out the signs of his having stopped in his flat. "As-yet-unpacked bag sitting by the bookcase; mail brought in and opened; milk, ditto; coffee cup and remains of bread roll on table, there; note to Mrs. Wassermann cello-taped to my door reading, 'Back from the country and will see you this evening, RJ.' All signs of human habitation in general and mine in particular. You noticed none of these pointers?"

Carole-anne squinted up at him as if she'd gone momentarily blind. "I'm not one to pry, am I?"

Curiously enough, this was true. He had given her a key and told her to answer his phone if she heard it, done more for her benefit than his. Jury and Mrs. Wassermann were the extent of Carol-anne's "family," as far as he knew. And he also knew just what that lack felt like. Anyway, a toss of his rooms would reveal nothing. He wondered if he even had a secret life.

Jury fell into a heap in his big easy chair. "Elaborate on 'zilch' or you'll be sorry."

She raised the coral-painted nail brush and sat back, gazing at her handiwork and wiggling her toes. "I guess it was a bad connection."

Any call from a Jury lady friend would be a bad connection if Carole-anne was taking it. "Did you put the receiver down and go in my kitchen to do one of your fry-ups while she was trying to talk to you?"

Carole-anne rolled her eyes in her best oh-God-grant-me-patience manner. "No. Lemme see. She was talking about soup."

"Soup?" Jury frowned, then his frown relaxed as he remembered the soup Jenny Kennington had served him when he'd last seen her. Melon and mint, smooth as glass. "She's a cook," he said absently.

"Oh? Well, I expect we all got to make a living." Condescension oozed from her every pore.

"She doesn't have to do it to make a living. She's just a superb cook."

"Really? Didn't sound like it. She was going on about what she was putting in it. The soup, I mean."

Jury studied Carole-anne for signs of subterfuge. "Somehow, I can't picture you and Jenny Kennington exchanging recipes."

"Not me, Super. I've better things to do with my time. I admit I wasn't attending all that closely. Said something about a pub."

"She's going into the pub business."

Carole-anne's look was disapproving. "I've always wondered about women publicans."

"Wondered what?" She'd never given women publicans a passing thought, Jury was sure.

"Well, I think it makes a woman a bit hard, don't you? Or maybe it's the hard ones go in for it." Daintily, she recapped the bottle of Koral Kiss and wiggled the toes of her other foot. Then she folded her hands behind her head, whose dazzling reddish-gold was illuminated by the light reflected up from the bright pink sweater—she looked like a sunset over the Salisbury Plain—and said, "Coarsens one, that's what I think."

"Well, it won't coarsen this particular one, lovey."

"No, I expect not; I mean, not someone who sounds as snobby as her."

No one could change a tune quicker than Carole-anne. So if Jenny couldn't be coarse, she could at least be a snob. "Snobby?"

"It's that la-di-da kind of way she's got of talking."

"Memory returned, has it?"

She thought for a moment. "I didn't say I *forgot*, did I? Only, she didn't say nothing—anything—worth remembering. You don't have time for a lot of chat." She sighed and shook her head wearily. The demands that other women made on his time and energy were scarcely to be tolerated. "You've more important things to do." Here she planted her two feet on the coffee table and studied the pedicure.

"Like counting your toes? In the time, Carole-anne, we have been sitting here imitating two people exchanging views, you could have delivered a parliamentary White Paper or the entire Report to the Commissioner, much less a simple telephone message." Jury slid down in his chair, glowering. "I'm getting an answering machine." He loathed them; Lord knows Carole-anne loathed them too, because *she* wanted to be his answering machine. How else could she screen his life? "Getting an answering machine" was merely an old, standard threat, in the category of "getting my lock changed" or "found a pretty woman for the first-floor flat."

Now she looked at him as if it were *he* who was the cause of this little fracas. "You needn't get shirty. You needn't keep interrupting. You needn't—"

"—resist the impulse to get the kitchen breadknife."

Infinitely patient, Carole-anne held up her freshly manicured fingers, patting air, calling for silence. "The reason I didn't *write* the message, if you must know—" pause for fabrication—"is because I knew you'd be tired, exhausted from your trip, and I didn't see any reason you shouldn't get a bit of rest before returning calls." She folded her white arms and tapped her Koral Kiss fingertips against their skin, lips pursed, waiting for him to come to his senses.

"Well? I've had my bit of rest sitting here with you. So what did she say?"

Carole-anne shrugged as prettily as she could. "Well, that's all, just about that soup."

Jury sighed, impatiently. "Anything else? Anything at all?"

She pursed her mouth. Deep concentration. "Oh, and she wants you to call, is all. But I expect you could have guessed that." With another fake yawn, and so as to distract him, she bounced up from the sofa and went to the window, where she might have been measuring for new curtains. "Your windows need cleaning. You should get a char, you should. Can't expect me to do *everything*."

"Just stand in front of it. You'll steam it clean."

"Who's that then?" She had her face plugged against the glass. "Who?"

"Down there, look."

Jury moved to stand beside her. Across the street, a rather dumpy, middle-aged couple were standing, talking. "Those two? I don't know."

"No, no, not them. Mrs. W.'s down on her steps with someone, some fella. Here, come over here."

Jury maneuvered around and close beside her, a pleasant proximity, he had to admit, and tilted his head against the glass. Mrs. Wassermann was outside, at the top of her downward set of steps, talking to a tall young man, who kept looking up, and Jury would have thought for a moment he was looking at them, there at Jury's window, until he realized that he was looking higher. Mrs. Wassermann was pointing.

In one swift move Carole-anne had gathered her belongings and headed for the door. "Got to get ready for work. Ta!"

At first he thought she was going to pound down the stone steps outside, but he heard her pounding, instead, *up* to her own flat. This he surmised was done so that she could slip into something of even hotter coral.

Jury himself went out and down.

"Mr. Jury! I did not know you had returned. Look, look, here is someone come to view the flat."

Which is what Jury thought, when he'd seen him looking up. The man was probably in his late twenties, nearly as tall as Jury, dressed in black leather. Totally. Black bomber's jacket, black trousers, tight. Brilliant hazel eyes, sandy hair, muscles beneath the leather, cheekbones planed for model or movie star.

Randy Tyrone.

At least that's the name Mrs. Wassermann gave out by way of introduction. Nobody, Jury thought, was really named Randy Tyrone. The grip splintering a few tiny, unnecessary bones in Jury's hand, Randy Tyrone (or whoever he was) said, in a voice modulated beyond belief, "Mrs. Wassermann told me about you. This should be a pretty safe place to live."

How clever. Jury did not return the smile; he was looking at the motorcycle—a Mercedes Benz, no less—parked at the curb. Sleek and shiny black, just like its owner. "That yours?"

Randy Tyrone nodded, mouth curved in a supercilious smile. "Gets me around quicker than a car."

"From where to where?"

"I'm an actor. Resting, at the moment. A spot of modeling between acting jobs."

"An actor!" Mrs. Wassermann was thrilled.

Jury didn't think "acting" had bought the Benz. A stint in Soho, maybe. With a regretful shake of his head, he said, "Golly, what a shame, Randy. You've come all this way for nothing. Place was just rented not fifteen minutes ago."

Mrs. Wassermann's mouth dropped. Then she said, "Why . . . Carole-anne never told me anyone was coming to see it. My goodness . . . I didn't see anyone." Helplessly, she looked at Randy Tyrone.

Jury pointed to the couple still conversing on the other side of the street. "Right there. I expect you must've just missed them." Gaily, Jury waved at the couple, who stared at him, at each other, and then waved back, but rather tentatively.

As Jury was listening for signs of Carole-anne, Randy Tyrone zapped on his black helmet, twitched a muscle in his cheek several times, sketched an abrupt goodbye to both of them, and (just as Carole-anne came out the front door) shot away in a black blur.

"Who was that?" she fairly whined, on the pavement, making for the middle of the street to get a better look.

"Just one of those messengers on bikes," said Jury, signing Mrs. Wassermann to keep still. She had lived long enough around him and Carole-anne to sense potential trouble; she nodded.

"For who, then?"

"Me," said Jury.

"On a *bike?*" She frowned. "Must've been important."

"Not really."

"Well, what was it, then?"

Jury yawned. "Zilch."

Thank God tea was born before Wiggins.

That was Jury's first thought as he walked into his office at Scotland Yard at four o'clock to find the detective sergeant with his hand poised over the electric kettle, just working up to a hiss and a screech, as if he wanted to grab it before it took wing. It did screech and Wiggins's hand did clamp down on it, and moved it toward the two waiting mugs.

"Tea's up," said Wiggins, with a beamish smile, when he saw Jury. "I knew you'd be here right about now."

Jury didn't know how he knew, but said nothing except "Not so much sugar this time, thanks."

"You know I don't use sugar these days, sir. Honey, that's the ticket."

"Uh. Not so much honey, then." Jury looked down at the massed papers that had landed all-anyhow on his desk, wiped his hand over them as if this action might disclose one that was important, then shoved the whole lot aside. "What'd you find out about the Tate art lovers?"

"Beatrice and Gabriel? Nothing yet; I'm expecting a call from C Division. How much milk?" asked Wiggins, keeping his priorities straight.

"The usual."

Wiggins poured a careless amount into the mug and set it before Jury. He then proceeded with the more serious matter of infusing his own tea with one or the other of the medications arranged in vials along the front of his desk. He picked up first one, then another little brown bottle, studied it with a care Jury doubted even the pharmacist had expended on the prescription, pursed his lips, shook his head, picked up the next.

Jury was in a state of ungovernable suspense. As long as he'd known him, Sergeant Wiggins had been dispensing pills, syrups, herbs, potions, biscuits, capsules, anodynes, and amulets, everything short of a necklace of garlic cloves to ward off evil spirits. The spirit world held no terrors for Wiggins; he was afraid of what crept and crawled along planet Earth, not ill-defined and amorphous masses from either Hell or Heaven. Planet Earth had spawned enough corporeal diseases for Wiggins to tolerate or even contemplate; he wasn't the least interested in the soul's ills. Jury watched him fix his gaze on a clear glass vial that held some viscous greenish stuff.

"What the hell's that?" Jury asked in spite of his oft-broken promise to himself never to inquire into Wiggins's medications.

"This? Oh, this is for my chest." Wiggins made a few experimental *rr-rrks* and *ahs*, not a cough exactly, more of an aborted laugh. "Chesty, sir, I've been these last few days since you've been gone. It's all this weather we're getting."

Jury sipped his too-sweet tea. "I've never known a day without it."

"Sir?" Inquiring eyebrow lift.

"Weather. Same old February stuff, to me. Damp and drizzle. Unless you're talking about the ozone again."

Wiggins had been making dark prognostications for some time now about the dramatic weather changes in Britain—and elsewhere, of course, but elsewhere could take care of itself, since he didn't live there—hot summers, worse winters. Such changes were ominous. "Next, it'll be hurricanes, tropical hurricanes," he had said last summer.

Having inspected the row of vials, Wiggins now was eschewing them in favor of one of his favorite anodynes—the black biscuit. This was a disgusting-looking biscuit, a black-as-bile biscuit that was supposed to make the digestive system fully operational. Wiggins enjoyed one or two at teatime.

Having completed his ablutions, Wiggins asked Jury about the case. After Jury gave him a rundown of the conclusion Macalvie had drawn, Wiggins said, brushing away black crumbs, "Probably right."

"Right? My God, I'd sooner bet blindfolded at Cheltenham races." Jury was not at all convinced of this, though.

"Well, remember Dr. Dench, sir."

Macalvie had locked horns with his friend Dennis Dench over a question of bone identification a few years back.

"Mr. Macalvie was right, then, too," said Wiggins. "And Dench was the expert. And *he was wrong*."

Jury shoved aside a stack of papers and clamped his feet on top of his desk. "He's talking funny, too."

Wiggins frowned. " 'Funny'?"

"For Macalvie. He's turned philosophical, mumbling about abstract notions of time, and so forth."

"Oh, he always was." Wiggins said this with calm assurance.

Jury stared. "*Macalvie?* Macalvie was always one of the most straightforwardly pragmatic people I ever met. He loves cold, hard facts. He's not a philosopher."

"He's not a forensic anthropologist, either. But he managed to be one when he had to."

"Oh, for God's sake," Jury muttered just as the telephone rang.

Wiggins picked it up, announced himself, listened, put his hand over the receiver, told Jury it was C Division about the Tate Gallery. Listened some more as he pulled over a pad and a pencil. "Slocum, that's her name? S-L-O-C-U-M. . . . Right. . . . Gabriel Merchant. . . . Uh-huh. . . . Bethnal Green, right. . . . Both of them? . . . Uh-huh. . . ." Sergeant Wiggins's expression changed dramatically; he banged forward in his swivel chair. Finally, he choked out a "ta very much" to the caller and hung up.

Jury waited. Wiggins was silent.

"What the hell *is* it?" asked Jury. "What's wrong?"

"It's these two, this Bea Slocum and Gabriel Merchant."

"Something's happened to them?" Jury was alert.

"No, nothing's happened. It's where he lives, sir. In East London."

Jury frowned. "So? A hell of a lot of people live in East London."

"Not on Catchcoach Street, they don't."

It sounded vaguely familiar, obviously not vague at all to Wiggins. "Catchcoach Street?" Jury turned it over, smiled, laughed. "My Lord, Wiggins, you're not talking about—"

Looking as if the atmospheric ozone had just burst another hole, Wiggins nodded. His voice was ominous. "Crippses, sir. White Ellie. Ash. And those—*kiddies* . . ." An involuntary shudder ran through him. He opened his eyes, then looked imploring. "I'm still feeling really chesty, sir. I was thinking of maybe going home early, having a quiet lie-down."

Jury was already shrugging into his jacket. "No lie-down, Sergeant. Two men. You know how it is; Racer says we've got to follow proper procedure." Jury beamed at him. "Just bring your black biscuits."

All things change, all is transitory, and you never dip your hand in the same river twice. Or piss in the same birdbath.

Unless you were a Cripps.

In the front garden—a mere dusty patch of earth—of the house in Catchcoach Street, a boy of perhaps four years was taking aim at a white plastic birdbath that was planted amidst the earthly delights of plastic ducks and a hateful-looking troll.

Birds were visibly absent, having drunk once too often already, Jury thought as he and Sergeant Wiggins stood on the pavement watching, fascinated.

A window flew up; a slab of pale face above an obese body appeared, yelling, "Petey! Stop that infernal pissin' and come get yer tea!" SLAM down went the window, rattling the panes, shaking the baby buggy sitting on the step by the door. Without bothering to collect his short trousers, Petey hightailed it through the door, leaving it ajar.

"I expect we don't need to knock," said Jury, peering in the carriage at the baby in its faded bunting. It was like turning back time for Jury, seeing that buggy. The first time he'd seen it was nearly ten years ago, when he and Wiggins had come to Catchcoach Street to dig up information about a suspect in a grisly murder case. They'd been more successful in digging the baby out from under the wash. The carriage was still doing double time as a laundry cart; Jury moved a towel and some flannels away from the baby's face and checked to make sure the tyke was breathing. Yes.

Wiggins shook himself loose of his own personal Cripps nightmare and mumbled, "Good Lord." Then he, too, peeped into the carriage. "Surely, that can't be the same baby, sir, as last time?"

"Probably there's always a baby of one sort or another." Jury gave the dented rattle a bit of a shake. The baby gurgled and drooled, its fingers clutching a flannel, either uncaring or unmindful of the dark fate that lay in wait for it, if not today, then tomorrow or the day after.

They entered what might dubiously be termed a "front parlor," where Wiggins just missed stepping in a bowlful of water with wires running into it, sitting on the floor. From the kitchen came a terrible din, sounds of kettles and jangling crockery, curses and giggles, White Ellie's voice distinguishable above the others from sheer volume. Then Ellie appeared, wreathed in smiles.

"Well, if it ain't the Two Rons back again! Wait'll I tell Ash—" She lifted her eyes ceilingward, adding, "Never mind. Come on in and wet yerselves!" Without waiting for them to answer, she dashed— waddled, rather—back through the kitchen door.

Wiggins, for once, wasn't backing away from her offer of refresh-ment, for his attention was taken up by the bowl of water. "What's *this* lot, then? Look, those are live wires, sir. That's dangerous. Burn the house down with that." Wiggins kept shaking his head.

"Probably," said Jury, glancing at the colored images jerking around on the telly. Some kind of cartoon show—

"You're in the way, mate," said a female voice from the other side of the room. The figure there was slouched, nearly buried in a dozen cushions scattered about the sofa. The red hair blazed as if the head itself were charged with electrical wires, like the dish on the floor.

Jury smiled. "Beatrice Slocum, isn't it? I'm from Scotland Yard CID."

Bea Slocum tried to appear bored, her interest aroused only by the cartoon characters. She clapped her hand over her mouth, gig-gling. It was a little like talking to Carole-anne Palutski.

"I'm Richard Jury; this is Sergeant Wiggins, Scotland—"

"Well, that there's Ren and Stimpy, so move, will you?" Her hair was a wondrous bluish-blackish-reddish color that one sometimes sees in adverts, and certainly looked dyed, the color of eggplant. She had a pretty face, spoiled by rainbow shadings of eye shadow—there must have been half a dozen colors vying. The face was soft and petulant, the mouth downturned slightly, signal that the soft petulance might, in ten years' time, harden into cynicism. She was dressed in a kind of ugly green flak jacket and sawed-off jeans. Her feet were stuffed into heavy, short boots. She was holding a remote in her hand and she raised the volume, and, apparently lured by the sounds of their favorite cartoon show, several Cripps kiddies burst from the kitchen into the living room, nearly bowling Wiggins over, then scattered like shot to distribute themselves across the floor, where they immediately started poking and pinching one another.

Said Jury above the TV noise, "If Ren and Stumpy—"

"*Stimpy*, sir," Wiggins corrected him. "It's all the rage."

With Wiggins, too, apparently, given the way he was so intently staring at the screen. "Don't sit on the floor, Sergeant."

Ren (or Stimpy) looked like a pull of taffy with teeth. The other looked like something Picasso had tossed out. Their time appeared to be taken up in bloodthirsty yowlings or finding ways to destroy whatever they came in contact with, with all the elaborate machinations that cartoon characters are given to, screaming, shouting, pinwheeling about the premises. No one was paying any attention to Scotland Yard, not even its own detective sergeant.

Naturally, Ren and Stimpy were an inspiration to the Cripps kiddies. For when Ren (or Stimpy) strangled Stimpy (or Ren), the older boy with the spiky hair made to do just the same thing to his little sister, shaking her like a rag doll until Jury clamped hands on him and pulled him off. If there was one rule the Cripps lads hewed to, it was never to pick on someone your own size, age, or sex; that way, you weren't so likely to get hurt. That the children hadn't changed over the last ten was, of course, the illusion created by more Cripps kiddies coming along to replace the ones who had got larger. If that taller lad over there was Friendly, he had grown a lot, but still had the sly and foxy look he had already honed to perfection when he was seven or eight. Yes, it must be Friendly, thought Jury, judging from the way his hand crept toward his crotch. Or perhaps such a movement was locked into the Crippses' genes. Just look at his father.

"Hey, mister, give us ten p. Go on, mister!" One of the smaller girls was yanking on his sleeve with a hand that bore witness to a tea of mash and catsup. Her boldness encouraged demanding howls from the others.

"Shut yer trap, Alice!" Here was the voice, if not of authority, at least of White Ellie. She came stomping back into the room with two cracked mugs of tea. These she held out to Jury and Wiggins. "Wet yerselves."

Jury's thanks were lost in the uproar created by Alice and Petey and the baby in the pram they'd managed to set wailing outside on the pavement. As for Sergeant Wiggins, well, it was the first time Jury had ever seen him look at a cup of tea with disrespect.

"'Ere now!" Wildly, she looked round the room. "Wherever's little Robespierre? Did ya go and leave 'im out again?" White Ellie went to the door and out to the pavement to rescue the baby. "Petey, you been pissin' in that birdbath?"

"No ma'am, no ma'am, no ma'am," Petey answered in a singsong.

"Takes after his da, Petey do. Disgustin', I keep tellin' 'im, and he'll wind up like 'im, too, screamin' in the streets. Just last week the Liar was rantin' and ravin' that Ash give 'er one in Mervin's lockup garage, but I says, 'Ha.' Wishful thinking, if you ask me. Well, you never did meet our Amy"—here she dragged a six-year-old out of the crowd and planted her before Jury. "Just a baby she was last time you was 'ere." She managed to make it sound as if Jury and Wiggins were annual visitors. "And this here's Alice."

Alice, a year or two younger than her sister, said hello by raising her cotton skirt so that the policemen could see she wasn't wearing knickers. Her grin was impoverished by several missing teeth.

White Ellie slapped the hand away and yanked the skirt down. Then she marched to the television and slapped it off, as if it too were up to salacious doings. "We got comp'ny!"

All the while, Bea's persimmon head had been bobbing here and there, first to one side, then to another, trying to regain her view of the telly. Defeated, she fell back against the faded cretonne of the sofa. Jury wasn't sure exiling Ren and Stimpy was such a hot idea, anyway. At least the cartoon had increased the attention span of the kids. Now, of course, they all had to amuse themselves again, and were bobbing around in a circle singing

> Piddlin' Pete, Piddlin' Pete,
> Piddles all over the toilet seat

which they thought rich with humor, or all of them did except for Petey himself, who stood bawling in the middle of the goblin ring.

White Ellie's injunction to "SHUT YER TRAP" warranted nothing. Sotto voce for no reason Jury could understand, she went on, "Thought you was the Social, come about Ashley. Up there—" she looked at the ceiling—"with 'er around the corner, the both a them, last week. Disgustin'. Bangin' 'er in me own 'ouse . . ." White Ellie could never quite believe that New Scotland Yard wasn't yet another arm of that police surveillance set up to expose the doings of her husband, Ash Cripps. "Well, I says, 'Ashley, you're bloody lucky it was the Liar spreadin' that story about Mervin's lockup, nobody believes what she says, anyways, know what I mean?' "

No, Jury didn't, but he took the opportunity to say: "It's not Ash we've come to see, Ellie. Actually, it's Beatrice, here."

Beatrice was stirring the kiddie stew by poking at the dancing ring with the broom handle. She looked up, surprised.

> Piddlin' Pete, Piddlin' Pete,
> Piddles all over his own two feet!

More wails from Petey, trapped in the center.

"Clear out and give the superintendent a seat!" shouted Ellie. "You, Aurora, clear them knickers and tights off that chair there." Whichever one Aurora was, she paid no attention, nor did the others, being much too busy with their game.

Jury did for himself, sweeping a few rags from the cushion beside Bea Slocum. "You were at the Tate with your friend Gabe. Where is he, then? It was Gabe I expected to see here."

White Ellie put in, "Kips on our sofa there, Gabe does. Lost his flat, so Ash told him he could stay 'ere till he got on his feet. And Bea, she's only stopped by fer tea. Bea's got a *job* over in Bethnal Green. Bea *works*." Unused to the notion of gainful employment, Ellie breathed real life into the word.

Jury said, "I thought you might've remembered something about the dead woman. Frances Hamilton was her name."

"Gabe might've done. Thing is, we separated for a while so's he could go to the Swagger exhibit and I could look at the J.M.W.'s—"

"The what?" asked Wiggins. He had apparently given up on the wire-laced dish of water for now and had his notebook out.

Bea fiddled a scrap of red polish off a nail. "Turner, you know." She apparently took Jury's and Wiggins's astonished looks to mean they didn't know who Turner was, and added, "J.M.W. Turner. He's a painter." She said this quite matter-of-factly, her information aimed at the knuckleheads who'd never heard of Turner. "Anyways, Gabe likes the Tate; we go there a lot. Gabe's a painter."

White Ellie hooted. "That one? Only thing he ever painted was Ash."

"Oh, give it a rest, Elephant. That was just a joke."

"Nearly landed Ash in the nick, that did. Some joke. See—" Ellie turned her full attention to Jury, spreading her great girth over the clean laundry—"drunk as two lords they got, Ash and Gabe, and Gabe, he's got out his pots of paint—"

"My paint, Elephant. *Mine*. Last I had, too. Gabe nicked it from my flat in Bethnal Green."

Ellie went on, "So Gabe, he makes a few dibs and dabs on Ashley. Then they think, well, what's the point of being only a little bit blue, so Ash strips right down until he's stark, and Gabe paints him blue, blue all over except for patches so's the skin could breathe, and then bets him ten quid he wouldn't run down to the corner that way. So I'm in here, givin' Robespierre 'is bottle, and what do I see when I look up. This blue thing goes streakin' by the window and pretty soon one of the kids comes runnin' and tells me his da just run by, and he was turned all blue—"

Now the counterpoint to this tale was offered by the kiddies, who changed their chant to

> Ash is blue, Ash is stark,
> Ash is always outta work.

"'Ere now!" cried White Ellie. "That's yer da ya be makin' fun of, so show more respect!"

> Da is blue, Da is stark,
> Da is always outta work.

As if there'd been no interruption, Ellie went on, "And don't think the Liar wasn't ringin' up the Old Bill practically before I could even catch me breath and get out there. So round come the cops and the Liar's out there directin' traffic and Gabe just laughin' fit to kill—"

Said Bea, as she cadged a cigarette from Jury's pack, "Ah, go on, Elephant. Give it a rest."

Jury turned his attention to Bea. "Is it possible Gabe saw Mrs. Hamilton—the dead woman—when he was going round the Swagger Portrait exhibit? And you were in the Clore Gallery?"

Exhaling a bale of smoke, she said, "He might've done. He'll be here in a minute. You can ask him yourself."

"Were you looking at the Turners, then?"

"Oh, well," she said, as if either the question were idiotic or any answer would be, "you seen one Turner, you seen them all, right? How many ways can you do light? is what I say." She was looking at Jury to see how he'd react.

Jury's reaction was even greater astonishment. Beatrice Slocum wasn't the girl he'd thought she was. Or the one she wanted you to think she was.

There was a brief scuffle out in the street, and Bea leaned over the back of the sofa to pull a grubby lace curtain aside.

The participants in this fracas were an elderly man with no chin; a woman in a waxed coat who'd probably looked middle-aged all of her life; a tall, youngish man whom Jury recognized as Beatrice's young man, Gabe; and Ashley Cripps. Jury certainly would have known Ash anywhere. Some sort of argument was in progress— shouting from the chinless man, waving of arms from Ash, a cane brought into play by the woman, which put her at considerably more than middle age.

Bea was turned round, looking over the back of the sofa. "Oh, bloody hell. It's the Liar again. She's out there with Fuckin' Freddie—"

Ellie threw up the window. "Get outta the street, Ashley. Get yerself in 'ere!"

With obvious irritation at this interruption of his dispute, he told Ellie to go fuck herself, he was busy, thank you very much, and returned to shoving his fist at the nose of the chinless man.

Disgusted, White Ellie waddled over to the front door and furiously across the pavement. Now there were five of them, and Jury decided he had better intervene, or at least go out and collect Gabe, if his investigation was to end this year. He walked out into the street.

To what must have been White Ellie's question, the chinless man was responding:

"Well, he f-f-f-f-fuckin' pissed hisself in me primulas, dihn't he? F-f-f-f-f-f—"

"Ah, *shud-dup!*" shouted Ash. "I never done no such thing."

"Seen 'im with me own eyes!" whined the woman Jury presumed was the Liar.

The tall young man was himself sticking up for Ash, claiming the Liar was exactly that and hadn't seen any such thing. Jury asked him if he was Gabriel Merchant.

"Yeah, tha's right, guv, but piss off for right now, okay?" It was apparently the password, offered in a friendly manner.

The collective voices had reached a pitch feverish enough to attract the attention of passersby, who were stopping with their dogs on leads and their shopping carts to watch.

"—and then he f-f-f-f-fuckin' pulls down 'is zipper an'—"

"I never! Elephant, tell 'er! I couldn't do, could I?"

The woman started whipping the air with her cane. "You did do, I seen you, I seen you—"

"Liar! Liar! Liar!" yelled White Ellie. "He couldn't, could he? I sewed it up, dihn't I?"

Ashley thought this was enormously funny, the two neighbors being caught out, as he thrust his pelvis forward. "Go on, then, go on, yank 'er open, Liar."

The woman gave a little gasp, either over the proximity of Ash Cripps's zipper or over being discovered in the act of living up to her sobriquet. The fly of his trousers was quite firmly stitched over. She turned, face flushed nearly to the color of the garnet at her throat, and stumped away. The chinless man (Fuckin' Freddie, apparently) stuttered out a few indecipherable words and made off after her.

Both Ash and Gabe laughed until they wept, arms round one another's shoulders.

"I hate to break this up," said Jury.

"Hey, well, I'll be pissed if it ain't Scotland Yard come round again." Enthusiastically, Ashley shook Jury's hand, pumping it up and down. "Hey, Gabe, this here's the police. Remember I told you about that case we was helpin' out with?" Cheerfully, Ash turned to Jury. "So what's it this time?"

Jury smiled. "If we could just go into the house. I'd like a word with Gabe."

"Gabe? Whatta you been doin', then? 'Avin' a piss in Fuckin' Freddie's primulas? Ah, shut yer mouths, ya little bleeders!" Ash said as they passed the kiddies, who had all collected outside to watch the fracas.

There was a bit of schmoozing and smooching between Gabe and Bea before he settled down comfortably beside her. He had remarkably blue eyes to offset his long and slightly greasy hair. "So, guv."

Jury nudged Wiggins away from the small bowl of water. "Sir," said Wiggins, getting out his notebook. He went over the facts as he had taken them down, meticulously, as always.

"What we'd like to know is whatever you remember about that incident at the Tate."

"Give us a fag, luv," said Gabe to Bea. She passed him a tin of tobacco and some cigarette papers and he carefully distributed the tobacco, pinched the ends together, lit up, looked thoughtful. But said nothing, and Jury prompted him.

"Did you see Mrs. Hamilton—the dead woman—elsewhere in the gallery?"

"Yeah, as a matter of fact. In the Swagger exhibit. Bea here didn't go with me."

Bea leaned her head, which was resting on his thigh, back farther so that she could look up into his eyes. "Why should I pay four quid to see a lot of women sitting on clouds with their feet on skulls?" She gave Jury a broad wink, ushering him back into the world of art appreciation.

Gabe made a noise of utter disgust. "Don't be daft."

"Can you remember if she was alone?"

"Far as I know, yeah. Those exhibitions can get pretty crowded."

"Do you recall exactly what she was doing?"

"Lemme see. I remember it was after the Van Dycks and I was studying that one by Reynolds of the Italian dancer. Some eyes she's got. That's when I noticed her. Looked sickly. Well, I thought she must be, for she hurried out—you know, the way people do if they're gonna—" Here he made retching gestures.

From the kitchen came a crash and the sound of raised voices and, at the same time, the kiddies spurting into the room and scattering like gunshot. The period of relative tranquility was obviously over.

"I never!"

"You did!"

"Never!"

And more from the kitchen, shouts and imprecations, until Ash came through the door holding a plate and fork, grinning for all the world as if his exit from the kitchen hadn't been accompanied by an aluminum cook pot hurled with breathtaking force, bouncing off the wall, bruising the faded browny paper, and clattering along the floor-boards.

The pot just missed hitting Ash, who was followed by a scruffy little terrier. The dog clearly wanted the plate Ash was hugging to his chest with his forearm. Ash collapsed on the sofa next to Wiggins, sending dust motes dancing. Generously, Ash offered Wiggins a share of his fry-up—a melange of chop, sausage, potatoes, onions, and beans—that turned the sergeant pale. Ashley was forking it up with relish. Mouth full to bursting, he inquired of Bea and Gabe, "How 'bout you kids, then. You had your tea?"

They said they were going down the pub as soon as the "interrogation" was over.

"Mr. Jury? Ah, he ain't half bad. Nossir, he helped me out once when the Social come round." Looking sad as could be, he added, "That pub closed, the old Anodyne Necklace. Things change." Ash shook his head.

White Ellie came steaming in with her own full plate—fried eggs and a mountain of beans on toast. "So I says t' this one 'ere"—and she nodded her head, hair the color of egg yolk, towards her husband, and took up the conversation in true Homeric fashion, in medias res—"I says, 'Ashley, you scare up twenty nicker for a ticket, when that Criterion opens, you'll be able to show yerself t' all the nobs in London."

A gurgle came from the baby carriage, but Robespierre was hidden by a cloud of faded blue wool, so Jury could not see if he was choking on the beans. Several forkfuls had gone in that direction.

Ellie continued talking and chortling. "That there theatre's got the swankiest toilets in London."

"Ah, lay off, Elephant," said Ash, who was dangling his lamb chop bone over the arm of the sofa, teasing the terrier.

"Well, better'n showin' yourself down them filthy toilets in Mile End."

Ashley Cripps had been inside so many times that he kept a little bag packed and ready near the door, like a runway model. He'd been up on just about every minor charge a man of any imagination could be—doing a newsagent, handling, dealing, carrying—but his forte was indecent exposure, which had got him his nickname, Ash the Flash.

Wiggins broke into this muttering argument, his curiosity apparently uncontainable. "I was just wondering, Mr. Cripps," he said, pointing to the dish of water and wires, "just exactly what's the, ah, theory behind that?"

Ash wiped his mouth with his dirty handkerchief and stuffed it back in his trouser pocket. "That there's my own invention, Mr. Wiggins, and right proud I am of it, too. See, when the mouse comes along for a drink a water, he gets fried. Place smokes right up."

Said White Ellie, "Oughta put a bit o' cheese in, Ashley. Mice are turnin' up their noses."

Wiggins frowned and said, "But I didn't know mice—"

Ellie was lighting up the cigarette she'd rolled and settling herself on the sofa amidst the cloud of laundry—clean or dirty, it was anybody's guess. Her descent into the broken springed cushions created a stir on the other end, and a face appeared.

"*There* you are. Thought you was going up to the Paki's for the beer," said Ellie, undisturbed by this Lazarus-like vision of the uprising moon face topped with spiky hair.

The girl rubbed at her eyes. "I was just havin' a kip, what's it to ya?"

This latest addition to the Crippses' ranks bestirred herself and rose, stretched as if now ready to meet the day, told White Ellie she needed a fiver for the beer, and left, stopping only to search for a garment (a scarf, as it turned out) in the jumble of the baby carriage before letting the front door bang behind her.

White Ellie put a pudgy hand on Wiggins's forearm. "You married, then?"

Wiggins quickly shoveled some towels and flannels to the side to give himself a few more inches of grace. He moved away from Ellie, telling her no, he was not married. Smart lad, she said, giving him a huge salubrious wink as if to say he was better off with a catch-as-catch-can relationship with the ladies.

Bea was now talking over the din of giggling kiddies fallen all in a heap on top of Petey. "Spend a lot a time in the Tate, Gabe and me. We like the V and A and the National Gallery, too, but the Tate's best, because it's on the Embankment and we like to walk by the river."

Jury smiled at the picture of Bea and Gabe that was reshaping itself in his mind, an odd mix of East Ender nonconformist, neon-haired, anti-establishment together with the Chelsea Embankment, cappuccino people. "So did Frances Hamilton," said Jury. "Spend a lot of time in the Tate, I mean. According to the friend she lived with. She liked museums, period."

Bea's face scrunched up into a little girl's thoughtful frown. She had turned her head to look out at what was now a bright and sunlit day.

Wiggins took down their addresses: Gabe's flat, which he hoped to get back into next week, was nearby in Catchcoach Street. Beatrice lived in Bethnal Green, where she also worked at the Museum of Childhood.

Jury rose, Wiggins following suit. "Thanks for your help—Bea, Gabe." Jury looked round the room. "And everybody."

He looked down into the baby carriage, which was now propping open the front door. Robespierre, unlike the shiftless Ashley Cripps, served a number of purposes from laundry hamper, to drawer, to door stop. Jury spent an idle moment contemplating the ferociously sleeping babe, wondering which of the children yelling outside on the pavement had once been the baby he had seen in this selfsame carriage. Aurora was a likely candidate, for she looked to be nine or ten years old. Jury did not want to ask; he was afraid of finding out that that particular baby had not survived this lot.

There was a whimper, and a crying out there on the pavement, and in the midst of whatever pain was being inflicted on whichever one of them, Jury found his heart sinking to think that tiny-fisted, flame-cheeked Robespierre would very quickly grow up to have spiky hair and lashless eyes and join the grubby ring outside.

How could time play such tricks?

He thought of the Avon, flowing between the verdant green banks beneath a cobalt sky. The ducks, the rush grass, the swans. It never changed. But that was a lie. He would never stand by that same river twice. Everything changed, nothing stayed.

Except the Crippses.

Jury sighed.

Jury had told Wiggins he'd meet him back at New Scotland Yard, but that he wanted to stop by Lady Cray's and talk to her nephew. The door of the Belgravia house was opened, not by the shy maid, but by a young man in a subtly checked lamb's wool overcoat. He looked like someone just on his way out.

"Oh, hullo. Are you looking for my aunt? I'm afraid she's just nipped round to Harrods."

Given his expression, Jury imagined the nephew meant it when he said "afraid." Given, further, what usually happened when Lady Cray "nipped round to Harrods," Jury could understand why. He smiled and introduced himself, explaining, before the young man turned even paler, that he was an old friend of his aunt.

From the drawing room, a woman's voice—or at least a female one, with more of a girlish timbre—called, "Who is it, Andrew? We'll be *late* for the *opening*."

Jury smiled slightly when Andrew ignored the voice. "Your aunt has spoken about you with a good deal of enthusiasm."

Andrew brightened considerably. "Yes, we get on famously."

"Could I speak to you for just a moment? I won't keep you, I promise."

"Of course. Come on in. My aunt told me about you." As they moved across the marbled entrance hall, Andrew said, "At Castle Howe, that's where you met. My God, but that must have been exciting, to be in on a murder, on catching a killer. Wish I'd been there. This is Adrienne. Armitage," he added. "Adrienne, this is Superintendent Jury. Scotland Yard."

Andrew now seemed pleased as punch that he'd found a Scotland Yard superintendent on his doorstep. Less pleased was Adrienne Armitage, who looked up with a massive sigh from a glossy fashion magazine she was riffling, and rolled her wide, lovely, slightly vacant blue eyes in one of those God-give-me-strength looks. She did not bother to acknowledge the introduction. "Andrew! We'll be late!"

"Never mind," said Andrew, clearly a match for all of her heaving impatience. "How can I help you, Superintendent? And sit down, why don't you?"

Adrienne had her fisted hand on her hip, holding back a near-to-the-floor-length glossy fur coat. The charcoal-gray suit was a designer, perhaps an Armani; the scarf casually draped around its deep-cut neckline was Hermès. The shoes, the gloves were Upper Sloane Street, he bet, and the smoothly cut blond hair she gave a little horsy toss to had recently been scissored by someone way off Jury's usual route. She walked about the room—here, there—standing before the fireplace, one gloved hand on the mantel, the other still pushing back that fur coat and raising her chin and tapping her foot. Jury decided not to sit down.

"I'm just making a routine inquiry into Frances Hamilton's death—"

"Do you really *say* things like that?" asked Adrienne Armitage, now snapping shut the silver case from which she'd taken a cigarette.

"It just slipped out, miss," said Jury, watching her take little jabs at her cigarette as she moved over to the long glass table and more magazines, which she began pushing about distractedly.

"Would you like something? Coffee? A drink, perhaps?" Andrew started toward the cabinet, but Jury stopped him.

"*Well!*" said his betrothed, in a stagy way. "I've been trying to get a champagne cocktail out of you for simply *hours*, darling."

"You had four of them at lunch. Sorry, Superintendent. You wanted to talk about Fanny, did you?" He frowned. "I know my aunt thought there was something peculiar about that, but—"

"*Daddy* will be *furious* if we don't leave this instant." But Adrienne's drawl and her turning over of pages did not attest to anyone's being in a hurry for anything, despite the fact all three of them remained standing. "You *know* how poor Daddy gets. . . . Oh, *look*, darling—" The magazine, opened to a page of two models holding the reins of two horses, was held forth for Andrew's inspection. "Doesn't this one look just like Gypsy?"

One of the women or one of the horses? And it was then that Jury knew who Adrienne reminded him of: his old love Susan Bredon-Hunt, although Susan's mannerisms weren't so artificial, so exaggerated. But Susan had also had a daddy and a horse.

Andrew sighed. "Adrienne, will you leave off, please? The superintendent's trying to get some information."

Jury smiled at her pout. All she was trying to do, poor girl, was keep Andrew's attention riveted on her, which spoke of a painful insecurity. "Did you know her, then, Miss Armitage? Frances Hamilton."

"Did I? Well, yes, I knew her well enough to lunch with."

Intimacy for Adrienne Armitage appeared to be measured in what sorts of meals one might share with another person. Jury smiled. "The thing is, her death was put down to complications of a heart condition; yet Mrs. Hamilton denied that she had any symptoms."

"That's right, she hadn't," said Andrew.

"Yes, she had," said Adrienne, head bent over her magazine. "At least, that's what she told me."

Andrew was clearly surprised. "*What?*"

"Well, that's what she said." Adrienne flicked through the fashion magazine, now holding its glossy pages at arm's length, cocking her head as if considering how she would look in the model's ensemble.

"Adrienne, put that down and pay attention."

She sighed, tossed the magazine on the table. "We were lunching at the Savoy. She tapped her chest and told me she was wearing one of those nitroglycerin patches and I asked her what they were for and she said her heart. Well, you know, when you get to a certain *age*, I expect you don't want to advertise its *ills*, do you?" She lit another cigarette.

Shrewd of her, thought Jury, and then wondered that Fanny Hamilton would have chosen to confide in a woman who seemed as lacking in empathy as Adrienne Armitage. Was it vanity calling to vanity? Jury wondered about Andrew's interest in her: she was beautiful, but shallow.

"Oh, a spot," she said, suddenly, dropping her face towards the top of her suit coat and scraping at a tiny spot that might be egg yolk. He smiled at the expression, fleeting, on her face before she'd dropped it; at the look of bewilderment, apparently that something so tiny might just cancel out the persona she had gone to such trouble to create, like tossing a pebble in a pool and watching the surface break, the circles of water ruffling. What she had so painstakingly assembled now had to be as painstakingly reassembled: it was rather like that montage of pictures she had earlier held out. The sable, the hairdo, the horse, the title—all the bits of her life scissored up and waiting to be pinned and pasted in place. *Oh, a spot.* Jury's smile deepened, watching her. Well, a spot had played hell with Lady Macbeth, hadn't it?

But Adrienne Armitage was no Lady Macbeth, certainly. And Jury wondered if he didn't now see something of what Andrew might see: a guilelessness that over the years had been just about trained out of her, but that yet could be resurrected; a painful insecurity, rather than a brittle self-interest, that generated all sorts of effort on her part to get the paper doll properly dressed and spotless. There was, beneath the long fur coat and designer clothes, something uniquely charming about Adrienne Armitage.

"So she hadn't told Lady Cray about this condition." Jury's mind was moving toward some connection between at least two of these deaths: Frances and Nell Hawes. "If she wouldn't tell Lady Cray, why would she tell you, do you think?"

"Oh, that's easy." She exhaled a thin stream of bluish smoke.

Jury frowned. So did Andrew. "What's that supposed to mean?"

"I'm a chain-smoker, darling. I might give it up when it's all right for ladies to take snuff or chew tobacco. Not before. Fanny was worse. Obviously, she shouldn't be smoking at *all*, really. Well, your aunt's trying to stop and thinks the world should stop with her, especially with a heart condition."

"Yes, I can see that," said Jury.

Bored now, or acting it, Adrienne merely shook her shining blond hair. As she stood there, the light informed her, breaking up into watery patches across her hair and coat and down her arm to the glass table, turning the skin more golden, the sable a paler brown, the tabletop a glistening, steely blue. And Jury heard again the voice of Brian Macalvie, saw him standing there in the vestibule of the cathedral, holding the skein of multicolored threads. *Try and see the colors apart from each other and it won't work.* In his mind's eye, Jury watched the colored threads fall from Macalvie's hand.

Rainbow mechanics.

2

BENEATH THE WINDOW of the New Scotland Yard office sat a small basin of water. Wiggins appeared to be concentrating on an electrical cord.

Still with his coat on, Jury sat down in his swivel chair. Why bother to ask? So he said, as calmly as he could, "Wiggins, there's not a mouse alive that Cyril couldn't sniff out across the length of a rugby field. Now get that bloody thing out of here."

Wiggins had set aside the cord to stir whatever concoction was steaming from another bowl atop his desk. "It's only an experiment. Are you worried, then, Cyril might get at it?"

"Cyril? Worried about Cyril? There is nothing you or I or Racer can devise, no traps, no tricks, that Cyril couldn't work out in two seconds." Jury's tone was rather dangerously level. "Why should I worry about Cyril?"

Wiggins pursed his lips. "I don't honestly believe it'll work, of course; I was just——"

"Wiggins, I'm not negotiating; get the bloody bowl out of our office." He smiled. "Out!"

Mustering all of his self-command, Wiggins rose stiffly and moved over to the window, remarking how exposure to the Crippses did seem to coarsen a person.

"Uh-huh. You'll find out just how much it coarsens a person when I paint you blue and run you stark past Racer's door." Jury shrugged out of his coat and sat down again. He looked down. "And be careful of the damned wire!"

But the sergeant was already holding the bowl in one hand and the wire upended in the other and heading for a tiny sink in the corner of the office. He was clearly unhappy about the experiment's being aborted in this way.

"Never mind, Sergeant. Maybe I can get an electrician to build you a miniature electric chair."

"Very funny, I'm sure." Wiggins reseated himself before his own steaming bowl. "Had your lunch?"

"No."

"Care for some soup? It's only instant chicken noodle, but it looks quite tasty."

Soup. Jury frowned over at the bowl. Suddenly, he was reminded of Jenny Kennington and her message—her *ostensible* message—to Carole-anne. He plucked up the receiver, dialed the Stratford number. He let it ring eleven times before he sighed and gave up.

"No thanks," he said when Wiggins asked him again.

"Well, it's about all I can take after that visit to the Crippses. Puts you straight off your food, that place." He lowered his voice as if White Ellie might be listening. "When I stepped into the kitchen you know what I found?"

Jury was scanning the mess of papers on his desk. He didn't want to know. "What?"

"The half-loaf had a hole right in the center and when I asked that one—Batty?"

"Petey."

"—why the bread had this big hole through it, he said, 'Had to get rid of the mold, dihn't I?' " Wiggins shivered.

Jury laughed. It was a fair imitation of squealing Petey's voice. He stacked the papers, then flipped through the messages. None from the commissioner. None from an ax-murderer. None from Jenny. Worthless. He shoveled them into a desk drawer. Now his desk was neat. He smiled.

"Did you talk to Lady Cray?"

"No. To her nephew. And the nephew's fiancée. Turns out Frances Hamilton was on medication for a heart problem."

"Which is what the pathologist said. Natural causes. You think the coronary was induced by something? Some shock?"

"Macalvie thinks so, with the woman in Exeter. Helen Hawes."

"But what's the connection?"

"The American Southwest. The women were both there at the same time."

Wiggins frowned. "That's a bit tenuous."

Jury nodded. But he was thinking about Gabe's description of Frances Hamilton leaving the Swagger Portrait exhibit so hurriedly. As if she were going to be sick. "Gastric lavage," Jury said.

"Pardon?"

"To remove poisons from the system, vomiting is induced." Jury sighed, leaned forward. "Well, I expect it wouldn't kill me to have a chat with this DCI Rush."

Wiggins said, after tasting another mouthful of soup, "I was thinking about taking a bit of a holiday myself."

But the prospect, thought Jury, did not appear to excite him. "You look a little glum, Wiggins."

"Frankly, sir, with you gone . . . well, I haven't all that much to do." He waved his free hand over his desk, cluttered with files. "Paperwork, that's about the size of it. Stuff nobody else will do."

He didn't have to explain that Jury himself was the only detective at New Scotland Yard with much of a demand for Wiggins's services. Wiggins, Jury had always felt, was underappreciated. His colleagues put Wiggins down as a rather irksome burden, with his pills and nostrums, neglecting to see that the sergeant's particular eccentricities were the very things that made him valuable. Witnesses were willing to talk to Wiggins; they forgot he was a cop. You don't much want to discuss the fact you fiddled an extra tuppence from the Social with some ice-eyed policeman flashing a shield, any more than you want to discuss your gimpy knee with Arnold Schwarzenegger.

The phone rang and Wiggins plucked it up, listened, said, "I'll tell him."

"Tell me what?"

"It's Fiona again. She's really upset. The guvnor's threatened to have Cyril taken away."

"He's been threatening that for years."

Impatiently, Wiggins said, "No, but *this* time he's got the cat locked up in a cage and won't let him out. He told Fiona to call the RSPCA to come and get him. I left a message, did you get it?"

"I'm not here, remember? Yes, I expect it's in the stuff I tossed out. Thought it was Racer wanted me, not Fiona." Racer seemed to wait, like a motorcycle cop, for Jury to crash through his speed zone. The radar gun could always pick him up.

Jury put his feet on his desk and asked, "So are you going to Manchester?" Manchester was Wiggins's only getaway destination.

Grimly, Wiggins nodded.

"Hardly a holiday." It would be Wiggins's sister and the sister's kiddies. Jury knew exactly how that felt. He himself had a sister and nephew and nieces in Newcastle. No more a Provence or Saint Kitts than was Manchester. His colleagues were always prodding Wiggins to take his hols in a sun-drenched or snow-drenched clime. *Swim, Wiggins; ski, Wiggins.* That was the same as giving him a choice between skin cancer and a broken leg. How fucking patronizing people were, Jury thought, falling in step with Wiggins's own depression, seeing him alone on some foreign shore or foreign mountaintop.

Jury was up and flicking his jacket from the chair back. "I'm going over to the Starrdust, Wiggins. To see Carole-anne. That is, if Her Glossiness is working today." Sergeant Wiggins loved the Starrdust in Covent Garden. "Not official, but you can come, if you like."

Wiggins sighed. "No, sir. I've all this paperwork to do on that Soho restaurateur."

Or "the Chink-restaurant business," as Racer always put it. It'd been going on for ages, for years. Jury moved towards the small sink.

"But aren't you going to do something about Cyril?" Wiggins was anxious.

"Yep." Jury was studying the wire, following its length to see where it connected up.

"UZ A ARUH CUH, or iz zat ser Cyuhl?"

Fiona Clingmore's diction was somewhat impaired by a white hankie pressed to her mouth. On the desk lay a lip outliner, a lipstick, and a mirror, waiting to repair the damage done by tears.

Jury, leaning on the water cooler, said, "Never mind, Fiona. It'll be all right."

Fiona wailed, unknotted the handkerchief. "This time he means it. I'm to call the RSPCA."

"Hullo, Cyril," Jury said.

The cat Cyril sat inside the wire cage in kingly fashion, tail lapped around his feet. He watched the water cooler; he liked the bubbles made when someone used it; the paper cup, usually full of water, that sat beneath the spigot provided him with a number of possibilities for experiment.

"He's on a rampage."

Racer on a rampage. "What else is new?"

Jury walked into Racer's office.

"JUST WHAT in *hell* are you doing here, Jury?" Two minutes later, Chief Superintendent Racer appeared. His eye fell immediately to the dish on the edge of the table. "And what in the *hell*'s a dish of water doing on my desk?"

"It's a mousetrap, actually." Jury placed the coiled cord beside it. He cleared his throat. "Not just a dish of water. Friend of mine invented it. Want to see how it works?"

No mouse, to Jury's knowledge, had ever been seen; none would want to hang around Cyril. Or Racer, for that matter.

"*NO*, I do not want to see how it bloody *works*! Get it out of here."

"Okay." Jury got up and started to remove the dish.

"What's the cord for? Those wires are stripped, for God's sake." Racer was leaning across the desk.

Jury shoved the dish back again. He uncoiled the wires. "One end is placed so. . . ." He demonstrated. "The other you hook up to an electrical source. Voilà—goodbye, mouse."

Racer blinked, first at the water contraption, then up at Jury. "That's ridiculous." He sounded uncertain.

"Mice love water. It's a little-known fact." It certainly was. He sat there and watched the wheels in Racer's mind going around. At least, he supposed there were wheels in Racer's mind; it was just that they seldom engaged.

Racer's smile came very slowly. And meanly. He hit the intercom and the weepy voice of Fiona came over it.

"Miss Clingmore, you can cancel that call to the animal catchers. Oh, and when you come back from the tea break Her Majesty has seen fit to grant to every layabout in the government, bring me a pint of milk." He flicked off the intercom. "So what in hell do you want, man? Thought you were dead."

"If wishes were horses," said Jury, walking out.

THIRTEEN

Covent Garden.

Jury got out of the car and stood looking over at the collection of shops that was now Covent Garden. It hadn't been so long ago that the old vegetable and fruit market had stood in that spot—a dozen or so years, perhaps?—before it had gone, taking its noise and grime and porters and cabbages with it.

When he'd been a lad, living in the Fulham Road, he'd come down here in Saturday dawns to watch them unload the trucks and set up the stalls, to listen to them yell and curse as they ripped the tops from crates and tossed the lettuces about.

Now here were a neatly tiered arrangement of health food and herbal shops; bookshops and boutiques; espresso bars, restaurants, and the inevitable ice-cream emporium. Jury sometimes thought if he saw one more Häagen-Dazs place he'd throw up.

Bound to be a Crabtree and Evelyn in all of this, so he crossed the cobbled courtyard and looked at the directory. Yes, he was right. He stopped to watch three acrobats with painted faces entertaining the crowd and was glad at least that Covent Garden provided a venue for live entertainment, although it tended to be canned and programmed. Searching out the Crabtree and Evelyn store, Jury looked over the rail, down into the well of lower-level shops and a yuppie pub called the Crusted Pipe. As far as split-level malls went, he supposed Covent Garden was rather a nicer one, perhaps with a bit more *quaint* than most—but it was still a mall.

He found the shop and purchased the potpourri and a silver-lidded jar to keep it in.

His route back across the cobbled yard brought him close to the flower market. But he didn't stop.

He must stop this reminiscing; he really must.

THE STARRDUST TWINS, Meg and Joy, were watching the sky. The "sky" in Andrew Starr's little establishment was the ceiling, which had been recently changed—by Meg and Joy, and they were viewing their handiwork. Behind artificial clouds which hung suspended from a freshly painted and stormy-looking sky, bright yellow lightning flashed. Somewhere, thunder rolled.

Off, on, off, on. Splintered light dashed across the ceiling. Meg applauded; Joy clasped her hands beneath her chin and jumped a little. It worked.

"Heat lightning," said Meg. Or Joy. Jury tended to confuse them, not that they looked so much alike, but that they *were* so much alike. They were Andrew Starr's shop assistants and they were in charge of the window—and in this case, of the ceiling. The Starrdust front window had become a major attraction on this little street, full of mechanical and electrical marvels dreamed up by Meg and Joy and far more entertaining than the Covent Garden performances. Jury had had to wade through a dozen appreciative kids outside, for the window had also changed recently.

Jury gazed up at the splendid ceiling. "It's wonderful. Where's Andrew?"

Still with their eyes on the ceiling, they pointed (both of them) toward the shadowy length of the shop. It was a very dark little shop. But that was part of its charm, for what lights there were seemed to swim toward the customers, veiled, misty, and moving.

The curtain of Madame Zostra's (aka Carole-anne Palutski's) silken tent was certainly moving, for a woman came racing out of it, slamming into Jury with the roughest of "pardon me"s and a face that looked infused with some of that heat lightning. She parted Meg and Joy as if she were Moses and rushed out of the door.

Carole-anne emerged from the tent and moved right across to the cake being cut up by Joelly, a newly hired stock girl who usually came to work with her three-legged dog. Its name was Joe. On the counter sat the richest-looking chocolate cake Jury had ever seen, with the tallest cap of deep chocolate icing he could imagine. It stood up in licks and spits, and Carole-anne's index finger was wending its way through a few of the spits.

"Super! Want some Chocolate Sin? That's what it's called."

"No, thanks." Jury never ceased to wonder how Madame Zostra kept that figure that could send all the traffic in Piccadilly Circus running counterclockwise. "Your client seemed upset." Carole-anne told fortunes. Sometimes with palms, sometimes with cards, lately with skulls, but never with accuracy.

"It's a *shame*, isn't it?" She accepted a slab of cake they could have used for the cornerstone at Canary Wharf.

"What's a shame?"

"Her hubby's having an affair—" a largish chunk of the cornerstone was forked into her mouth—"whim a tartith li' seketry—"

It was like listening to Fiona talking to her mashed-up hanky. "Tartish secretary? That what you said?"

Carole-anne nodded.

Jury frowned. "And why was she confessing this to you?"

"Oh, it was me told *her*, naturally."

Jury's frown deepened. "And just where did *you* come on this nugget?"

"Wavelengths. I'm psychic, you know."

Don't comment, a small voice warned. He commented. "As a matter of fact, I don't know."

Carole-anne pressed the tines of the fork down into chocolate crumbs. "Oh, yes. Even when I was ever so little, I seemed to be able to see things nobody else could." She licked the fork.

"You still do."

The sarcasm went unnoticed. "Well, that's what I'm telling you. I expect you don't know anything about the New Age?"

Don't comment; the voice was more alarmed. Jury knew that to ignore this warning would be to lose himself in the labyrinthine ways of Carole-anne's circuitous conversational routes. If he pursued this absurd New Age thread, he would only have himself to blame when he ended up staring at the Minotaur. He looked from her lapis lazuli eyes up to the lightning-bolted ceiling and wondered if Zeus would toss one at him. . . . My God! She already had him going in circles. *Don't comment, don't comment*, the voice clattered.

He commented. "What I know about the New Age is that its followers wear their hair long, travel in caravans, and end up in Wiltshire or Sedona, Arizona." In his mind's eye, Jury saw the newspaper clipping on the wall of the Rainbow's End.

The Minotaur had herself another helping of cake. *Plop* went the slice onto her plate. "See, the New Agers know all about raising your consciousness. We're all of us a little psychic, if only we practiced. Even you." She looked him up and down. "More or less."

"In other words, even I could have told your unfortunate lady her hubby was getting it on with his shorthand typist."

"No. And one wouldn't put it like that."

"Wouldn't one? Well, one certainly messed up one's relaying of Lady Kennington's message."

"Ohhh." Disgust. "Are you *still* on about that? I *told* you—"

" 'Soup' was the word. Did she tell you—now think carefully—that she was 'in the soup'?"

Dawn broke. Jury could see from the way her mouth dropped, her fork stopped midair, and her blue eyes shone with sudden light that she really *had* made an honest mistake. Anyway, he knew Carole-anne well enough to know that if anyone (pretty ladies included) left a message suggesting trouble, she'd make sure to convey it.

"Wait a tick. That *is* what she said. Gee, Super . . ." The beautiful eyes looked ceilingward, as if calling on the psychic powers that had temporarily deserted her.

"Never mind." He smiled at her.

The blue eyes regarded him. Sympathetically, slightly patronizing. "Well, maybe you are."

"Am what?"

"Psychic."

A thunderclap made both of them jump. Zeus commenting.

2

INSTEAD OF unpacking and repacking his suitcase (which Jury considered an absurd waste of time) he decided to open the bag and let the contents air. While this airing proceeded in the living room of his flat in Islington, Jury looked at his mail—his bills and circulars—and stared at his telephone, thinking he really must buy an answering machine, much as he hated them. His flat was not a touchstone of technological wizardry: no VCR, stereo, CD player, voice mail, fax machine, or surround sound (unless Carole-anne's conversations counted). At the moment he didn't even have a television. It was not a snobbish disdain for what the telly had to offer; it was because he had loaned his set to Carole-anne. He calculated, as he went into his kitchen for coffee, that the loan had taken place about a year ago. Once, when he was up in her second-floor flat, watching some mindless show and drinking beer with her, he had asked her how she got around the TV licensing fee. She'd said she had a "special arrangement" with the installer. This had been in her pre-Starrdust days, so she wasn't providing free palm readings, and Jury was curious as hell as to how she had hoodwinked the licensing authority.

The kettle whistled (despite his standing there watching it) and he stirred instant coffee into a cup. No matter what brand he used or how strong he made it, instant coffee always tasted watery and metallic.

Back in the living room, he tried ringing Jenny again. Still no answer. He sipped the coffee that tasted of nickels and stared at the telephone, willing it to ring. It didn't. He sat down and shook out the paper, looking for a follow-up account of the death in Wiltshire. It should have provided the media with a bit of gristle, if not with meat. He was surprised that no columnist had capitalized on the bizarre resting place of the dead woman, hinting, perhaps, at arcane religious rites and sacrificed virgins. Something like that. Here was a column on the inside pages, but not much, and nothing new. Detective Inspector Gordon Rush's name figured prominently, but his comment was "No comment."

Jury looked over the edge of the paper and glared at the telephone that refused to offer up its secrets, its hidden messages, its trapped voices. He closed his eyes and Lady Cray's turquoise sculpture swam before them. Not unusual for that part of the country, turquoise and silver. Last year, the windows of Harrods had been done up with stuff from the American West: fringed jackets, boots, Indian blankets, silver jewelry and belts. He looked down at the picture of Chief Inspector Gordon Rush in the newspaper and thought he looked decent, intelligent, approachable, even with a touch of humility, the way his head was bent that way.

There was no denying that all three of these women had apparently been in or near Santa Fe at the same time. And you might put the deaths of the two older women down to some sort of heart thing, but the younger one? That seemed very unlikely. Macalvie was right; the Wiltshire police should be running tests for poison—but what kind? Well, there was little to connect the three dead women except for a thread or two. But he had to agree if you pulled a thread it often unraveled a lot of material.

Again, he looked over at the telephone, thinking that if she didn't call, he would have to stop over in Stratford-upon-Avon. Not an unpleasant prospect. He smiled, remembering the first time he had ever seen Jenny Kennington. Her anxiety had made her irritable, truculent, unforthcoming, even somewhat rude. These were postures Jenny would never strike in her own interests, but only in the interests of others, in this case the stray cat Tom. Jenny seemed so resolutely packed inside her own body, so there. He recalled what Gertrude Stein had said about Los Angeles: there's no there there. With Jenny, it was the opposite. She was so there; she was so very much *there*. And where in hell was she?

Then through these drowsy reflections came the unfamiliar strain of piano music: not "music" precisely, but bunched notes. He might not have recognized them as piano notes, had he not known that in the flat overhead, the vacant one, was an old grand piano. Jury sat up suddenly, staring at his ceiling. There had always been that piano ever since the three of them—Jury, Mrs. Wassermann, Carole-anne—had lived here. No one knew where it had come from and it was the only piece of furniture up there. Not even Mr. Moshegeiian knew the origins of the piano; he could not remember any of his tenants having one. Jury remembered his saying, with his little purse of a mouth opening and shutting on a laugh, that perhaps it would attract "an artiste."

Plink. Keys on the high end of the scale. *Plink.* Slightly lower. *Plunk, plunk.* Silence. Perhaps Mr. Moshegeiian had sent someone over to clean and air the place. Since when? Jury scratched his head. Moshegeiian never did anything; he left it up to Carole-anne. But Carole-anne's virtuosity was exercised only in interviewing prospective tenants (for all the good it did them). Clanging pipes, dripping faucets, creaking boards, falling plaster—these were not in Carole-anne's provenance, their course not decided by crashing stars or colliding planets. Pipes and plaster were Jury's job.

Plink. Plunk plunk plink. He kept looking upward. It was as if a child might patiently be trying to teach himself a tune. He left his flat and climbed the stairs to the first floor (each flat taking up one entire floor, which seemed spacious until one realized how narrow the terraced house was). He stood outside the door for a moment, listening. He heard nothing. He knocked, lightly. No answer. He knocked again. No answer, again. Jury scratched his head again in perfect cartoon rendition of a puzzled man. He listened, ear close to the door.

A mystery.

"PIANO MUSIC?" Mrs. Wassermann looked at him curiously. Then she looked down at his feet. "You've forgotten your shoes, Mr. Jury."

As if only crazy shoeless people heard piano music. "I went upstairs and knocked. Nobody answered and the music stopped."

She was twisting her intertwined, chubby fingers, and seriously considering this problem. "Do you think it's the dog?"

Jury blinked. "Well, no, I actually *didn't* think that. I still *don't.*" Sarcasm fell wide around Mrs. Wassermann. "I don't know what you're talking about, Mrs. Wassermann."

"The dog in the first-floor flat." As if that were adequate, she turned toward her kitchen. Jury trailed after her as she said, "I'm just taking my nut-and-ginger cookies out of the oven, Mr. Jury. Your favorite. Come and have some."

Mrs. Wassermann always assumed everything was Jury's favorite. "Why is there a dog in the first-floor flat?" He didn't want to ask why it was playing the piano. The dog itself was enough to contend with.

She stopped and turned. "You mean Carole-anne didn't tell you?"

"Tell me what? That she let the flat above me to a dog?"

Mrs. Wassermann, who seldom laughed, did now as she bent down to open the door of the oven. "It belongs to the new tenant, of course. He moved in this morning while you were at work."

Jury was stunned. Then he was mildly furious. "*What* new tenant? I talked to her not two hours ago. She didn't say anything to me about letting—"

Mrs. Wassermann stood there with her big red oven mitts on, shaking her head. "I *told* her she should wait until you returned. 'Wait until Mr. Jury returns, Carole-anne,' I told her." She raised the red mitts toward the kitchen ceiling as if enjoining either God or the dog to hear her pleas. Then, her stagy bit over, she bent to slide the cookie sheet out of the oven. "But Carole-anne said it would be perfectly all right, since he was your idea in the first place."

"My idea? Mine? Mrs. Wassermann, I don't know what in hell— excuse me—I don't know what you're talking about." He said this slowly and evenly, as if calm would restore the Islington house to its former three-person occupancy. Sans dog.

"Well, it's very strange. He's *your* friend. That's what she said. 'Stanley's a friend of the super.' "

"I don't know one living soul named Stanley."

Now Mrs. Wassermann looked very upset. "You *don't?* But Carole-anne stood right there. . . ." Sadly she shook her head. "Why would she lie about that?"

Oh, ha. "What's he like? I mean besides being extremely good-looking, somewhere in his mid-twenties, early thirties, very available, and—colorful, let's say?" "Flash git" would be nearer. And he'd just managed to get rid of Randy Tyrone, too. That flat had stood vacant for years with Lord only knew how many people turned away by Carole-anne because they didn't meet the Palutski standards.

"So you *do* know him!" Mrs. Wassermann held out a plate of cookies.

Absently, Jury took a cookie, shaking his head. "I'm merely listing the credentials. Does this Stanley shill in Piccadilly or Oxford Street with his performing dog?"

Inwardly, he fumed. Bloody *dog* upstairs. To say nothing of bloody Stanley. Jury muttered under his breath as Mrs. Wassermann poured him a glass of milk.

"Now, now, Mr. Jury. It is definitely not like you to lose patience. Your patience is your most lovable quality." She patted his arm and held out his glass of milk.

He drank. "I don't get it. Why'd she say he's my friend?"

"Because it is you who introduced them."

"*Me?* Look, Carole-anne's gone round the twist, or something. She's been doing too much star gazing. I think we should be worried about her." Jury held out his glass for a refill and munched his cookie.

"We've never had a dog before."

This did not strike Jury as being of primary importance. They'd never had a Stanley before, either. "What kind of dog?" What a stupid question.

"Labrador. Stanley says he'll be a good guard dog for all of us."

Oh, hell, people that wanted in *always* said that. "When somebody breaks in, he runs them off with Mozart? Or maybe he tells us, 'Now, if you hear Adagio in G Minor, it means they've got guns'?"

Mrs. Wassermann sighed. "You're not taking this very well. I told Carole-anne you'd be upset. I said, 'Carole-anne, dear, Mr. Jury—' "

"Okay, o-*kay*. What's this guy do for a living? I mean besides shill?"

"He plays gags. I'm out of milk." Mrs. Wassermann was peering in her fridge.

Jury stopped in the act of picking up the cookie plate. "He plays *gags*?" He thought he was going quietly insane, right here in Mrs. Wassermann's kitchen.

"But that's all right. The dog will be down in a moment. It's nearly one." She was rinsing out the pint bottle.

Was he actually having this conversation? Or had he fallen asleep upstairs and dreamed it? He clutched the plate of cookies, as if its concreteness would lend him strength.

There was a knock at the door. A sort of knock, anyway.

Mrs. Wassermann went to the door with the empty bottle and didn't even bother checking the peephole before opening it. Obviously, the visitor was expected. And welcome. "Come in, come in and meet your new neighbor."

A dog of a beautiful caramel color entered. He was wearing a red bandanna round his neck.

Jury looked at the dog. Where had he seen this dog before? Where?

Mrs. Wassermann reached down, held out the bottle, and the Lab took it between his teeth.

Where *had* he seen this dog with a bottle in his mouth—?
"STONE!"

"You see, I knew Carole-anne wasn't lying."

"Is Stanley's last name Keeler?"

"See, you do know him. Carole-anne wouldn't lie."

"Stan Keeler's a professional musician." Jury remembered Stan's club, the only one he played in—the Nine-One-Nine, that small and smoky blues cellar where Jury had gone to question him about the case he'd been working on. Stan was an underground musician with a dedicated underground following. A great guitarist. "Stan plays guitar, Mrs. Wassermann."

"That's what I said." She waggled her finger at him.

"You said he plays gags."

She nodded, happy that Jury seemed to be his old pleasant self once more.

"Stan Keeler." Jury bent down to give Stone's back a good rub. Stan played gags and Stone played piano.

FOURTEEN

Jenny hadn't been in the house on Ryland Street. He had been worried, decided perhaps he could ask Sam Lasko to keep an eye out. But then he had decided not to mention Jenny; it was absurd suspecting something had happened to her simply because she'd been out so much. She was starting up a business, after all.

Sam Lasko paused and looked away, thought for a moment, shook his head as if he couldn't believe what was in it. "You'd think with all the work on my desk Lincolnshire wouldn't be asking me to keep an eye out."

Immersed in his own reflections, Jury almost thought he'd voiced them. "What?"

"I *said* I've got too much to do without following somebody around for the cops in bloody Lincoln."

Jury didn't know what he was talking about, except that Lasko wanted help. Jury's help. "Look, I'm sorry, Sammy, but I just don't have time to—"

Paying no attention to what Jury didn't have time for, Sammy opened a file, turned it so Jury could see it. While he talked, Jury recollected that case eight years ago in Stratford that Sammy had got him to investigate. Americans, too, in that one.

"Are you listening?"

"No."

Lasko looked so bereft that Jury felt irrationally guilty. "I'm on my way to Wiltshire, Sammy. I only stopped here to see a friend."

"Lady friend?"

"Someone I've known for years. Anyway, I'm on my way to Wiltshire."

"Who in hell ever goes to Wiltshire?" Lasko never stepped more than a foot beyond the city limits of Stratford-upon-Avon unless a case demanded it. "You're not talking about that American? The one they found at Old Sarum? You mean the Wiltshire police asked for help? Hard to believe."

"It's pretty involved, Sam. No, they didn't ask for help from us. And I'm sure they don't want it, either."

Especially Chief Inspector Gordon Rush, he thought, sliding from Lasko's desk.

FIFTEEN

"A Roman privy," said Gordon Rush. "Helluva place to drop dead. Funny." But he wasn't amused.

Jury was sliding a necklace over his fingers, one found among the dead Angela Hope's effects: a semicircular silver pendant, like an upside-down crescent moon, studded with turquoise and with a turquoise bird inset on a bar. He turned from this to the file and the morgue shots, spread out before him. He pulled one of the photos closer. "You don't think maybe she just slipped? If she was, say, trying to come down this worn grass above the garderobe?"

"No. She would have clawed dirt, grabbed whatever she could to break the slide. She didn't." Rush held up his own hands, turned the palms.

"Uh-huh. Then what—?"

"Could've been pushed, could've been murdered before and brought there." Rush shrugged. "A lot of things could've happened."

"No one saw anything?"

"No one *to* see anything. What tourists there were had already left, and the ticket kiosk is out of visible range; I mean, the National Trust people who were selling tickets were inside."

"And it was one of them that found her. What in hell was he doing on the site at five a.m.?"

"Said he liked to go there, liked to walk early and see the sunrise. Anyway, she died ten hours prior to that. Probably around sunset, just about when they'd be shutting down. Around six." Rush was in the act of lighting a cigarette.

Jury picked up the necklace again.

Rush watched him studying it. "She's a silversmith. Was, I mean."

"Turquoise and silver is fairly common in the American South-west."

"You, too?" Rush finally lit a cigarette with the lighter. The Zippo clicked three times like a tiny metal mouth.

Jury raised his eyebrows. "Me, too?"

"There's a divisional commander in Exeter—name's Macalvie—with a flea in his ear. I used to work under him. Mad Dog Macalvie, we called him."

Jury swallowed laughter. "What's the flea?"

"A connection between my lady and his—"

Lord, but they were possessive as lovers, weren't they? thought Jury.

"—because there's a Santa Fe address in his lady's address book. Something to do with a place or a road called—" still flicking the lighter, Rush thumbed his memory as if it were a Rolodex—"Canyon Road. Angela Hope had a shop there."

The silver crescent swayed on the chain looped over Jury's finger. He studied it. He said, "But it does seem damned coincidental."

Rush tossed the lighter on his desk. " 'Coincidental' is precisely the word."

Jury took Lady Cray's turquoise sculpture from his mackintosh pocket. "This was brought back by my lady—" he smiled briefly—"from New Mexico. Albuquerque, perhaps. Taos or Santa Fe, perhaps. Any tourist who's found her way to Albuquerque would almost certainly go the extra fifty miles or so to Santa Fe. Or so I'm told." Those windows in Harrods had been a real treat. Sensational, the Southwest looked. And the big attraction in the Southwest was Santa Fe.

Rush picked up the turquoise block. "Who's the little guy?" His finger tapped the silver flute player.

"Kokepelli," said Jury. "Some god or other. Indian, I expect. Could we assume, for the sake of argument—?"

Rush put this down in a hurry. "I'm not known to do much for the sake of argument, Superintendent." The smile was just slightly superior.

Jury ignored him. "Frances Hamilton died in January, couple of weeks ago. The cause appeared to be heart trouble. Like Angela Hope. And she had been in New Mexico this past November. Probably in Santa Fe, although I haven't verified that. The thing is, there was no reason then to question her death."

MYNDERSE LIBRARY
31 Fall Street
Seneca Falls, New York 13148

"So what's changed?"

A woman named Helen Hawes, Jury wanted to say. But if Rush knew he was here at Macalvie's insistence, the man would clam up completely. Jury hated egos getting in the way of investigation. Macalvie, who was supposed to be consumed by ego, would have been far more interested in the connection between the women than in whether some other police force might be "interfering" in his investigation. "The question's been raised whether she might have been poisoned."

Rush was turning the Zippo round and round in his hand. "Why's that?"

Was he being deliberately obtuse? "She apparently got quite ill before she died. The symptoms sounded much the same as the American woman's."

"You're exhuming the body, then?"

"Possibly. Of course, you wouldn't have that problem," said Jury.

"The symptoms of a coronary mimic those of a number of poisons. Nausea, vomiting. But since no one saw the effect of whatever it was, we can't say what she went through. Were there convulsions? Coma? So it's difficult to say whether the cause was natural or drug- or poison-induced." Rush looked at him and turned the lighter.

"You said a cousin flew here to identify the body."

"Dolores Schell. She just left. Two days ago."

"No closer family? Parents? Siblings?"

"Siblings, yes. Or one. A younger sister. The cousin volunteered because she thought the sister would be too upset. And the kid's so young."

Jury sat back. "How young?"

Rush flicked his eyes over the papers before him. "Thirteen." He flicked the top of the Zippo. "Name's Mary."

Jury picked up the photo of Angela Hope, facedown on the ground. "Mary. What about relations? I mean, who's going to take care of Mary? Her cousin?"

Rush shook his head. "Don't know." His smile was thin. "We're not Social Services."

Jury said nothing. He waited for more information.

Rush picked up the silver chain, swung it. "Cousin said she'd made this. As I said, she was a silversmith. Her shop was called the Silver Heron."

"On Canyon Road."

Rush nodded. "Mr. Jury, if the only thing you've got connecting one American and one Brit is Santa Fe, vomit, turquoise, and some Indian god, well . . ." Another shrug.

Jury knew he'd got everything he was going to get, and it was certainly more than he came in with. He smiled. "Would you mind if I had a copy of that photo of Angela Hope?"

Rush shrugged again. "Why should I?"

Jury stood, pocketed the turquoise sculpture. "Thanks for your help." There was no sarcasm meant; he didn't blame Rush, who handed him a copy of the morgue shot. There were at least six in the file, like a set of graduation pictures. That thought saddened Jury. "Probably a wild goose chase," said Jury, smiling to dissipate any negative waves that had been circulating between Rush and himself.

"Wild heron chase," said Rush, offering Jury a gallows smile.

SIXTEEN

Two hours later, while Jury was looking out of a window over the roofs of Exeter, Macalvie was on the phone to someone in his telecommunications division.

"New Mexico State Police and Santa Fe—" Macalvie thought for a moment—"Violent Crimes Division."

Jury turned from the window, eyebrows raised. "Violent Crimes, Macalvie?"

Macalvie tossed the address book on the desk and sat there in silence. His arms were tight against his chest, hands warming in his armpits. He was still wearing his topcoat; he usually did, even though the radiators were hissing away. Jury recognized it as one of those peculiar Macalvie silences and turned back to the window to study the rooftops, the sliver of the Exe River that he could see away in the distance. In the silence that followed, he looked at the river and wondered about Jenny. The silence drew out.

Then, with his usual precognition (Macalvie could teach Carole-anne a thing or two), he scooped up the telephone receiver midway in the first *brr*. "Macalvie." Pause. "Uh-huh, go ahead, I'm writing. . . . Angela Hope, uh-huh, that's her. . . . Silver Heron, Canyon Road, Santa Fe. Home number's what?" Macalvie grunted, wrote. "What about this other five-oh-five number? . . . Area code, yeah . . . Where's Española, then? They don't know her? . . . Nothing? . . . Thanks." He hung up and sat there frowning, first at the wall, then at Jury, as if Jury had been the one at the dead-end Española number, disclaiming any knowledge whatever of Angela Hope. Now, Macalvie was up and moving towards the door. "Let's go."

"Go where? I've done my bit, remember?" Jury followed him.

"Saint Peter's."

"Mind telling me why?"

Macalvie's long-suffering secretary was seated at her desk, head bent over paperwork. As Macalvie passed, she asked, "May I take down the Christmas decorations now? The tinsel's dusty." To Jury, she added, "It's February, after all."

"You got better things to do," answered Macalvie.

Her voice floated to them as they made their exit, "That's not what you said when you wanted them up."

IN THE PARKING AREA of the cathedral yard at least a dozen buses were pulled up. More schoolchildren, but these without uniforms, were cavorting about the green, chasing each other, making mischief. Probably they were here for some sort of learning experience or historical expedition to enrich their education. A very fat boy was being chased by three girls in coats or sweaters. Jury doubted they had much interest in the martyrdom of Saint Boniface or the burning of the abbey. Several others were standing staring at an old woman with a bicycle carrying sacks of feed who was tossing it out for a flock of pigeons. She seemed to be holding a discourse, not with the children but with the birds. Close as that lot would ever get to Saint Francis, Jury mused.

MACALVIE WAS by now on familiar terms with the three ladies all seated at a long table opposite the quire, who were embroidering— cushions for chairs, by the look of it. They all nodded and greeted Macalvie. They might have been sisters, with their varying degrees of plumpness and rosy complexions and graying hair. Macalvie seldom bothered ingratiating himself with witnesses by way of getting information; he was, however, given a warm welcome by these three, who appeared delighted to see him again.

Given that Helen Hawes "had a heart" anyway, her collapse did not come as a complete surprise. Only the circumstances were surprising. Still and all, her dying here in Saint Peter's, and dying while in the act of inspecting the rondels that were in small part the result of her own handiwork, was probably far better than in a hospital bed. Thus, whatever unpleasant elements attached to a sudden death were mitigated by her having died with her boots on, so to speak. And to all of this was now added the elements of intrigue and mystery (in the persons of Macalvie and Jury). Mystery had now turned from the religious to the secular.

Macalvie had taken the photo out of the file, but before showing it around had explained to them that they certainly didn't have to look at it if they didn't choose to; that it was a shot of a dead woman—although there was nothing at all gruesome in it, just the face, the eyes closed. "A morgue shot, we call it."

It was obvious their curiosity had completely overridden any delicacy in the matter and they were nodding even before his lengthy (for Macalvie) explanation was finished. At the phrase "morgue shot" Jury could feel the little frisson of anticipation pass down the table.

But he went on: "We're wondering if this woman might have been known to Mrs. Hawes. Angela Hope, an American from Santa Fe. If each of you could look at it separately, before you confer, it would help. I'm not really expecting any of you to identify her. But if there's anything about her that you associate with Helen Hawes . . ."

As instructed, the three passed the photo from one to another. They did not speak. Their eyes did not meet. More impressive still, Jury thought, they did not flinch. Gertie, Ruth, and Vi were used to detail, to a microcosmic view of life, if their long application to the elaborate stitchery of rondels and cushions and chasubles was any evidence. They could also follow instructions, and could also bring a great deal of concentration to bear on a subject. Having studied the photo, they looked off in different directions—toward the Lady Chapel, a tomb opposite, down the nave. Finally, they demurred. Apologetically, they shook their heads, almost in unison. No, they couldn't think of any connection between this dead woman and their fellow tapister Nell Hawes. Macalvie told them he appreciated their help and if they did recall anything, they had his card.

As Jury and Macalvie turned to leave, Vi asked if they'd talked to Annie Landis.

Macalvie said he hadn't. "Is she a tapister, then?"

"Yes. And she'll be at home, I expect." Vi gave Macalvie the address, then paused, looking sad. "She's taken a bad turn. It's really a shame."

" 'Bad turn'?"

The three of them bent their heads over their embroidery. They might have been praying. Again, Vi said, "See, she's just recently got her lab report. Well . . ." Her voice trailed off.

Vi stopped speaking and Gertie picked it up. Her head still bent with the others, red silk wound about her finger like a thread of blood, she added, "We always set our clocks by Annie. I recall the gentleman who takes care of the cathedral clock—well, I recall his looking up the nave to see Annie Landis come in one morning and then cast his eye up to the clock and say, 'Good Lord, two minutes off!' Yes, we set our clocks by her. Time and tide and Annie Landis. That's what we said and what we say."

Jury smiled over this rather poetic turn of phrase, yet mildly shocked by this reference to what might be present, or what might be past. It was as though Annie were already gone. He looked at Macalvie slowly folding a stick of gum into his mouth; he seemed to be reflecting on Vi's news and Gertie's words.

After some silence, Macalvie finally said, "Thanks for your help, ladies." His eye swept down the little row. "Come on," he said to Jury. He walked away, past the great clock, and up the nave.

Jury followed. Outside the cathedral entrance, he asked, "To where?"

"Annie Landis's house."

As he followed him to the parked car, Jury protested. "But if she's ill, really ill, Macalvie—"

"Probably she'll be glad of the company." Macalvie yanked open the car door.

"*Company*? Macalvie, we don't exactly fall into that warm and comfortable body of well-wishers known as 'company.' "

Over the bonnet of the car, Macalvie gave Jury an affectedly crooked smile. "Maybe *you* don't. Not with *that* attitude."

What? thought Jury. "What 'attitude'?"

Climbing into the driver's seat, Macalvie called, "You coming? You staying?"

Jury got in, slammed the door. "You're a treat, Mad Dog."

"Now I *know* you talked to Rush." Macalvie slammed the gear into reverse and the tires spit gravel.

2

JURY HAD never seen Exeter's waterfront before, its old quay and canal, its new condos. The river from here stretched all the way to Topsham (Macalvie had told him), passing weirs and warehouses, discos and pubs along the way. Much of the waterfront was built more or less into the side of a cliff, a high rise of red sandstone with part of the city wall above it.

Annie Landis's cottage was set back near the top of stone steps that twisted and turned up the cliffside. It was whitewashed, neat and narrow, and Macalvie was about to let the dolphin door knocker drop when they heard raised voices from within. One raised voice, actually, a man's, answered by the subdued voice of a woman.

The argument proceeding inside and very near the front door seemed to turn on whether he was leaving or staying. Or rather, it was clear he was leaving and she wanted him to stay.

"Just down the pub, for God's sake; just to stop with my mates for a drink."

Her voice, much less distinct, said something to the effect that "a" drink was likely to stretch for hours and after all, she'd just got this bad news—

"Mum . . . you can't always be expecting—"

"Tea." The voice was plaintive.

"No, I don't want any tea. Can't you understand? It's *my* life."

Funny, thought Jury, I got the impression it was, at this particular point, hers. He watched Macalvie fold another stick of gum into his mouth in that ruminative way of his. Jury had finally realized that Macalvie did this when something upset him, something that for one reason or another, he wasn't permitting to show.

The door opened with a yank. They were looking into the angry face of a young man, who bore an astonishing resemblance to the woman behind him. If they'd been mother and daughter, only the years that separated them would have kept one from taking them for twins.

"Oh. . . . Who're you?"

The question was not belligerent but genuinely inquiring as he looked back over his shoulder at his mother. "Somebody for you,

Mum. I'll see you tomorrow." And he smiled and took the steps fleetly, several at a time.

She shook her head, her hands turning an embroidery hoop round in her hands. The piece of linen stretched across it was shot through with brilliant strands of silky thread. That Annie Landis had been weeping, copiously, was evident. "Ravaged by tears" was a phrase Jury had seldom had occasion to use; in her case, though, it was the first thing he thought of. Annie Landis looked as if some heavy object had struck her, landing with terrific force. Everything about her seemed askew—the neckline of a cashmere sweater yanked to one side; a leather belt drooping across one hip; a wave of soft reddish hair rising upward like a flame from her temple. She looked lopsided, out of alignment, like a reflection in a divided mirror.

And there was no doubt in Jury's mind that that was just the way she must have felt.

Macalvie took his identification out, told her who they were, apologized for the intrusion, and explained what they wanted. "We'd like to ask you a few questions about Helen Hawes. It won't take long."

Her eyes refocused on Macalvie, then shifted to Jury. "Nell? Ah. Poor Nell. Come in."

The three of them then stood in the front parlor in much the same way they had stood in the hall, arranged awkwardly just inside the door; they could have sat on the sofa or on the floor—that was what her vague gesture toward the interior of the room implied. Her hand, still holding the hoop, moved in an aimless way toward a couple of armchairs with cretonne slipcovers, their large pastel roses fading into a monochromatic blur.

Annie Landis looked like that too, rather: skin that must have been rose and ivory, once; hair, gold-tinged; eyes the color of young grass. And though only the ghost of those colors remained now, blending into the pale beige of the sweater and skirt, Annie Landis had the sort of looks time might try to erode, but would never succeed in doing.

"You wouldn't," said Macalvie, his hand tilting toward his mouth in the gesture of one drinking, "happen to have a cuppa, would you?" Jury had never before heard Macalvie ask a witness for anything. Wiggins, yes; the sergeant was always conniving and maneuvering as close to the tea and scones as possible.

Instantly, Annie Landis's face and form underwent a transformation, seeming almost magically to straighten out, to realign themselves. What had looked like an image dispersing in water now recast itself into the appearance of a very attractive woman. "Oh, yes, indeed I do. As a matter of fact, I've just made some."

She was an Englishwoman after all; first and foremost she could produce a cup of tea and certainly for the Devon and Cornwall Constabulary—not to mention Scotland Yard. She left, her step almost brisk, and while Macalvie whistled behind his teeth and ignored Jury, there came from a kitchen the rattle of cups and tinkle of glass. In less than two minutes she was back, rolling before her a double-tiered butler's table, set out with Spode and a blue glass plate of iced cakes and biscuits. Clearly, this is what she'd got ready for her son.

"That your son who just left?" asked Macalvie, echoing Jury's thought.

She had sat herself down to pour the tea. "Yes, it was. Jimmy." She was even smiling a little now. If there was anything more calming than this ritual, Jury couldn't imagine what it was. He thanked her as he accepted a cup adorned with a transparent slice of lemon.

Macalvie had his own cup balanced on the cretonne arm and was munching on one of the cakes. Then he reached for a biscuit. "He live with you, does he? Jimmy, I mean."

She shook her head. "No, he doesn't. He hasn't done for a few years now. Young people need to have space to themselves. It's tiresome living with parents." Her tone held no rancor. She handed the plate of cakes round again.

Macalvie helped himself to another and commented on their richness. Macalvie, who ordinarily didn't seem to have the time to say "hello" or "goodbye," was comfortably settled back in his armchair, sipping and chewing. It was Jury who reintroduced the subject of Helen Hawes.

"Nell, yes. We called her Nell, not Helen." She paused for a moment, her teacup held aloft as if she meant to drink, but she didn't. Instead, she set it down, gently, and gathered the cashmere sweater around her, as if the room had suddenly grown chilly. "That was so sudden."

"We understand she had a history of heart disease, though."

"No, not exactly. I mean, heart 'disease' isn't the same as heart 'trouble,' is it? It wasn't the sort of thing that should have caused that reaction. Although I expect it could."

"What?" Macalvie asked. "What 'sort of thing'?"

Annie Landis picked up her cup again, then replaced it. "I was used to Nell's heart episodes. I think it's called ventricular fibrillation. And she took medicine for it, had done for several years. Occasionally, she'd forget or would stubbornly refuse to have it refilled. Nell could be stubborn like that. 'Oh, I'm right as rain; what do I need this stuff for?' I'd tell her the reason she was 'right as rain' was because of that 'stuff.' If she didn't take it, she'd become ill. But she seemed to be fine as long as she wasn't without it. And she wasn't"—here Annie Landis looked brightly at Macalvie—"without it, was she? The vial was right there in her purse."

Jury smiled at her. "You're observant, Mrs. Landis."

"Yes. Most of us are, you know, in the society. Perhaps it comes of doing all of that close work."

Macalvie shifted in his chair. "There's not much doubt it was her heart. Coroner's report put death down to that. Have you had thoughts?" For Macalvie, that was an incredibly lachrymose question.

"Of course." She leaned her head on the wing of her chair and all but closed her eyes. "That day. Five of us were sitting at the table, the one near the quire where we always sit and do our work. Nell said she was tired of stitching and wanted to have another look at the rondels, that she hadn't really seen all of them along the west nave. She left her purse there and it was open; that's how I knew she had her medicine with her, because the little bottle rolled out. And so she walked away."

"That's the last you saw of her before she was taken ill and collapsed?"

Annie Landis nodded. "I find it peculiar. Well, I expect you do too, or you wouldn't be here." Her smile lingered on Macalvie's face and moved to Jury's.

There was a silence. Then Macalvie, who seldom revealed information about any case, surprised Jury by asking, "You've read about the body of the woman found at Old Sarum?"

She frowned. "Yes." Again, she looked from Macalvie to Jury. "Are you saying there's a connection?"

Macalvie looked up at the ceiling, apparently considering. "Mrs. Hawes spent a holiday in the States fairly recently."

"Several months ago she did. She liked to travel. Every two or three years, just about, she'd go abroad. Europe, usually. Three or four times to America."

"The Southwest."

"The last time, yes, to the Southwest. That was back in October . . . no, it was November, I think. Nell always liked to travel in months when it wasn't so touristy and wasn't so expensive."

November, thought Jury. The same month in which Fanny Hamilton had gone to the States. "Did she talk about it? Did she meet anyone in particular? Did she seem her usual self when she came back? And since then?"

"Do you think something happened in the United States? I believe she went to—Arizona, possibly. Yes, she mentioned—wait a moment, what was the area?" Annie Landis frowned mightily, trying to remember. "It sounded more like an intersection than a state. . . . Oh, yes. Four Corners. Where four states came together. I think she said you could stand there and put your foot in all four states. Utah, Arizona . . . New Mexico? I forget the fourth." She shook her head. "Well, that's all I recall her mentioning. Nell really didn't chatter about things the way a lot of us do. Well, the way *I* tend to do."

Jury doubted that, very much. "But there was no reason to believe that anything had—happened to her, that she was acting differently, or anxious, or—"

"Nothing. Nothing at all."

"What about your son?"

Macalvie's question came out of left field, surprising both of them.

"My son?"

"I expect he knew her, didn't he?"

Annie said, "Knew her, yes. Slightly. But he's only twenty-four, Mr. Macalvie." She smiled. "I doubt she'd have held much interest for him."

"What sort of contact did Jimmy have with her?"

Her smile indicated she thought this line of questioning pretty useless, but she said, "Very little. Occasionally, he'd drive her somewhere. To the shops and so forth. She hadn't a car, see. And if she needed a lot of groceries it was hard for her, with the buses and all."

Macalvie had his notebook out. "Where was your son on his way to this evening?"

Her expression changed with the reminder of the earlier scene. "The pub. Probably the Pelican, since it's where he's likely to meet his friends."

Carefully, Macalvie wrote this down. Like an edict or like a sentence, Jury thought.

"But I don't think Jimmy can help you much, Superintendent."

"Maybe not." Macalvie's smile was a flash in the dimness. "Still, I might just have a word with him."

"But I don't understand why Nell might have had some connection with this dead woman—girl, wasn't she?—in Salisbury. It's so hard to believe."

"We don't know." Macalvie asked then, "Ever hear Mrs. Hawes mention a place called Coyote Village?"

Annie Landis looked surprised and then thoughtful. After considering this, she shook her head. "No."

"It was written in her address book." Macalvie drew the small leather book from his pocket and reached it across the tea trolley. Annie Landis took it, slowly leafed through it. Macalvie went on: "My assumption is, Mrs. Hawes might have picked that up in the United States since the only numbers in it turned out to be in New Mexico."

"No, she didn't."

"Pardon?" Macalvie raised his eyebrows.

"I'm just telling you she didn't get it there."

"I think she must have, Mrs. Landis. If you look on the inside of the back you'll see a bit of the price tag is still stuck to it—the bit that shows a dollar sign. It must have been bought in the States."

Annie reached out and returned the notebook. "I'm not saying it wasn't bought there; I'm saying it wasn't Nell's address book."

"She could have had more than one."

"Of course. But this one wasn't hers. Look at it."

Macalvie looked at it and frowned. "So?"

"It's leather, Superintendent. Nell never bought anything made of leather or any animal hide. She was quite adamant about it. She was a vegetarian, too. Animal exploitation was one of the very few things I would ever see her get truly angry about."

Macalvie was staring down at the little directory. "It's very small. Perhaps she didn't notice—"

With undisguised annoyance, Annie Landis said, "Didn't *notice?* Superintendent, she didn't even wear leather *shoes;* and that's not easy; you have to go to a bit of trouble to find shoes totally absent of leather. Didn't *notice?*" She looked away, shaking her head in wonder at such a misconstruction. *Men,* her expression might have read. "You'd be better off not trying to force the facts to fit your theory."

Jury's mouth nearly dropped open. He coughed to mask a bark of laughter. Macalvie? Force *facts?* Pigs might fly.

She continued as she pulled a clip earring from her ear and rubbed the lobe. "Wouldn't it be more sensible to accept the obvious?"

It was the first time Jury had ever seen Macalvie look at a witness with open admiration. He smiled as he asked, "And what's the obvious here, Mrs. Landis?"

"That it belongs to somebody else. And call me Annie."

WHAT JURY ADMIRED about Brian Macalvie was that the man never wasted energy in trying to justify himself—his theories, his assumptions, his mistakes (mistakes, of course, being rare). That Annie Landis had in a sense bested him (an occasion even rarer than Macalvie's making a mistake) had surprised him, but did not bother him. Annie, thought Jury, was absolutely wrong about one thing: Macalvie never cut the facts to fit the theory. Never. His theories were sometimes outlandish, but even those were, in the end, not really strange at all, not when looked at from another perspective.

They were at the bottom of the steps and walking along the quay where the mists from the Exe threaded along the bank and under the bridges, before Macalvie commented on what she had said. "Why *was* I assuming it was hers?"

Jury stopped. "The address book? Pretty obviously because it was found in Nell Hawes's flat. A scrawl, a few numbers, a couple of words. The point is, there was no reason to believe it belonged to somebody else, so you'd hardly have the damned writing analyzed, would you?"

"Whose? Whose is it? If she picked it up somewhere, found it, whatever, it must have been in the States—it was sold there, at least. The numbers are from there. . . ."

Jury saw fog-shrouded lamps ahead, flickering like old gaslights, a cluster of buildings, people. "Where are we going?"

"The Pelican."

As if he didn't know.

3

THE PUB LOOKED as if the river mist had been skimmed from the water and blown inside, the way smoke hung like a ceiling and threaded its way in and around the customers. The Pelican wasn't too crowded, but crowded enough for the collected voices to dull the sound of the throbbing jukebox. Despite the smoke, the place was bright with light and color—color of clothes, of the jukebox sending up rainbow reflections, of glass globes on the tables, sheltering candle flames—red, gold, blue.

Jimmy Landis, still with his coat on (which Jury thought interesting, as if the lad might have to leave suddenly), was drinking at the bar with a friend. "What's this in aid of, Macalvie?" Again, thought Jury, as if I don't know. But he persisted. "You don't really think the kid can help?"

Macalvie didn't respond, beyond telling Jury to find a table; he just walked up to the bar and Jury watched him produce identification, and motion for the boy to follow him over to where Jury was sitting. There was no sheltering from the noise. The only empty table Jury could find was by the wailing jukebox. But Macalvie liked jukeboxes; liked them, that is, as long as they played "his" music: Elvis, the Beatles, Frank, Patsy. Presently, some country-western singer was sawing off several bars about his woman packing up and driving off. They were always setting off like this in American country music—women leaving men and men leaving women alike, piling their bags in cars and taking off across country. Was it all those miles of roads that made for all this broken-hearted travelling?

"Superintendent Jury," said Macalvie, introducing Jimmy Landis. "Scotland Yard's CID."

Jimmy Landis smiled the ghost of a smile, nodded, and sat down with his half-full bottle of lager; he polished off most of that immediately. Wheeling colors from the jukebox seemed to run like little rivers across one side of the boy's face.

"Mrs. Hawes?" he repeated the name Macalvie asked him about. "A friend of Mum's. I scarcely knew her."

"You drove her around."

"Sometimes. How did you—?"

"Kind of chauffeur."

"Sometimes. She lived alone."

"Like your mother."

Macalvie's tone was level, almost expressionless. It was guilt, Jury supposed, that brought Jimmy Landis's head down to study the bottle of lager and moved his fingers to pick at the label.

"Something wrong?" asked Macalvie.

Jimmy. Mid-twenties, his mother had said, but he looked so young, or perhaps it was the look of fear in his eyes, the near-transparency of his skin. His skin had a pallor that made him seem all the more vulnerable. It was the way in which Jury had seen his mother's face, her complexion from which all the color had fled. Jimmy Landis's skin was like his mother's; Jury imagined the boy often took on his mother's coloration. It made him think of a London sky during those fleeting moments between first light and real sunrise when the sky is wiped clean of all color, between that first line of gold and the rising sun. Looking at Jimmy sitting there, trying to hunch down into his coat, Jury thought of the bleak skies on a winter's day in Newcastle where his cousin and unemployment lived, and the hunched figures of boys grown old from the dole and from drink.

Then he realized that the connection here was another Jimmy, the snooker-playing Marquess—also dark, thin, and tall. From there it was only a bleak winter road back to Old Washington and that bed where Helen Minton had lain, her arm dropped over the side, hand almost sweeping the floor. He had never really been aware before that Helen had looked, in death, like the portrait of Chatterton. Chatterton with his icy, pale skin. All of this washed over him in a few seconds of looking into the face of Jimmy Landis.

The boy exploded. "I don't get it. What *is* this? You talk about Mum; you talk about Nell. What is this? It was her heart. Why does this need Scotland Yard? For God's sake!" he added for tough emphasis.

"We just had tea with her," Macalvie continued. "With your mother."

Nothing. Grimly, Jimmy picked at the beer label.

"Hated to see it go to waste."

Jury breathed, "Macalvie, come on."

"Your mother's sick, we were told."

"So what's that got to do with anything?" Even the reflection of the jukebox's pulsating colors fled from his face. It looked bleached.

"For you, kid, I'd think it would have to do with *everything*." When Jimmy didn't respond, Macalvie sighed, said, "Tell us what you know about Helen Hawes."

"Nothing. I told you. Just drove her a few times to get groceries, things like that."

"In total silence."

"What?" Jimmy frowned up at him, head still bent.

"You never talked. Never."

"Well, for Christ's sake, of course we *talked*."

"So?"

"Not about anything that makes a difference—"

"How would you know that?"

Jimmy's wail of frustration far outshone the country singer's rendition of "Walkin' After Midnight." "The weather. My mum. My job. Look, what *is* this?"

Jury cut in. "Sometimes you hear things that don't register at the time. She might have talked about herself, people she knew, trips she took. That's all we mean, Jimmy."

Macalvie said, "I need a drink." He got up.

As he rose, Jimmy looked from one to the other, mustered enough sarcasm to ask, "So what is this? Bad cop, good cop?"

"No. Bad cop, bad cop." Macalvie nodded at Jury. "Be careful. He turns on you."

Watching Macalvie walk off, Jimmy then looked at Jury as if he were, indeed, souring right before the boy's eyes. And he asked it again, the only question left in the world: "Look, what *is* all this? Am I suspected of something?"

"No. This death is not totally explicable, that's all." In fairness to Macalvie, Jury kept his tone level, though unthreatening.

"You mean it wasn't her heart?"

Jury looked over toward the bar, where Macalvie was standing three deep with the other customers demanding attention from the one girl who was working the beer pulls. The crowd in the Pelican generated a lot of heat and there was the pervasive feeling of hot breath and warm beer. Jimmy Landis still hadn't taken off his coat. Neither had Macalvie. Macalvie, Jury always thought, must sleep in his coat. Well, they had something in common.

He answered Jimmy's question. "Yes, probably. But a lot of things can bring on an attack. Did you know Nell Hawes well enough that her death affected you?"

"If you mean, was I sorry—yes, I was sorry." He continued to strip away bits of the label on the empty ale bottle. "Nell was nice." He looked up and as quickly looked down again. "Talked a blue streak, though."

"Really? Your—everyone else said she was rather quiet. Reticent." He had not wanted to mention Jimmy's mother.

"Yeah. Well, for some reason she talked to me. You know, when I was driving her to Sainsbury's or somewhere. The chauffeur. You know. Anonymous." He smiled for the first time since he'd sat down.

Jury returned the smile, said nothing.

Jimmy shrugged, as if disdaining his own insight: "Except probably it wasn't that. See, Nell didn't have any kids."

Although he certainly hadn't judged the boy to be lacking in insight, still Jury was a little surprised by this comment. Also, by Jimmy's implied admission that he had filled for Nell Hawes a role that he was failing at with his own mother. If he had been Macalvie, he would immediately have asked him about those rides and what Nell Hawes might have told him. Well, he wasn't Macalvie, and he didn't even know why he said what he did:

"When I was a kid my mother had a friend that I used to go with every week to the park. I mean one of those little green squares surrounded by terraced houses that residents only were allowed to use. You had to have a key to get in. She had one, and she'd unlock the gate. I always thought this was—I don't know, incredible. Wonderful. To have a key that unlocked the park gate."

Jimmy had stopped scraping the label with his thumbnail and his eyes were intent on Jury's face. Jury hadn't noticed before, since the boy had been keeping his head down, the color of his eyes. Darker green than his mother's, more intense.

"This woman loved flowers, but she was nearly blind. Not totally, but forms, she told me, swam together when she looked at them. She couldn't distinguish between the little benches in the park and the trees that overhung them, much less between the various kinds of flowers in the beds there. And she had been a painter, a watercolorist, and a very good one. Her name was Amy and she was known for her courage. No one ever heard her complain, or get angry. No one ever saw her cry. I couldn't believe Fate could play such a horrible trick on someone. It was like a pianist having his fingers paralyzed; or a runner having his legs cut off; or a singer losing her voice." Jury nodded toward the jukebox. Jimmy looked too, both of them hypnotized by its swimming colors—oil mixing in water—and the throbbing voice, still, of Patsy Cline. Someone in here really liked Patsy. "Like Patsy Cline being struck dumb. Well, what Amy liked was for me to describe the flowers, that is, tell her what kinds were planted in different seasons, and then she'd paint them. They were remarkable; they were so true. 'The hand remembers,' she used to say. And then after she'd done that, she'd paint what she could actually see. This turned out to be blobs of colors. Colors all running together. And once, only once, did she get so frustrated she threw her paints and her brushes down and chucked her book of watercolors straight across the grass. 'Oh, God! That's all I see! Just a lot of melting colors!' She was crying, she was nearly *wailing*. 'I want to see edges, I want to see outlines, but all I see is melting colors.'

"And something inside of me just—exploded. *I* started crying, but not out of sympathy or empathy. I was furious, more and more furious, not at her but at life in general. 'I wish *I* could see that!' That stopped her, stopped her cold.

"She looked at me, that is, as well as she could do, you know—a little out of kilter, a little squint-eyed. 'See what?'

" 'A lot of melting colors. But no! I have to see *everything*!' And this seemed to me to be the most unjust and outrageous thing—that I had to see *everything*. Hard edges, outlines. We were both crying then, and then we were laughing. I asked her not to tell my mother, I don't know why. I told myself it was because I didn't want Mum to think I'd been callous, yelling at blind Amy, making her life harder . . . but that wasn't the reason. I still don't know the reason."

Jimmy's eyes were still on him, childlike in their intensity. Jury recalled the little park, the dark green of the September trees, the cool ferns and damp mosses. His eyes were that shade of green, exactly. He started to say something, but stopped.

They listened to a few bars of "Crazy" and Jury said, "Nell Hawes. Anything you can remember, tell me."

"You mean that trip she took?"

"That. Anything."

"It's been a few months."

"Things come back," said Jury, wryly.

"She really liked it, the West. Or the Southwest, I expect it was. Colorado, New Mexico . . . Santa Fe, and—what was the name of the other place . . . ?"

"What about Santa Fe?" asked Macalvie, back with two pints and a bottle of ale. He sat down, still with his coat on, drank off nearly half his pint.

"I think she liked it because it's mystical. She was telling me about 'channels' and 'auras,' stuff like that." He raised his bottle. "Cheers. Oh, Taos. That was the other place she liked. It means 'the way,' she told me. Chinese, or something. Very mystical she thought the Southwest was." Jimmy drank and thought. "Nell was religious. Or spiritual, I expect you'd say. 'Everything runs together,' she'd say. She said the American Indians had a lot to teach people. She talked about a 'rainbow path'—something one of the tribes believed. I think she said it was like a path between the earth and the sky."

Macalvie grunted. He slipped twenty pence from the little hill of change he'd dumped on the table. He got up and hung over the juke-box for a moment, running his thumb across his forehead, apparently deep in thought as to what record to play, then slid the coin in. When nothing happened immediately, he kicked the jukebox. Then he sat down. As the voice of Patsy Cline filled the room with another help-ing of "Walkin' After Midnight," Macalvie asked, "What about other tourists? Did she mention anyone she met over there?"

"No one in particular, no."

"How about unparticular. Anyone at all? Any of her own coun-trymen, for example?"

"Americans, she said. Not surprising," he said dryly, shooting Macalvie a slightly insolent look. "But no one I remember—oh, except she said she had dinner with a family from New York, and, yes, there was a woman 'teamed up' with her for a few days. Saw the sights."

Macalvie had taken out his tiny spiral notebook, uncapped his pen. "What about this woman?"

Jimmy frowned, trying to remember, then shook his head.

"Did she mention places she stayed? People who come back from trips are always raving on about the high price of food and hotels."

Jimmy thought for a moment, took a pull on his bottle of ale. "She didn't, though, I mean she didn't name any particular place. Did talk about how pricey everything was, especially in Santa Fe. 'Even that little B and B,' she said. Because it was so near the center of town. But that's all."

"Easy enough to check." Macalvie made a note, then asked, "Did she mention a place called Coyote Village or the Silver Heron?"

"No . . . Canyon Road," said Jimmy, suddenly. "I remember that because I liked the name. That's where she ran into her, this woman." He shook his head again. "Maybe I'll remember more."

Patsy Cline walked her heart out as the three of them sat in silence for a few moments.

"Was it you?" asked Jury of Macalvie. "Playing Patsy Cline?"

"She helps me think. Okay, Jimmy. We have your mother's address but not yours. I understand you don't live with her?" Macalvie managed to invest this comment with as much reproach as he could.

Almost absently, Jimmy gave him the address; he was frowning at the pen poised over the notebook. "That was it; I remember, now."

"That was what?"

"The notebook. Or address book, rather. It was when we were driving to Sainsbury's on the Monday, and Nell was looking for something in her purse, tossing stuff out, you know, the way women will do. And she came across this little address book. She said, 'Drat, I forgot to send this off to her.' I asked, Who? It was the woman she'd got on so well with on the trip. It seems this woman—what did she call her?" Jimmy rubbed at his temple as if to dislodge this bit of information. "Frances, that was it. It seems she'd handed Nell her address book to write down her address and number and something had happened right then so that Nell forgot to give it back. She meant to post it, she said."

Macalvie had pulled out the address book in its sleeve of polythene and put it on the table. "That it?"

"Why, yes. Where'd you get it?"

"Amongst her things."

Jury asked: "That's what she called her? Frances?" When Jimmy nodded, Jury said, "They were all Americans that she met, you said."

Jimmy nodded again. "Could one of them, this Frances, have been living in London?"

Jimmy frowned. "Well, she could have done, of course. But Nell didn't say that."

"Okay. Time to go home, Jimmy. But make yourself available, will you?"

Jimmy brought the bottle down on the table, totally perplexed. "Home?"

"Yeah, it's the place halfway up the steps with the door and the windows. You'll be wanting to say goodnight to your mother, I imagine."

Jimmy laughed uncertainly. "I still got some drinking to do. Hardly had a chance to talk to my mates, me sitting here cracking with you two." He was sounding tough again, but not too.

"Oh. Too bad, because this place is closing." Macalvie drank off his pint of bitter.

Jimmy was totally surprised. "It's not even half-nine yet. What're you talking about?" He looked around as if to assure himself people weren't bolting.

"Call it early closing." Macalvie was up and pocketing his cigarettes, his change. "Time to go home. Unless you'd like to come along to the station with us?"

"What in hell is this?" Jimmy was back to his former line of questioning. But he had finished his ale and was standing up.

"It's a choice. A nice cup of tea with your mum or along to headquarters." Macalvie shrugged as if to say, No problem.

Patsy's voice walked them out the door into the cold night air.

"I DON'T THINK I can handle it." Jimmy's words were all but inaudible.

There was a silence during which Macalvie made a movement toward the boy and Jury thought he was going to relent and put a comforting hand on his shoulder. The hand went to the shoulder all right, but it didn't look comforting—more like the grip of a bird of prey. "Poor. Fucking. You," Macalvie said.

Suddenly, Jimmy exploded. "Where the hell do you get off, telling people how to live their lives? You come in here like Judgment Day when you don't know anything about it; you don't know me, you know nothing about me; you don't know me and my mum!"

He sounded in his near-to-weeping rage as Jury remembered himself sounding that day long ago in the park with Amy. And he knew why he'd told Jimmy about her.

Macalvie was taking all of Jimmy's verbal abuse in much the same way he did when he waited for one of his own men—or women, like Gilly Thwaite—to come back down the ladder of near-hysteria, Macalvie having frustrated them to within an inch of their lives. When Jimmy finally came down a few rungs to nothing more than a sputter, Macalvie said, "Goodnight, then. We'll just watch you up the stairs to see you don't get mugged."

Jimmy stomped furiously upwards, turning once in the middle to hurl one remaining insult at Macalvie: "*Fuck YOU, Commander!*" Then he continued up the stair.

Jury loved that "Commander," as if this particular "fuck you" weighed in with a lot of rank.

"He has a point, Macalvie." Jury had his hand on the other's arm and was trying to turn him toward the quay.

Macalvie was looking upward. "Is he inside the house yet or just skulking around in the dark waiting to make a run for it?"

"Will you come *on*? You're not his bloody minder!" Jury pulled him toward the quay and the river.

"We find out the dates when your lady—Fanny Hamilton—was in the Southwest, where she stayed. Easy enough."

Jury sighed. "This is an extremely tenuous connection you're making."

His face still turned upward, Macalvie said, "Nell Hawes and Angela Hope both in Santa Fe. Fanny—or Frances—Hamilton, ditto." His sigh was awfully theatrical. "If I could take a holiday, I'd go. Too much on my platter at the moment."

"There's *always* too much on your platter. Me, hell, I have nothing better to do than take off for the American Southwest."

"Looks like it." Macalvie craned his neck upward, squinted.

"No."

"Suit yourself."

"Angela Hope was found in *Wiltshire*. Nell Hawes died here in *Devon*. Fanny Hamilton, *London*. The American embassy and the American cops will not be interested in the last two. Ditto, Wiltshire Constabulary."

Calmly, Macalvie answered, "Obviously. That's why we ought to go there."

" 'We' seems to have a trickle effect. Down to *me*. I do have a life over here, you seem to forget." Jury was thinking of Jenny and not being able to contact her. It was frustrating.

"Not much of a one."

Jury turned his face upward, too. It's true, he thought sadly. The black matte of the sky was crowded, more than usual, with stars, as if a star gun had sprayed it with star bullets. Then, unaccountably, he smiled, for the image made him think of Covent Garden and the Starr-dust. A few moments passed in total silence and he found himself irritated by Macalvie's upward staring. "What the hell are you looking at?"

"Dark matter."

Jury winced. He was sorry he'd asked.

"You've read about dark matter, haven't you?"

"No, that's just one of the many things I haven't read about. Come on, I'm tired." Jury yanked Macalvie's sleeve.

Macalvie, however, wasn't going anywhere. "It's got something to do with gravitational pull. The first mass they found they calculated to be trillions of miles long. That's *trillions*, Jury. This is matter so huge it's *unimaginable*. That's what gets me. It's unimaginable, but it's calculable."

"Is this going to be another 'deep time' lecture?"

Macalvie turned his squint on Jury. "I'm not talking about deep time; I'm talking about dark matter. Can't a person even look at the universe without being persecuted by you?"

"A person, yes. You're not a person. Come on. I don't feel like standing here in the middle of the night talking about the universe."

Macalvie now squinted at his watch. "It's only ten bloody o'clock. That's the middle of the night to you?"

"How can anyone who's so damned literal stand around talking about deep time and dark matter? What's wrong with you? Usually you can only see what's at the end of a gun or a torch or a microscope. What's all this philosophizing about?"

As if the question weren't clearly rhetorical, Macalvie answered, face turned skyward once again, "Dark matter. I told you."

"What? Am I hearing correctly? Are you saying you think there's such a thing as an unsolvable crime?"

"That's right. Stop to think about it: They have enough facts, the scientists. The physicists, the chemists, the astronomers. They have enough facts with which to calculate. With which, I expect, to actually prove it. But that 'prove' is in quotes. Because how can you prove something you can't imagine?"

Jury had started pacing back and forth, there on the cold quay. "Macalvie, cut it out. You know and I know there are only two reasons for not solving a case. You either don't have enough information or you do have the information but just can't put it together. That's it. Fini."

Macalvie shrugged, dug his hands in his trouser pockets.

"Oh, come on, Macalvie. You have to agree with that. If we can't come up with a connection between Fanny Hamilton, Nell Hawes, and Angela Hope, it's either lack of information or inability to think straight." When Macalvie didn't answer, Jury added, "There are plenty of cases I haven't solved. God, there might *even* be a case *you* haven't solved. Lack of information. Bad thinking. For you, of course, it could only be lack of information. There's nothing metaphysical about it."

But Macalvie merely shook his head. "Maybe not. Because it's— unfathomable."

"That's ridiculous. Impossible. And are you saying *this* one is that sort of crime?"

Macalvie snorted. "How could I be saying that, for Christ's sake, when we don't *have* all the available information." Macalvie yawned. "What point does he have?"

"What? What are you talking about?" Jury's mind was still working at metaphysics.

"Jimmy. You said he had a point."

That was Macalvie. He never forgot anything, no matter how insignificant. "Let me tell you something you probably won't like—"

"How thrilling."

"For such a good cop, for someone with such a subtle mind, you sure as hell see things sometimes in simple terms. You don't seem to be able to imagine the possibility that life can be extremely complex—"

"No? What was I just talking about, then?"

"—or that people are slaves to ambivalence. His point was, you can't tell people how to live."

"The hell I can't. Well, come on. Let's *go.*"

Jury sighed. "You're just like he is."

Macalvie stopped. "Like Jimmy Landis? Me?" He clapped his hands to his chest. "*Moi?*"

"Yeah, *toi.*"

"And how do you work that out?"

"You're both so scared somebody might die you can't even take your coats off."

They walked in silence for some minutes.

What Jury was thinking about was the girl, the little sister. How old? Twelve, thirteen. Angela Hope had, apparently, been her family. Now her family was gone. He said, "Two or three days. Four, tops." Jury looked out over the river. "Because I want the information and I know you're wrong."

Macalvie was lighting a cigar. When he had sucked in to his satisfaction, he flicked the match toward the river and asked, "Can you leave tomorrow?"

"No."

The next day, Jury left.

SEVENTEEN

To any casual passerby in the rain who glanced through the windows of Ardry End, Melrose was sure he and his aunt must present the very picture of warmth and conviviality, snug as could be before the fireplace, drinking tea and sherry, the old dog at their feet.

But why would anyone casually pass by in the middle of a dark downpour? He realized he'd been thinking of Miss Fludd for the hundredth time. And would have started in on a hundred-and-one, had his manservant, Ruthven, not been standing over him at the moment, telephone receiver extended, drawing him from dreams of Paris and Miss Fludd. It was a fantasy he'd had a good deal of trouble supporting, even before the telephone's interruption, given that Agatha was beached on the sofa opposite, the tide of the pouring rain not powerful enough to suck her out through the door, despite its having floated her in.

These watery images, however, had led him from Paris and Miss Fludd to Baltimore's National Aquarium and thence to the writer Ellen Taylor. Her book *Windows* lay on the arm of his chair. He had put it down, inspired to pick up his own. Until Agatha's early morning intrusion, Melrose had been having a lovely time, drinking a coffee and writing the next installment of *Gin Lane* and the adventures of Detective Chief Inspector Smithson and his wife, Norma. Smithson and Norma were also seated before a fire, theirs at Gravely Manor; they too were drinking coffee (and Norma, champagne, as always). It pleased Melrose how these two partook of his own pleasures and pastimes.

"*So you see, darling,*" said Norma, "*that alibi is . . .*"

What? What about the alibi? Melrose scanned the page before to find out. Couldn't he even keep straight which alibi belonged to which character? Well, he hadn't, after all, picked up *Gin Lane* since he'd gone to Baltimore. He frowned a little, his mind only partly taking in Agatha's deployment of the fairy cakes, the rest of it on the telephone receiver Ruthven was forcing on him.

"It's Superintendent Jury, my lord." Ruthven sounded self-satisfied, even smirky. He knew that Agatha's presence meant any conversation with Mr. Jury would be conducted in code. Ruthven was very fond of Richard Jury, whom he referred to as "a gentleman of the old school," and who, despite being titleless, somehow (in Ruthven's estimation) made up for Melrose's having given up his earldom, his duchy, his marquessry.

Melrose listened for a few moments; then he said, "*Again?* Good Lord, but we just got back. . . . Hospital? *Wiggins* is in hospital? . . . What sort of accident? . . . Nothing serious? For Sergeant Wiggins, everything's serious. . . . Oh, all right, if you won't tell. . . . Yes, I'll stop in and see him. . . . I was going to London anyway. . . . Uh-huh. . . . Merchant—wait a moment, let me get a bit of paper—" He looked about the end table, when Agatha, in one of her rare moments of helpfulness, handed him a small silver notebook, the cover adorned with a crest. It looked familiar, somehow. "Go on. . . ." Melrose wrote as Jury talked. "Gabriel Merchant. . . . The Crippses? You're joking. . . . I remember. Ah! Lady Cray. I should be glad to see her again. . . . Slocum, Beatrice . . . the couple in the Tate, right? But if you've already talked to them . . . How could there be any relation between . . . No, I don't have a facsimile machine—why would I have one of those? I can barely manage dialing a telephone. . . . All right, send it express. I'll get it before I leave. What do the telephone numbers have to . . . Commander Macalvie . . . Well, isn't he always?" Melrose laughed, then stopped laughing when he realized sheer surprise had him repeating what Jury was saying while Agatha was sitting there, all ears and fairy cakes. Lord, wouldn't he ever learn to take calls *outside* when she was in the room? So he sat there for the few moments remaining, stony-faced while Jury told him why he was nipping off to the States. Again. And they'd been back for only a week. Finally, they said their goodbyes.

"What was all that about?"

He was saved from answering at all while she trod on her own question. "And you didn't tell me you were going to London!"

"It's my annual visit to Mr. Beaton."

"Who on earth is he? I've never heard of him." Which fairly well settled Mr. Beaton's existence.

"My tailor. Was my father's tailor. And *this*—" Melrose held up the silver notebook—"I believe was my mother's."

Wide-eyed, Agatha asked, "Whose?"

"M-U-M's. Lady Marjorie's. You do remember Lady Marjorie, the Countess of Caverness?"

Agatha settled for telling him not to be silly; she certainly wasn't settling for the truth.

He sat there brooding for some moments over Jury's call, until pulled from his reflections by his aunt's voice, together with the sudden appearance, at the long window, of Mr. Momaday, emblazoned in a flash of lightning. Mr. Momaday was the new groundskeeper; he stood outside now like a skeleton in a Barbour jacket, drenched.

Melrose went to the window, threw it up, and got a lashing of rain on his face. He listened to Mr. Momaday's guttural vowels and watched his rather violent gesticulations.

"Close that window, Plant!" yelled Agatha. "It's raining!"

What a brilliant sleuth. To Momaday he said, "Yes, yes, I understand." Melrose didn't but he slammed down the window anyway.

This did not, however, deter Mr. Momaday, who apparently assumed Melrose was as conversant with him through a pane of glass as anywhere else. Mr. Momaday's mouth kept working.

"Whatever is that Momaday person on about? He's quite crazy. I told you that when you hired him."

Agatha hadn't, of course, told Melrose any such thing. She was delighted to have someone new to order about the house and grounds. Melrose had hired this groundskeeper, not to manage his pheasant and grouse, but to manage the occasional hunter who came poking about his property. Momaday roamed around in his green Barbour jacket and gumshoes, shotgun broken over his arm, looking purposeful and doing nothing. But that was, of course, what Melrose wanted him to do: nothing. Nothing but project a sense of danger. He had been hired from amongst several candidates precisely because he was fairly useless and would, therefore, leave both Melrose and muskrat alone. Mr. Momaday looked the part, too: gaunt and with a sort of cuneiform skull, a forehead permanently formed into runnels. And Mr. Momaday also had supplied the unexpected bonus of keeping Agatha out of the drawing room and in the copse, for now she had someone new for whom she could fashion fresh hells.

"If you're going to London, you can stop in at Harrods and get me some of their Norfolk ham."

"If you want ham, go to Norfolk. I'm not going to Harrods Food Hall. I wouldn't surface for days." He looked at his manuscript page again, frowning. What alibi? He couldn't remember so he drew a pig. The ham was doing more to inspire him than his own imagination.

The moving pen supplied Agatha with fresh ammunition: "Are you still writing that silly mystery thing?"

"No." Melrose went on writing.

She sighed and finally sat back on the sofa. "What's Martha cooking for our dinner?"

Our? "Haggis. And some mashed turnip. Washed down, I think, with a single-malt whisky."

"*Haggis?* Good Lord, you don't really eat that stuff. I don't believe it."

"I eat and drink and recite Mr. Burns's ode to a haggis. That might be the name, actually: 'To a Haggis.' 'Cut you up with ready slight—'" here, Melrose pretended to wield a knife—"'Trenching your gushing entrails bright—'"

"That is absolutely disgusting!"

"You won't care to join me, then? It does get a bit, well, like a revenge tragedy when Ruthven stabs the skin."

"*You could, you know, make an appointment,*" said Norma. "*After all, Jonah has never met you.*" Yes! That was an excellent idea! And "Jonah" was a popular name, he thought, with psychiatrists.

"A nasty, low dish." Agatha, apparently still on the haggis, shuddered. She surveyed the wasted tea table and said, "I'll just have Martha wrap me up a few of those cakes to take with me. I'm sure she's got more in the kitchen." She raised her eyes and said, "I don't know what you think you're writing, Plant."

Melrose didn't answer. He had drawn a fountain and was now settling a little statue near it. Unable to think of anything that Smithson might tell a psychiatrist, he was drawing little pictures on the manuscript page. This garden gnome was no doubt inspired by Trueblood's absurd plot to get through the doors of Watermeadows.

The voiceover of Agatha thrummed on, but he ignored it, returning to thoughts of the Fludds and Watermeadows. Miss Fludd clearly could not be living at Watermeadows alone, unless . . . Could she have come in advance of Lady Summerston? Perhaps as a paid companion, or something like that? Oh, surely, the girl would not be working in that capacity. Damn it! How could he have been so stupid as not to ask her anything? What a remarkable conversation. Not a moment's worth of practical exchange of information in it—

"Since you've come back from the States, there's no question but what you've changed, Plant; I really think it too bad." *Thrum, thrum, thrum.*

Melrose found he had doodled in three chickens by the fountain. He turned his gaze to his ceiling, an Adam ceiling that he found soothing, its elegant spirals and garlands almost soporific, and wondered why he hadn't thought of the extremely simple overture of inviting the Fludds (assuming "Fludd" was some sort of family name) over for tea. Surely, it would be a neighborly thing to do; Watermeadows was, after all, the property next door to his—although the acres and acres of land in between must have put the distance at perhaps half a mile. Still—

"What are you doing?"

Melrose looked up. The thrumming, he noticed had stopped, like the sudden cessation of a vibrating string. "Hmm? Oh, I'm just making a list for Momaday."

"List? What sort of list?"

"Things we'll need." Melrose sketched in the tiny snout of a pig. He had had little to do with pigs, true, but he quite liked them, he decided. This one had a pot belly, like one of that Korean lot. Or was it the Vietnamese pigs? "Feed, fertilizer. Probably a tractor."

"What? Why would you need a tractor?"

Melrose drew a fence around his farm animals. "It's for the farm. Or farmling, perhaps. I don't want to overextend myself. We'll need the tractor to turn over the loam. Loam." He repeated the word, liking the sound of it. Earth had such nice words connected with it: "soil," "loam," "moss," "moor" . . .

"You must be mad! This is Ardry End! Why, it's . . . it's a manor house!"

"No, it isn't."

"It would be if it were a bit larger."

"If it were a bit larger, so would Mrs. Withersby's cottage."

Outraged on behalf of Ardry End, on behalf of the late Earl of Caverness, Melrose's father; on behalf of the late countess, Melrose's mother; on behalf of the crystal and carpets, the diamonds and Derby, Agatha rose in indignation—but first not forgetting to wrap up in a napkin the scones that remained on the Derby cake stand—and announced: "I've done, finished, I wash my hands!" She gathered up Lady Marjorie's silver notebook and said, "You need a psychiatrist, Plant."

"But it's only to get information, darling," said Norma.

Melrose's smile was sly. At least it would save *him* from seeing a psychiatrist. Writing, he decided, was wonderfully therapeutic.

EIGHTEEN

He made it to Heathrow with over a glum hour before his flight, but, of course, the airlines always wanted you there with *three* to spare. Most of the time was taken up with depositing his hired car together with a hefty surcharge for not returning it to its original London source. He'd driven it from Exeter.

Bad boy, the grizzle-haired and slightly matronly booking clerk seemed to be saying. Still, she settled for telling him how *fortunate* he was that her firm was one of the bigger car-hire companies, and thus could accommodate the vicissitudes of their customers. And *furthermore*, he hadn't notified them in advance—

(Here the stapler banged down on the tissuey order forms.)

—which was *always* the understanding, and even *more so*, you're fortunate it's our firm—

(Tissuey papers were being stuffed in an envelope.)

—because the others would never—

"Furthermore," said Jury, breaking out his ID and shoving it up to her face, "the day I think Dame Fortune smiles upon me just because I'm using some particular bloody car-hire firm is the day I quit the Murder Squad." He never used that term; there was no "Murder Squad." Quickly, she stepped back, and then, with a diffident forefinger, pushed the envelope across the counter.

"Thank you," said Jury, as he pocketed it and smiled, brilliantly, which reassured her.

Brightly, she said, "When you next need to hire a car, sir, remember—"

You wouldn't dare, said his glance.

"I fancy DimeDrive," she whispered. "Down there." Elaborately, she pointed.

Rapport restored, they saluted each other in a comradely fashion.

SOMEONE STEPPED AWAY from one of the pay phones just as Jury came up to the kiosks; for that, at least, he was grateful. Usually, you couldn't get near them.

No answer, still. He had about given up expecting one, paid little attention to the distant double note of Jenny's cradled telephone receiver.

He thought a moment, dialed Stratford police headquarters, got himself put through to Sammy Lasko. All right, Lasko shouldn't, as a detective inspector, be called upon to go looking for one's tearaway friends (the image of Jenny Kennington being a "tearaway" rather amused him). But his failure to find her over the last three days was making him more and more apprehensive.

"Lasko," said Sammy, managing to sound tired, bored, and intrigued all at the same time.

Jury told him what he wanted; that Sam Lasko would send somebody around to check on a friend of his. "Her name's Jenny Kennington, Lady Kennington, and she lives in Ryland Street, one of those little cottages."

There was a silence that managed to sound "troubled" on the other end of the phone. There was the sound of Sammy's breathing. Heavy. "Kennington?"

"Yes." Everything in Jury's body tightened, not just his stomach. He felt an adrenaline rush that would help an Olympic runner off the starting line.

"Hold it just a tick, Richard."

Oh, my God. "Just a tick" was quite long enough for his mind to fill up with more lurid pictures of broken and mangled bodies lying by equally mangled automobiles along the Stratford–Warwick Road than Jury wanted.

"Richard." Sammy was back and seemed to be rattling papers. "I just wanted to make sure. This is weird, one weird bloody coincidence."

"Weird" he could stand; "weird" was okay, for, given Lasko's tone, "weird" definitely did not mean "dead." Relief flooded him. "Meaning what?"

"I was telling you about that case in Lincolnshire. You weren't listening. CID up there in Lincoln wanted me keep an eye on a lady who's involved in a murder investigation—"

Jury was ahead of him. He gripped the phone. "You're not saying—"

"Jennifer Kennington. Listen, where in hell you calling from? Sounds like an airport."

"It is. Are you telling me *Jenny's* one of their suspects?"

"Witness, witness. What I *am* telling you is, I've been looking for her too." Pause, troubled. "You going somewhere?"

"The States. What do you mean you've been 'looking'? Can't you find her?"

"No. Maybe she's scarpered, as we quaintly say over here; as they quaintly say in the U.S. of A., she's boogied. So where're you going? Which part?"

"Santa Fe. And that's ridiculous, Sammy; Jenny wouldn't 'scarper.' " How did Jury know it was ridiculous? The public-address system blasted. Calling his flight? He checked his watch. Time yet.

"Maybe," said Sammy, equably. "Anyway, she's not at home. Santa Fe, huh? Why don't I ever get sent places like that? Hell, you just got back."

Jury was rubbing his temple, as if this action might get through to his brain. The awful thing was, of course, that she had called *him*, and clearly for help. He had a sudden unreasoning rush of anger at Carole-anne. . . . No. It wasn't her fault. Jenny had made the one try, and he wasn't there, and that was it. "Sammy, do me a favor." If anyone owed him a favor, it was Inspector Lasko, and Lasko knew it. "Remember Melrose Plant? If I give you his Northants number, will you get in touch with him?"

"Plant? Plant—oh, the duke. Sure, I remember him."

"Earl. Or, rather, ex-earl. Don't call him 'Lord Ardry.' He gave up his various titles some years back."

"Why? Politics? Does he want to sit in the House of Commons or something?"

"Plant? Hell, no." Jury remembered a little lecture Plant had given once on nobilary entitlement. But all he said was, "I don't know why. Ask him, don't ask me."

Jury fumbled out his address book, recited the number, which Lasko repeated after him with the studied rote of a child. "I can try ringing him myself, but I think he's in London today. At any rate I'll leave word with someone there to tell Plant you'll be calling."

"My pleasure. But why am I?"

"To find Jenny." Again, his hand gripped the receiver. "She's not in any danger, is she?"

"Don't see why she would be. Maybe she's just staying with a friend; maybe *she's* gone to London." Then he added, uncertainly. "Only I told them all to stay put in Stratford."

Jury thanked him, rang off. Another flight call.

Jenny.

Scarpered.

Boogied.

Hell.

JURY LEANED against the uninviting plastic surround of the phone and held a brief argument with himself. Jenny was a friend and she'd called him for help. He wouldn't go. But he'd promised Macalvie. He would go. It was a wild goose chase, damn it. He wouldn't go. It wasn't his case, dammit. He wouldn't go. He rubbed his head. No. Macalvie had never chased a wild goose in his life.

He found Plant's number and rang up Ardry End. Yes, Mr. Plant had indeed gone up to London, only a little before noon. Ruthven told him this, conveying extreme sadness and sympathy that the superintendent wanted to speak to Lord Ardry and Lord Ardry wasn't to be found in his usual place.

"If you're in London, sir, you might be able to find him at his tailor's. That would be in the Old Brompton. I can let you have the number. He has been known to spend a good deal of time with Mr. Beaton, they being old friends. Mr. Beaton was tailor to his late father—"

Jury interrupted. "If you could just give him a message for me, Ruthven. I have to catch my plane in another fifteen minutes or so. Simply tell him that Inspector Lasko, Stratford-upon-Avon CID, will be ringing up about a matter I'd like him to take care of for me. It's rather important."

Ruthven assured him he would convey the information immediately. Mr. Plant would probably be returning late that evening.

Stressed, Jury automatically went for the pocket where he usually kept his cigarettes, finding instead the packet of pills Wiggins had pressed on him during a recent flu epidemic. With directions. A small sheet of paper was inside the packet. Looked like some sort of colored code. He took it out, studied the damned thing, tossed it away. Bad enough a gift of pills without the additional suffering of decoding them.

He could have chewed up an entire pack of Players or Silk Cut at this point, and made for the magazine and newspaper kiosk. With what he felt was impressive self-control, he kept his eyes away from the counter, the case, the racks where Temptation Beckoned.

From the multitude of magazines—was there one for *every* subject?—he chose a couple and then found, amongst the rows and rows of paperbacks, one of Polly Praed's books. He was surprised that Polly was airport-popular, as she was always making it sound as if her books weren't selling, or they were being remaindered, or going out of print, or the object of book burners. Polly was an extremely pessimistic woman. The cover was lurid; he was sure the content was not.

Jury put his purchases in Temptation's way—he could not avoid the cigarette display, for it was directly behind the cashier and her computerized register. She looked over it somewhat sadly, shaking her dark blond hair away from her shoulders. Tobacco-brown, he thought, was the color. How ridiculous. And her eyes were merely light brown, not nicotine-stain-brown. Longingly, he looked at the colorful display of cigarettes as one might observe the skyline of some exotic land that grew the more enticing as it grew the less corporeal, balanced along a shoreline that receded in the watery dis—

Oh, shut up! he screamed inwardly. Jenny's scarpered and you're thinking about a *smoke?* Is it absolutely necessary to get poetic about a killer habit? But then he stopped in the middle of this self-flagellation: Wait a moment, old son. The trouble was that, yes, one bloody well could wax poetic about tobacco. Wasn't that, indeed, the trouble? One *could* remember many, many times when a cigarette was an integral part of some pleasant, lovely experience. One could remember standing perhaps on a balcony overlooking a sea the color of jasper, drink in one hand, cigarette in the other; or the comfort of a cigarette as you stood at the window watching someone walk away. It was a loss, and no matter how much you rationalized and turned your inner eye to the hideous X-rays of ruined lungs, there was still, superimposed over that deadly picture, the other: the balcony, the sea, the cigarette, the whisky, the sunset, the window, the smoke, the rain. It was a loss as exquisitely painful as the loss of love or beauty, because although viciously neither it had insidiously wedded itself to both.

You devils, he thought, glaring at the rows of glossy packets.

At least he thought he had merely thought it, until the cashier jumped. "What?"

Jury blushed, apologized. "Sorry. I wasn't meaning you, but them."

She looked around, turned back to him with an uncertain smile. "You, too, then? I been trying to stop for ever so long. Haven't had one for a week; don't know how much longer I can hold out. Especially working in this place. I been thinking of joining one of them groups, you know, like Alcoholics Anonymous, only for smokers."

"For me it's been two weeks. It's hell." He slapped a packet of mints and one of chewing gum on the counter. "I hate mints. The gum's not so bad, but I never chewed gum before."

"Me neither." She rang up these items, slipped them into a bag. "I don't think I can last. All you need to do's look at me to see I'm going fast."

This was said in a tone of such gravity that Jury had to laugh. And she laughed in response. "Tell you what," he said. "Let's make a bet. Or a pact, say. I'll be gone maybe three or four days. When I get back to Heathrow we'll check up on one another. But we should get some sort of prize—" He looked across the top of this counter to one behind that held costume jewelry, perfume. "Anything there you'd like?"

All of this pact business made her excited, slightly breathless. "Well, I'll tell you the truth. I've had my eye on that bracelet—" She slipped from her stool and reached into the glass case and came out with a bracelet of small colored stones that didn't look to Jury as if it were worth holding your breath over. To each his own.

"All right, if you can hold out, I'll buy you this."

She beamed with the novelty of this idea. "Now, what about yourself? I got to give you something."

He doubted, looking at her, she had two pence to rub against each other. "You can give me a kiss." He smiled at her indrawn breath, her look of uncertainty. "I'm safe. I'm Scotland Yard CID. Here." He showed her his ID.

Now she was completely hooked. She smiled. "That's all? Just a kiss?"

He nodded. "It's enough. What's your name?"

"Des." She blushed and said, "It's really Desdemona, but I hate it, so I made it just Des."

Jury touched his hair in a mock salute. "I'll see you in a few days, then, Des."

As he moved up to security and tossed the bag on the runner, he looked back. She waved. Jury thought of where he was going. He had heard about the light in the American Southwest, about the skies, about the sunrises and especially the sunsets.

Could he possibly make it through a Santa Fe sunset without a cigarette?

He waved to Des.

Maybe. Just maybe.

NINETEEN

"OD'd on black biscuits, did you, Sergeant?" asked Melrose, then silently berated himself for being so cavalier. He pulled up one of the molded plastic and tubular-legged chairs in Wiggins's room in Fulham Road Hospital.

Looking literally pure as the new-driven snow, as he lay between ice-starched sheets, hands folded on the top one, Sergeant Wiggins replied, with a sniff, "Police are supposed to keep going, no matter how sick we are; if one of us gets run down or ill, well, we're not supposed to mind. It's quite unfair, it is."

Melrose reached into the parcel he had brought and pulled out a packet. "You're absolutely right, Sergeant. I only wanted to make sure you were allowed these." He put the black biscuits on the bed, and the rest of the bag with it. While Wiggins inspected the parcel from HealthWays, Melrose looked round the spartan room. In its distilled whiteness, there appeared to be only one floral offering, a rather wistful-looking bunch of Michaelmas daisies clumped with a spray of fern soaking in a tall glass. Before this was propped a card with another "Wiggins" name on it. Melrose deduced this must be from one of the Mancunian Wigginses. He was upset that there weren't more flowers, more of a recognition that Wiggins was, after all, hospitalized. Not even from Jury. Probably too busy darting off to New Mexico.

But Wiggins seemed well satisfied by Melrose's gift. He drew first one thing and then another from the brown bag: rolls of crystal mints, a couple of packets of Fisherman's Friends, herbal tea, digestive biscuits, and a handsome ceramic cup emblazoned with a W. "This is most awfully kind of you, Mr. Plant." He pulsed with pleasure. "You know, it's not at all pleasant to be trapped here, all day long, no one much to talk to and nothing to do."

He did not, Melrose observed, seem at all trapped. He enjoyed turning and re-turning the top of the sheet and smoothing the whole works out. Melrose still did not know what had brought the sergeant to this (he suspected) highly enjoyable hospital end. "So if it's not the Black Biscuit Death, then why're you here? Tests of some sort?"

"The superintendent didn't mention what it was?" This was put in a tone of mild surprise and also relief.

"Not a word. Only that it wasn't serious."

Tearing off the cellophaned top of the black biscuits, Wiggins pursed his mouth and appeared to be thinking this over. "It's not serious, no. Just an accident. Stupid of me. A little job I was doing for Chief Superintendent Racer, an electrical thing. Got a bit of a shock, see—" he offered the packet of biscuits to Melrose, who gently declined the treat—"faulty wiring, I expect. You'd think a CID sergeant would know better than to go mucking about with electricity."

Melrose hadn't the vaguest notion what the sergeant was talking about, but he didn't pursue the matter. Instead, he reached into his pocket and brought out the paperback he had also purchased. "There's this, too. It's absolutely right for the situation."

Wiggins carefully wiped his fingers on a tissue before he sat up a bit straighter and took the book. "Well, now. *The Daughter of Time.*" He pressed the book to him and seemed to be studying the ceiling for a syllabus that would tell him whether he was familiar with its contents, whether he'd read it.

"Josephine Tey."

"Oh, yes. A very fine mystery writer." He studied the cover. "No nonsense about them back then. Perfectly straightforward, dead-on detectives. Professionals like me, or amateurs such as yourself—" benignantly, he inclined his head—"no women, no gays, no lesbians, no whores, no animals. No cats. I've noticed cats are enjoying a certain cachet." Wiggins zipped the pages of the book back and forth with his thumb as if he were about to shuffle cards, then he sat forward. "Would you mind giving these pillows a plumping?"

Melrose did so, patting and pushing, and Wiggins settled back with a satisfied sigh and his new book. "*Now* I remember: this is the one where her detective's flat on his back in hospital!"

"That's why I chose it. An historical case. He comes up with a rather slippery solution to the question of the murders of the princes in the Tower of London. King Richard being the chief suspect. Our detective clears his name. More or less. His lady friend, I believe it was, brings him all sorts of books and other information and he puts it together. Now, what I thought was that if I were to fill you in on whatever details I happened upon in this Tate Gallery–Exeter Cathedral–Old Sarum show, the two of us might come up with something."

Wiggins, clearly excited, was nonetheless thumbing slowly through the first few pages of his book, looking quite grave. This was serious stuff, then. "What you mean is, that with the super in the States, we might on *our* end be extremely helpful. And don't forget there's also Commander Macalvie. We can get his input, too."

"Commander Macalvie never did strike me as the person to 'input,' " Melrose said dryly.

Wiggins's retort was that the issue had never arisen before, and, don't forget, *he* was the patient. "Mr. Macalvie and me, we understand one another." He seemed a trifle hurt that Melrose did not realize Wiggins was not just another patient in hospital in Macalvie's eyes.

"Uh-huh." Melrose hoped his plan to amuse Wiggins wasn't going to backfire.

As if taking sustenance from Josephine Tey, Wiggins stroked *The Daughter of Time.* "It's a good idea. Tell me, then, whatever you know about this case." Wiggins settled back, aligning his new book with his sheet and his crossed hands.

"Unfortunately, not much, not yet." Melrose told him the little Jury had told *him.* One piece of information was about Macalvie's having come across an address book in Nell Hawes's possession and the phone numbers in it. Melrose had called Commander Macalvie for a few more details, which he shared with Wiggins. "Besides Angela Hope's shop, there's a pharmacy, a hotel, and a private residence, where the party claimed not to know anyone named Frances Hamilton or the Hawes woman or Angela Hope."

"That's the lady found at Old Sarum." When Melrose nodded, Wiggins said, "They said they didn't know her? This Hope person?"

Melrose nodded again.

Wiggins looked deep in concentration as he studied the photocopied pages. "It seems odd, doesn't it? I can see a tourist would set down the number of the hotel or a restaurant or some shop she wanted to go to—"

"And I can see a tourist might meet somebody in her travels who would give her his phone number, too. What's odd about that?"

Wiggins looked at his new paperback as if he were going to kiss it for coming up with this grand idea of solving mysteries from hospital beds. "Well, nothing at all. Except it's odd that the person then would disclaim any knowledge of the party." Carefully, Wiggins smoothed his sheet. "Why are you so sure it's a telephone number?"

Melrose was completely surprised. "Because . . . I just told you; the New Mexico police apparently rang it. It was answered. Whoever answered said he didn't know what they were talking about."

Wiggins shrugged. "Obscene telephone callers often use random numbers."

"What does this have to do with obscene calls?"

"It doesn't. That's not the point; the point is the randomness. Given all the telephone numbers there are—Lord knows what the figure would run to—a person could come up with an authentic telephone number purely by accident. Just because there *is* such a number doesn't mean it can't be something *else* besides."

Melrose thought this over. It was, actually, possible.

"So if the number's of whatever we're looking for is the same as this number in—where?"

"Española."

"Española, it could still be coincidence." Gently, Wiggins closed his eyes and folded his hands across his book, managing to look like the Wise Hermit in the Cave.

Melrose felt abashed, embarrassed by what he now realized had been a rather patronizing attitude towards the sergeant. For it was certainly a thought. A very good thought. It was just that Wiggins, for all of his virtues, had never displayed much deductive prowess. Wiggins's value lay in his loyalty, his methodical note taking and attention to detail, and especially in his being able to mirror the fallibilities of witnesses. They were able to identify with Wiggins. No one in the sergeant's presence felt the need to be infallible—to be brave or strong or healthy. Kleenexes could be brought out, snifflings and snufflings begin, heads and joints ache, tears fall like rain. Jury (Melrose thought) was good at this sort of thing himself. But Wiggins was better; Wiggins was Everyman. Those were his virtues, not deductive brilliance.

Thus, Melrose was completely taken aback by Wiggins's having brought up a point that no one else had, including Commander Brian Macalvie. They were all assuming that here were several telephone numbers.

"What do you think it might be, this number?" asked Melrose, feeling inept.

But the Wise Hermit kept his eyes closed, fluttered his hand (rather dismissively), and said, "Well, we'll just have to put on our thinking caps, sir." He yawned.

"Yes. We will." Melrose rose. "I'll be going, then. To do some thinking."

Wiggins made no move to detain him, nor did he open his eyes.

At the door, Melrose heard a snore coming from the bed, a series of snores, catching in Wiggins's throat. He lay there, mouth open, jaggedly snoring away, his head on a short pillar of fluffy white pillows, hands crossed on *The Daughter of Time*.

The Hermit asleep in his cave of clouds.

MELROSE'S FIRST STOP was at the nurses' station, where he spoke to Matron about the possibility of getting a private nurse for the sergeant. Yes, of course, that could be arranged. Melrose gave her his address and telephone number and said he would be responsible for whatever charges were incurred, only not to tell the patient that this nurse was a private nurse. Matron understood.

His second stop was at a florist in the Fulham Road near the hospital. Here he put on his thinking cap and came up with a short list of names. He then directed a pleasant woman to make up various bouquets, took four white cards from the rack, and wrote four different names. He changed his handwriting for each of them. He gave the florist his instructions for delivery, telling her the bouquets should be delivered at four different times, not all together, then paid her a king's ransom and went whistling on down the Fulham Road.

TWENTY

Mr. Beaton, Melrose's tailor, did not "maintain an establishment" in the heady environs of Mayfair or in Regent or Bond Street. Amazingly, Mr. Beaton had his shop—or to be more precise, his rooms—on the first floor above a sweet shop in the Old Brompton Road, near the Oratory.

Melrose liked the sweet shop too, and always stopped in it, hoping that this time the person behind the counter would be a little gray lady in purple bombazine, lace collar, and cameo brooch, who would smile diffidently as she plied the metal scoop in the tilted glass jar of gummy bears. This person existed only in his imagination, or, possibly, was patterned on someone in his childhood, which, he liked to think, had been full of sweet shops. The shop girl here today was certainly not this person; she was a slack-faced girl with frizzed yellow hair, who was sitting reading and chewing gum and, given the look she shot at Melrose, would be far better off in a chemist's dispensing cold poison instead of here in such aromatic premises dispensing lemon drops.

Well, she didn't bother him beyond the limits of her first chilly stare and he merely wanted to gaze at the rows of thick glass jars and the displays of boxes of Cadbury's and Opera Assortments. He asked for assistance, and the girl tossed aside the gossipy magazine, unfolded herself from the chair and tugged down her sweater. Melrose purchased tiny amounts (to the shop girl's everlasting annoyance) of lemon sherbets, fizzy bears, Smartees, sour bats, toffees, and Rainbow Crystals. He did not want the sweets; he wanted to watch the little engine of sweet-buying hum along: the aluminum scoop; the weighing up, and the frown this always seemed to elicit; the depositing into small white bags; the quick screwing of the tops. He paid for these six little screws and asked that they all be placed in a larger bag. Naturally, she did not want to do this, for no other reason than it was written into the shop-assistant script not to want to do what the customer wanted—and to so indicate by either grimace or posture or overall manner, or even by outright words. Hers was grimace. Melrose absolutely beamed at her, which annoyed her still further, her large lifeless eyes retreating as soon as they could behind the armor plate of tabloid newspaper.

Melrose stepped out of the door of the sweet shop, comforted by the knowledge that the prototype was still around, that Style still existed, that shadows still danced in Plato's cave. From the sweet shop he turned into the next door and walked up the darkish steps to the first floor and Mr. Beaton.

Here in Mr. Beaton's combined living and working quarters, the existence of Style was verified. Mr. Beaton looked, simply, like a tailor. If Beatrix Potter had been interested in people as she had been in animals, she would have drawn Mr. Beaton. He was small to the point of delicacy, with a domelike head that glistened in a cone of lamplight; wore rimless glasses that he never looked through, only over; and sometimes a green eyeshade rode high on his forehead; but *always* there was a tape measure round his neck. Mr. Beaton had always had an apprentice, several different ones over the decades. They were interchangeable. This young man had a shock of brown hair, wore glasses also, and like his Master, was very polite and decorous. In this shop, one could die of decorum.

Melrose forgot, from year to year, how he would always enter these rooms with a sigh of pleasure. Nothing had changed; nothing ever would. Mr. Beaton had been his father's tailor, and had been apprentice when the elder Mr. Beaton had been Melrose's grandfather's tailor. There was a nucleus here of persons so tightly knit that Melrose found it nothing short of miraculous, and could, therefore, forgive himself for the sentimental notion that nothing changed here in Mr. Beaton's. Having little to do with the present, Mr. Beaton had plenty of room for the past. Oh, yes, he read the papers, and knew that governments came and went ("Conservative, Labor, Sociopath," Mr. Beaton would chuckle), but that made no odds to him.

On one or two occasions, Lady Marjorie—Melrose's mother—had accompanied his father here, had sat silent and smiling while Mr. Beaton took his measurements. Had never interfered, had not spoken unless her husband asked her opinion about materials or colors, had sat quietly with folded hands and either gazed out of the wavering glass of the casement windows, then probably as now covered with a patina of umber dust that gave the scene below a slightly golden glow; or seated at the round table, chin in her hand, looking at the framed photographs of Beaton ancestors. The windows were still streaky with dirt, and the ancestors still arranged on the table in pewter or dark wooden frames. And if she did speak, it was always to compliment his skills.

Melrose knew all of this because Mr. Beaton had told him. Lady Marjorie, Countess of Caverness—now there was a lady, there was a lady who deserved a title!

"My lord." Mr. Beaton's brief nod was in no way obsequious, but an acknowledgment of old ways and traditions. Melrose had never told him that he had given up his titles, because it would have been too disturbing to Mr. Beaton, too much an indicator that carelessness and slovenliness were rampant, or that modernism was afoot. Modernism had had nothing at all to do with it, and God only knew, certainly not carelessness.

"I've just got in this very fine worsted—" here he nodded his apprentice toward a curtained alcove where he kept his bolts—"that I think you will find satisfactory." The tall young man brought it out, a heavy bolt of dark gray wool. Mr. Beaton drew down a corner for Melrose's inspection. "It feels like silk."

Melrose drew the dark gray material through his fingers. It did not feel like silk; it felt like air. "Mr. Beaton, this is ethereal. How can wool be so light?"

The question was rhetorical; the tailor smiled and shrugged—an infinitesimal movement of the upper body. All of Mr. Beaton's movements were like that, graceful but parsimonious, as if, being so small, he were intent upon husbanding his energy for the task at hand.

For Mr. Beaton, it was not enough simply to be exquisitely dressed. It was also de rigueur that no one should know you were doing it—a man wore his clothes as he wore his sainthood: without advertisement.

Then the fitting would be over and the apprentice would bring in tea and wafer-thin biscuits as tasteless as the Eucharist and they would stand about with cups in their hands, chatting. Mr. Beaton always stood. He seemed to think sitting down was necessary only to see how cloth strained over the knee or rode up the calf. And when one stood, well, one *stood*. He always instructed his gentlemen to assume the same posture they would normally do—not to stand stiff as starch, not as they had been forced to stand in dancing class with books on their heads. Clothes were meant to fit facts, not fantasies.

When tea was done, the fitting was finished. It was a ritual in which everyone was secure and knew his lines.

Smiling, Melrose took his leave and retraced his way back down the steps and out in the Brompton Road. He could only describe himself and this day as "in fine fettle," a phrase that had a pleasant metallic tinkle to it, and everything along the Brompton Road looked rich and thriving, as if the scene were made of British sterling. The sun was out, the shoppers bustled. Colors and sounds swept by and around him, jostled him just as elbows or umbrellas might do, and he wondered if the Old Brompton Road had undergone some Wordsworthian transformation, concrete, metal, and glass becoming one with a strangely natural setting. That long white banner flapping down the side of the Oratory like a waterfall; the road like a river running past the rocky excrescences of cars.

Melrose felt so totally *London* he could have wept.

2

O AIR! O sunlight!

Melrose escaped the travails of the Jubilee Line, walked from the Pimlico station, and crossed over to the Chelsea section of the Embankment, woozy with the Thames and Westminster up ahead. The Vauxhall Bridge behind him, the dark lacework of Waterloo Bridge off in the distance before him. He stopped, shielded his eyes with his hand, and looked toward Westminster Bridge and thought again of Wordsworth.

His dark blue (non-Beaton) cashmere coat open and swinging round his legs, Melrose walked along the Embankment once more imbued with the Spirit of London. Expansive, poetical, free of the shuddering Underground darkness, he watched a speedboat zip along the river, a sailboat bob, looked upward to where the sun was minting the tiny treetop leaves like coins, and blessed the Aboveground.

He entered the Tate Gallery, feeling a need to recover some sense of his own form by looking at others'—paintings, sculpture. In the anteroom of the Swagger Portrait exhibit (which had been held over) he paid for his headset. Melrose loved recorded guided tours because he loved having stories told to him. This one was told by an actor who had a fine, precise voice, one that registered enthusiasm for the paintings without sounding pompous or unctuous.

Some paintings! The first ones were wonderfully ostentatious, depicting feet on skulls with their subjects sitting on clouds; then there were the beautiful Reynoldses and the glamorous Van Dycks, with their subjects looking so grand and dignified they were removed from real life. A ride on the Jubilee Line might shake up you lot! thought Melrose, with a superior little smile.

He followed the injunction of the actor to stop the tape as he moved into the next room. Covertly, he glanced around at the other gallery viewers. This one, a middle-aged woman, had removed her headphones; that thin young man was swinging his from his hands; and most of the visitors didn't even have any. Free spirits. He shrugged. Or poor. He started the tape again, listened to comments upon the British School, and agreed, yes, the subjects seemed a little more relaxed, more natural, not so full of swaggery self-importance. . . . Oh, this one of Mrs. Siddons! The unbelievable texture and color of that velvet! Maroon? Dark, dark brown? How glorious!

Then, through the door, Melrose saw a portrait that stopped him in his tracks. He did not know who the subject was (discovered, eventually, it was a Mrs. Chambers), nor the painter (discovered, too, it was Lawrence), but it was so overwhelmingly beautiful and so strongly resembled the portrait of his mother hanging in the dining room of Ardry End that Melrose honestly felt as if an enormous hand had fallen against his chest and shoved him back. He knew for once the exact meaning of one's breath being "taken away." The eyes! The yellowish light reflecting upwards from the dress, suffusing the skin of this woman. At first glance, and from beyond the doorway, he had thought this one portrait was separately lighted, for it seemed to be a source of light.

Melrose gazed at Mrs. Chambers for a long while, and when he could stand it no longer, left and dropped off his headset.

He found Room 9, which housed the Pre-Raphaelite paintings, and then found the bench that Mrs. Hamilton must have been sitting on and sat down himself. It was where Jury had said it would be, just in front of the portrait of Chatterton and the Holman Hunt. The Holman Hunt was not there; probably it had been moved. But the Chatterton certainly was there. Not, certainly, a painting that would ever have been included amongst the Swagger Portraits. There was no swagger in Chatterton. Not, perhaps, the most auspicious choice of painting to be sitting in front of, in his present mood.

He wondered how other people dealt with loss, of loss of persons and places. For they seemed to do it better than he himself, but then, how would one know? And why assume that everyone had to deal, anyway?

He thought of Nancy Fludd. Her name wasn't Nancy, but he thought it fit her, and he was tired of calling her Miss Fludd. How did Nancy deal with her diminished world? How did she explain, rationalize, inhabit, color, frame it? There were probably a lot of people so intent upon the future that they found the past almost superfluous. The young, he guessed, must be like this. When he himself was young, did he ever feel regret or remorse? Probably not. Probably just as callow as this Beatrice and Gabe couple, who hadn't even noticed a woman dying beside them.

He recalled what he had felt standing in the doorway of the last room of the Swagger exhibit, the breath knocked out of him, the hand against his chest, and when he then returned his gaze to the portrait of Chatterton, he wondered, had he something in common with this woman he didn't even know, Frances Hamilton?

Sadness overwhelmed him; he judged it to be sadness and not despair, for he had always thought of despair as having no identifiable source. The source of his sadness was easily identified, stretched back to that whole bad business just before his mother died in their Belgravia house, lasted for how long? Months? A year? For what had seemed an endless time to him then. That Belgravia house that he had sold when he was thirty because he could no longer feel at home in it or even comfortable in it.

In his mind's eye he saw himself in the dimly lit sitting room at the rear of the house, filled with exquisite furnishings whose outlines he could no longer make out, staring through the french window into the garden. Why, he wondered, was there always a garden in tales of love and betrayal? Eden, he supposed. *Thus leaf goes down to leaf, thus Eden sank to grief*.

And that meant a serpent. Nicholas Grey.

Affable, handsome Nick Grey. Friend of his father; shooting companion in the wilds of the Scottish Highlands; fishing mate in the icy trout streams of Wales. It was the Nick Greys of this world who could make good use of Mr. Beaton's professional abilities. Or perhaps not, he observed. Perhaps not. Mr. Beaton's "gentlemen" were not merely figures, like mannequins, on which he would hang his clothes. His customers were, well, "gentlemen," persons of quality. And Nick Grey was anything but "quality."

In that sitting room, where Melrose watched himself staring out of the window, he could also see the figure of Nick Grey over the months, the years, really, in one spot or another—slouched in one of the armchairs with a whisky in his hand; leaning against the ivory marble mantel, smiling; sitting on the library ladder, a volume from the bookcase open in his hands, and he looking puzzled. Gibbon or Virgil was far too much for him. Most was too much for him.

Melrose watched his mother moving like a ghost through the garden.

He thought about the women he'd known, and knew. He did not think he was too critical of women; indeed, the reverse was more likely true. His heart was too easily snared. But, then, he believed in love at first glance (although he was not absolutely sure of the depths of such love). For it was clearly of unconscious choosing, and not of conscious. Then, something got in the way, barred his path, like a fig-ure in a passage or on a pavement that he couldn't get round.

And in the last several years alone, there had been several: Polly Praed, who had so intrigued him in Littlebourne that first time. It could have been her. Or it could have been Ellen, whose very asperity was lovable. And, of course, Vivian. But it was too difficult believing Vivian had any romantic inclinations towards him at all. They'd been knocking about together for too long. Still. It could have been any of these women, if he were to try a bit harder (although it still eluded him, just *what* he was to try . . .). Yet, his vision always got clouded over by the ghost in the garden.

"I'm—sorry."

Melrose came out of this trance with a jerk, looking up to see who she was and why she was sorry. He had utterly forgotten he was in the Tate, a public place.

"I'm sorry." She said it again. Her face was a mask of concern. "I hate it when someone breaks in on me in this sort of way. But you do—or did—look, well, in a bad state. I thought you might be ill."

Her embarrassment and her confusion as to whether she should have spoken at all were all too evident. He smiled at her, hoping to relieve it. What went through his mind was that here he was sitting on that same bench as Frances Hamilton had sat. And here was a Beatrice come to his rescue in a way the other Bea had certainly not helped Mrs. Hamilton.

Dark red hair, wide mouth, pale face, sympathetic. Not beautiful, but memorable. At any other time, he would have made some witty comment, asked her to come for a coffee, or if he might give her lunch. But not today.

"Is it the Chatterton?" she asked, pushing her dark thick hair back with a wedding-ringless hand. "That painting is upsetting, I think." She glanced from the portrait back to Melrose.

It could have been you, was what he thought.

But what he said was, "Yes. It's the Chatterton."

TWENTY-ONE

"I'm sorry—" was very nearly the first thing Lady Cray said, and Melrose was instantly reminded of the woman in the Tate.

"—that I made Fanny out to be sillier than she was." Lady Cray handed Melrose a thick cut-glass tumbler filled with an inch or so of Virginia Gentlemen. She had told him it was Fanny Hamilton's favorite drink. "Cheers."

They both raised their glasses and drank. The liquor was smooth, but sweet as mead. Despite the rather cloying taste of the whisky, he was glad to have it; he was especially glad to have the plate of chicken sandwiches the little maid had brought in. After the long morning's trials, he had, on sinking back into the several silky pillows of an ice-blue armchair, realized that he was exhausted. By now it was after four o'clock and he still had other visits to make.

"I think I gave Superintendent Jury the wrong impression. Unfair of me." She too sank back into the pillows of the sofa, her glass in both of her hands, her eyes trained on the ceiling.

"Never too late to amend it." He smiled and thought how pleasant it was to sit in this room, not unlike one of those in Ardry End, and to be talking to a woman distinctly *dissimilar* to his aunt. What a difference in company and conversation! She was probably the same age, perhaps a bit older than Agatha. "Richard Jury is particularly interested in the trip she took to America. That is, the part of her trip *after* she went to Pennsylvania."

Lady Cray's frown deepened as she looked upward in thought, as if it had been brought on by the plaster cherubs whose chubby hands bore up plaster draperies. "Superintendent Jury seems to think there's some connection with a woman who died in Exeter." She sighed. "I have no idea how he makes this connection."

"I'm not sure he's the one making it. There's a divisional commander who seems to be, but this particular policeman is seldom wrong."

Somewhere, flute music played from the recesses of a room beyond this room. Flute music and then a deep sort of chanting. It was utterly unlike the melodic strains Melrose was used to. He mentioned the music.

"Fanny's. She brought it back from the Southwest. Native American, I believe. I find it very restful."

"So do I." Melrose thought for a moment, then asked, "What was her nephew like?"

Lady Cray reflected on her answer to this question. Perhaps, having shortchanged Fanny Hamilton, she wanted to be sure she didn't do the same to the nephew. "Honest. He was honest. I was struck by that."

Melrose nodded, drank his drink, and waited for her to go on.

"You know, if you're like that, you mightn't have many friends. People find you disturbing, and you find other people, well, shallow. Because people who are not honest will talk about anything in the world except what they truly think and feel. We don't do enough of that, I think. Most of us waste most of ourselves most of the time." Lady Cray inspected her glass.

Melrose murmured agreement as he looked past the marble fireplace to the french windows and the little garden. The flute was by turns distant, eerie, haunted, clear, close. "And she went to America straightaway." He watched the delicate branches of an ornamental willow lift in a stiff breeze and fall again into the drained concrete of an oval pool. He thought of Watermeadows. He thought of Hannah Lean. Poor Hannah. "It must be the worst thing imaginable. To lose the person most important to you. I don't know how I'd handle that."

"You've had to, haven't you? Your parents are both dead."

He did not turn his face from the overhanging willow and the empty pond. "Yes," simply.

"Well, then." She finished her drink.

Well, then.

Light had turned milky, nearly opaque and thick like fog, dense. The border of dahlias bent as if the light weighed too heavily. Light seemed to have crept into the room, not in shafts of sunlight or blue dawn or some late-afternoon rainbow diffusion. It had crept in.

"Do you have a picture of him?" he asked.

Lady Cray looked at Melrose, puzzled. "Of whom?"

"Sorry. Of Philip Calvert. Given Mrs. Hamilton was so fond of him, I'd imagine there were photos. Snapshots."

"He was murdered," she said, as if in answer to his strange question regarding the photograph.

"I was just thinking about something, something when I was sitting in the Tate. And I wondered—" Melrose broke off, not even sure what he wondered, then or now.

Lady Cray smiled, indicated the wall behind and to the left of the sofa where he sat. "Not very observant, are you?"

He turned toward that area of the wall between the two double doors leading to the long foyer. On the eight or ten feet of wall space above the moulding were arranged paintings of various sizes and variously framed. The largest in the top row, a portrait of a young man, was lit by a small lamp. Melrose got up and, then, as if a walk across the room would seem a rude departure, said, "May I?"

Lady Cray nodded.

The portrait showed Philip Calvert seated in a fancy Victorian chair drawn up to a small table, the sort of useless bits of furniture one often encounters in portraits, chairs and little tables too delicate to serve a purpose other than to rest an elbow on or position a hand or make a jaunty display of cap and scarf. All of these were here: Philip Calvert's elbow rested on the table, his hand supporting his head; the other hand was furled against the end of the chair arm; a soft wool cap carelessly listed against the base of the lamp as if it had been tossed there (which of course it never would have been, not against that lamp) together with a pair of driving goggles. A dark cashmere scarf drifted away from his neck and fell along the arm of the chair, as if he'd been in the process of pulling it off. "Jauntiness" being, as it would seem, the effect aimed for. A young man, stopping between drives in his sporty car, barely able to restrain himself in the chair for all of this brushwork. But the composition itself was totally at odds with Philip. Yes, he was smiling, but it was fleeting, one could tell. It made Melrose think of that pale and empty sky behind him from which the coil of birds had fled so swiftly, as if pursued by that encroaching light. All of the colors here were mournful variations of brown. The brown at the top of the canvas was so dark it was nearly black, and this melted down into sable shadows, then into the coffee color of lampshade and dubious drapery. The few colors in the weave of the cap—burgundy, flecks of hunter green—were so dark and dull they bled into their background. And so Phil Calvert's pale face and light brown eyes approached a stage of near-translucency, caught as they were within these dark surroundings.

Melrose thought it was a wonderful little portrait, but something of a contradiction, its subject out of synch with his surroundings. It was all too redolent of comfort and privilege, of casual elegance. Too rich, much too rich. From what Jury had told him about Philip Calvert, Melrose wondered if the young man hadn't been trying to escape all of that. And he said as much to Lady Cray.

Emphatically, she nodded. "That is exactly so. In a nice way, he used to argue with Fanny, for she, having so much money, naturally wanted him to share it. Money made Philip uncomfortable. It does so, with some people. I've never had enough to acquire that particular posture."

Melrose said: "He does not look happy."

"No. He does not. But I do not know why. For he seemed to be—not 'happy,' perhaps, but sure enough that he was doing the right things for himself that he was fairly content."

In silence, they studied the portrait. Then she said, "But Mr. Plant. You're surely not suggesting that *that* particular crime has something to do with *Fanny's* death?"

"No. Philip Calvert's murderer was discovered. I don't mean it in that way."

"In *what* way, then?"

Melrose smiled. "I can tell you a theory favored by a friend of mine in Long Piddleton. That is, if you're prepared to hear something pretty damned silly."

"Say on. Silliness, my dear, is my stock in trade."

"Come on, Lady Cray. I know you, remember? You're anything *but*."

She winced and dropped her hand from his arm. "Oh, don't exaggerate my virtues so. I am many things *but*. So, let's hear the silly theory."

"She calls it 'the Stendhal syndrome.' "

"The what?"

Melrose explained. "Art addicts, such as Stendhal was, might conceivably collapse in front of great paintings."

"Good Lord. Are you suggesting that Fanny—who was hardly that impressionable when it came to great art, anyway—took in too much at the Tate?"

Melrose answered obliquely. "I walked into the Swagger Portrait exhibit, and when I suddenly came upon one of the portraits, I felt as if I had been horribly—*hit*, you know, as if a wall of hands had forced me back. I expect that's what people mean by having the breath knocked out of them." He thought she would speak, inquire as to which portrait it was that had affected him so singularly, but she didn't. Perhaps Lady Cray was respecting a privacy that he himself had intruded upon without wanting to.

Lady Cray's finely arched brows drew together. "What was Fanny looking at?"

"Chatterton."

Her gaze returned to Philip's portrait. "But there's no resemblance, really."

"Oh, I think there is."

Again, that frown. "Chatterton, from all I remember, was very young—"

"Seventeen."

"—indigent, friendless, and worst of all, exposed as a plagiarist. Something like that. An artist, yes, and so was Philip. But I don't see any resemblance, beyond that."

"Well, I wonder about the temperamental similarity." Melrose motioned with his hand to stave off an objection. "But that's not the point. That isn't what I mean. I mean something much simpler." Melrose nodded at the picture. "He would have looked different when he was dead."

"Naturally, but Fanny didn't see—"

"Didn't see him? No. But the manner of his death would have been described to her. Philip Calvert was lying on a sort of bed-sofa. She didn't see him. All the worse. She imagined him. My guess is she would have seen him lying like Chatterton, thrown across a narrow bed. Even the books, the papers on the floor. At least, that's what Richard Jury was told about the appearance of Philip Calvert's body."

When she turned her head to look at him, her silvery-blue eyes glinted. "Be sensible. There could be no possible reason then for Superintendent Jury to relate Fanny's death to the death of this unfortunate woman in Exeter. And God knows, not to the body found outside of Salisbury. They were not *all*, I presume, admiring the painting of poor, dear Chatterton?" Lady Cray was moving from the portrait of Philip back to her place on the ice-blue sofa as she said this.

"No. But your friend Mrs. Hamilton and Mrs. Hawes were apparently in Santa Fe at the same time."

"Mrs. Hawes?"

"Helen Hawes was the woman in the cathedral. And the dead woman found at Old Sarum was from Santa Fe." He said this to the portrait rather than to Lady Cray. For some reason, he had grown almost enamored of the light in it, the infinitesimal dots of gold that were sprayed across the scarf and table; the sheen of the boy's skin. He cocked his head to one side; it all bothered him inexplicably. Then he turned to reseat himself and accept a fresh drink.

"At the same time?" She gave a short laugh as she topped up his glass. "Well, so were a thousand others, I expect."

"They're not dead."

She looked at him, shrugged slightly. "Of course, that's true. I'm being dense."

From his inside jacket pocket, Melrose withdrew the photocopied pages Jury had sent to him. "Look at this, will you?"

She took the pages, studied them carefully, before asking, "Should this be familiar to me? It appears to be an engagement book."

"One of those little address books. You probably haven't seen the book itself, but what about the handwriting?"

"Are you suggesting it's Fanny's?"

"Asking. It was actually in the possession of the woman who died in Exeter Cathedral, only it wasn't hers. The Exeter police are sure of that."

Lady Cray frowned over the pages. "It's difficult to say. . . . But it looks like two *different* hands, doesn't it? See here—" she handed the pages back to Melrose—"the C and the *o* in 'Canyon' look quite different from the ones in 'Coyote.' What an odd name, 'Coyote Village.' But I don't understand—" She looked up at Melrose. "If it was found with this other woman's belongings . . . Haven't I told her again and again, those precise little numbers of hers were absolutely impossible to read. Her nines looking like fives, and so forth." Lady Cray sighed deeply and sat back, eyes nearly shut. "Poor Fanny." She sighed.

As if a confusion between nines and fives had been the death of her.

Well, perhaps she was right. It was no more unlikely than the Stendhal syndrome.

Melrose smiled and thanked her and took his leave.

TWENTY-TWO

When he saw the Cripps kiddies hammering on dustbin lids, Melrose thanked the Lord that this time he hadn't driven the Rolls into Catchcoach Street. Last time, he'd had to pay them protection money. He counted five of them—no, six, for there was one in the center of the ring—and, of course, they couldn't have been the same six. This was just another set. He imagined the Crippses came in sets.

But there was no mistaking the Cripps look, passed on from generation to generation—whey- or pudding- or pasty-faced; bleached-out hair and eyelashes; eyes so colorless they were nearly transparent. The Crippses all looked as if they'd gone round in the washers down at the launderette just one too many Mondays.

But what their looks lacked in color, their actions made up for. Melrose stood across the street, just to observe their latest game. Five of them were engaged in marching round in a ring where, in the center, stood one benighted sixth—being somewhat androgynous, hard to tell whether boy or girl—blindfolded and holding a potted plant. Those in the circle were either banging the dustbin lids, or putting what appeared to be tools to other purposes. A garden rake served as a pole to which a tattered Irish flag was tied. A hoe bore a hand-lettered (and naturally misspelt) message—*DOWN WITH FUCKIN MAJERS*. The theme of this demonstration was taken, apparently, from the morning's headlines about another IRA protest, one of the perpetrators taken into custody, which was the reason for the kiddies' sentiment. Their sympathies lay with any organization which could wreak havoc. It was unclear why they had taken one of their own to play the part of prisoner, however. But Melrose supposed the Crippses would have it both ways if they possibly could, thereby losing no opportunity for mistreating anyone or anything they could, be it Country or Cousin.

He also wondered why the garden tools, given the state of the bit of earth that lay between front door and public pavement. The other residents of Catchcoach Street might conceivably refer to similar patches as "my bit of garden." But the Crippses' looked in a state of turmoil, clumps of weedy earth churned up, mounds of dirt beside gravelike holes, as if making way for whatever had died inside—dog, cat, gran.

It looked like that, yes. But Melrose was quite sure the over-turned earth was not waiting to receive any Audenesque honored guest. No, these dugouts would serve no utilitarian purpose. No poet would be buried here, no beloved pet. The Crippses did not waste their time on fine feeling, nor were they even pragmatic. That old child's saying "A hole is to dig" found its ultimate expression in the Crippses. No, feelings were a waste. There was always too much to *do*. Like torturing one another or driving the neighbors round the twist.

Or, if it was truly a lucky day, a *stranger*.

Seeing this one crossing the street towards them, the kiddies suspended all activity in an eyeblink and watched the Stranger with a voraciousness that all of the coyotes in New Mexico were eyeing Richard Jury with about now.

He drew abreast of them, smiled and asked pleasantly, "Mum home?" The point being that—unless Mum or Dad came to the door—there wasn't a hope in hell of crossing the Cripps threshold until this lot gave its permission. "Or Dad?" added Melrose, removing one of the small bags of candy from his pocket. He took out a fizzy bear and made himself chew it although it tasted like liquid sugar.

Twelve eyes—no, ten, for the sixth seemed to be too stupid to remove its blindfold and just stood with its mouth open—followed the progress of hand to mouth. The toddler had draped its sticky self around Melrose's leg to yank and yell.

The oldest of the bunch, a boy of perhaps ten or eleven, took over. Pretending to disdain the fizzy bears, he glared at Melrose. "So 'oo wants ter know?" and to the toddler he yelled, "Put a sock in it, Spanky!" and gave the child a right wallop across its rear, thereby ensuring an increase of volume.

"I do," returned Melrose, calmly taking out another bag, this one of lemon sherbets. He sucked on one and watched a couple of the kiddies lick their lips. Number six was still waddling around with its blindfold, arms thrashing. "I'm a friend," he added.

"Oh, *yeah*? Mebbe she be home, mebbe not."

"That fairly covers it, doesn't it?" Melrose took out a third bag and peered into its contents. Smartees. Ugh. He shoved two in his mouth and chewed slowly. The middle girl (of perhaps six) was jumping up and down, clutching herself as if the very sight of Smartees gave her a sexual thrill. She danced backwards toward the door, calling out, "I'll get 'er, I'll get—"

"*Shaddup!*" yelled the biggest boy, running to grab her back and making her fall in one of the freshly dug holes. Briefly, she cried and then gave it up to come back to where the action and the sweets were. Furious with Melrose for possibly making him lose control of the consortium, he stood hands on hips and repeated, "Mebbe so, mebbe not."

"Make up your mind; I haven't all day." Out came the bag of Rainbow Crystals, to audible "ooohs" and "aaahs." The toddler unleeched its dirty hands and turned its runny-nosed, runny-eyed face up to Melrose and flailed its small hands towards the white screw of sweets. Melrose pinched up the colored sugar and popped it in his mouth. Four bags were now in evidence.

The blindfolded one had blundered around and was now running into the toddler. The older one yanked him back and told the "stupid, bleedin' li'l prick" to take off the bloody blindfold. The little girl who had been dumped in the dirt gave her brother a whack with a trowel.

Melrose drew out bag number five, buried his nose in it, then fingered out a Devon toffee that looked hard as a rock. Be damned if he'd eat that. He returned it to the bag.

The child, now minus blindfold, made a swipe at the bag, missed, and started to urinate very near Melrose's shoe.

"See, see!" yelled one of the girls. "Look what ya made Petey do!" The girl who had yelled this and the one who'd scrambled from the hole joined hands and swung each other round and round, singing

Piddlin' Pete, Piddlin' Pete
Give him somethin' sweet to eat

whereupon they collapsed in giggles.

When the last bag came out—the sour bats—they all went berserk, even the ringleader, at the realization there were *six* bags and *six* of them. They shouted, they screamed, they lunged for the bags which Melrose was holding beyond their reach. He had an uncomfortable moment recalling a shuddery scene in a Tennessee Williams play in which some poor devil is set upon by a bunch of horrid urchins. Well, he thought, he probably deserved it for so blatantly taunting Crippses.

Then, at the height of the game, the front door flew open, and White Ellie herself appeared, Dear Old Mum, in flowered overall. "You lot get in 'ere—" Then she saw Melrose. "Well, I'll *be!*" And she kept repeating this as she waded through the dirt, debris, toys, and mangled tools to where Melrose stood so that she could pick each of her kiddies off him as if she were dead-heading roses. "Now you get in t'yer tea!"

"Just a moment," said Melrose, stopping them to bestow on each a white screw of sweets.

They grabbed, they yelled, they laughed, danced, they tore away to their tea, snatching at whoever's white bag was not fixed firmly in his or her hand.

DESPITE THE CUT-OFF SCREAMS, breaking crockery, and the voice of White Ellie layering all the other sounds like a big thunderclap, Melrose was relaxing serenely in the parlor, congratulating himself on the use he had made of the sweets. He thought himself especially clever, since he hadn't purchased them with the Crippses in mind. Whatever in the world had made him buy six bags? God was in his Heaven, clearly. So now he felt rather pumped up, some of the old confidence come back, the bit that had drained out of him upon discovering Sergeant Wiggins might be smarter than he himself was. No, Wiggins had never outwitted the Cripps kiddies. *He* had outwitted them. The point was that it was all but impossible to outwit the Crippses, they being totally witless. And then in the midst of all of this self-congratulation he pursed his mouth and frowned. Was this, though, something a rational man could take pride in? Had he, perhaps, well, *lowered* his expectations of himself . . . ?

As he waited for White Ellie to reappear with his cup of tea, he went back to smoking, to blowing smooth little smoke rings in air. Here was certainly a place where one didn't have to wonder if smoking was permissible since it was obvious, glancing round the parlor, that everything else on God's green earth was. Big-armed chairs and sofas abounded, jammed in as if the parlor were a secondhand shop like Ada Crisp's; stuffed in and piled up with old pillows and mountains of laundry waiting to be sorted by an act of God. Above the cold fireplace hung the head of a bobcat (probably brought down by some of the kiddies) that could have stood a bit of touching up by the local taxidermist. Table lamps rested on the floor, shades splayed as if to spotlight the carpet's faded cabbage roses like nocturnal lights in a garden. In one corner sat a dish of water which Melrose found puzzling. Leaning forward, he saw that wires seemed to be running into it. He shrugged and sat back to survey the wallpaper. This paper was fresh (well, Cripps-fresh), for he recalled the old wallpaper having a different pattern. But it was still familiar to him, as he knew it was the same as the wallpaper in the kitchen. So they must have found a few old rolls and redecorated. It was covered with those big, horrible-looking flowers (the name of which escaped him), the sort that had wide petals open around drooping stamens that closely resembled phalluses. The resemblance here had been marvelously enriched by the crayon-wielding kiddies. The similarity now was even more striking and quite a little conversation piece, he imagined, when guests came to call. Still, it fit the general graffiti-like theme, for doors and sills had been inked and Crayola-ed with various obscenities. He wondered if the two buckets stationed beneath damp spots on the ceiling were really for catching drips or for Piddlin' Pete. Both, probably.

White Ellie's voice preceded her. She chugged into the parlor with two mugs of tea, a small plate of iced biscuits, and one of her long-winded anecdotes, already in progress.

". . . an' there be Rasputin, chuckin' the bleedin' furniture straight out the upstairs window, an' that wouldn't a been so bad except—'ere." She handed Melrose his tea. "I sugared it fer ya."

(Melrose murmured his thanks and turned the lipstick smudge on the rim outwards.)

She dropped into a deep dark armchair, redistributing a pile of laundry and resetting a balloon of dust. Her cigarette danced as she talked and seemed magically to cling to the corner of her mouth. "Except 'e's got this 'ere bonfire like going, and there goes me mum's antique petit point chair right on top of it. So I yells at 'im, 'Rasputin, ya bloody fool, the fire brigade'll be 'ere any minute—' "

Melrose waited smilingly and patiently for her to conclude her saga of Rasputin's Guy Fawkes adventure. White Ellie had a way of beginning her tales in the middle, with her interlocutor being totally in the dark about who the characters were or what their relationship to her was. She would have been a match for Homer, except that White Ellie would never manage to make the ends meet, as Homer had.

". . . shed, that's wot! Rasputin decides it'd be a right laugh to burn t'shed out back and then 'ere comes t'Old Bill round *and* the Social—that's Missus Esposito lives down the street, an' don't *she* ever stick 'er long nose in. I says, 'Wot's the Social doin' chasin' t' fire brigade?' "

Her buzzsaw voice *brrr*ed away, rising to a screech or lowering to a whine as Melrose drifted in and out of a gentle fuguelike state, broken first by the volcanic eruption of kiddies out of the kitchen and up the stairs; second, by a commotion beyond the parlor window, which was partially open, even in February. He turned to look out and saw two people standing more or less in the middle of the street, obviously arguing, ignoring a Morris Mini trying to maneuver round them. The man was small, stooped, with a terrific overbite and a chin that disappeared into his neck; the woman was sharp-faced and shrew-voiced.

White Ellie hove herself from her chair, walked to the window, and yelled at this couple to "shaddup, I got company," which invited a few hurled insults and did nothing to make them stop. She slammed down the window. "It's the Liar and Fuckin' Freddie. Make me sick, they do. Fight fight fight an' right outside me window. Where was I, then? Oh, yeah, well, Rasputin—"

Melrose looked over the plate of biscuits she had set beside him, selecting the one with the smallest amount of pinky icing. They were quite revolting looking, but appeared to be clean enough, and he wanted to be as good a guest as she was a hostess. As he bit into the chewy biscuit, his attention was diverted by the appearance of a very small mouse that had taken up a station by the dish of water on the floor. Definitely giving it the once-over. Well, he simply had to know. He interrupted the tale of Guy Fawkes revelries (the fire brigade, the entire police station) to point out the mouse to White Ellie.

She leaned way forward to twist her head to see. "Oh, that's Ashley's mousetrap. That there's Narcissus." Then she returned to Rasputin.

Mousetrap? Narcissus? Perhaps they really were in the land of the Lotus-Eaters. "Just a minute. How could a dish of water trap a mouse?"

"Well, it don't, do it? It's one of Ashley's inventions. Now, them electric wires in the water is to electrocute any mouse that takes a drink. The only one even comes for a deco is Narcissus there. Friend of ours, Gabe Merchant, named him that." When she grinned, a touch of gold winked in the light.

Ah! A wedge, a crack in the door—the mention of Gabe provided a smooth transition to the matter at hand. Not (he reminded himself) that one needed to use cunning with White Ellie. He watched as once again she wrestled her huge girth out of the chair and waddled to a shelf from which she plucked up a square of paper or cardboard. This she handed to Melrose. "See? Gabe painted 'is portrait."

Melrose couldn't help but smile at the little drawing, later water-colored in, of a mouse by a water dish. It was extremely fetching and whimsical and put him in mind of Beatrix Potter. Two bright little eyes appeared to be asking, "Would you fall for this lot?" At the bottom the artist had penned in the name "Narcissus."

"Cause 'e always be lookin' at hisself, Gabe said."

Gabe, Melrose was pleased to discover, was imaginative.

"So I leave a bit of biscuit out fer that there mouse, but don't tell Ashley. 'E'd be ever so disappointed." She lit another cigarette and waved out the match. "Was a dead mouse out in t' kitchen I brought in and put by the dish. Died from natural causes, it did, but Ashley didn't know that. Oh, he was ever so pleased. 'Elephant,' 'e says, 'Elephant, there's genius up 'ere,' an' taps 'is 'ead. A genius Ashley ain't."

Melrose smiled, then laughed. He handed back the drawing, saying, "This painter, Gabriel Merchant? That his name?" White Ellie nodded. "He was in the Tate with a friend of his—"

"Bea Slocum, right."

"They were both in the Tate when a woman named Frances Hamilton died."

White Ellie let out a hoot and slapped her thigh. "Weren't they ever? Well, there Bea sat and this lady falls on 'er. I never."

Melrose marvelled that it did not occur to her to question his visit, or to question his question. In White Ellie's world, it was all part of one giant tapestry, the warp and the woof, Rasputin and the Tate, the mouse and Melrose, the garden on fire and sudden death. White Ellie's approach to life was almost metaphysical.

"Richard Jury wanted me to talk to them. Mr. Merchant has been staying with you, he said, and I was hoping he'd be here."

"Aw, Gabe's down t' the nick bailin' out Ashley. Bea, well, she'd be at work still. Not gone five 'as it? Bea lives over in Bethnal Green. Works at that kiddies' museum. Like t' take me own kids, but they'd tear the place apart." She sighed. "Right bright girl is Bea. Fools people. But I don't know what else either a them could tell ya. The super and his sergeant, they've asked a thousand questions. I think Bea and Gabe told 'em everything." She leaned forward, breathing onions on him. "You don't think they'd something to do with it, now?"

Melrose shook his head. "No, I'm sure the superintendent doesn't think that. I'll tell you why he wants me to talk to them: because I'd be a fresh pair of ears and because sometimes, as I'm sure you agree, a person can actually know more than he himself realizes he knows."

Sententiously, she nodded. He doubted White Ellie could ever know more than she realized she knew.

"This Gabe is obviously very observant. And his girlfriend, as you said, is bright. From what Jury told me, she said some rather surprising things about art. Both of them made . . . *observations* that just might suggest they saw more than they knew. As I said." He shrugged. "Very likely the Hamilton woman died of natural causes—" he couldn't help his eye flickering to the water dish—"but there are things that have happened, subsequent things that make us wonder if Mrs. Hamilton's death isn't somehow connected."

White Ellie smoked and studied something on the ceiling. "Subsequent things," she murmured. Then, looking around the room, she said, "Where's them kids got to?"

Melrose was suddenly conscious of the background racket having stopped.

"Always up to somethin', it's turrible, turrible." White Ellie *tch-tch*ed but made no move to look for them. Instead she lit another cigarette.

"You said Ash was in the nick?" Ashley Cripps was, Melrose remembered, the Man on the Dole, the paradigm of the unemployed.

"T' Bill picked 'im up in Bethnal Green this time."

"But Superintendent Jury just saw him here, a day or two ago, wasn't it?"

She snorted. "Don't take long to go showin' hisself in the public lavatory down the Underground. Bea was *that* mad, and I don't blame 'er. 'All them kids, Ash,' she told 'im. 'Fancy some poor little girl goes to the toilet and what does she see? What?' Well, Ashley really takes umbrage at that, as you can imagine. 'I *never!*' 'e says to Bea. 'Think I'm a bloody pervert, the way you talk!' "

"How long will they hold him?"

"Not long. Gabe went down there to get 'im out. Only, I do wish Ashley'd stick to round 'ere; it's ruddy embarrassing, it is."

This was said in the tone of one who wished her nearest and dearest would stop patronizing a shop belonging to a competitor.

Putting down his mug, Melrose rose and said he'd got to be going. "I'd really like a word with Beatrice Slocum. You say she's working at the Museum of Childhood?"

"Right you are. But you only just got 'ere. I enjoy a nice chin wag with an old friend now and again. Thought mebbe we could go along to the pub for a pint." She struggled up out of the depth of the sprung-cushioned chair. "Necklace is gone, worse luck."

She was speaking of the Anodyne Necklace, a narrow old pub that had stood at the end of Catchcoach Street. It made Melrose sad to hear it was gone. "That's bad news. What happened?"

"Ah, you know them breweries," White Ellie said, waving the breweries away. "Got took over by Charrington's. Twice the price and half the beer, now. They got one a them awful glittery big balls, you know like they put in discos, hangin' from the ceiling."

By now they were at the door, where the rat-faced dog was waiting to sink its teeth into Melrose's trouser leg.

"'Ere, Basker! Get yerself off!" White Ellie gave the dog a thumping kick but her slipper was too soft to do any damage.

The dog clung and clung until Melrose gave it a swipe. He was wondering where the kiddies were. Fifteen minutes of silence boded ill, he was sure.

Out on the pavement, up and down White Ellie looked. "Beats me where them brats got to."

"I'm sure I'll find out. Goodbye, Ellie."

MELROSE THOUGHT he was getting off fairly cheaply. Only six quid. They'd ambushed him at the corner, saying they'd walk him past the butcher's for just a quid apiece. (Protection money had gone up just like everything else, he supposed.) When he questioned this enterprising scheme—"Why should I pay anyone to walk me past the butcher's?"—they told him the butcher was insane and whenever he saw some toff from the City he went for his meat cleaver.

"I'm not from the City. Nor am I a toff, as you put it."

"Yeah? Well, he don't know that, do he?" came the reasonable answer.

So he'd paid them off—even the toddler, who had her sticky little hand out—and walked the rest of the block with them until they came to a shop owned by one M. Perkins, and featuring: Choice Meats and Game. Melrose couldn't imagine a great deal of a demand for "choice meats," much less "choice game," in this particular area, but as he looked in the window he saw a pleasant, round-faced gentleman in a spanking-clean white apron arranging little bouquets of mint on a platter holding a handsome joint. Leg of lamb, thought Melrose, smiling brightly at the butcher. The man returned the smile and waved cheerily to the Crippses, even blowing a kiss to the toddler, who had her small hands and face mashed against the glass and was licking at it.

They passed on. Melrose reflected, "Strange. He seems quite a pleasant chap."

The older boy looked up at him, shaking his head as if he were truly dim. "A *course* he does. I tol' you you'd be okay long as you was with us, right?"

And this said, they all ran away, giggles floating back in the icy air as they twirled and turned and skittered away like leaves.

TWENTY-THREE

Except for the red hair, with its unreal eggplant tint, Melrose would have thought her to be one of the visitors. She was standing in front of one of the many glass cases housing nostalgic holdovers from childhood, this particular one being a very large and intricately furnished dollhouse. He found this glimpse of her—her face reflected in the glass and superimposed over a small kitchen and dining room filled with minuscule bits of dishes, oil lamps, fruits and vegetables—a ham on the table ready for carving, even—this glimpse showed a face with a wondering expression, head tilted slightly, mouth an *o*. In her hand was a jeweler's loupe.

"Miss Slocum? Beatrice Slocum?"

Suddenly, she turned and the child was quickly replaced by the rather bored adult. "Do I know you?" But the up-and-down, quick assessment suggested she wouldn't mind, after all.

"No. My name is Melrose Plant. I'm a friend of the Crippses."

Her eyes narrowed to a squint. "What? *You* are?" She seemed to want to add, "Not bloody likely."

He nodded. "I've just come from Catchcoach Street. Ellie Cripps told me you worked here and I was wondering if we could talk. I'm also a friend of Superintendent Jury."

She moaned. "Not *that* again? Not that bleedin' lady in the Tate? So *now* what?" She moved away from him, going behind a counter and inspecting the tiny accessories used in the dollhouse.

Melrose followed. "I can't say I blame you. You must be pretty sick of the whole thing, especially as you didn't really see anything you think might be helpful."

Irritated, she started slapping things into her purse. "I certainly didn't. Gabe and me—I expect you've talked to Gabe, too?"

"No. He wasn't around this afternoon. Mrs. Cripps says he's trying to get Ash out of custody."

This at least put her into a better humor. Her giggle was as fresh as any of the kiddies'. "Oh, God, yes. I told him, I told Ash if ever I found him anywheres round my territory again I'd give him a proper thrashing. Anyway." She sighed and continued stuffing her bag.

"Look, if you're leaving work, perhaps you wouldn't mind having a bite or a cup of coffee or something and we could talk. Just for a few minutes."

She pursed her mouth. "Mmnn. There's that new caff Dotrice opened up near Vicky Park. I wouldn't mind. But I'll have to clear out of here first. Just take me a few minutes if you want to look around. Wander about, why don't you?"

He did wander about.

It struck him as rather an odd place for somebody like Bea Slocum to be working, but, then, he didn't really know her, did he? He looked over the dollhouse up a few steps to his left; it was really a cabinet, cleverly converted into several rooms. He was fascinated by the detail, the tiny glasses on the dining-room table, the miniature vegetables ready for cooking in pots as small as a fivepenny coin. He passed to the next big window. Here was Dingley Hall, quite a handsome manor house. Its occupants seemed very busy here, descending and ascending the sweeping staircase, probably assembling for the tea that was about to be served on a table round which were collected tiny chairs in the Queen Anne style.

Melrose climbed a few steps to the second level and found himself amongst the trains: electric, steam, pull-alongs; engines and tenders, locomotives, carriages, Pullman and passenger, every kind he could imagine. There was a long glass case that had been set up with track, rolling stock, miniature buildings and people—a countryside that the train would run through, provided you put twenty pence in the slot. He watched a boy of five or six do just this and the train started rolling. The boy stood with his hands clasped behind his back, rocking a bit on his heels, his gaze intense. He did not appear to mind sharing his twenty pence with a stranger; however, when the train came to rest, the boy looked up at Melrose with the expression of a crony who'd been standing drinks and was wondering when the other fellow was going to be in the chair.

Melrose pushed his own coin in the slot. The boy nodded, and they both turned to watch the locomotive move out of the station into open country. The boy's eyes tracked the train's progress. He was not disposed to talk, which was fine with Melrose.

Melrose frowned at the little train, snaking its way through a tunnel. It had started him wondering whether, when he was this lad's age, he'd had some sort of setup like this. He could not remember having had one; this annoyed him. After some hard thinking, he came to the conclusion that, no, he had never had a train, which annoyed him even more. Why hadn't he? Didn't every boy whose family could afford it have a train? After a while he became aware that he had adopted the boy's own posture—hands clasped behind him, tilting forward and backward on the balls of his feet. Quickly, he dug his hands into his jacket pockets.

With no comment, the boy left to continue his way round the exhibits, and Melrose moved to the several cases housing miniature shops. There were a provisions store, a fish stall, the Tiptop General Store, a milliner's shop where a porcelain shop assistant gestured with her tiny pearl-white hand towards tables and shelves of little hats. The largest of these shops was the butcher's, quite amazing in its approximation to the real thing. Sides of beef, joints of mutton all hung in a row beneath the roof; ducks and chickens and other fowl hung neck down. One bowler-hatted butcher occupied the doorway; another, in the dark recess of the shop, sharpened knives. Mr. Jurvis, Melrose was sure, would appreciate the scale to which the shop and its contents had been drawn.

He walked along a few steps to a display of models of boys and girls engaged in old games like Hot Cockles and Bull in the Park. The girl with the hoop reminded him of J. M. W. Turner's fanciful painting in the Tate. Had he played such games? If he had he was sure he would have been It.

He passed along to the building bricks, construction kits, old Bayko building sets, and could not recall one single one of these he had had as a child. Frowning, he moved to a large case of the sort one would find in Brighton at the Old Penny Palace. Inside were wooden black-faced sheep who would give their rendition of "Baa Baa Black

Sheep" for 20p. Everything seemed to cost 20p, and he'd run out of coins. Melrose bet he'd seen any number of these coin-operated toys along the piers of Brighton or Liverpool—

Oh, for heaven's sake, he said to himself. You've never been in Liverpool in your entire life. Only once to Brighton, and that was with Jury. Yet, there must have been holidays by the sea. Still, he could not call up one scene of himself as a child with a pail and sandy, sunburnt legs. Why had his childhood been so blighted? He frowned deeply. He would ask Ruthven, the repository of such memories. Good, stout Ruthven and, to a lesser degree, his wife, Martha. How old was Ruthven? Well, no matter, for he appeared to be in robust health. Then, as usually happens in the moment you start considering your own or another's mortality, you think you've got to sort out everything before everyone drops dead. He would ask Ruthven the minute he got—

A movement behind him brought Melrose out of these reflections; a hand was pushing a coin into the slot and the wooden sheep began to baa to the tune. He turned to see Bea standing right behind him.

"There, how's that?" she said cheerily. "You can sing along if you like."

Melrose studied her expression, to see if he could detect any irony in it, but he could not. He didn't answer, though.

"Probably, you'd like the peep shows. They're just back there—" she gestured towards the back of the room.

Huffily he said, "I'm sure I had quite enough of peep shows when I was a lad."

She ignored the tone. "Did you used to make them up out of shoeboxes? That's what we did. Inside the box you put little things and then stick a hole in the end—"

"Yes, that's about what we did. Except ours were very fancy. We had regular scale-model . . . things. Let's go to this cafe, then, what do you say?"

Her face brightened. "It's what's near where I live. I live in one of them blocks of flats the Social tossed up. It's French, the cafe. Kind of posh?" She made a question of this, unsure as to whether Melrose was into poshness. "Kind of expensive."

He smiled. "Damn the expense. Let's go."

*   *   *

IT WAS as Bea had described it: a posh little restaurant, probably over-priced—posh, certainly, for Bethnal Green, which was hardly an afflu-ent area, having as its neighbors Shoreditch and Spitalfields, and, not far away, Stepney and Limehouse. Perhaps Dotrice heralded gentrifica-tion, the promise of invasion by Trueblood's WEMs, who might be spending the rest of their week (their working week) in Bethnal Green.

If anything was the bellwether of such a movement, it was a restaurant. London loved its restaurants, perhaps even more than London loved its West End theatres. Eating out was almost obligatory, and every new little restaurant that sprouted was solemnly noted, patronized, criticized. It made Melrose sad, studying the exterior of Dotrice, the way the old pubs had refurbished both their looks and their food to cater for this new clientele.

Finally, the maître d' came to lead them to a table. A surprising number of customers were already dining, so they must have come before 7:30. Good God, was this a new trend, then? Dinner at seven? Melrose shuddered slightly, as he followed Bea to a table. If one couldn't while away the evening hours between eight and ten at din-ner, just how was one to fill them? Watching the telly? The couple at the table beside them were eating dessert! They'd be finished by 7:45 if they weren't careful.

"Something wrong?" asked Bea, who'd parked her bag on the floor and was fanning open her napkin. "You look awful."

"Wrong? No, no. Just thinking about that woman dying in the Tate. About death. You know . . ."

Bea was not interested in death, only the menu. She read it avidly, tongue caught between her red lips.

Well, it *was* a sort of death, wasn't it? Through dinner by six or seven? Whole horrible vistas opened before his eyes, such as Agatha turning up at his door yet again in the evening, her meal taken in Plague Alley finished, so plenty of time to bike up to Ardry End for her port and biscuits.

No! He would simply return to the Jack and Hammer and stay until closing if it came to that. But the Jack and Hammer was the aper-itif, not the pears and port. He didn't want his daily routine disturbed.

Looking round the room, softly lit, rather art deco–ish and with a lot of Lichtenstein and Duchamp prints on the walls, he wondered if a pub had once stood on this site. The old pubs were going; think of the ones in Docklands: the Town of Ramsgate, the old Grapes no longer catered for the fisherman, the wharfinger, the workingman. Now they were all done up and over for the upwardly mobile professional who lived in one of those renovated warehouses. It was no longer the fish cart clanking and rattling along the cobbles, but the tires of Jaguar XJ-6s and BMWs hissing through the rain.

The waiter handed Melrose a wine list. That at least was something he could deal with while Bea clucked over the menu (the prices! Cor!). Melrose insisted she not bother about prices, that she have whatever she wanted, and when she said she fancied the steak and potatoes *frites* he was not surprised.

The waiter was, though, when she asked if the *frites* meant, was they fried? His nose seemed visibly to lengthen as he informed Madame that, yes, they were. Melrose ordered a bottle of Château Latour, and for himself only an appetizer of foie gras with lime.

As the waiter swanned off with the order, Bea wrenched round to watch his departing black-clad back. "Cheeky bastard. Like to chuck me straight out the door, he would. That's all you're having, just that appetizer?" she protested.

He said he'd had a very late lunch and couldn't tuck into some elaborate main course. Actually, he was looking forward to his cook Martha's *boudin blanc* with mustard sauce. It was a dish he especially loved because it kept Agatha absolutely away. "Disgusting white sausage" was her assessment. Spiced apples, sauteed to go with it, he imagined. Surreptitiously, he checked his watch. He could be back in Long Pidd by ten o'clock, perhaps even nine-thirty if there wasn't too much lingering about in Dotrice.

Still, he liked Bea. He liked her open enjoyment of the costly interior, the obviously moneyed diners, the French menu. He tasted the wine, pronounced it exceedingly good, and the waiter poured. He watched Bea take in this heady environment, quite different from her cheese salad or egg mayonnaise sandwich, and smiled. There was something about Bea (and about Gabe, too, from what he'd heard of the man) that really didn't fit the funky picture of two kids smooching in such an upmarket venue as the Tate Gallery. He said so.

Bea was picking the radicchio out of her Salade Dotrice, and answered, "Ah, that's just Gabe's way. Likes to see if people react." Around the rim of her large salad plate she deployed bits of the radicchio. "You know, he wants to see if people get shocked. It's to study behavior, he says. Says it helps his painting. Can't imagine how." She sipped her wine, chewed her Bibb lettuce. "Anyway, we weren't really concentrating, know what I mean? I was looking over his shoulder at that painting on the other wall, A Grey Dawn, something like that, real sad it is—"

"But then Gabe might have had his eyes open, too."

She shrugged. "Coulda done, yeah." Lining up some more radicchio bits, she shrugged again. "So?"

"He might have noticed something."

"If he'd seen something, he'd've said. Didn't say anything to me."

"Tell me again exactly what you were doing. I mean for the hour or two before Mrs. Hamilton died."

She made a noise of impatience. "How many times do I have to tell it?"

"Perhaps many times more. In a story's retelling, it often changes."

"Not this story, it don't." With the handle of her fork, she pointed at her chest. "Not my story."

"I'm talking about details, tiny things. Things that might have gone missing—such as you just told me. You had your eyes open. Perhaps Gabe did, too."

She slumped back, prepared to give him a bit of a hard time. But then her steak arrived, and she brightened. The waiter cast a doubtful eye on the circle of radicchio leaves that ringed the salad plate he was removing.

While she cut up the filet into small bits (as if she were feeding the cat) she told him how she herself had gone along to "have a deco at the Turners," while Gabe had gone to the Swagger Portraits.

"And he saw Frances Hamilton there, too."

"So it's him you should be talking to, not me, right?"

"I want to talk to him, yes." Melrose looked into the dregs of his wine. "But you might be more observant than he is."

Surprised, she stared at him. "'Course I'm not."

"Those miniatures and that jeweler's loupe you were using to look at them." He smiled over at her. "That was interesting. You place them in the dollhouse, right?"

Bea popped an evenly cut square of meat into her mouth, looked at him, shook her head. "You got a point you're making, or what?"

"Probably not. I don't know."

"I don't either." Bea forked up a dainty bit of filet, chewed thoughtfully. "Here's this lady drops dead because of her heart, or something like that, and the cops, even Scotland Yard, they're all over it." More chewing as she shook her head. "How come? And how come that CID detective is so interested in Gabe and me? Huh?" The tone was one of mock challenge as she leaned toward him.

Melrose smiled and refilled their glasses, the waiter's job, but the waiter was busy tossing some greens around in a bowl. Caesar salad, no doubt. They always made such a fuss of a Caesar salad. "Superintendent Jury rather liked the significance of you and Gabe sitting directly in view of Dante Gabriel Rossetti's Beatrice."

"He did, did he?" She chewed with some deliberation, ran the forefinger holding her fork beneath her nose, and said, "Fuck him." Then she speared another morsel of steak. "Ditto you. Nice, this," she added, waving the meat on the fork.

Melrose laughed and sipped his wine as he regarded the Lichtenstein on the wall beside them. "You like these prints, Bea?"

Without looking up from her tiny mountain of potatoes *frites*, she answered, "If I want to look at cartoons, I'd sooner watch *Ren and Stimpy*." She flicked a disdainful glance toward the print. "Nah."

He watched the waiter brandish the clay bottle of olive oil over the huge bowl. "Do you like Art? Capital-A Art, I mean?"

"Some." She shrugged off Art, drank half her glass of wine, ate her potatoes.

"No, not 'some.' A *lot*. A whole *lot*. People who are merely waiting for other people to finish viewing something, an exhibit or a room full of paintings, might just wander through the rooms. Or go down to the restaurant and have a coffee. Said people do *not* go off to have 'a deco at the Constables.' "

"The Turners. J.M.W. I don't much like Constable."

"Yes. My point exactly."

"You ain't got a point. But you can fill me up again, ta very much." She tapped a stubby finger against her glass.

"Since the two of you didn't have ten quid between you, you generously let Gabe go along to the Swagger exhibit."

"What's generous? Who wants to see a bunch of overdone portraits of a lot of toffs, anyway?"

He smiled. "How did you know that's what that particular exhibit was about?"

"Pretty obvious, ain't it?"

"No, it ain't. At least it ain't to me. And I'm not stupid—"

Her expression suggested he might do well to reassess that opinion.

"—and the catalog says the term 'swagger' was coined by the Tate's curator."

Bea frowned. "What's all this in aid of?"

Melrose swirled the wine in his glass, wondered if they were in a nonsmoking section, decided not to ask and lit up a cigarette. He knew Bea smoked from the nicotine stains between her fingers, so the smoke wouldn't bother her. "You paint, don't you?" It was a shot in the dark.

"What?" She made a face and stabbed at her steak. "Oh, don't be daft!"

Melrose exhaled a gentle stream of smoke and watched it curl and disperse. "Probably better than Gabe."

Her mouth, open to receive a forkful of potatoes *frites*, remained open as she lowered her fork. "Oh, *don't* be daft!" she repeated. Furiously, she chased bits of meat around her plate like a billiards player potting balls. Plate clean, she then laid down her fork. "Even if I *did*—"

(Meaning, she did.)

"—what's it to do with this lady pegging out there on the bench?"

"I don't know. Except I imagine you're far more observant than you let on. I would imagine that what a painter sees is almost indelibly impressed upon his mind or his inner eye. Perhaps even if he doesn't consciously recall it."

"Bloody hell." She said this without emphasis. "So out of the corner of me eye I see some guy in a black mac and Ray-Bans brush up against this Mrs. Hamilton and stick her with a needle. Something like that?"

"Not exactly. I'm actually more interested in reactions to art from someone who's extremely sensitive to it."

Her mouth pulled back over pearly teeth in an expression of utter disbelief. "You are a lousy detective."

"I'm not a detective." Melrose studied the Duchamp a bit farther along the wall from the Lichtenstein.

"You are a *lousy* detective." She held out her glass for more wine.

"You said that."

He poured; she drank.

Then she asked, "What in bloody hell does art have to do with this?"

Melrose was silent for some time, raising his eyes from the dark red depths of his wineglass to look at the prints. "You like Turner. Do you like the French impressionists?"

"What I like is the looks of that sweet trolly. Just look at that chocolate-chocolate thing. What is it?"

Melrose didn't look and didn't answer, beyond raising a finger to signal the waiter. While she eyed the trolly, he studied her. She was obviously intelligent—*extremely* so—and perceptive. He was surprised Jury, or Wiggins even, hadn't seen through the punk empty-headed act. That act (Melrose imagined) was assumed to fool "society," but probably also to fool her boyfriend, Gabe. Possibly even to fool herself. Right now she was regarding him, winding a lock of that ridiculous eggplant-tinted hair round her finger. Her eyes were expressionless, as if nothing about him were registering. They were also a cool, clear pale green. The color reminded him of ocean water at the shore's edge, running in, moving out.

The waiter appeared at the table and explained that the chocolate "thing" was a combination of mousse, cake, crumbled praline enveloped in a bittersweet chocolate glaze. Bea said she would have a piece "with a dollop of that whipped cream on it." The waiter smiled bleakly at this lily-gilding, but obliged. No, nothing thanks for Melrose himself except for coffee.

"Her nephew was killed not very long ago," he said, when the waiter had moved off to serve other diners.

Bea's head came up from her dessert plate and her careful apportioning of chocolate bites. She looked puzzled.

"Mrs. Hamilton's nephew. He was murdered. In the States."

"That's terrible. You think it's got something to do with how she died?"

Melrose shook his head. "Not directly, no. That matter was cleared up, pretty much. But there are other things related to it."

"What things?"

"A couple of other deaths, possibly. The police aren't sure." He wondered if she'd read about the body found at Old Sarum. "Do you read the papers?"

She just looked at him. "Nah. Never learned, me. Sign my name with an X, too." She slid the fork from her mouth, licking off the bits of chocolate.

"Sorry. I didn't mean to sound so patronizing. What I meant was, have you read the papers recently? About the young woman found dead at Old Sarum?"

That made her stop her chocolate-laden fork in midair. "God, you don't think it's to do with *that*?"

Melrose shrugged. "Don't know." Perhaps he shouldn't have said anything. He was not sure what he might, and might not, tell these people he was questioning. It was all so nebulous, the relationship so . . . well, impossible, really, that he couldn't imagine he was giving away secrets.

"They didn't say how she died. How did she?"

"I don't know."

She returned her attention to her final tidbit of mousse. "Don't know much, do you?"

"No. What sorts of things do you paint?"

"Never you mind." Done, she sighed as she carefully lay her fork across her plate. "That was a treat. I could fancy some brandy." She looked behind her for the waiter.

"Still life? Landscapes? Big squares of color à la Rothko?"

"Why'd you want to know? You'd only tell Gabe."

Melrose rolled his eyes. "*Don't* be ridiculous. Do I act like someone who'd grass on you?" He raised two fingers to bring the waiter.

"Dunno, do I?" She regarded the Duchamp with a frown. "I paint in blue."

"Blue?"

She nodded. "Blue. That's all. Every kind of blue ever invented and some of my own. I got blues you ain't *ever* seen."

Melrose opened his mouth to comment but could think of nothing to say.

"So when Gabe painted Ash blue, I thought it was some kind of message. Didn't get half mad, did I? I thought maybe he snuck into my digs and nosed around. Nobody noses around my digs."

Her small face took on a sharp, feral look as if warning Melrose, in case that was what he was thinking of doing.

"I beg your pardon? Painted Ashley Cripps *blue*? You did say that?"

"Yeah. Didn't your CID mate tell you?"

"He forgot."

"So it was a bet or something stupid. Ash ran around stark—except he was blue. Probably just to shock the Liar." She smiled serenely when the waiter set down their double cognacs. Two gorgeous snifters, brandy glowing with reflected candlelight. "You are *not* cheap, I'll say that for you. Cheers."

What *wouldn't* she say for him, he wondered as he smilingly raised his glass and touched hers. "Thank you. Tell me: why are you drawn to the Turners in the Tate?"

"I told you. The light. The way he does light. When I get depressed, I go look. Great stuff, it makes me feel better. But so does this." She sipped her drink, licked her lips. "What's all these questions about Art, anyway?"

"I just wondered how intense your reaction was to Turner. I wonder—" Melrose frowned slightly, raised his glass to see how her image would be distorted through the liquid—"if Art can kill."

"You're *joking*." She gave a brief, cut-off laugh.

"You believe it can cure."

"I do?"

"You just said so. Turner takes care of your depression."

"Bloody hell, that's not exactly kill or cure."

They drank their brandy; he paid the bill.

A NIMBUS of yellowish light surrounded the iron sconces set high in the brick wall of the restaurant, turning the misty rain to gauze. It was a light rain, but it could seep into your bones, Melrose knew. As they waited by the curb for a cab, he removed his topcoat and held it over Bea's head, tentlike.

Surprised, she looked up at him. "A real gent, you are!" She laughed. "Now, Gabe, he *hogs* the umbrella." She threw up her arm, waved her hand. "There's a cab down there."

But the driver didn't see them. The cab looked to be making a U-turn to head back the way it had come. Suddenly, an ear-piercing whistle made Melrose jump. He looked around to see Bea with her little fingers positioned in the corners of her mouth. A second whistle rent the night. The taxi backed up, headed toward them.

She shrugged at his raised eyebrows. "Learnt that when I was a kid."

As the cab crawled toward them, its headlamps glowing through the rain, Melrose said, "You'll never need Mace."

The cab pulled to the curb and he started to hand her into the backseat. She paused and asked, "What about you? Ain't you coming, too?"

He shook his head. "I'm going to walk."

"Walk? In this muck?"

"I don't get to London much. And I like to walk."

Uncertainly, she said, "Suit yourself." Then she held out her hand; her grip was surprisingly firm and strong. "Listen, thanks. That was ever so lovely, and so are you. For a toff. I've been wanting to go there for the longest time. Nobody else at the museum has been." She revelled in this knowledge.

"Then I'm glad we have." He scribbled his telephone number in his small notebook and ripped out the page. "Here. If you think of anything, or if Gabe does, just ring me, will you?"

Bea crumpled the bit of paper into her pocket. "I will."

"Once we sort all of this business out, if we ever do, I'll come back and we'll have dinner here again."

She smiled broadly. "Right you are. Only next time, you eat a proper meal, hear?"

"Absolutely. Goodnight, Bea."

In the cab she rolled down the window. "Next time you come, I'll let you see some of my paintings, if you like."

He leaned down to the window. "I'd like." He thought, if her painting was like her, it would be interesting. Bea, with her purple hair, her odd language slippages (East End up to West), her clear intelligence, her Turner and Rothko. Her hundred shades of blue.

"Ta," she said.

He backed away, slapped the cab as if it were a toy car he could control with a key or a remote, one he could send on its way or make come back.

Only, he couldn't.

Her face, receding and white in the dark interior, was pressed against the rear window as her hand made a backward, forward wave like a metronome.

Or it could have been you.

* * *

HE DID walk, too. He would be late home, late to Martha's *boudin blanc*, but over the last hour, he had lost his appetite. Or, rather, lost his urgency to get back to Northants.

So he walked through the wet streets of Bethnal Green while the mist turned to something more trenchant, a businesslike rain, an unsporting, un-English rain that dropped straight down, bulletlike, cold and soaking.

He walked and wondered what was the matter with him that one day's coming up to London should leave him feeling so disoriented, depleted, and alone. And different. He felt different, that was all. And that, old son (Melrose told himself), is likely the reason you should stick to your port and books.

Past dark doorways, an alley or two, he walked. Past a few shops—fishmonger's, greengrocer's, Hovis bakery. It was only nine, and yet the bleak quiet of Bethnal Green was what he'd expect to encounter in the hours after midnight. The still street and shuttered windows, the lowered blind of the greengrocer's, the webbed grate before the jeweler's windows, all of this fairly shouted *absence absence*. The street was swept clean of companionable sounds: no tires hissing past, no dogs or drunks rattling dustbins, no distant cries, cut off. The London night might as well have fallen into step beside him to let him know how alone he was.

Sorry, guv. You're in Bethnal Green, mate, not the bloody country. Not the friendly fireside and the snoring old dog for comfort. Bethnal Green, old son, and don't you forget it. Be wise to stick with what you know and not to go thinkin' too much about it, know what I mean?

But Melrose kept on walking and the rain let up, returned itself to that gauzy mist, perhaps weary itself with its sudden wrathful turn. He stopped to listen, heard nothing, started up again. He was not sure where he was and he was too sad to care.

He had come to a little cul-de-sac, a blank wall in front of him that was decorated with an ancient poster, an advert for Rountree's cocoa. And that, as had everything else that had happened that day, set the past before his eyes. *You won't escape, guv.*

Melrose bowed his head. It was as if by some act of humility he could exorcise sadness and remorse. Yet he did not really know from what source these feelings had sprung. As he looked at the fading, graffiti-riddled, and peeling poster, a verse from childhood came to mind. He was surprised by it:

> A splotch of mud on a Beggarstaff man,
> A splotch and that is all.
> Yet it blinds the eye of the Cocoa man
> On a Bethnal Green dead wall.

PART TWO

Sunset, Santa Fe

Jury sat on the rooftop of the La Fonda Hotel and watched the sun reflect off the western face of the Sangre de Cristo Mountains. He breathed in the weightless, dry air of New Mexico and watched that band of gold widen and diffuse, turn pink-gold that widened again and deepened to orange and red across the dark mountains.

He was too used to the bleak and often bitter dusks of London, where color was nonexistent and light, pragmatic. Light in London served its utilitarian purpose: being there, outside the window at six or seven a.m. to let him know it was time to get to Victoria Street; or at the other end of the day, its dying telling him he'd better take his torch along.

Jury was sitting on the roof of the La Fonda with Jack Oñate, the Santa Fe policeman, who had told him which mountain range that was, and that there were as many as seventy-three mountain ranges. Oñate had said that when he was a kid he'd had to memorize all of the names in school. But he had forgotten them by now, couldn't recall any of the Northern range, just the Sangre de Cristos out there, the Sandias, the Jemez, the Ortiz—the better-known ones—and maybe a few more.

The fifty-mile-or-so trip from the Albuquerque airport in the hired car had opened Jury's eyes to a wilderness of silvery sage and cottonwood, of land studded with the dark green of piñon and juniper. It might not be the most beautiful landscape he'd ever seen—there were, after all, the Lake District, the Hebrides—but this one was certainly the most unearthly. It didn't look real. He noticed the registration plates of the cars that passed him bore the legend Land of Enchantment. That fit.

Jury and Jack Oñate, along with several other guests braving the February cold to catch the sunset, sat on folding chairs, bottled beer in their hands, gazing out towards the Sangre de Cristos. Jury asked about snow.

"On some of these mountains it never completely melts," said Jack. "I go camping sometimes up in the San Juans and if you dig under that snow you get ice. Glacier snow, I call it."

"How far off are they?" asked Jury, squinting at the mountain range.

"I don't know, maybe twenty miles."

"They look so close."

"Here, thirty or forty miles looks like walking distance. It's the air, see. The air's so clear."

For a while they were silent, watching the sunset, and then Jack Oñate, with a back-to-business sigh, slapped open one of the files he'd been carrying in a beaten-up briefcase.

"Angela Hope," Oñate read from the sheet of paper, the manilla file open across his knee. He took a pull at his beer, set the bottle on the cement roof. "Thirty-two years, five-foot-six, brown eyes, dark brown hair. Angela Hope had an artsy little shop over on Canyon Road, where everyone and his brother has an artsy little shop. She lived some fifteen miles outside of Santa Fe, between here and Española. That's the 753 exchange we called where the people never heard of her. The 473 and 982 exchanges are Santa Fe. But 753, that's Española. Angela and her sister have this isolated little place in several acres of desert. The sister's pretty young. Thirteen, but acts older. Her name's Mary. Then there's a housekeeper, Rosella Ortiz, been with them ever since they came here. She's Indian. Cochise, maybe, or Zuñi."

"You didn't mention this cousin, Dolores Schell. The one who identified the body."

"Right. Schell's Pharmacy, that's her. Her dad was the pharmacist and then when he died, Dolores took it over. It's over on Old Pecos Trail."

"She's a pharmacist."

Oñate nodded. "Now, the Schells have been here a long time."

"She married?"

Oñate shook his head. "Lives by herself in a house over in El Dorado. A semi-swank development outside of town. I get the impression she and Angela weren't all that close." He shrugged. "Not unusual; *I* got cousins I ain't even seen."

"The Schells have been here a long time, but not the Hopes? Where are they from, then?"

"From the East." Jack Oñate thumbed the papers. "New York. Hmm. New York money, or at least some kind of money. Parents died when their private plane went down." He retrieved his bottle of beer. "So what do you guys figure?"

"Not much." Jury shook his head, watched the blue mountains turn grape-dark.

"What's 'not much'?"

"Nothing."

Oñate nodded. "I'd say that's not much." He returned his gaze to the file. "Her friends say she was nice, talented, nice, spiritual, nice, generous, nice. No deviations from that list, so no enemies, or none we heard from."

"What about men? As they say, 'significant others'?"

"Hard to tell, but this one guy, Malcolm Corey, might have been. He also has an artsy little shop on Canyon Road. This one's a gallery. He claims to be a painter—who doesn't around here?—but what he really is, he says, is an actor. He says."

"How'd he react when he was told about her death?" Jury leaned over to see the address in the file and wrote it down.

"Pretty shocked. Might have gone pale but with the guy's tan, it's hard to tell."

"You don't sound overly fond of him." Jury watched a long streak of magenta diffuse and spread into pale pink and lavender underlined with dark gold melting like caramel. "You said this Corey's an actor?"

"No, I'm saying what *he* says. There are a lot of movies made around here. So they need extras for big scenes, or just people wandering around the streets. That's the sort of thing this Corey guy does, except he wants you to think he's really set for big roles. Claims he has this shop of his as a 'hobby.' He paints when he's 'resting between roles.' That's what these actors say when they're out of a job. Meaning Corey's not much in demand as a movie guy. Anyway, he's got a high-profile agent. You want to talk to him, he just might be over at Rancho del Reposo. That's one place they're shooting. It's a high-priced sort of hotel, main lodge and casitas, several miles outside of town."

Jury held his bottle up to the light, brooding on its emptiness. "Then you get a lot of California types here?"

"Oh, hell, yes, but not just because of the movies. They flock here from Southern Cal. They *love* it, think they've 'discovered' Santa Fe."

"You've lived here a long time?" Jury thought he could sit here, slumped in this chair, feet resting on the porch railing, for the rest of the night. He was tired, but not with a London bone-tiredness. He felt as if a lot of tension were seeping out of his body, leaving him feeling wilted.

"All my life. It used to be so different. Now it's citified, know what I mean? Sophisticated, trendy, beautiful—but in a whoring kind of way. Paid to be pretty, paid to keep itself up."

Jury laughed. "This place isn't cheap like that."

"Who said cheap? Believe me, this is one place in the U.S. of A. that is decidedly not cheap. You can see the way the edges are rotting away, though. You drove here, you came on Cerrillos Road."

"The highway with the string of motels?"

"Right. Cerrillos Road is like afterbirth; it's the mess left behind because of tourism. Don't get me wrong; I don't hate tourists. In fact, it ticks me off when I hear these fancy store owners complain. Where the hell would they be without the tourists? Who is it spends the money? But it's the concept of 'tourism' that gets to me. It's like a monster the city itself created and now the monster's clumping around town demanding a room for the night." Oñate sounded sad. "Hell, another ten years, old Santa Fe'll be gone."

"You could say the same thing about old England."

Jack Oñate shook his head. "It'd be pretty hard to bury England under a pile of turquoise and carved coyotes and cactus. I just don't think a culture can stand this much hammering. Want another beer? You've been doing everything with that empty except standing it on your head."

Jury grinned. He'd been watching two women at the end of this row of sunset watchers light up cigarettes. The women were good-looking in a perfectly coiffed, enameled sort of way. But it was the cigarettes that made him salivate. "Yes, I want another. Do you smoke?"

"I used to. Gave it up some years back. Why?"

"I'm trying to quit." He watched the threads of smoke from the freshly lighted cigarettes turn a bluish-pink against the mellow umber of adobe wall. "But then I see that—" Jury nodded toward the women, both with cigarettes held within bare inches of their moist, red lips— "and it's like . . . sex. It's lust; it's a hunger, devouring. When I watch, I *lust* after them. The cigarettes, not the women."

"Took me years to stop. Must've tried two dozen times." He got up and clapped a hand on Jury's shoulder. "So, listen, man; let's have another beer and talk about stuff." He went off towards the rooftop bar.

Talk about stuff. That, and the childlike expression on Jack Oñate's face, made Jury smile; it took him back to the years he'd spent in the house of his uncle, after his mother's death, after the home he'd been put in. He was nine or ten. Behind the house was a long garden that emptied onto deep fields of grazing land belonging to some well-to-do farmer. There was a shed, a fairly large one that served as shelter for whatever farm animals might be stuck out in the fields in rain or snow. There was his best friend, Billy Oakley, a couple of years older than he, who used to nick his dad's cigarettes and sometimes his whisky. They would sit in the shed and make themselves ill, and often, a cow or a sheep joined them for company. Billy Oakley's favorite word was "stuff." It sufficed largely for anything he didn't understand, anything beyond his comprehension. His dad did "accounting and stuff"; women had "tits and stuff." And a couple of years into the shed visits Billy's mother died. It was "leukemia and stuff."

Jack Oñate resettled himself and handed Jury another beer. He sighed. "Angela Hope. I didn't know her myself. Only to see, that is. Her and her sister."

"I'll want to talk to anyone you know of who *did* know her. Who else besides the perhaps-boyfriend Corey and the little sister?"

"Well, there's some of the other people on Canyon Road. Since she had her business there, it stands to reason they'd have known her. On one side there's a Ms. Bartholomew. Sukie Bartholomew. My God—" Jack looked at Jury—" 'Sukie' Bartholomew. Go figure." She's into crystals, tarot cards, stuff like that. But you get more of that in Sedona. Actually I think this Bartholomew woman is from there. Which is kind of strange. Most of them leave Santa Fe to *go* to Sedona. Spiritual place, they say. 'Vortexes' and stuff. Some kind of magnetic center that's supposed to be real spiritual. Holes in the ground. They call them vortexes. Me, I call it mystical shit."

"You're talking about Sedona, Arizona."

"Yeah." Jack looked over at him. "Even in your business, you've heard of Sedona?"

"Coincidence. I just happened to read something in a newspaper about it. New Age people, that's what they were called."

Looking down at his notes, Jack continued. "I get the impression no one who does business on Canyon Road really knew Angela Hope all that well. Except maybe for this Sukie person, I mean, they had tea together sometimes. Probably that ginseng, herbal junk." Oñate studied his bottle label as if to compare ingredients. "And as for these two Brits of yours, Frances Hamilton and Helen Hawes—" Jack shook his head—"there's even less there. They both stayed here—" he pointed down at the roof "—for two days, and the Hawes woman was here longer. This Frances Hamilton checked in for the two days before they left. But no one I talked to—not the desk clerk, not the maid, not the dining room hostess ever saw them together."

"Could Frances Hamilton have been staying somewhere else before that?"

"Sure. But I thought you only wanted to know where they were together. I can ask around some more—"

Jury shook his head. "Thanks, but I can do it."

Oñate thought for a moment, then asked, "Did she have money?"

"Frances Hamilton? Yes, quite a lot."

"Then try Rancho del Reposo. It's maybe ten miles the other side of Santa Fe."

"Right." Jury glanced at Oñate's notes. "Anyone else?"

"Then there's this scientist type, Nils Anders. *Doctor* Anders, I should say. He was a friend of Angela Hope. Again, how good, I don't know. He's over at the Santa Fe Institute. All I have is, he's a friend."

"What's the Santa Fe Institute?"

"It's where all kinds of scientists hang out thinking up weird stuff."

Jury rolled the cool bottle across his forehead, and said, "What kind of weird stuff?"

"It's like a think tank. All kinds of scientists—physicists, biologists, mathematicians, chemists—they get together and knock ideas around. They use computers a lot; they got more computers in that place than Macintosh." Jack tilted his bottle, took a long drink. "They're mostly into something called 'complexity theory.' "

"What's that?"

Jack shrugged. "Some theory of the way the universe acts. It's after 'chaos.' Don't look at me; I didn't make it up. It's got something to do with order. A kind of order."

Macalvie might like that, thought Jury, returning his gaze to the dark mountains. He was getting hungry. There must be a hundred terrific restaurants in Santa Fe. "Where is this place?"

"Hyde Park Road. You go like you were headed for the ski basin or for that spa up there—"

"I'm not skiing or spa-ing, so you'll have to direct me."

Jack nodded. "What I think is, if Einstein had been around when there were places like this Institute, he'd have gone there and chilled. You know?"

"And Dr. Anders. Which particular kind of weird stuff is he into?"

"Anders . . . Anders . . . Anders . . ." Jack was whispering, leafing through the file pages. "Weird stuff . . . weird. . . . Ah, here it is: Ph.D., psychology. Ph.D., sociology. Ph.D., *mathematics*. Hell, I'm impressed. Guy's got three of them." He went back to the notes. "You going to see him? And the rest of them?"

"I imagine, yes. Right now, how about dinner?"

"Okay. Incidentally, Rich. These people at the Santa Fe Institute, they are *not* dumb." Jack repeated this, his mouth an O, silently mouthing the words NOT DUMB.

Jury leaned over towards him, also mouthing, NEITHER ARE WE.

TWENTY-FIVE

Canyon Road, the sign said, and given that the other streets Jury had passed were not posted with turquoise and brown wooden signs, he assumed that this one was one of Santa Fe's prime attractions. So variously and brightly painted were the adobe and wood buildings that bordered each side of the narrow, winding street, he thought he might have come upon one of those "Prettiest Villages in England." They were selling either Native American crafts, or art, or food. In the summer months he imagined it would be a touristy hell, but now, in February, it lay quiet and golden, sunlight reflecting off turquoise and blue and rose-colored paint.

The Silver Heron was located around a bend and about halfway along. It was, like most of the shops here, very small, one room in front and one in the rear about the size of a walk-in closet. This must have been where Angela did her silver work. The small room was windowless, the only furniture a very long wooden table—something like a refectory table, but higher—and a high stool drawn up to it.

She had not been an orderly person, Jury thought. Her tools were lying in disarray, none of them returned to the wooden box fastened to the wall that was clearly intended for them. Tiny silver shavings were strewn, confetti-like, across the length of the table, mixed in with bits of colored stone. There were little piles of these semiprecious bits—agate, coral, malachite, azurite, black onyx, obsidian. On one end of the table sat a block of turquoise similar in size and design to Lady Cray's piece. There were a couple of small machines Jury couldn't identify, an acetylene torch, goggles to wear when using the torch, what looked like a hand grinding-machine, and a couple of jewelers' loupes. On the outer edge of the long table were dark scars, indentations of blistered, blackened wood that suggested burning cigarettes had been parked there, lighted ends out. Angela Hope had been a serious smoker. For no reason other than his recent conversion, Jury counted fifteen of these marks, evenly interspersed in a line along the edge and creating a dark design. He could not help but smile at the sign of Angela Hope's addiction and he wondered how often she'd tried to stop and couldn't. He felt a kinship for her. The state of her worktable made it look as if Angela had simply risen from the high stool and walked out for a cup of coffee. And another cigarette. An air of expectancy, of imminent return, hung about her workspace. With a small camera he'd brought along, he started snapping pictures.

Back in the showroom itself, there were the usual glass display cases and the usual shelves lining both walls. One display case he was fairly sure held Angela's own work. It had a fineness of quality—the turquoise clusters set in hammered silver—that the pieces in the other case lacked. Also, every piece in it was turquoise or silver and turquoise. Even his uneducated eye could see the difference between that case and the other which held pretty but undistinguished jewelry. There were pins of abalone and coral, intricately worked gold and silver bracelets, bolo ties, and some of the Hopi and blackware pots that were so popular. On the wall opposite were shelves of books, a stereo, a row of kachina dolls that were not for sale. All of this together with the two armchairs positioned on either side of a rosewood table created a homey atmosphere, disturbed now by dust and dead petals fallen from a vase of withered roses. In one corner sat an aluminum coffee urn and plastic cups and a sign that invited customers to help themselves. The commercial side had been tempered by these efforts to create an atmosphere of welcome. He could imagine that Angela herself might sit in one of these armchairs and talk with a customer. It was more than likely, since she created original pieces of jewelry for people, that this would be the case. Talking over designs, taking measurements of wrists and ring fingers.

Feeling himself to be a voyeur, he opened drawers, went through notebooks and papers. Yes, Angela was a messy person. All manner of things had been shoved in together—letters, bills, accounting books. And in the general mess were the indications of someone trying to stop smoking: a packet of plastic filters, one used, the others forgotten; nicotine chewing gum; another filter, tar-stained. So he'd been right. Soul mate. He smiled a little. Again, he wished he'd known her.

Jury drew out one of the accounting books, recently dated, and opened it, hoping that perhaps Angela was one of those shopkeepers who entered names and addresses of customers who had bought from her once, hoping they would buy from her twice if the name was added to a mailing list. Angela wasn't that sort of shopkeeper. For tax purposes, she had kept records. But for all Jury could see, she didn't have a mailing list, and certainly hadn't collected personal information about her customers. Her salesmanship probably stopped at handing out her little cards, the name of the shop silver-embossed across its surface. Phone number, fax number, doing double duty, the same one that had turned up in Fanny Hamilton's address book.

He left the desk to study the silver work displayed in the glass case and on the shelves on the left wall. Her work seemed very fine and elegant, smooth and unemblazoned with the geometry of Indian designs he'd been looking at in the shop windows around the plaza. There were a number of crosses. Oddly, the crosses were the most elaborately worked of all the silver pieces. Both sides had been executed with circles, vines, curls—minute intaglio designs barely discernible, since the crosses were so small—an inch long at most, some little more than half. He picked up a bracelet inset with an oval turquoise and was surprised by its lightness and the airiness of the silver band.

On the middle shelf sat three turquoise sculptures similar to Lady Cray's, but of different sizes, slightly different in design. They were roughly the size one might want for a paperweight and he supposed that might be the purpose a customer who insisted on something utilitarian would put the block of stone to. Lady Cray's use of it was purely aesthetic. He wished Angela Hope were alive to appreciate that.

He wished Angela were alive, period. Holding the smallest of the turquoise and silver squares, he sat down in one of the armchairs. This one was banded round the center with silver, accented by a small bronze lizard. It looked a little like a belt with a bronze buckle. Neither of the other two turquoise blocks had bronze accents; perhaps she wanted to experiment with something different. What Jury was fairly certain of, having searched a dozen jewelers' windows near the square, was that this particular adaptation of turquoise to silver was unique with Angela Hope. He had seen nothing at all like this.

Jury was reaching the same conclusion as Macalvie. Only Macalvie had leapt to his immediately. Jury was not enthusiastic about such leaps—they were a little like leaps of faith, he thought, with nothing but the tenacity of instinct. Yet, his instinct was uncanny. Macalvie, however, would not call it "instinct" at all: he would call it something like meteoric calculation, such a swift taking in of facts that the conclusion would only appear to have been reached through "instinct." His facts were not precisely other people's facts.

Too many coincidences had piled up to ignore Macalvie's theory. This turquoise block, Frances Hamilton's visit to Santa Fe at the same time Nell Hawes had come here. Both had stayed at the La Fonda. Both in November. He set the turquoise block on the wide arm of the chair and drew out the same photocopied pages he had sent to Melrose Plant. This errant telephone number belonging to a person who had never heard of either Nell Hawes or Frances Hamilton. Jury studied it. Something odd about that number, he thought. It didn't resemble the others, nor had it been entered like the others that had been written carefully into the small lined squares.

Jury got up, checked the stereo, saw there was a CD in place, and punched the Play button. Flute music, notes as clear as crystal, filled the air. It was soothing stuff, he thought. It fit the country. Well, no wonder, it was Native American music. To the right of the stereo was a long row of books. An eclectic mix. Sharing the shelf with a number of works about Indian culture and some of archaeology were an assortment of Nancy Drews. He pulled out *The Secret of the Spiral Staircase* and leafed through it, loving the illustrations. Nancy with her flashlight, Nancy in her white socks and saddle shoes. Halfway through the book, he noticed marginalia, comments such as "obviously!" or "use your brain!!" or "I saw this coming a mile!!!" That last appeared near the end where the villain was (apparently) unveiled. Someone—the younger sister, Mary, perhaps?—had fancied herself a much better detective than Nancy Drew.

He replaced the revisionist Nancy Drew and read the spines of the others. *Sarum*, the fictional work about Old Salisbury and Stonehenge, which had also been given several thorough readings. Several volumes by writers who had popularized types of mysticism, such as Alan Watts. *Persuasion* by Jane Austen, a Raymond Chandler mystery, a couple of books by local writers.

One of the unfamiliar titles interested Jury. It had been written by Nils Anders with the odd title *Shattered Light*. Odd for a scientist, that is. Jury took it over to the armchair and sat down. The small picture on the inside of the dust jacket was of a man who clearly didn't enjoy having his picture taken. His head was tilted, his eyes cast down, as if finding down there something infinitely more interesting than the camera. Early middle age, perhaps not even that—late thirties, maybe. What Jury could see of his face appeared to be handsome, but given the angle, hard to say. Hair lightish and somewhat curly. The eyes were impossible to read, of course, being cast down. His mouth was slightly open, as if he'd been caught in the act of speaking. And in the bit of bio here there was a string of letters after his name that suggested even more degrees than Jack Oñate had mentioned. A couple of awards, too. Funds for his work happily supplied by several organizations.

Jury opened the book at random and was immediately lost in a labyrinthine description of light and its effects that he could no more understand than fly to the source of it. Jury tried again: he started on the first page, far more accessible since it was constructed as a sort of conversation between Dr. Anders and someone who had interviewed him a while back. They were having a little chat, this interchange apparently made use of by Anders to draw the lay reader into the book. It was effective, too, since Dr. Anders was no mean writer himself, with a certain flair for description—surroundings, people (especially the obviously vapid woman doing the interviewing)—a writer that Mary Hope might not even edit. It also had the advantage of delivering a message to the reader: Look, you're not as smart as I am, true; but then you're not as stupid as *she* is, right? Jury almost laughed. A clever ploy, and a necessary one, for the reader was about to be plunged into a universe that seemed to be made up of anything but solids: particles, lasers, equations, theorems, pis.

Given that he was such a "pure" scientist ("whatever that means," added Anders), did he believe in anything? His reaction to this question was given in such sardonic words that Jury thought surely the interviewer would have jumped and run. But his answer was quite simple. "Light." Simple, but strange enough that Jury could fairly hear the indrawn breath of the woman, the breathy little laugh, the disbelief. "Yes, but what *else*?" she asked.

"There is nothing else," he answered, tossing some papers on the table and immediately beginning to bury her in a morass of numbers.

Jury looked up, frowning. There *is* nothing else?

His mind seemed to tumble, something in the manner of the tumblers in a safe when one turns the combination. Things both clicked into place and blew away, helter-skelter. Unfortunately, the clicks were dependent on what had literally blown away and would have to be gathered back, raked in like tumbleweed across a dusty plain, before it would make any sense. He knew of no other way to describe his state of mind.

Thus, he closed the book, shook his head to try to clear it. The dust jacket was quite beautiful, showing a vision of the cosmos, silver bursts of nebulae against a blue-purple background, and all overlaid on something that looked like a broken mirror. Well, *Shattered Light*, he expected.

He started to return the book to its place on the shelf, paused, slipped it into a big pocket on the inside of his coat.

There were a few volumes of poetry, a thick Robert Frost, a thinner T. S. Eliot. *Four Quartets*. Here was a series of mystical flashes Jury had read more than once and, on the one hand, been moved to a point of fear; on the other, found impossible to comprehend. Jury approached most poetry with apprehension, timidity even, and with insulated gloves on. Poetry could catch you unawares. He opened *Four Quartets* and saw that here too sections had been heavily underscored and the occasional cross-reference written in the margin.

Who then devised the torment? Love.

Abruptly, Jury snapped it shut, eliding the next words in that act. He did not want to read about lost innocence. Or roses turned to dust. Or dry fountains.

What Jury wanted to do was avoid the deep for the shallow water, which Eliot would no doubt consider as self-consignment to Purgatory. Well, at least it wasn't Hell. Love. Love was rather terrifying. Something so hard to find should not be so easily lost. He closed the book and thought, again, of Jenny; he ran through his memories in that ominous state of mind that prophesies disaster. His memories of Jenny were, actually, few: on the other side of a grave; alone in that great empty house she'd been forced to sell; and in that pawnshop off Saint Martin's Lane, where she'd tried on a ring Jury was buying for someone else; and, lately, in Ryland Street. Years had separated these meetings, making them that much more emblematic, rich with unstated, perhaps unconscious meanings.

Jury much preferred to skate on the thin ice of consciousness. And he was beginning to think that thin ice might be all the ice there was.

Opening the book again, he looked at the title page. Nils Anders had given this book of poetry to Angela Hope. Angela Hope was taking it all very seriously.

THE WOMAN who came into the shop and demanded to know his business finally introduced herself as Sukie Bartholomew. Her favorite posture appeared to be the one she now adopted: one arm across her midsection, one hand cupping the elbow of the other arm, the other hand holding a small black cigar. The two arms formed an L that might have served as a frame for the viewer to look at Sukie Bartholomew. She was fighting hard to project an image; she wasn't winning. She was not attractive—raw-boned, thin, possibly in her late fifties, but still wearing blue barrettes to clasp and hold back her shoulder-length hair. It was mouse-brown and blunt-cut. But the color had been highlighted so that wispy little strands gave the impression of silver dust. Too many visits to the local hairdresser had resulted in hair the texture of straw.

Sukie Bartholomew was waging a war with herself over her looks. No lipstick, but there was that glimmery brown eye shadow; an uncompromising haircut, but carefully highlighted; an outfit that fairly screamed "I won't bow to fashion," but one that belonged on a girl of fifteen, not a woman of fifty-plus. Jury noted these contradictions because he inferred they spelled trouble. A difficult woman, uneasy with herself, dissatisfied, and therefore dissatisfied with the rest of the world. It was as if she eschewed the trap of femininity, the little embellishments that made women attractive to men. Jury had not really thought of it before, but the women he admired were not ones to do pitched battle with themselves over a bit of nail varnish or a dab of lipstick. He thought of Fiona, whose fountain of youth was gathered in her sponge bag rather than in her medicine cabinet, and that reminded him, again, of Wiggins. He *must* remember to send flowers. He smiled at the morning sunlight streaking the shop's polished floor as all of this passed before his mind's eye in a few swift seconds. He must have raised the smile to Sukie, for she asked,

"Something funny?" The tone was surely more hostile than such a smile had called for.

"No. Not at all. You remind me of . . . someone, that's all."

"Someone pleasant, I trust?"

Her expression was gratingly coy. The smile that accompanied this primping tone was more unpleasant than the frown had been.

"Yes. Very pleasant."

With a much-beringed hand, she flattened the already flat hairdo against her cheek. "You're here about Angela, I suppose. Terribly sad."

Jury doubted she felt sad at all. "When did you last see her?"

"Just before she left. We saw one another often. We had coffee, you know, that sort of thing."

"You knew her well."

Slowly, she drew in on her cigar and exhaled thin streams of smoke through her nostrils. Jury's eyes tracked the upward spiral of smoke.

"She didn't really talk a great deal about herself, about her feelings. People don't, you know. That's one of the problems."

He was not about to ask which one, or what the others were. It was clear she'd have gone straight off the topic of Angela Hope and onto herself in an eyeblink. He made his smile as ingratiating as possible. "I'm told she lived outside of town, some miles away, with her younger sister."

"Mary. Difficult girl. Angela herself was much more malleable."

His eyebrows rose fractionally. Strange sort of thing to want a friend—or anybody—to be. Malleable.

"Tell me about this U.K. trip of hers. Had she any particular reason for going to England?"

"Angela was extremely interested in ancient cultures, in ruins, stone circles, and so forth. She *loved* Mesa Verde. She was fascinated by the Anasazi culture." Sukie smoked her cigarillo and looked at the floor. "So I guess it didn't surprise me she'd turn up at Old Sarum."

"It must have surprised you she'd turn up dead, though." Jury pulled the small photos from his notebook. "Do you remember either of these women, Miss Bartholomew?"

" 'Ms.,' please." She took them.

"Sorry." It was better than "Sukie," at least.

After no more than a glance at the snaps of Nell and Fanny, she held them out to him. "No."

"They were probably in Canyon Road, both of them, in November. Are you sure? Mind having another look?" She sighed, studied the likenesses. "It's just that so *many* tourists come along here." Again, she shook her head, returned them.

"But not in November."

"You'd be surprised."

"Busy old place, Santa Fe. But I was told November was a slack month, or at least as much as trade here ever slackens." When she didn't respond, he said, "They're British citizens, actually. Names are Helen Hawes and Frances Hamilton. One's from London; one lived in Exeter. That's the West Country in England. I don't expect that means anything to you?" When she shook her head, he went on. "They were both here at the same time, one definitely stayed at the La Fonda Hotel, and we have reason to believe both were in Canyon Road. There's reason to believe they might have met over here, in Santa Fe or perhaps somewhere else—Arizona, possibly—and, you know, hitched up together. Not strange, as they would have felt compatriots."

"Are you saying they had something to do with Angela Hope? Is there a connection?"

"It's possible. What about her friends? Did you know any of them?"

"Not really, no. She was very friendly with someone who works at the Institute—"

"The Santa Fe Institute?"

"You've heard of it?"

Jury nodded.

"Scientists. They work on rather elaborate theories, I'm told. She saw a lot of Dr. Anders."

"Anyone else?"

"There's Malcolm Corey. Most of us know him; he's got one of the galleries."

"Is her sister around?"

"No. At least I haven't seen her in the last few days. Probably at their house. It's near Chimayo. No, somewhere around Tesuque. But not *in* Tesuque."

"Had Angela Hope no other family?" They were standing near the window, and Jury looked out on the street, at a low roof that served as an awning across the stone patio, where several white tables were set out to gleam in the sunlight, despite the cold.

"None I know of."

"What will her sister do, now?"

Sukie Bartholomew shrugged. "Go on as she's been going, I guess. She's pretty competent, from the little I can gather."

Nobody is that competent, thought Jury.

She nodded toward the window and across the street. "Malcolm's right there, if you want to talk to him. He always has his coffee over there around ten."

Jury looked again at the table and saw a blond-haired man sitting coatless in the cold, slumped down in the white metal chair, face turned sunward. True, the sun was strong and the air gentle, but still it was February.

"Makes me cold just to look at him."

She snorted. "Malcolm sacrifices comfort to his *mise en scène*. I don't know why he left California. Imagines he's an actor. *Imagines* he's a painter. Awful stuff he does, big streaks of this and that. He always sits over there around this time. Having coffee."

Jury was dying for a cup of coffee or tea. And a cigarette. He bet he hadn't missed one inhalation, one indrawn breath of that cigar she was smoking. How was he supposed to keep his mind on his job without a cigarette?

He thanked Sukie Bartholomew and made his way across the street.

TWENTY-SIX

Sunburnt blond hair, slicked back and slightly damp, as if he'd just spent his customary hour at some indoor pool; Italian-cut trousers, sneakers, no socks, sunlamp tan. You could just tell.

"Malcolm Corey?"

In the slightly smug smile, there was the look of the freshly anointed, the face turned upward again as if to receive the blessing of the sun. "Why?"

"It's about Angela Hope." Jury flipped open his warrant card and smiled as if extending the blessing of Scotland Yard.

The eyes cast themselves down to come into contact with the warrant card and Jury saw the smooth face go a little slacker, then tighten in a frown, deepening lines from nose to mouth. Not so young, after all. Past forty, Jury decided. "Mind if I sit down? I could do with a cup of coffee."

It was pretty clear that Malcolm Corey minded; still, he removed his sneakered foot from the chair opposite, shoving it a little in Jury's direction. From the manner in which Corey held his head to one side and arranged his features, one could tell that he was finding a role to play and an audience to play it to.

"I heard about Angela. Pretty awful."

A waitress with a headful of bobbing blond curls appeared with a cup of frothy cappuccino. She wore an embroidered skirt and many ropes of colored beads. She also wore a less than happy expression, looking at her customer.

"Thanks, m'dear," said Corey, showing white teeth. "You care for one?"

Jury nodded. She strode away. Everyone in Santa Fe seemed to stride, rather than walk.

"She was a friend of yours, is that correct?"

"Judi?" Malcolm Corey looked at the departing back of the waitress, puzzled. "Judi? You're interested in my sexual conquests? Oh, sorry, I thought you meant our server. You mean Angela?"

"I mean Angela."

"I knew her pretty well, yes. We're all on Canyon Road here." He nodded in the direction of the Silver Heron. "Angela was a silversmith, I guess would be the word. Or turquoise-smith. That's what she did, silver and turquoise. Nice stuff." He had taken but one sip of coffee before turning his tan face sunward again, eyes closed.

"That's what I understand. What I don't understand is why a Santa Fe silversmith would wind up dead at Old Sarum. Can you cast any light on that?"

That he could probably cast light wasn't the question; which kind of light was. Malcolm beamed his face up to the sky. "The Sarum part doesn't surprise me." He was looking at Jury now and extracting a vial of pills from his white jacket and inspecting it.

Sukie Bartholomew's response. Jury sighed. "Why not?"

"Because Angela was nuts about archaeology, digs, things like that. Standing stones, mystical circles." From the pill bottle he took a yellow tablet that Jury recognized (wouldn't anybody?) and started to reseal it. Then he arched his eyebrows in a question and extended the vial to Jury. "Valium?"

"No thanks. Had mine."

He crushed up his tablet with the back of his spoon and sprinkled it, like cinnamon, across the froth. He smiled his toothy smile. "Santa Fe style."

"Getting back to you and Angela Hope—" He gave the curly-haired waitress a smile that she didn't appreciate. Her look was fixed on Corey as she set down Jury's coffee.

"Who linked me with Angela Hope, incidentally? Sukie Bartholomew, I bet. What a bitch." Now he was popping the top from an aspirin bottle.

"Not really. Sergeant Oñate of the Santa Fe police. You spoke with him, remember?"

He gave a grunt of affirmation and spooned the Valium foam from his cappuccino.

Yummy. Jury looked down at his own delicious-looking brew and wondered why in hell he was feeling so superior to just about everybody else in Santa Fe. "You *were* her friend, though?"

"Implying a sexual liaison?" Malcolm Corey tossed back a couple of aspirin tablets which he washed down with the small glass of milk at his elbow. "Rough night."

Jury smiled briefly in sympathy. What we put ourselves through, he thought. Valium. Aspirins. Milk to coat the stomach. Perhaps because of his work, Jury was a comparative stranger to "rough nights." Drink had never been one of his problems. It was not a strength, though, merely a lack of inclination and time. When he looked at the Valium-aspirin-milk melange, his desire for a cigarette blessedly waned, at least for now.

"Why's Scotland Yard interested in this?"

"Well, the thing is, you see, she died on British soil." (Sounded pompous enough, he supposed.) "We're just working together with the New Mexico police on this."

"Uh-huh. Scotland *Yard*, though? Isn't Old Sarum in the west of England somewhere? You guys go out there, do you?"

"Old Sarum's outside of Salisbury. Wiltshire."

"It just sounds goddamned heavy-duty, getting you guys in on it."

"No. I'm just helping out the county police over there. Angela Hope died in extremely peculiar circumstances. And we still haven't determined the cause of death."

That seemed to stump him. "I just assumed—"

"What?"

He shrugged. "I don't know. Natural causes, I guess."

"Certainly, that's possible. And if she'd collapsed, say, in Salisbury's High Street, probably she'd have been taken to hospital and that would have been the end of it—" *Not if Macalvie were in charge,* Jury added to himself, smiling. "—but instead she died rather dramatically at Old Sarum. Papers make a meal of that sort of thing. From all we could determine, she'd gone there around sunset, or just before the place closed."

Malcolm Corey nodded and gazed at the sky. "Sounds like Angela."

"Does it?"

"Spiritual sort of girl. She was always clambering around through pueblos, Canyon de Chelly, Chaco, places like that." He sighed, as if with relief, and tipped back his chair. The Valium had probably kicked in. Jury wondered if Valium helped nicotine withdrawal. "Angela was intrigued by ancient cultures, especially Indian culture. Hopi, Anasazi. She spent a lot of time driving back and forth to Mesa Verde with Mary."

"Sorry, but what's Mesa Verde?"

Malcolm looked at him with the mild contempt he probably reserved for tourists. "Mesa Verde's famous for its ruins—cliff houses, that sort of thing. Anasazi ruins."

"Mary Hope was interested in all of this, too?" Somehow, it didn't sound like the editor of Nancy Drew.

He nodded and rubbed at his temples. "Because Angela was and probably wanted the company. Mary loved Angela. She's thirteen-going-on-a-hundred. Hard to take."

"Meaning what?"

"She looks at me as if I were a total eclipse."

Jury laughed. "Was she jealous? Of your relationship to her sister?"

"You're back on that again, are you? Got sex on the brain. We didn't have that kind of 'relationship.' " He leered. "Not that I didn't try."

Jury believed him. Malcolm wasn't the sort to admit to a failure at a sexual conquest. "If she was interested in that sort of thing, what about this New Age movement?"

"Angela wasn't into that. That's Sukie Bartholomew's move. Bitch. Met her? She's got the shop right next to the Silver Heron. Sells aroma-therapy junk. Crystals and so forth."

"She'd been to Sedona several times, though?"

"Hasn't *everyone* been to Sedona?"

"I haven't. There were an American and a British woman over here who we think might have known Angela Hope."

"Oh? Is that significant?"

"I think so. They're both dead." He produced the photos of Helen Hawes and Frances Hamilton. "Ever see these two women on Canyon Road?"

Malcolm shook his head. "No. This is strange. But it sounds like coincidence to me."

"Could be. But when you get enough 'coincidences' together, well, then it looks more like something else." Jury looked across the way at the little jewelry establishment. "Mrs. Hamilton took a turquoise block with a silver figure of Kokepelli engraved in the side back to London. To me, it looked a lot like Angela Hope's work. Does it look familiar?"

"Silver and turquoise is pretty common here." Malcolm was lining up the arrows on the aspirin bottle top again. "My head's killing me. And I'm on call, too." He frowned deeply.

" 'On call'?"

"The movie. You must have seen the crews around the plaza. It's a nothing part, no lines, but—" He shrugged, and then, as if the movement pained him, rubbed his temples.

Suddenly recalling that Wiggins had fitted him out with a supply of Wiggins anodynes, Jury drew out the plastic bag. Inside the one small bag were several even tinier ones. Seven of them. Seven, each with a letter and a color. Jury had promptly tossed the code away. He was surprised he hadn't tossed out the contents with it. He lined up the seven packets on the table. "There's something here might help." Jury frowned over the colored letters and numbers. What the hell was "H"? Could be headache, could be hangover—since Jury didn't have hangovers, this must be headache. Then he wondered *why* he was debating the meaning of the "H," since none of this stuff would do anyone any whacking good. He looked at the three bags with carefully colored-in numbers. The "H" being red meant that any packet with a red dot went along with it.

"Might I ask what all that is, Superintendent?"

"It's something my chemist made up for me. One in particular for an ailment is good, but two in concert works miracles." Jury shoved over the one marked "H." "Headache. And this one with it will take care of whatever goes with it. Nausea, et cetera."

Malcolm frowned, looking down at the two little plastic bags. "Looks like herbs to me."

Jury merely grunted in reply. Probably, that's exactly what the bags contained—herbs. Wiggins and Mrs. Wassermann putting their heads together, no doubt. He still remembered Wiggins with that goddamned rue up his nose, supposed to be good for the sinuses, that was. Rue, rosemary. If the two of them had been around, Ophelia would have been the picture of health.

"I'm not much on herbal remedies," said Malcolm doubtfully. "Give me my chemicals every time, thank you. Why won't people face it that Valium and Percodan have kicked Mother Nature's ass?" He rattled the vial.

Valium and Percodan weren't a patch on illusion, lies, and Sergeant Wiggins. "I agree, usually. But this stuff, taken in combination, will evaporate that head. Trust me." Trouble was, Jury couldn't figure out the combination. Color-marker letters were supposed to be in league with the colored numberings. 2.2/3–5. What in the hell was that supposed to mean? Maybe the 2.2 meant two doses. Why in hell was he trying to figure it out, anyway? He shoved this little bag across to Malcolm. "Now, what you do with this one is take two doses."

Malcolm frowned. "Two? How much is that?"

"One dose is three milligrams and the other one is five." Jury looked steadily into his eyes. "But you only take two times three. I know," Jury said in a tone meant to reassure. "It's very complex."

Malcolm scratched his head. "God, your chemist should be up at the Institute with the rest of them. So how do I take this stuff? Just put it on my tongue?"

"Beef tea is best."

"What's that?"

"Like bouillon." The pert-looking waitress was just then setting down two more coffees. Malcolm asked her for some beef bouillon or consommé.

As if pleased to give him any bad news she could, with a shake of her Bo-Peep curls, she said, "If it's not on the menu, you can't have it."

"Why? *You're* not on the menu and I've had—"

Red circles blossomed on her cheeks as she stared at him in a fury. She flounced away; Malcolm shrugged.

Jury was beginning to like Malcolm Corey. He wasn't as stuffy as he'd first seemed. More sardonic than conceited, perhaps. "Tell me more about Angela Hope."

"Not much that I know. They live outside of town, and I think there's a housekeeper, some old Indian woman. I've never seen her. The parents died years and years ago, so I guess Angela had to have some help when Mary was little, someone to take care of her. Though, frankly, there's one person I'd stake my life on not needing care."

"Tough kid, huh? But we all do, some time or other. Need taking care of. I get the impression you and Mary aren't mates."

That he took to be very funny. "To say the least. Not just me, however. Mary looks at you as if she's looking straight *through*, looking through to the something or somebody stupid enough to set you in her line of vision in the first place." He laughed, looked behind him as if there might be such a person back there. Probably just restless for his beef bouillon. "But as I say, I'm not the only one. Mary's gaze must have absolutely *evaporated* Sukie Bartholomew where she stood."

"She's only a little girl," Jury protested.

"Uh-huh. Well, she was very protective of Angela. I wondered sometimes who took care of who in that twosome. Mary saw Sukie as a threat, I think."

"Was she jealous of the Bartholomew woman's friendship with her sister?"

Malcolm made a sound in his throat disdaining such a ridiculous notion. "Jealousy is one of those mundane and mortal emotions Mary doesn't stoop to."

"Come on." Jury laughed. "You make her sound less than human."

"Or more than." Malcolm reflected. "I think she talks to trees and coyotes. Actually, she's got this coyote that she's trying to convince me is a dog. Some dog."

"A *tame* coyote?" Jury laughed.

"Is it? Beats me. That's why I give the damned dog a wide berth."

The waitress was back with the cup of bouillon and set it before Malcolm without comment. She left, rather hurriedly.

"So I stir this stuff up in it?" When Jury nodded, he sprinkled the contents of both packets into the broth. Jury watched as he sipped. "Hmm. Doesn't taste bad." He wrinkled his nose. "Get a whiff of marjoram, I think. Maybe sage."

"Uh-huh."

"How long's it supposed to take to work?"

"Ten minutes. Faster than Valium."

"Sukie sells a lot of crap like this—oh, sorry. I don't mean *this* is. Sukie just goes in for old Indian remedies. Roots. Rocks. Tree bark."

" 'Rocks'?"

"Yeah. Pebbles and so forth." He blew on the bouillon, drank the rest.

Jury would have to take this cure home to Wiggins. "What kinds of pebbles?"

"Who knows?" Malcolm leaned down, stretched out his arm, scooped up a little earth between the flagstones. "Like these." He picked out a few broken bits of rock. He was leaning back again, face raised skyward, eyes closed.

"Let me ask you something: if Angela Hope was murdered—?"

The eyes snapped open as if a host of flashbulbs had just gone off in his face. "*Murdered?*"

"It's possible."

"Angela murdered? You're asking me, can I think of anyone who hated her enough to kill her?" He shook his head. "No. And, anyway, if it were someone from around here, that person would have had to hop a plane to Britain." He frowned. "Only one who's done that is Dolly Schell, her cousin."

"To identify the body."

"So she'd be leaving it a little late, wouldn't she, for murder?" Malcolm said sarcastically.

"There's money. Love. Revenge. As motives, I mean. Not just hatred."

Again, he shook his head. "Didn't have any money I know of. I seriously doubt Angela would have done anything to warrant revenge. And I don't think Psyche would actually kill her for love of yours truly." He flashed Jury a smile.

"Competition?"

"Well . . ." The syllable trailed off. "She's been watching us, you know, ever since you sat down." But he didn't look in that direction and neither did Jury. "A real bitch."

"Yes, you've mentioned that before."

"Have you got the Santa Fe Institute on your little list? There's some guy, some scientist over there, who seemed to know her pretty well."

"Anders. But I haven't talked to him."

Malcolm rubbed his temple. "I still feel like shit."

"Hasn't been ten minutes yet. Trust me."

"Oh, I do, I do," he said without conviction.

For a few more minutes they sat there, Malcolm with eyes closed, slouched in his chair. Jury looking directly across the street into the shadowy face of Sukie Bartholomew. He waved. The face quickly disappeared.

"Hey." Malcolm suddenly opened his eyes. "You're right; it's mostly gone."

"Good. Well, I'll be off." Jury got up, pocketing the remaining plastic bags. Looking down at the one labeled "N," he sighed. "Wouldn't happen to have a cigarette, would you?"

"I don't smoke."

"Thank God."

TWENTY-SEVEN

If ever a photograph didn't do justice to a person, it was the dust-jacket photo of Nils Anders. It had not, among other things, given any indication of the man's intensity, although the book itself would probably have conveyed that. He was considerably more handsome than the photo allowed, and was, in person, as engaging as he appeared in the opening pages of his book. Jury stood inside Anders's office at the Santa Fe Institute thinking that if the man had decided to become a priest, a missionary, or a guru he'd have had no trouble in winning apostles. If he'd become a serial killer, God help us all.

On women, he must have wrought absolute havoc.

Certainly, the woman talking to Anders when Jury entered was one who had fallen under his spell, given the way she was looking at him. Jury hung back in the doorway and heard her extending a dinner invitation.

To which Anders replied, "I don't think I can make it, Dolly."

"Even you have to eat," she said, as if he were generally thought of as someone more than mortal.

It was clear to Jury that Dr. Anders wasn't aware of his effect on this woman, or of his turning down her invitation. Her face, when she turned to leave, was a mask of woe. Jury stepped aside as she swept through the door, barely glancing at him. He smiled. She didn't.

Anders offered Jury a molded plastic chair and sat himself down on a wooden swivel chair. As Jury told him his reason for being there, Anders swung backwards and forwards, slowly, rhythmically. Then he stopped and the chair creaked a little.

"Angie." He shook his head briefly, looked down at nothing and then past Jury, again at nothing.

That he said nothing else surprised Jury, for Anders struck him as a man who would be in constant motion, charged with energy that he could release only in act or words. But instead, Anders sat for some moments, having uttered the name only; Jury was rather glad to hear it shortened, as that bespoke a kind of closeness. But Anders neither verified nor denied that closeness.

Jury went on. "I understand you were a very good friend of hers, Dr. Anders."

"I was, yes." Then Anders looked at him, slightly surprised. His changeable eyes darkened. "You mean sexual?"

Jury shrugged slightly. "It's just a question. You don't have to answer it, certainly."

Anders's look dismissed such a possibility. "I don't have much time for women, Mr. Jury. Love affairs are too consuming." He paused and looked off into that space again. "I was in love once. . . ." His voice trailed off; his tone a little wondering, questing, quizzical, as if recalling a poorly formulated hypothesis, an inconclusive experiment—something he might still be turning over in his mind and wondering where it had gone wrong.

"Why do others seem to think the two of you were lovers?"

"I don't know." Anders laughed. "You'll have to ask *them*, won't you?"

He rocked in his swivel chair. His smile was such that Jury had the uncomfortable sense he was serving as a source of amusement for Nils Anders, who then asked, "Why's it important, either way?"

"I don't know, Dr. Anders; that's the truth. I'm just trying to get a fix on Angela Hope. What her life was like."

Anders nodded, clasped his hands behind his neck, tilting sideways slightly. It was a boyish gesture, as if he might be about to zoom off, pretending he was an airplane. He said, "That's reasonable. Assuming, of course, it's reasonable you're here in the first place." He flashed Jury a smile, totally disarming.

It was a point in his favor, Jury thought, that he wasn't at all interested in who had given Jury this impression.

Then more soberly, Anders said: "Angela. Yes." The eyes literally appeared to cloud over, blue evaporating to a wintry gray. "Don't think my attitude trivializes Angie's death. That left me feeling very empty. Angie was someone I really liked, liked to be around, liked to talk to. There aren't many people I feel that way about. They'll waste your time, give 'em half a chance, in mind-numbing social chat. Angela didn't do that; when she talked, she talked about things that were important to her."

"May I ask what they were, those things?"

It was snowing now, flakes as big as stones, and looking heavy as them too, in their weighty descent. Anders's eyes were fixed on a point out there somewhere and Jury felt impelled to follow the direction of his gaze.

Nothing except big flakes of snow drifting onto the winding road that had probably once divided empty land but which now twisted through million-dollar properties. Jury waited, but Anders didn't answer.

"Dr. Anders?"

"Hm? Oh. Sorry. I was just looking at the snow. It looks backlit, doesn't it? Angela. Hmm."

Jury followed his gaze. "It reminds you of Angela?"

"Not directly. But then, few things are direct, are they. Light is my, ah, thesis, I'd guess you'd say. Focus. I wrote this book—"

"I saw it, on Angela Hope's shelf." He didn't tell Anders he'd borrowed it.

"The title is just another way of saying 'scattered consciousness.' "

"Meaning?"

"Meaning . . . meaning. It's too simple to say 'lack of focus.' But that's the best I can do at the moment." He smiled. "My mind's muddled today."

Meaning, really, that Jury's probably was. The human condition. Jury smiled, too. "What things was Angela interested in, can you tell me?"

"Sure. Besides her work, the culture of the Hopis, the Anasazi, myth, ritual, the land—I mean, this country. It's very beautiful, isn't it?" Jury nodded; he went on. "She thought it all had something to do with personal salvation. Hers."

"In what way?"

"It's very difficult to understand somebody else's 'way.' I'll tell you one thing; she had a lot of respect for silence. That's tough for people. Well, not for me; I'm off in one world or another, in one of my fugue states. An irritating habit, I've been told more than once, by more than one. Angie had a sort of mystical turn of mind. . . ." He paused, frowning. "But, to tell the truth, well, I hate to be patronizing, but it was the trendy sort of mysticism. You know, reciting mantras, or praying in a corner given over to icons and candles. That sort. Not muscular."

Although Anders didn't actually scoff, Jury imagined it was only because Angela Hope had been a good friend. " 'Muscular'? What do you mean?"

"The sort of mysticism you have to take to the gym and exercise until you sweat buckets. Saint John of the Cross. T. S. Eliot. That kind."

"*Four Quartets* was in her bookcase. She certainly appeared to have given it a good thumbing through."

"Uh-huh," said Anders, noncommittally.

"Was she enthusiastic about your own work?"

He laughed. "Would have been, I'm sure, if she'd understood it."

Jury smiled. "I read a little of the book. I guess I opened it somewhere in the middle. I have to admit, it's too deep for me."

"Never start in the middle. Never."

"How do I look at a circle, then?"

Like everything else about him, Anders's laughter was engaging. "Okay, dammit, you've got me."

"I wish I did. I wish I could understand this sort of abstract thinking."

He snorted. "Surely, you're not going to tell me your thinking is all evidential?"

"Yes, I expect it is."

Nils Anders started ticking points off on his fingers: "You don't know Angela Hope, you don't know why she died, you don't know if you'll learn anything in Santa Fe. Yet here you are, five thousand miles from home, sitting in that chair."

"No, you're wrong. There *is* evidence to indicate I *should* be here, sitting in this chair." Jury smiled, told him about the connection between the three women, the notebook, the whole strange chain of events.

"That's not evidence; that's inference. Abstraction. Because there's a shadow, there must be a man. Plato's cave, though that wasn't Plato's point."

Jury shook his head, smiled. He relaxed even more. He was up for a game. "Actually, I expect the reason I'm here is a friend of mine, another cop, looked at the deaths of Angela Hope, Helen Hawes, and Frances Hamilton and made a wild surmise."

"*Yes!*" The other man's fists shot into the air, like some kid who'd just hit the jackpot on the fruit machine or won the pools. " 'Wild surmises' are precisely what I mean. Life is a wild surmise as far as I'm concerned. Trouble is, most of us refuse to entertain that idea; it's too frightening. We refuse to see that a so-called totally irrational hypothesis is more dependable than a conclusion drawn from demonstrable premises—"

Jury interrupted him before Anders could get too caught up in his theories. "The reasons for murder are not so philosophical. They're more straightforward."

Nils Anders's eyebrows seemed to orbit. "Oh? Are we talking about murder?"

"I think so."

Then, with a slightly self-satisfied air, he folded his arms, said, "Okay, I'll bite."

Jury laughed. "I'm not sure I want to be bitten by you."

"I want to hear the straightforward reasons." He had reached behind him and pulled down a copy of his book, plucked a pen from his pocket, and scribbled something on the flyleaf. That task finished, he picked up a sheet of paper and started folding the corners neatly.

"Money, revenge, unrequited love, greed—well, money again— rage. And so forth." Jury felt slightly uncomfortable.

Anders stared at him. "That's *your* idea of 'not philosophical'? Hey, *hey*—" his hand shot out for the telephone—"let's call Plato, let's call Kant." He dropped the receiver back on the hook. "Mr. Jury, your terminology is not exactly slam-dunk, not precisely the ball thunking through the hoop. Leaving aside your odd understanding of the term 'philosophical,' where did you ever get the idea that the other term, 'straightforward,' was its antithesis?"

"Look, Dr. Anders." Jury felt his own tone and smile were a trifle condescending. "I mean 'clear.' You know what I mean."

Dangerously condescending, he decided when the other man's fist came down and made the papers on his desk jump. "Like hell I do!" Anders leaned forward and fixed Jury with blue eyes so intense they might have nailed him to the wall. "People are always saying 'you know what I mean.' How can I, when *you* don't know what you mean." Then he sat back and smiled. The three-second fit having dissipated completely.

Jury shook his head. "This cop—divisional commander, he is— would love you."

"The wild surmiser?"

Jury nodded. "He's been driving me nuts talking about concepts like 'deep time.' The thing is, I've always regarded him as the paradigmatically rational policeman. Yet, myself, I've always thought of as operating more on emotion and instinct. Seems I'm wrong. I seem to be the more rational one and the more superficial in my thinking."

Nils Anders sighed as if the student were being a deliberate dullard. "Mr. Jury, 'rational' has nothing to do with depths and surfaces. And it's not the *opposite* of 'emotional,' either. Why do people persist in that belief?" Anders's face took on an expression of genuine puzzlement, as if the stubbornness of humankind was totally beyond his ken. "What we're given to call 'emotional' can have its own underlying 'rationale.' Look at human behavior. Completely Janus-faced." He finished creasing his paper airplane. "I've decided there are four kinds. Two are benign—let's say the 'I love you' that means 'I love you,' and the 'I hate you' that means just that. Two are malignant— the 'I love you' that means 'I hate you,' and so forth. And all of these have their own rationale." He smiled at Jury. "And superficial, you are *not*. I know."

"How?"

"Because you've been sitting here—" Anders sailed his paper airplane over Jury's head—"for over a quarter of an hour, talking to me. Most people cut and run after five. We here at the Santa Fe Institute are definitely not the first choice of hostesses to fill in at dinner parties."

"Too bad. You might make the damned things more bearable." Jury tried to recall the last time he'd ever been to a dinner party. In Bradford, in Yorkshire—hadn't that been it?

"Thanks." His expression sobered, his tone became somber. "You think Angie was murdered?"

"It's possible. Accident's more likely, I expect." Jury shook his head. "Did she strike you as suicidal?"

Anders gave a disbelieving little laugh. "If you thought that, you wouldn't be here." He picked up a sheet of paper and started folding it as he had the other one, making a paper airplane. To his working fingers he said, "I would think Scotland Yard would do a lot of demystifying." The plane sailed from his fingers, was borne by a current of wind around in a circle, and finally landed by a filing cabinet. He regarded its fall and sighed. Then handed the book he'd written in to Jury.

"Well—thank you." Jury opened it, read the inscription. He smiled. Then he said, "The pathology report suggests Angela's health was delicate. Did you know if she had a heart condition?"

Anders shook his head. "I know she caught every virus that came down Canyon Road. Also had migraines."

"Oh? In that case she might have had a lot of medication at her disposal."

"Forget it," said Anders, laughing. "Not unless you can OD on ginseng or slippery elm or goldenseal. Angela didn't take the stuff. An overdose of Tylenol 3? Nope. The only time she'd ever take medicine, she said, was 'in extremis.' Dolly's worst customer."

Jury was momentarily confused. "Whose worst customer?"

"Dolly. The one who didn't wait to be introduced. The one who was in here when you came. She's a pharmacist. Dolly Schell."

Jury was surprised. "You mean *Dolores* Schell?"

Anders nodded. "I forgot. The police had her over there to iden-tify the remains. That's right. That must've been hard."

"I rang her last night; she wasn't in. I want to talk with her."

"Try the pharmacy. It's on Old Pecos Trail. 'Worst customer' because Angie hated doctors, so she didn't have prescriptions to get filled. I think maybe she blamed the medical profession for her mother's condition. Breast cancer, a too-late diagnosis."

"The parents died in a plane crash, the Santa Fe police told me."

"Yes, but her mother was close to death as it was. The late diag-nosis—maybe that was her mother's own fault. Angela was very bitter about doctors, I can tell you." He shrugged. "But that was probably just an excuse to keep from going to one. Most people think up excuses for fear, don't they?" He seemed to be concentrating on the paper plane, disappointed in its performance. "You haven't talked to Mary, have you?"

There was a change—a change of tone, a change of atmosphere. It was charged with something Jury couldn't put his finger on. He looked at Nils Anders, but the man had his eyes down.

"Not yet. I don't know where she is."

"School."

"It's Saturday."

"No kidding? Well, Mary's got her own agenda. Angela spent a lot of time looking for her." Anders laughed. "She found her once out in the middle of a stretch of desert about a mile from their house, out there with her dog, sitting on a rock. She asked her what she was doing. Mary said 'Nothing.' Angie said, well, she had to believe her. She's got this dog whose name is Suma—"

"Mr. Corey told me about it. He thinks it's a coyote, not a dog." Jury smiled.

Nils Anders smiled. "I bet it is. Mary claims it's mostly German shepherd because people don't look too kindly on coyotes at their heels. Anyway, it goes everywhere with her. Its *nickname* is Sunny. I love that." He started laughing. "I can't get over that, you know. The dog has a nickname."

"You like her, then?"

Anders looked surprised. "Mary? Hell, yes, of course I do. Who wouldn't?"

"I can name two people." Jury did.

His tone was scoffing, his hand waving that double-opinion away. "Sukie Bartholomew is a bit of a bitch." There was no rancor in the tone, though. He might have been stating a natural law.

Jury laughed. "Well, there you share the opinion of Malcolm Corey."

"Him. Mary isn't your stereotypical thirteen-year-old. I suppose if a kid loses two parents, both together . . ." He paused. "They had money, the parents, I mean. She inherited, he made it. The Darks—the mother was Sylvestra Dark—had a bit of money. Martin Hope had more. But you don't see any evidence of it in Angela or Mary. They live pretty simply."

"Angela was about twenty years older than Mary?"

"About. Angie was—thirty-one, I think. Thirty-two, perhaps. Very close, they were." He was quiet for a moment, turning again to look out of the window. "This is really tough for her. Did you try the house?"

"I rang the number this morning. No answer."

Anders frowned and chewed his lip. "Rosella—the house-keeper—is nearly always there." He was running his thumb back and forth across his forehead, abstracted. "Mary's probably just out . . . doing whatever Mary does. Mary's quiet—no, that's not right. 'Silent' is a better way of putting it." Then he smiled. "I could be trying to get something out of her—just by way of ordinary conversation, and she can stand right there like a monument to the monosyllable. 'Yes,' 'no,' 'yes,' grunt. But on the other hand she's highly imaginative. Or impressionable. Or both. Stuff spews out of her like volcanic rock." Anders turned his clear gaze on Jury and said: "She thinks Angie was murdered."

Jury was surprised. "What motive does she attribute to whoever—?"

"I told you. Mary's not big on details." Nils Anders turned his gaze to the window.

Jury felt it again. The suddenly charged atmosphere.

TWENTY-EIGHT

It was almost nostalgic in its way; it reminded Jury of any number of chemist's shops he'd been in when he was a kid—the narrow aisles, the crowded shelves, the flannels and plastic shower caps hanging from pins at the corner of one shelf. Except, of course, they didn't have soda fountains in chemist's shops in Britain. Too bad, he thought, looking at the marble countertop, the chrome shakers, the wooden stools that any kid would have loved to twirl on. There were a couple of kids there now, older ones, a boy and girl slurping up soft drinks. Behind the counter, a tall, skinny boy was reading a magazine called *Flex*. Muscular reading for one with no biceps, Jury thought.

Dolores Schell was in the rear, bent over a workspace, reading what he saw to be prescription blanks when he came up to her. "Miss Schell?"

Surprised, she raised her head. She was wearing horn-rimmed glasses, and not very fashionable ones. She was rather small, and thin and (what Jury thought of as) "nervy." Her movements were abrupt, almost jittery. The most that could be said for Dolly Schell was that she was pleasant-looking. When he approached the counter she was filling an amber-colored vial with tiny white pills. At the sound of his voice, a few of the pills spilled onto the counter. Nervy, yes. Probably why she was thin.

"My name's Richard Jury. We met—or nearly did—about an hour ago. I'm with Scotland Yard CID. I'd like to talk with you for a moment?"

"Is it about Angela?" He nodded. "Go ahead." She was unscrewing a big jar of tablets, started funneling a portion into a smaller jar in front of her.

He smiled. "I was thinking we might sit down."

She smiled too, again briefly. "Sorry, but I can't stop right now— your name was—?"

"Jury. Superintendent, CID." He flipped out the ID again. Somehow, he didn't really think she needed to be reminded.

"I'm backed up with prescriptions and some of these people will be in for them." Here she held up a small sheaf of white squares and waved them, in case he didn't know what a prescription was.

"Okay. Do you mind talking while you work, then?"

"Not at all. Excuse me, though."

Here she disappeared into the shelves of medicines, and through them he made her out hidden in part by the rows of bottles and jars, so that what he got was a view of bits and pieces—a square of white coat, a patch of brown hair, fingers with unpainted nails. The metal shelves ran horizontally, the bottles and jars stood vertically, so that what he saw was an oddly tense arrangement of squares and oblongs when he looked through them. His eye was caught by a row of cobalt blue, amber, and amethyst apothecary bottles of the sort one sometimes sees adorning a chemist's window. Silently, he read off the names—tonic pills, castor oil, Ague Cure—as he watched Dolly Schell through the open spaces between them. She worked, unruffled by his presence, calmly and competently. Either Dolly Schell, he thought, was extremely good at hiding her feelings, or else the subject of her cousin Angela didn't give rise to them.

She returned with several other bottles in her hands. Jury said: "You went to Wiltshire to identify your cousin."

"Yes. I did."

"I understand Angela Hope has a sister. Why didn't she go?"

"Because she's only thirteen. And Angela was Mary's only family. I don't know; it seemed pretty awful to have her go over there for that reason." She shrugged slightly. "I offered to go in her stead."

"You and Angela were close?"

Dolly Schell was measuring liquid into a small plastic container. "No. We weren't. We didn't see one another much. I don't think she liked me, to tell the truth." Her tone was sad, as she tapped the white tablets into a small envelope.

"Was Angela Hope one of your customers?"

Dolly looked up at him then, with an ironical smile. "Only in extremis. Angela believed more in herbs and the hand of God." She went back between the shelves to return the jar. "I don't think she ever walked into a doctor's office around here."

"And when was she?" Jury raised his voice slightly to reach her.

"Was she what?"

"In extremis."

"Oh . . . I didn't mean that literally."

"Figuratively, then?"

Dolly was back again, this time with a smaller jar of pinkish pills, tiny ones. Now she wound a roll of blank labels into an Underwood that looked old enough to be an antique. She pecked information onto a label. "Angela got migraine headaches that simply wouldn't respond to goldenseal and sassafras root." Here, she looked around with a guilty little smile. "I gave Angela some Tylenol 3, a prescription drug, of course. You going to run me in?"

Jury smiled. "Haven't the authority. You told Detective Inspector Rush she'd had rheumatic fever as a child."

Dolly nodded. "Yes, that's right. I don't think it was severe, but something like that can cause trouble later in life." She pulled the completed label from the typewriter. "Fortunately, she didn't often get migraine headaches. You know how they are. Can make you quite sick."

Jury thought of the medical examiner's findings, the vomit at the site of the death. Migraine, he knew, could be awful, could be blinding. But he doubted very much it could have catapulted Angela Hope into that deep, dark stone well.

Dolly stuck the label on an amber vial and slipped that into one of the small white envelopes on which she had already made some jottings. Then she picked up a container of a rather startling pink liquid that Jury thought might fit Wiggins's plans to medicate the universe. "What is it you want to know, exactly? I'm not sure I understand why you're here, asking questions."

The tone was free of antagonism, merely matter-of-fact. Jury answered, "A divisional commander thinks your cousin's death might be related to another death he's investigating."

"Nobody said anything to me about a related death." She was looking at him hard.

"When you spoke to the Wiltshire police—Inspector Rush, wasn't it?—there was no indication that the other women's deaths were tied to Angela Hope. Or that the circumstances were suspicious. We're still not sure that this is the case."

"Other *women*? You mean, there's more than one?" Her eyes were large as she held the bottle of viscous pink stuff in midair.

"Possibly."

"God." She set the container on the table and nervously wiped her palms down her white jacket. "God," she said again.

Jury told her what he could and Dolly Schell forgot all about her jars and vials as he did so. "But that's—" she searched for words— "that's rather unbelievable. And why are you searching over here, in New Mexico, rather than there, where it happened?"

"We're doing both."

She returned to her medications, picking up the bottle of pink stuff, setting it down again. "Aren't you reaching a conclusion . . . ?" She paused and shook her head, again searching for words. "Aren't you looking possibly at the wrong side of the coin? How do you know it's not the other way around? Someone in your country meant to do away with one or both of these women and Angela got in the way?"

Dolly Schell was no fool, he thought. "You're right; that's certainly possible."

Jury watched her for a moment in silence, watched her dexterous movements, hoping she'd get to the end of her prescriptions, for he was finding the eight-by-eight enclosure a good venue for claustrophobia. Wiggins would have loved it. Paradise, really, sealed up with all of these nostrums, anodynes, potions—which was, Jury suddenly realized, the way in which the sergeant must have construed whatever was in the jars and bottles. Not mundane "pills" and "syrups" but substances with properties verging on the magical.

"What are you smiling about?" Dolly was screwing a lid back on the huge jar.

"Was I? I was thinking of a colleague of mine. He'd love this place. Your little room here."

"Oh? Doesn't strike me as awfully lovable."

"You're not a hypochondriac, Miss Schell."

She had recovered enough to laugh. "Everybody's a hypochondriac. And call me Dolly, will you?" The jars were back on their shelves, the vials secure in their white packages. She looked around, satisfied. "Well, that's done. I can get Billy to watch the store for a while. He's only reading his muscle-building magazines, anyway." She went off towards the soda fountain, spoke to the lanky youth, and was back. "If you'd like, there's a coffee bar next door."

Now Jury laughed. "In this town, there's always a coffee bar next door."

IN THE NUTMEGY, cinnamony environs of next door's coffee-cum-book-shop, they sat on benches overwrought with flower-patterned pillows. Dolly ordered latte; Jury had plain strong coffee.

"They just can't leave it alone, can they?" said Jury, nodding as a tray of varying cups of froth was carried by. Dolly looked at him in question. "This." He raised his cup of plain coffee.

She laughed. "It's not just Santa Fe. Cappuccino and latte are a national plague these days. Well, an international one, maybe. You have espresso bars. I was in one in Salisbury. So there."

He shook his head. "You were in a *bar* in Salisbury. A *bar* bar. Where the landlord laid on an espresso machine."

"Okay, you win. Anyway, Salisbury's beautiful."

"Yes. The cathedral, did you go there?" She nodded. "I'm sorry about the circumstances."

She lowered her head, "Yes."

"You said you and Angela weren't close."

She raised it. "Shall I tell you the truth?"

"I'd prefer it to lies." He smiled.

Dolly leaned back against the many-colored cushions and sighed. "I said Angela didn't like me very much. That may or may not be so. But I do know that I didn't care for Angela all that much."

"Oh? Why not?" Jury thought he could see why. It would be difficult for a woman as plain, as nondescript as Dolly Schell to care for someone as pretty as Angela Hope. And probably as talented, artistically, as Angela Hope.

She shook her head, studied her cup, a hint of a smile raising the corners of her mouth. As if she were chiding herself. "I guess I was jealous. I resented the way luck just seemed to walk in her door." Dolly sighed. "Let me tell you a little of my—of our—history, okay?" Jury nodded and sat back. "I've lived all of my life here in Santa Fe. Or Albuquerque. My dad had this drugstore and I guess I just followed along. I was the only child. I suppose I'm not terribly adventurous and

I'm used to a small town. But Angela and Mary's parents—I have a hard time calling them 'aunt' and 'uncle' because I scarcely knew them and hardly ever saw them, so I can't think of them as 'family'—anyway, they were absolutely the most confirmed New Yorkers. I don't think they ever got west of the Hudson. All of their travelling was the other way—Europe, Antigua, Kyoto, Turkey, places I've only read about. Both of them were physically beautiful. I mean *really*. The movie-star looks you see wandering around this town. My Aunt Sylva—that's what we called her—was my dad's younger sister, but you'd never know it to see them together. Sylvestra Dark Schell was her name. 'Dark' was my grandmother's maiden name but she was nothing like my gran, I can tell you. Sylva would have liked this place now; Hollywood all over it. But then, she hated the Southwest; she loathed New Mexico, called it Hicksville. So she went east and ended up in Manhattan and married Martin Hope. My father's dead; he died four years ago, cancer. And you know, I guess, the Hopes were killed when their jet—*private* jet—crashed into some mountain in some tiny country with an unpronounceable name." She fingered her cold coffee cup. "I sound cold-blooded. But I never knew them, you see. They'd probably like Santa Fe now; it's been discovered; it's raised the notion of chic to a frenzy. Thirty years or so ago it was a pretty sleepy place. Parts of it still are, don't misunderstand. It's not all lipstick and sequins. But it's too—*publicly* gorgeous, if you know what I mean. It's such a *scene*."

Did she consider herself "behind" it, Jury wondered, like an unappreciated stagehand switching sets and working pulleys? Few jobs he could imagine were more "behind-the-scenes" than that of a chemist. A job that isolated you, yet one that was very exacting. He knew his local landlord at the Angel, but not his local chemist (allowing, of course, that the former got significantly more business from him than the latter). Sergeant Wiggins was the only person he could think of who'd know his chemist if he met him on the street. It was doctors who got the credit. Did Dolly Schell feel herself underappreciated in what obviously struck her as an overappreciated "scene"?

Jury said, "An American Mecca, it must be now. Go on with your story."

"Well, Sylvestra escaped to the East and married Martin Hope. He was a rich builder, of what I'm not sure. Houses, high-rises, I don't know. They were killed seven years ago when Angela was twenty-five and Mary was six. Angela's a lot older than Mary, but they get—got—on really well. Which surprises me because they're so different. Mary is practical and down-to-earth as an old no-nonsense lady. Stubborn like one, too. Since they hadn't any family back east, Angela decided to come out here. When she was young, when she was a child, she visited us several times. When Martin and Aunt Sylva went off on one of their spectacular trips and didn't want to be saddled with a kid, I guess. I didn't like her then, either." And in the petulant but still beguiling gesture of a teenager, Dolly flipped her straight brown hair back from her neck.

Jury smiled. He liked her directness. "Did your father and mother like Angela?" When her face flushed and her mouth tightened, he thought he must have touched a nerve.

"My mother died when I was a baby, when I was barely one year old. As to my father: yes, he liked her. It was very hard not to like Angela. See, she was exactly like her parents—charming in her helplessness. I *hate* these helpless types, mostly because I don't think they really are, they're just too lazy to develop a backbone, so they lean on other people's backs. Look, she was twenty-six when she decided to come here. With all of her money and all of her contacts, she still had to have someone to lean on, someone to look after her. So she picked Dad."

"And did he?" Jury meant the question to be volatile.

Dolly dipped her head, said she wanted more coffee, was silent for a few moments as Jury beckoned the waitress over. "Yes." She went on in a flat voice. "Angela had a way of making people want to take care of her."

"That must have been—pretty difficult for you." He sensed how inadequate the words were.

"Then he died." She looked away, into the dark aisles of the other room that housed the books.

Jury wondered if, in some part of her mind, she saw a connection between these two things—the coming-on-the-scene of Cousin Angela and the death of her father—some irrational cause-and-effect. He supposed that as a child, especially as the *only* child of a widower, she had been the center of her father's life.

She continued: "Angela liked to think of herself as one of these New Age people. You know—crystals, vortexes, channeling. Nonmaterialistic, spiritual. Easier to think of yourself as disdaining material goods when you've got them, or have the money to get them, isn't it? Easier to turn down a Mercedes if you're driving a Jag."

Jury smiled. "Yes, I expect so. And Angela had the material goods?"

"Oh, she certainly did. A pretty big inheritance is my guess. Martin Hope wasn't poor."

"And who does the money go to? Her sister?"

"Probably."

"What about you?"

Dolly frowned a little, reflecting on this as if the idea really appeared to be new to her. "It's possible. But she'd have to have made a will, and people like Angela often don't. Can't be bothered, or something." She shrugged.

"Careless of practical matters, was she?"

Dolly nodded. "Or pretending to be."

He smiled. "Odd thing to say. Why would she bother pretending to be impractical?"

"If you wanted to impress somebody of your otherworldliness and poetical nature."

Dr. Anders, for instance, thought Jury, though Dolly Schell was way off base if she thought dreamy impracticality would get very far with Nils Anders. "Anyone in particular she might have been wanting to impress?"

Dolly blushed, and her eyes, behind the big-rimmed glasses, darted about as if they wanted to flutter away. "Well, no. Nobody in particular."

Jury didn't want to press the point of Dolly's attachment to Nils Anders. "So Angela and her sister lived by themselves . . . where, exactly? I know it's outside Santa Fe. I'd like to talk to Mary."

"Ha! Lots of luck." Dolly sipped her fresh cup of latte.

"Oh? She's difficult to talk to, is she?"

"Well, she's sort of—scarce."

Jury laughed. " 'Scarce'? What's that mean?"

Dolly sat back and twisted the cup on the saucer. "Just that, one, she goes off by herself a lot; and, two, you can talk to her, or think you're talking to her, and she's all the while tuned you out. She works at the pharmacy off and on. You know, just being there for when people come in to pick up medicine. Or at the soda fountain. But only occasionally, when Billy—that's my delivery boy—and I are gone at the same time. But she's very smart, I'll give her that." Dolly sighed. "Doesn't like me much, though. She senses how I felt about Angela. And she and Angela got on really well—Mary's passionately loyal—in spite of their ages and in spite of their being so different." She looked at her watch and quickly started gathering up her coat, her purse. "I have to get back; Billy's not all that reliable."

As she half-rose, Jury put a restraining hand on her arm. "Dolly, can you think of anyone at all who might have wanted Angela dead?"

Surprised again at the thought her cousin might have been murdered, she sat back down. "She died of a coronary, or something like that, didn't she?"

"A policeman in Devon thinks she could have been poisoned. You probably know, it's a little difficult to determine unless you know what you're looking for."

"But she didn't know anybody in England."

But she did, Jury thought: she knew Frances Hamilton and Helen Hawes. That was the problem. He said, "No. Here. Enough to follow her to the U.K.?"

She stared at him. "Like *me*, do you mean? Do you want to see my passport?"

"I wasn't thinking of you, Dolly. I wasn't thinking of anyone in particular. That's why I asked you the question."

Relaxing a bit against the back of the booth, she seemed to be thinking this over. She shook her head. "I can't imagine. It'd be easier to imagine somebody doing away with Mary." She smiled.

Jury didn't. "Why?"

"Look, I'm only kidding. It's just that Mary's a lot more difficult to get along with than Angela. Angela was kind of . . . vague. Well, that's not the right word. Mary's anything but vague. I get the feeling she's looking straight through me sometimes. She's a lot closer to the ground than Angela."

"The same thing Dr. Anders said." Her discomfort at the mention of that name was evident. "He was a good friend of Angela, was he?"

Dolly looked away. "Most people liked Angela," she said, evasively.

"Somebody didn't." Jury tossed some bills on the table and got up.

TWENTY-NINE

The desk clerk at the La Fonda approached Jury as he was contemplating the menu posted outside the hotel's restaurant. He was trying to decide between the huevos rancheros (given he'd skipped breakfast that morning) and the Old Santa Fe Trail Platter, comprised of enchiladas, beans, posole, and red and green chile sauce, when the young man handed him a message.

"The caller said it was important, that I should give it to you as soon as you came in." He was as impressed by Jury's being a British cop as he would have been had Jury been a casting director.

Jury thanked him; still, he hovered. The lobby was crowded, the dining room was packed. Jury had seen another one of those film "shoots" as he passed by the plaza, taped off like a crime scene, a lot of Santa Feans or tourists surrounding it, stopping to gawk.

He asked the desk clerk if there was any place at all, any restaurant he could go to that wasn't jammed.

"No," said the clerk. But he smiled as he delivered this unembellished response and still gazed at Jury as if Jury might land him a part in *Priestly of the Yard* or *The Whitechapel Horrors*, whatever Scotland Yard's latest venture might be. Finally, he sailed off to tend to the incoming guests.

Jury read the short message from Jack Oñate, telling him to call immediately, that it was important. He looked around for a bank of public telephones, looked through the people flowing in and out of La Fonda's entrance—rich people, pretty people, California-tanned people—and finally located a phone around the corner near the elevator and slotted in a quarter.

*   *   *

"YOU FEEL LIKE going to Colorado?" was Jack Oñate's enigmatic question when he took the call.

"No. I feel like having the Old Santa Fe Trail Platter. But now you mention it, I might have to go to Colorado just to get some lunch. Where did all of these people come from in February? What's in Colorado?"

"Aspen, Telluride—to mention two things. You should see Colorado before you leave."

Jury sighed. It was clear that Jack was going to spin his nugget of information out as long as could. "What's so important, Jack?"

"Are you gonna be surprised."

"Great. Surprise me." Jury studied the Mexican tiles encrusting the wall in front of him.

Sound of cellophane or other substance crinkling and rattling and when Jack's voice came back over the line, he was eating. "Okay. Coh-wada Stah Cup—"

"Jack. Swallow, will you?" It was like trying to talk to Wiggins when he was shooting up nose drops. Jury ran his finger over the intaglio design of the tile and reminded himself he hadn't sent Wiggins any flowers. Well, he'd be back in a couple of days.

"Sorry. There was a Colorado state cop in here this morning and he and a couple of other guys in here were jawing about Mesa Verde." Jack must have taken another bite of whatever—pizza, sandwich—for Jury heard sounds of chewing again. "Well, he was talking about the ruins—the big ones, like Spruce Tree House and so on, and then the smaller ones, the ones that are known only by numbers. And guess what?"

Jury sighed. "I can't. You're going to surprise me, remember?"

"Well, sometimes they assign names to these lesser ones. Just for the fun of it, I guess."

A silence lengthened during which there was more rattling of paper and Jury prompted him. "And—?"

"Yeah. One of them's named Coyote Village. If you're going, fly from our airport and rent a car there. Otherwise, it'll take you maybe six hours."

THIRTY

The guard at the gate to the park handed him a map of Mesa Verde and told him that he wouldn't have more than an hour, since they closed the park at sundown. As his hired car crept along the winding road the sun blazed on the windscreen as if it hadn't heard the guard's prediction. Right now, it was a cold, blue day of high-piled clouds and air like glass. By the roadside, delicate white flowers he couldn't put a name to were interwoven in tufts of silvery grass.

He knew exactly how to get to the ruin whimsically christened Coyote Village. About fifteen miles, and another two past the visitors' center; *why* he had undertaken this short trip was somewhat more obscure. Perhaps he'd find something; more likely, he wouldn't.

He must have missed the wooden sign, supposed to be on the left, for he found himself near one of the principal attractions, Cliff Palace, pulled the car into the car park and got out. From the mesa top, Jury looked down into the canyon that wound under the cliff. Built under the edge of a cliff in a space like an amphitheatre was the pueblo. It was a cavernous three-and-four-tier living complex built like steps, its roofs becoming porches. The Anasazi had built this literally from sticks and stones. It was enormous; Jury guessed there must have been over two hundred rooms. He stood looking for some moments, hunching into his coat. What had happened to them, the Anasazi? Where had they gone? *Why* had they gone? What were they running from that would make them leave everything they'd built? It was, Jury realized, a dangerous line of thought, for it only led him back to Jenny's disappearance. Surely, "disappearance" was overstating it. Yet, when he looked at that cliffside and thought of a whole vanished civilization, he was not comforted. The cold breeze stirred, blew clumps of tumbleweed over to the rim where he stood. Finally, he got back in his car, the only one in the car park. He headed back, keeping a closer lookout for Coyote Village.

HE STOOD beside the car, listening. He could hear nothing but some dim, distant birdcall, so faint that he thought he might be imagining it. Music.

It wasn't birdsong that he was hearing, but a flute playing. When he came out on the clearing, he stopped dead. A young woman was playing a flute, a slow, sad piece, in a private ceremony of her own.

She was of less than average height, and thin, boyish-looking. Her hair was dark brown, and like mahogany, long and straight, tinted red by the dying sun. She was dressed entirely in black. Relentlessly in black: black leather, black wool, black cord jeans. Milky light, but strong, poured through the trees. Light that pearled the flute also shimmered on the material of a shirt with a high collar buttoned right up to under the chin. The jeans were stuffed into black boots. Only her face and her hands were uncovered and, by contrast, illumined against the dark clothes and hair. She stopped playing and gripped the flute before her in her two hands, stared at the site for a moment, and then turned her head to stare at Jury.

And he saw she was (he thought, with a smile) rather glowingly made up. Glossy lipstick, heavy purplish eye shadow, black eyeliner. All of this was in strange contrast to the somber gear she was wearing and in contrast to her actual age, which he had clearly mistaken. She was a girl—a child, nearly—not a young woman. What he had taken for boyish thinness was actually an undeveloped figure.

Jury stood there in a moment of confusion as they regarded one another, and he wouldn't have guessed, had not the dog emerged from the undergrowth and into the clearing. It certainly looked like pictures he'd seen of coyotes—the long, thin legs and long, foxlike muzzle; the lips were black as pitch and bordered by white hair; the silvery coat the color of sagebrush or the tufts of grass he'd passed back there. And the eyes that looked transparent, colorless. The dog loped over to stand at a point between the two of them, ears set forward, ice-water eyes wide and boring into Jury.

Jury coughed lightly and (he hoped) in a friendly-seeming way. "What's your dog doing?"

"Nothing. Just saying 'Hello.' "

"I've never seen police dogs say 'Hello' that way."

Reasonably she said, "Well, he's not a police dog, is he?" Then *her* eyes, the exact same color of the dog's, bore into him too. "Are you another policeman?"

"I don't know about 'another,' but, yes, I'm a policeman."

Her shoulders slumped. He heard her breathe, "Oh, goddamn."

Jury kept his eyes on the so-called dog, judging its greater or lesser display of tension. Judging, actually, the distance between the dog and himself. "Are you Mary Hope?"

Her frown deepened. Then she pursed her mouth and chewed at her lip. In an unconsciously female-coy gesture, she flipped her long hair back over her shoulder. "Mary Dark Hope." She sighed and pointed off toward the carpark. "The car's out there."

"The car?" He took a step forward and, alerted, the dog moved. It was like some American Mob movie with the wiseguy's bodyguard going for his gun. Jury took a few defensive steps backward. "What's he doing?"

She sighed. "He's just being friendly." She paused and Jury could all but see the wheels go round in her head. "That's why I call him Sunny." She added, "That's the way German shepherds are. You're not a state trooper? You didn't come about the car?"

"I'm not." The dog seemed to relax at this announcement, so Jury added, "I'm from Scotland Yard."

Her head tilted slightly, regarding him. It was a tiny movement, one of the few she'd made since she saw him. She stood motionless, still gripping the flute. Mary Dark Hope and coyote made a good twosome.

"Then I guess you're not going to arrest me."

Jury considered his reply. Soberly, he said, "Not yet."

It was clear she liked that answer. "But I guess you want to talk to me."

Jury smiled broadly. "I certainly do."

THE REASON for all "the goo" (she told him as they walked the path back to the cars) was that she had to look older, old enough to drive. Old enough to get through the park gate. All the way here from home she'd been afraid of being picked up by a state trooper.

They were standing by the car she'd driven, a dusty old Ford. Jury was peering through the driver's side window. "Telephone books?"

"I had to make myself taller."

"You drove nearly three hundred miles sitting on telephone books?"

As that was what she'd just told him, she didn't bother answering, but leaned against the Ford and kept her eyes riveted on the far mountains. The eyes were so pale they were almost colorless, clear as ice. Jury had never equated beauty with colorlessness before—but then, there were diamonds, weren't there? There was brook water, there were iridescent raindrops—

There was vodka, there was gin, he heard the voice of Diane Demorney chime in to his inventory. He laughed.

"What's funny?" Mary Dark Hope blushed slightly; surely, he must be laughing at her.

"Nothing. Nothing at all. I'm sorry; a friend just came to mind." He paused. "It must've been important to you to get here."

Still, she didn't answer. Why should she? He might just laugh again.

"Could we go someplace and talk? Get something to eat, perhaps?"

This suggestion enlivened her a bit. "There's a coffee shop in Durango where we always went—" Her eyes turned quickly forward again, looking out over the mesa where the setting sun blazed for a moment, before finally sinking.

Jury did not ask her to amplify as to the "we." "I'll drive," he said dryly, opening the door. "Do you think I'll need the telephone books?"

She ignored this, looked at his Dodge Dynasty. "What about your car? Is it just going to sit?"

"It's a rental; maybe the park police will help out getting it back to Cortez. If I explain," he added, ominously.

"I'll drive, then," she said, starting to get into her car.

"Out," said Jury, stacking the telephone books on the floor.

She opened the passenger door and ushered her dog into the front seat.

"No," said Jury, "the dog goes in back."

She shrugged her indifference at this arbitrary law, but got out and opened the rear door. "Have it your way, but you'll be sorry." She slammed Sunny's door, got back in front, slammed her own. "Sunny's an awful backseat driver."

Not nearly so bad as Mary Dark Hope, he discovered ten miles along the curving mountain road, as the fading red glow of the sun reflected on high-built clouds and turned the cloud bank deep pink, spread across mesa and sagebrush. Jury thought it was magnificent.

"Painter's sun," she said, and went back to negotiating every turn for him, announced every lay-by and every precipitous drop well in advance, every advancing car and every car following, and generally criticized every single move Jury made.

All Sunny did was punch Jury's shoulder occasionally with his forepaw.

Mary Dark Hope wondered aloud how in heaven's sakes Jury had ever made it all the way here by himself.

Jury wondered how he was going to make it all the way back.

THEY STOPPED in Durango for coffee.

All three of them.

Durango, Colorado, sat in a bowllike declivity, shaped by the surrounding mountains. The air was so clear and pure it was like breathing at an impossible altitude. Jury took great gulps of it as they walked through the door of Mary Dark Hope's favorite coffee house (no wonder, since it permitted animals).

Mary was still talking about Jury's driving, saying that it was probably because he was English, and that they drove on the wrong side of the road, on lanelike roads, and in toy cars.

"*Look*, will you cut it out about my driving?"

She was peering at the pastry display, moving along the counter and looking at the pedestaled plates. "I was only giving reasons for it, that's all. I'll have two jelly doughnuts and a cheese danish. And a chocolate éclair." Raising her eyebrows at him, as if he might try to refuse this repast, she explained, "The other doughnut's for Sunny."

"Do you want something to drink? Hot chocolate? A soft drink?"

"No, I want cappuccino." Her tone was slightly condescending. They were, after all, in an espresso bar.

He refused to get three of them, however. "The dog can drink water," he said. "It might have to drive."

That little witticism was about to misfire, her expression told him.

"Don't say it." Jury carried the two cups and she followed with a plate of pastries. The doughnut went under the table where Sunny had been lying, peacefully watching the proceedings.

They sipped, they munched. His driving momentarily forgotten—or set aside—she told him about Durango. "It's a real old-fashioned cowboy town, you can tell. It's got wide streets and a lot of saloons."

Jury looked around the espresso-cappuccino-coffee bar at the beautifully booted women, the soft leather clothing and silk scarves, the tiny cups and tiers of croissants and tried to imagine it packed with cowboys. Underneath the table, Sunny gnawed at the doughnut as if it were as tough as a steak bone.

Mary sat, calmly eating her pastry. He watched her blow on her cappuccino, making designs in the froth with her breath. Her eyes were cast down, lashes long and thick. A knockout, thought Jury. That's what she's going to be—a knockout. And he was disturbed by this thought; she was, after all, only thirteen. Yet, there was about her a distressingly ambiguous sexuality, as if the woman were laying claim to the little girl. He had at first mistaken her for a young woman, and realized now that it was not wholly owing to the heavy makeup. He wondered how men reacted to her, what feelings she aroused in them.

There had been no further reference to Angela's death since the implied one: *I guess you want to talk to me.* And Mary certainly didn't seem inclined to bring it up. So Jury simply took a direct approach. "I'd like to talk to you about your sister."

Mary stopped spooning up the froth of milk, but she did not look up.

"I know you and your sister liked to visit Mesa Verde," Jury went on. "Was that one of your particular spots?"

She nodded and spooned up the rest of the froth. Then she said, "There might be spirits there."

"Spirits?"

"Well, Angie believes in spirits. So does Rosella. Maybe that's why Angie did, because Rosella talks about things like that so much."

"Rosella is the woman who takes care of you?"

"Uh-huh." She was cutting the rest of her pastry into small pieces.

"Is she by way of being, well, a legal guardian?" Jury wondered what fate lay in store for Mary Dark Hope.

Her dark hair swung when she shook her head. "A couple of ladies from the Social Services came around day before yesterday." The memory caused her to look over at Jury with her icewater eyes.

He was glad he was not "a couple of ladies from Social Services." He smiled. "Rosella's been with you long enough that I imagine she'd be considered a suitable guardian, despite the lack of blood relationship."

If Mary was relieved, she didn't show it. She just went on looking.

He could understand how adults might contemplate her with awe or anger; she was that inexplicable and self-contained.

"You were playing the flute for the spirits, then?"

"No. For the memories."

He looked at her, her face now turned toward the plate, empty of food but for one small square of pastry and the éclair. Her hands, lacking employment now, could do nothing but turn the plate slowly round. Jury felt a little ashamed; his question had been condescending. *For the memories.* "I'm truly sorry, Mary, about Angela."

"You haven't told me anything, though."

Jury told her how they had found her sister.

All the while, she contemplated her chocolate éclair without eating it. "Look at this, will you?" From his inside coat pocket Jury drew the photocopied paper and smoothed it out on the table. "It's a page from an address book."

For a moment, she regarded it with a slight frown. "It says 'Coyote Village.' What are the numbers?"

"Telephone numbers, presumably."

"Is it Angie's telephone book?"

"Does it look like her writing?"

"No."

"Did anyone else you know of like to visit this particular site?"

"No. Tourists mainly like to go to the big ones—Balcony House, Spruce Tree House—like that. One of the reasons Angie—" Her head dipped; he could not read her expression. When the face came up again, it was as remote as the moon. "*Angie* liked it because nobody much turned up there and she—*we*—could have it to ourselves. Angie liked to think." She picked up her éclair, bit the end off.

Jury refolded the paper, creases weakened by much use, and returned it to his pocket. "My impression of your sister is that she was by way of being more interested in the spirit than in material things."

"That's why we don't have a dishwasher." Having summed up the spiritual life, Mary licked a bit of custard oozing from her éclair.

"Did she tell you about Old Sarum?"

She looked left to right as if to search out the source of this queer question: "What's to tell? It's some ancient excavation or something that goes all the way back to—" She consulted her fund of Sarum knowledge, found it wanting, ended with "—many years ago." The tongue came out to catch another custard drip. "It's a famous historical site. You should know; it's yours." Having handed over Sarum to Jury's personal estate, she slid down again to give Sunny a bite of her éclair.

Jury played his fingers tattoo-wise on the rim of his cup, decided not to throw it, and waited for her head to reappear. When it did, he asked, "Did Sarum have some special meaning for your sister? *Special*, is what I'm wondering."

"Not exactly, but look: if you loved rocks and ruins, and Angie did, wouldn't you want to see it? And Stonehenge? That's there too. Nearby." She glanced at him as if his knowledge of England needed shoring up.

"I'd want to see it, yes."

She shrugged, drank her coffee, went on. "She never went to England before and she liked the idea of seeing all of this stuff."

They drank their coffee in silence for a few moments. Then she said: "People cause their own death."

"I beg your pardon?" He was mystified.

"If you were a Zuñi, you'd understand."

"Zuñi?"

"You know, the tribe. Rosella's a Zuñi." She paused, reflecting. "She has to go back to Zuñi Pueblo several times a year."

"Oh. Why?"

"The women have to stick close to the pueblo. Zuñi women hardly ever leave because they make so much money with their silver and turquoise. But mostly it's because Zuñi women are expected to be good wives and cook up feasts for the Kachina actors and be admiring onlookers at the dances. Even after a woman dies she has to go to Kachina Village and do the same things all over again. I'd say that sucks, wouldn't you?" She didn't wait for an answer. "Zuñi believe you can cause your own death."

"Do you mean as in suicide?"

Vigorously, she shook her head. "Not like that. You can *mean* your own death and not even know it; you can *intend* it. Like—" She was casting about for a way to say it. "Like, you could have what you think is an accident, you could cause yourself the accident. Or else, you could cause your death by mourning for someone for too long, by keeping on being miserable." Here she paused and studied her black clothes and was silent, raising her eyes to some far-off horizon out there in the cappuccino crowd, the roomful of espresso drinkers. "Like heartbreak," she added.

He was stunned by this and did not know what to say. He took the photos from his pocket and placed them before Mary. "Do either of these women look familiar to you? I think they might have visited your sister's shop last November. Or, at least, this one." He tapped the picture of Fanny Hamilton.

She paid them serious attention, picked up each little picture, studied it, set it down. "Why do you think that?"

"Because Mrs. Hamilton—that's the name of this one—took back a turquoise sculpture, turquoise with a silver band round the center. Angela's silver work was distinctive."

"That's because Rosella taught her, that's why Angie was so good at it. It's the kind of work the women do in the pueblo."

"I saw several blocks of turquoise like that in Angela's shop."

"Aren't you supposed to have a search warrant to go into people's houses?"

"I have one. You want to see it?"

"Never mind."

"One thing I was looking for but didn't find was a mailing list, or an accounting book that lists addresses of customers."

"There's a Rolodex."

"I saw that. But it appeared to be more of a personal listing than a business one."

"I don't think Angie kept very good records; she had an accountant or a tax person to take care of stuff like that. Angie wasn't organized. I kept on telling her she should expand. She could have done much more business than she did, but she just said money didn't mean all of that much to her, and she'd rather spend her time in places like

Sedona. It was better for her spirit." Mary shrugged. "Well, money means a lot to *me* and I can't stand Sedona. She knows some flaky people there. They all go out and hang around the vortexes." Mary shrugged again.

"Mary, what did you think when you heard about the way Angela had died? I'm sorry to ask this, but you knew her better than anyone. And this all must have seemed incredible to you." She didn't answer for such a very long time that Jury was ashamed of himself for asking such a speculative question. Yet the girl seemed to be such a direct and self-controlled person he had nearly forgotten this was her own sister who had died. "I'm sorry. Let's just drop it."

But she must still have been turning the problem over. "I wondered how they did it," she said.

"How who did what?" Jury was puzzled.

"Killed her."

"You think someone murdered Angela?"

It was her turn to look at him. "Well, sure. Of course. So do you or you wouldn't be here."

"Why would someone kill Angela?"

"Rosella says it was witchcraft. You know—killing someone long distance." She shrugged. She turned her eyes back to the pictures. "You think maybe they were customers? Or what?"

"I think so."

"Well, but . . . who are they?"

"This one was from Exeter, that's about a hundred miles from Salisbury and Stonehenge. This one, although she's actually American—" he picked up Fanny's snapshot—"was living in London—had been for years."

" 'Was' living in?"

"They're both dead." He pocketed the pictures.

At last he'd said something interesting. And as if the announcement had surprised even Sunny, Jury felt the dog shift, roll over on his foot.

In a nervous gesture, Mary licked her lips. "You think it's got something to do with Angie."

Jury nodded. "Yes."

"Why?"

"That's what we're trying to work out."

"Were they friends? Let me see their pictures again."

Jury brought the photos out again. "We don't even know that, but there's reason to believe they met over here. Both of them from the U.K., it wouldn't be unusual for them to strike up a friendship, however slight. They both booked rooms at the La Fonda. At least for a couple of days."

After studying the pictures for a moment, she said, "It's hard because so many people come along Canyon Road. Maybe somebody else saw them. Who else did you talk to?"

"The lady who has the shop next to the Silver Heron— Bartholomew."

What Mary thought of Sukie Bartholomew was fairly clear from her expression. About Nils Anders she was considerably more enthusiastic. "He's nice. He says I'm a soliton."

"A *what?*" Jury laughed.

"A soliton. It's one of their words. It means 'self- . . .' " She cast about for a definition. "It's like 'self-dependent,' or something. Anyway, somebody that can take care of themselves."

"I can believe it. I get the impression that your sister wasn't intimate with many people."

Mary shook her head. "She wasn't. With Dr. Anders, mostly. I don't know why she liked Sukie. And there's Malcolm; did you talk to him?"

"Yes, I did."

Disdainfully, Mary said, "He says he's an actor. That's when he's not being a painter. And they're *always* making movies around Santa Fe. If I see Robert Redford one more time I'll throw up."

"I saw some shooting going on in the plaza. Is that the same film?"

"Probably. Most of it's going on over at Rancho del Rip-off. That's a kind of dude ranch ten miles away." She paused. "What about Dolly? Did you talk to her?"

The question was too casual, Jury thought. He hadn't brought up Dolly Schell yet, avoiding it because of its potential for causing her pain. "Your cousin. Yes, I did."

"She went to England to—identify Angela." Her voice was bitter, but she didn't look at Jury. Suddenly, she slid down and looked under the table. "Sunny's asleep."

"He's a pretty quiet dog." Jury would pursue the Dolly question later.

"Unless he gets riled."

"What riles him?"

"Well, I don't think he'd take to anyone coming after me with a club or an ax. He walks up and down Canyon Road and people kind of disappear into doorways." Her little headshake, her tightening of the mouth told him what she thought of that. "Can you believe it? They think Sunny's a coyote."

She pronounced it "ky-yote."

"He does rather look like one, Mary."

Exasperated, she said, "He does *not*. Have you ever seen a coyote with that kind of silvery eyes?"

"No, but I've never been eye-level with one, either. Where'd you find him?"

"Walking around" was her vague answer.

"Him? Or you?"

Impatiently, she said, "He was out in the desert, just a puppy, nosing around a buzzard skeleton. I guessed he was hungry, so I gave him my ham sandwich."

"What were you doing in the desert with a ham sandwich?"

Oh, he was just too much, the tight little mouth indicated. "Probably the same thing he was."

"Looking for buzzard skeletons?"

"Nooo." Her mouth was a circle around the long, drawn-out syllable. "I always go there on Saturdays and take my lunch."

Still she didn't say what she "did." Maybe nothing. A soliton? He smiled. "You should be . . . I don't know . . . at the cinema with your friends. That's what I used to do on Saturdays." Had he? He could think of no Saturdays . . . but, yes, hadn't there been an Odeon? Down the King's Road, or was it the Fulham Road? He thought he saw himself standing outside, reading the adverts, the posters. . . .

She was staring at him, or glaring. Mary Dark Hope seemed to favor the latter. She looked, looked away, glanced back and away, the opportunity for barbed ripostes seeming so plummy, she simply couldn't decide on the best one and gave up.

Jury smiled slightly, now dimly aware as to why he was being an arsehole (in his own eyes, also), for he was presenting himself as a target. If you'd just lost someone you greatly loved (and there was no doubt in his mind that Mary loved her sister), it would be a relief to have some big booby—especially a policeman booby—sitting across from you and at whom you could take potshots.

"Anyway, it's not a real desert. It's a painter's desert. It's not real anymore." The tone was no longer sarcastic, but sad.

He watched this child in her coal-black clothes, so resistant to ordinary childish activities, and wondered if it was matter-of-fact Mary instead of a more spiritual Angela who had (in the words of Nils Anders) "run the show." She was so down-to-earth, so unethereal, Jury wouldn't have been surprised to see not shoes but roots at the end of her long, straight legs. Images ran together in his mind; those so-called Saturdays with friends—had there been those? The Odeon cinema down the street (the King's Road, yes, he thought for sure now); the park where he helped Amy do her watercolors. . . . Perhaps it was that remark about the "painter's desert" that had brought this back. . . . Jury looked up.

Mary's face actually wore a look of startled concern, and her clear eyes were clouded over, as if he were, against her will, slipping away. . . .

But all she did was to shove her plate back and say "I'm done" and look around the room as if they could all go home now. She slid down again, reached to grab Sunny's lead.

Jury could feel the dog shaking itself awake and together. Sunny's head appeared out from under the table. He regarded Jury with his silver eyes.

THE PASTRY FIX didn't last long for Mary, and around nine they stopped for dinner outside Chama in a rustic little restaurant offering no particular cuisine. They ordered steaks and french fries with side orders of green chile and posole. He asked her, during the meal, about Dolly Schell and the Schells' relationship to the Hopes. He kept it as neutral as he could. She answered calmly, giving him no information that Dolly herself hadn't, and kept on cutting up her steak.

They ate largely in silence, but there was no strain to the silence. It just was.

The steak was good, but the posole with green chile Mary said was not very authentic. Rosella could do much better. When they finished, she insisted on taking the steak bones—one for Sunny (who'd been left in the car this time), and one for whatever strays they might see along the road. There were always strays, she said, and now there'd be dead dogs since they'd crossed from Colorado into New Mexico.

She was right. They hadn't driven more than five miles when their headlights caught a stray dog along the side of the road looking ghostly gray, its yellow eyes pricked by the beams. Mary told him to stop so that she could toss out the bone.

And she was right about the dead dogs, too. Two hours later, they passed a dog, a large dog lying dead by the road. "That's one," Mary said, grimly.

The moon was up, a full moon, huge and yellow, sailing ahead of them. Looking at it and almost without thinking, Jury said, "We used to call that a bomber's moon."

Why was he talking about the War? Such an event to Mary Dark Hope must seem as remote and irrelevant to her experience as a landing on the moon up there. Dusty and dull as some bloody old history book. So he was a little surprised when she repeated the phrase.

"Bomber's moon." She appeared to be considering this.

"There were blackouts; London was utterly dark."

"So if the moon was really bright, the bombers could see their targets."

"Yes."

"Did you go down in air-raid shelters?"

"Yes."

Again, she seemed to consider. "Did you ever get caught before you could get there?"

It took Jury a few moments to answer this. "Yes. A few times." He added, "Especially at the end of it."

Mary Dark Hope leaned her head back against the seat, the moon apparently forgotten now.

He was wrong about that, though.

She said, "When you were a kid, it must have all been awful real."

In her mouth, it sounded as if the reality had grit. Had muscle, as Nils Anders might say.

Then she said, "It's not like that anymore. It's a movie moon."

Ten miles later, the other side of Española, between there and Tesuque they saw another dead dog, one that looked like an Alsatian, lying off on the shoulder. And only two miles farther on, another one.

Jury said, "That's three. My God."

"Land of Enchantment," said Mary Dark Hope.

The movie moon sped away, ahead.

THIRTY-ONE

After Bethnal Green, the journey back to Long Piddleton and Martha's *boudin blanc* had restored his spirits; now, the pleasure of his late breakfast was augmented by the absence of his aunt. She had got into the practice of turning up at early and unwelcome hours, but there was no sign of her now as Melrose lifted the silver domes on the sideboard and saw the buttery eggs and the succulent sausages. It was nearly ten o'clock when he began filling his plate and getting that creepy feeling one does when one feels watched. He turned from the lavish sideboard and stared out of the window. It was Momaday. Really, the man simply must stop *lurking*.

Melrose set down his plate, went to the window, and cranked it open. "What are you *doing* out there, Momaday?"

Mr. Momaday touched the brim of his cap, greeting Melrose as if they always exchanged information through the window, and said, "Got a message, m'lord."

Ruthven and Martha, his wife, who couldn't get out of the "my lord" habit, had unintentionally indoctrinated Momaday.

"Message? From whom?"

Momaday's answer was oblique. Melrose knew it would be. "Well, 'twas give me by some boy come up from t'village." The man looked all around, crafty as a spy.

"Where—oh, listen. Go round to the kitchen, will you?" Melrose was freezing there in the chill air cutting through the casement window. It also annoyed the life out of him that he was being called away from his sausage on a Momaday goose chase.

The kitchen, redolent as always with the voluptuous, spicy smells of that day's meals, was inhabited by Martha, floured to the elbows, and Ruthven, eating a wedge of toast before a small grate.

Naturally, Melrose's appearance made Ruthven snap to attention, and to get to the kitchen door before Melrose did. The butler did this without appearing to hurry at all. Both of them, Ruthven and Martha, sniffed Mr. Momaday into the room.

It was hardly surprising, thought Melrose. After all, the two of them had been with the seventh earl and the countess long before Melrose was born. They had served as the nucleus of a sizable staff— maids, tweenies, chauffeurs, gardeners—and took it in stride that it was now left to them to run the place alone, with the help of a couple of cleaning women from the village. The old gardener, Mr. Peebles, had finally retired (making official, Melrose said, what he had actually done years before), making way for Momaday.

But this delivering messages to His Lordship was definitely treading in Ruthven territory. Melrose took the several-times-folded piece of dirtied paper from Momaday, posing the question: "Well, why wasn't the message delivered to you, Ruthven?"

Momaday tread on the butler's toes further by answering for him: "Warn't here, were he?" He managed to insinuate that the moment His Lordship's back was turned, Ruthven was out on the tiles.

"It was necessary," said Ruthven stiffly, "for me to go into the village, to Jurvis's, to pick up the saddle of lamb. And Martha was visiting her cousin."

The message was from Dick Scroggs, telling him that Mr. Jury had called the Jack and Hammer, not being able to get an answer from Ardry End. It went on to tell him that Mr. Jury desired him to ring Inspector Lasko in Stratford-upon-Avon.

It desired him, if the truth be told, to *go* to Stratford-upon-Avon.

"WHY DON'T we have a fax machine?" asked Melrose of Ruthven later that same morning, and in an uncharacteristically pugnacious manner, as if it were all Ruthven's fault. "We *don't*," he continued, looking round at the deficient butler's pantry, which did double duty as an office, "even have a computer."

"We've only just acquired the typewriting machine, my lord." Ruthven added, "Which seems adequate for our purposes."

Melrose was not sure he liked the sound of that, since "our purposes" meant the typing up of *Gin Lane*, a task that Ruthven had undertaken with alacrity. He loved sitting with rolled-up shirtsleeves at the antique walnut writing desk, his accounting and inventory books shoved aside, typing away with abandon. He had become extremely proficient with two fingers. He kept Melrose's handwritten pages locked away in the desk (for reasons neither of them could fathom) and was now reviewing His Lordship's notes relative to his recent London trip. Melrose had written up some of them and would simply dictate the others.

Dictation usually required Lou Reed pounding away in the background of the sitting room. For some reason, this made Melrose's creative juices flow. He was especially fond of the rendition of "Marshal Law," which he would often play when Agatha was sitting on the sofa like an old gray seal, stuffing in fairy cakes and drinking tea.

. . . I'm the marshall in this town . . .

would conjure up further visions, visions of Clint Eastwood, someone else Melrose liked. Whereas Lou Reed could send Agatha screaming away, Clint Eastwood was the apotheosis of dark and bedeviled Silence. When Clint stood there before the fireplace mantel (stood, that is, in Melrose's imagination), his silence was so palpable, took on such shape and substance, that Melrose could further imagine dust-cloths dropping over chairs and sofas, especially over any place Agatha sat, covering sofa and its occupant, so that as she continued to talk, her mouth moving under the covering, darkening as it sucked in air, ghostly and muted. And if Melrose's imagination was not quite up to this Special Effect, Clint would simply take out his gun and shoot her. That happened sometimes.

Melrose was dictating the bit about his meal in Bethnal Green, being quite colorful in his description of Bea Slocum (whom he recalled now with real fondness), occasionally pausing for Ruthven to catch up. It was to send this lot to Richard Jury in Santa Fe that he wanted a fax machine.

"Well, who has one? Someone must."

"I wonder but what Mr. Trueblood might have one, m'lord. Being in business as he is."

"Good Lord, I hope not." What Trueblood got up to without the help of technology was bad enough.

Ruthven thought some more as he flexed his tired fingers. "You might inquire at the Wrenn's Nest. Mr. Browne would likely have one." Ruthven gave a sniff of distaste.

"I'm not asking him for any favors. There must be another."

They both thought. Then Ruthven said, "I wouldn't be at all surprised if you'd find one at the Blue Parrot. You know, Mr. Sly likes to be up on the latest of everything. A bit pushy, Mr. Sly is." Ruthven coughed gently as his fingers hovered like fairy wings over the keys.

The Blue Parrot was but a short distance from Ardry End (a fact that Dick Scroggs had often noted with a withering glance at anyone from that end of town who might be disposed to have a drink in Sly's establishment). It was about the same distance from Watermeadows as from Ardry End. It was the thought of Watermeadows and Miss Fludd, perhaps more than the fax machine, that made Melrose clap Ruthven on the shoulder. "Brilliant! Get me the fax number of Jury's hotel. If Sly doesn't have a fax machine I'll go on to Sidbury."

2

SLY DID HAVE a fax machine. And he was delighted that Melrose Plant wished to use it, offering its use as if he were doing the customer a personal favor while all the time he was charging an arm and a leg.

Trevor Sly stood behind his copper-lined bar like a child's stick-figure drawing, impossibly tall and thin, washing his hands, as usual, in his best Uriah Heep manner as he said, "That'll be just three pound per page, Mr. Plant." His several-toothed smile would have looked marvelous carved on a pumpkin. Sly had returned from his living quarters with Melrose's three-page fax to Richard Jury.

"A bit steep, isn't it, Mr. Sly?" Melrose nodded toward the beer pulls and added, "And give me a half-pint of that Cairo Flame stuff." Melrose felt as if he needed a sudden jolt. He placed three five-pound notes on the bar—for his three pages and the beer. "Have one yourself."

As Sly's long-fingered hand closed round a glass, he said, "Three pound is only but a trifle more than what it costs me, Mr. Plant, as it's going to the States, now isn't it? And one has to consider the convenience, too."

"What convenience? You're out here in the middle of nowhere. The potholes on that half-mile of road down here nearly took out my muffler. You ought to fix it—it can't be doing business any good." Melrose cared not a jot about road or business; he had been hoping Miss Fludd would emerge from one of the Blue Parrot's shadowy corners. The room was, alas, empty.

Trevor Sly had given Melrose an opening to probe her whereabouts: " 'Convenience' might apply to people who live within walking distance and don't drive." Carelessly, he added, "The Fludds, for example." He paused. Sly said nothing; he was looking off past Melrose. "Has, ah, Miss Fludd been in lately?"

"I don't know but what I preferred the camel to her."

At this conundrum, Melrose started. "What in hell are you talking about?"

Trevor Sly had apparently been lost in contemplation of his newest acquisition, for he pointed a bony forefinger toward the door. "My lady, Mr. Plant." Melrose turned to look at the plaster-of-Paris figure of the painted Arabian woman who served to advertise the menu of the day. "The camel was a bit cleverer, I think." He cocked his head.

"Also moth-eaten." Melrose was annoyed they'd got off the subject of Miss Fludd. "Anyway, what the devil difference does it make, you never have those specials."

Sly's smile managed to convey both sycophancy and superiority. "Now, that's not quite true—"

"The hell it isn't. The meat's supposed to be lamb and all you ever have is beef mince."

"I don't deny that once or twice that's happened, but—"

"Ha! All right—" Melrose slid from the stool and walked over to the menu holder, tried to make out the pseudo-Arab script, and said, "I'll just have an order of this *fatta* stuff. It says here it's 'lamb stew.' " He marched back to his stool.

Trevor Sly said serenely, "Well, now of *course* that dish ain't ready yet, Mr. Plant. Trouble is, I've to depend on Mr. Jurvis, haven't I, just like the rest of you, only with me it's crucial, and here his lad was to bring my order at nine sharp, and it's already gone—" Sly looked around and above him at a clock face implanted in the shoulders of a Sphinx (as he seemed to favor hollowed-out objects)—"half-eleven, and him not here as yet."

Melrose sighed and shoved his half-pint across the bar for a refill. So now it was the fault of Jurvis's Fine Meats and Game.

Sly went on: "I went in Tuesday, regular, as is my way, to place my weekly order. Well, it does create a problem, when one is in the restaurant business. And no sign of that delivery van yet."

Melrose thought maybe he'd just stick around until the van came and bribe the delivery boy, if need be, to tell him whether there was any lamb in Sly's order. He felt irritable, excitable sitting here trying to work out a way of reintroducing the subject of Miss Fludd as he watched Sly draw him another half-pint. He said, "Just where does most of your custom come from anyway?"

"Northampton, I'd say. The young people like my disco nights. That's every Saturday. And there's people come from Sidbury, too, even though the Jack and Hammer's closer to them." At this he simpered with pleasure. "But a lot of my trade's right off the road, so to speak; you know, people on the way to Northampton wanting to stop for a bit of a drink or a meal."

"A lot of people like beef mince."

"Oh, you are a caution, Mr. Plant."

"Well, there aren't many locals come here, do they?"

"Well . . . no-ooo—" Sly pursed his lips. "Mostly, those that live in Long Pidd of course frequent the Jack and Hammer. More convenient, as you say."

"So, actually, you don't have many regulars, do you? I mean, there aren't that many actual homes right around here." Six or seven, and four of those were probably five miles away. That left two. "I mean there's *me*, of course . . ." Melrose drank his Cairo Flame and waited. Nothing. He sighed. "And now, there's this Fludd family—"

"Mr. Trueblood stops by occasionally when he's out antiquing. Said he'd spotted a nice series of pyramids, and would I like them. It was his thought I could spot them about the room, you know, one in each corner, like with the palm to go with it. But I don't know. Be a bit, well, overbearing, don't you think?" In the rear, a telephone jangled. "Back in a tick."

Well, at least it saved him answering that incredible question, he thought, as he looked around at all of the pharaonic items on display: miniature gold pyramids on every table, the odd cardboard Sphinx set here and there. Glumly, he studied his glass and wondered how he'd put down nearly a whole pint of Cairo Flame.

Trevor Sly came writhing back through his beaded curtain, dragging the black telephone on its long extension cord. "It's for you, Mr. Plant."

"Me? Must be Ruthven—"

"No, it's a woman." Sly leaned across the bar, all ears.

"Hello . . . Diane? How did you know I was here?" Ruthven, of course. Melrose sighed. He did wish Ruthven wouldn't bruit his whereabouts to all and sundry. But, she said, it was quite important. Would he *please* stop by and let her give him a drink?

"No. Sorry, Diane, but I'm—quite busy. Waiting for a fax, and all that."

Trevor Sly wiggled his eyebrows as if he were in on the deception.

Irritated, Melrose turned his back. "Jury's supposed to fax me."

"But I think I've worked it out, Melrose. How it was done."

Melrose held the receiver away from him, then drew it back. "What was done?"

"How they were *mur*-dered," she said, impatiently.

Melrose looked up at the ceiling fan, turning dustily. That should be a treat.

3

IN DIANE DEMORNEY'S arctic living room, Melrose sat sunk in a shapeless white leather chair that reminded him of an ice floe. He did not like this chair and never had, but it was either this or the settee (Diane herself commanding suzerainty over the long sofa), and if he sat on the settee, he'd have to share it with the cat. Melrose despised Diane's cat; the feeling (he knew) was mutual. It had squinty golden eyes buried in a mess of soft white fur and an enormous, showy tail that it liked to flick in a warning gesture whenever Melrose looked its way.

At Diane's insistence, he accepted a preluncheon martini, which he did not intend to drink, not on top of the Cairo Flame, but he had agreed to it to be sociable.

He looked around the living room, done so relentlessly in white—carpets, furnishings, slipcovers—that Admiral Byrd would have felt at home. Even the paintings were mysteriously white on white, form sinking into background, redundant against the white walls. Sunlight, in this room, did not bisect carpets in golden rhomboids, or stripe sideboards and walls with delicate lemony fingers. Rather, it flashed and knifed, sparred with mirrors, cut across paintings, looked for a duel.

Diane herself, as if not to disturb the arrangement, was wearing a fine white wool outfit of perfect cut and subtle drape. Her very black hair (also cut and seemingly draped either side of her chin) was a wonderful contrast to all of this. Melrose had to hand it to her: she was always *dressed*, always, whether on her way to market or to the Jack and Hammer or London or college gaudy. He admired that a person could be so self-respecting, she'd go to all of this trouble for no reason beyond her reflection in a mirror, and would also manage to do this in Long Piddleton. Long Piddleton was (except for Marshall Trueblood) pretty much a fashion vacuum. Vivian, for instance, who would dress to the nines in Venice, bumbled about over here in her dusty-colored skirts and jumpers, uncaring.

Whether she really had anything to tell him was anybody's guess; she could do, or it could have been a ruse to get him here. Though Diane was usually too clever to stoop to ruses. In any event, she was evading his pointed questions, so he had been telling her about his London visit while she stirred the martini jug with a long glass icicle-wand which was full of oil in which hundreds of tiny silver stars were suspended. A sudden flash of sun lit the glass stirrer and moved off in its laser search. Melrose only hoped it would rest its pinpoint beam on the cat. *Zap.*

In the midst of talking about the Tate Gallery, he looked around at the brightness and said, "I wouldn't be surprised but what Turner would like this room." As she raised her black eyebrows in noncomprehension, he added. "The painter. J.M.W. Turner."

Diane's mouth formed in a thoughtful little moue as she looked off towards the big bright window and he knew she was exploring her mental Rolodex of tidbits . . . *Tolstoy* . . . *Trieste* . . . *Tristram (& Isolde)* . . . *Turner* . . . *Tutenkha—back up a bit, yes, that's it!* "Turner's black dog."

"What?" She was outdoing herself.

She took a long time with her white cigarette holder and her Silk Cut, screwing in the cigarette, then waving the lot at Melrose for a light. He heaved forward in his chair and lifted the cigarette lighter. Now, with cigarette, martini, and Turner firmly in hand, she sat back, looked up at the ceiling through a ribbon of smoke, and told Melrose the story:

"There's one of the paintings—I forget which one—"

(Naturally, thought Melrose.)

"—in which he's painted a long terrace beside some river or other—"

(Thames, Seine, Rubicon, Styx.)

"—the terrace being lined with houses, trees, and heaps of other things—"

(*Heaps* of things.)

"—and a long wall, all in the most dazzling sunlight, the sunlight striking the wall. *Well*. On this wall is a black dog, standing there, facing the river—" She smiled, almost conspiratorially, over the rim of her big glass. After sipping, she set it down on the glass coffee table.

"Well? Well, what?"

"He'd finished the painting, and just left it to dry, and one of his painter friends walked in and looked at it. He cut the dog out of black paper and pasted it in!" She sat back, beaming. "The dog was just an afterthought."

The cat flicked its tail.

"My. That's—" He wondered if Bea Slocum knew this about J.M.W. Probably not. But, unlike Diane, who wouldn't know a Turner if she ran into a wall of them, Bea knew them, chapter and verse. "—really interesting." Which it was, he supposed, in some weird way.

"I wonder why his friend didn't just paint it in," said Diane, chin cupped in hand, ruminatively.

Melrose looked at her. "The varnish. The painting was—" Hell, why bother. "Diane, you told me on the telephone you had something important to say. About this case Jury's working on?"

She refilled her glass, getting down to business. "I've been thinking . . ."

Oh, that's a treat. Melrose held his glass out to be topped up. "Yes?"

"I started thinking about what could be the connection among these three women. I mean, how they could have been murdered. If they were, of course." She lit another cigarette and went through her lazy exhalations. "I worked it out." She sighed a little, smoked, swung her foot.

"You did? You mean, you worked out how they were killed?"

Now she studied her crimson-painted fingernails. "Um. The earphones."

Melrose felt as if he'd seized up, like the engine of a cheap automobile. "I beg your pardon?"

"*You* know. You said you did it yourself, at that exhibit of portraits in the Tate. You purchased the guided tour. Probably, so did— what's her name?" Melrose was too stunned to answer. And the question, apparently, was rhetorical anyway. Diane did not give a fig for victims. "And the second one, whoever, was in Exeter Cathedral. Now, you know as well as I they nearly *always* have those taped tours of cathedrals. Just to check it out, I rang them up. Guess what? There's a guided tour of those—whatchamcallits—?" She snapped her fingers in an effort to jar her memory. "Those embroidered things. Those cushions."

"Rondels. You're talking about the rondels."

She nodded, pleased as punch. "Now, I bet the one woman picked up the tape of the portrait collections and the other—didn't someone say she was a tapestier?—"

"Tapister."

"A tapister. Wouldn't you imagine she would have listened to one of those tapes?"

Melrose blinked. "Diane, the tour of the Swagger Portraits was done by an actor. He didn't scream out 'PREPARE TO DIE'—"

With an expression of total disdain for his thickness, she said, "My *God*, Melrose, don't you see? The *murderer* switched the tapes!"

He took a long drink of his martini and leaned back in his chair, but since it allowed no real support, he found he was nearly supine. He gathered himself together and sat up. "How?"

" 'How?'? How what?"

"Did he or she switch the tapes."

Here, Diane gave a little flick of her fingers, waving this trivial question away. "I expect any number of ways—*you* should be able to work that out; *you're* writing the mystery! Ask what's-his-name? Inspector Smithson!"

"That's different, for heaven's sake!"

Eagerly, she leaned forward now, clasping her hands round her knees. "But Melrose, *if* someone could do it, it *would* be perfectly plausible, now wouldn't it?"

"If someone could do it . . ." He swigged his drink. "Well, it's that wearisome old 'if' . . ." He chortled (a bit drunkenly? crazily?) and held out his glass to be topped up again. "I mean, if I could grab that knife blade of sunlight on the wall, I could stab your cat, too."

The cat flicked its tail, raised its rump, and *meeeeowwwed*. Diane cuffed it.

"And another thing." Melrose grinned through gritted teeth. He was close to hating himself both for squashing her pretty theory on the one hand and for discussing it on the other. "And another thing," he said again, "it wouldn't work for the young woman they found at Old Sarum, would it?"

"Why not?"

He stared at her, dribbling a bit of his martini as he took his glass from her hand. "Well . . . because they don't have recorded tours of places like Sarum and Stonehenge."

In genuine astonishment, she raised those jet brows and said, "But Melrose, they're famous sites. Stonehenge is one of the most visited *monuments* in the entire world! Old Sarum and Stonehenge are— hundreds of years old!"

Melrose studied the dagger of sunlight now lying across his polished shoe. Perhaps he could grab it up and smite himself, rather than the cat? "I think. I, uh . . . think . . ." He looked up at her rather hopelessly. "I think they expect you, well, when it comes to a place like Stonehenge . . . either you get it . . . or you don't."

Really? said her expression.

THIRTY-TWO

Sam Lasko sighed, the weight of the day's vanishing apparently on his shoulders, taking witnesses with it. "I told her not to leave," he said, almost miserably, his hangdog expression like a dad's whose errant child had gone off in a fit of caprice. "Material witness. Well, that doesn't look good, does it?"

They were walking in the cold dusk past the stone patio of the pub across the street from the park and the River Avon. It was not yet open for its evening trade. Lasko paused, looked up at the façade of the Dirty Duck, as if its refusal to switch to London opening hours were only another stab in the back. "I could use a drink," he said.

They walked on.

"You don't know that she *has*," said Melrose in answer to Lasko's sad statement as to the unreliability of Jenny Kennington. "Left, I mean." He watched a family of ducks ("family" was his own invention) scavenging the riverbank in the far distance for bread left over from that day's takings. Not much in February, he imagined; not many tourists crowding the banks and tossing out crumbs and popcorn and chips to the swans. It was quite beautiful; it always was. Misty sodium lights had just turned themselves on along the path that joined the Royal Shakespeare Theatre and the little church that was the playwright's burial place. Melrose added, "She's just not at home." Now, there was a clever bit of deduction. He felt Lasko's eyes on him. Lamely, he added, "I mean—what about her friends? Might she be visiting one of them?"

"Of course, I checked that out, didn't I?"

"Yes. Sorry." It was all this running around that was dulling his wits. He'd intended to make straight for Stratford-upon-Avon first thing that morning but had instead allowed himself a lie-in following his visits to the Blue Parrot and Diane's.

Lasko asked, "Is this lady a particular friend of Richard's? He seems to be concerned." Lasko's face clouded over, as if this might add to his difficulties.

It certainly added to Melrose's. "Apparently," he responded, impatiently. What was it with Jury and women? Either they died, or turned out to be murderers, or were otherwise totally unsuitable. And now this one had disappeared. According to Lasko. Melrose doubted it. He did not know Jenny Kennington very well—he did not know her at all, come to think of it. Only one time had he actually seen her, and that was at a distance; furthermore, it had been at a funeral. She'd been standing way off, the other side of the grave. But he did know a great deal of her history, that having been an important part of the case in Hertfordshire where she'd lived. And Jury had talked about her on occasion. Consequently, he felt he knew her, knew something of her, that she didn't sound like the type of person who would run off.

As they turned the corner of Ryland Street, Lasko said, again, "She shouldn't have scarpered."

THE HOUSE on Ryland Street, only a short distance from the pub, had been their destination. Seeing the Dirty Duck opening, though, they'd stopped for a drink and a chat about old times.

Now as they walked the short distance to Ryland Street, the breeze coming off the Avon had a tang to it, almost medicinal, and Melrose thought of Wiggins, laid up in hospital reading Josephine Tey. The spartan room came to mind, its antiseptic whiteness relieved by now (he hoped) with bright sprays of color. He'd forgotten to send flowers from himself. Well, that could be the next round.

At the door they were met by a chewed-up black tomcat that looked as if it had just escaped from Borstal. Melrose at first mistook it for a piece of misplaced garden statuary, as it sat there looking scraped, chipped, and dusty.

The cat decided to bristle at sight of the intruders, the hair along its back standing up like a Mohawk on a Piccadilly Circus punk. Actually (thought Melrose, tilting his head) the resemblance was remarkable.

"You wanna see the warrant? There." Lasko unrolled the search warrant and held it out to the cat.

"Thank God you were first one in," said Melrose.

The cat became very starchy, got up and turned its back and swayed out of the hallway.

Melrose and Lasko followed it into the small front room. Melrose immediately made for the kitchen and inspected the floor. A foot from the wastepaper basket stood one bowl of water, clean and topped up, and two dishes of food, one wet, one dry, both partly eaten. He inspected the half-eaten canned food closely.

"All right. Lady Kennington's about and it's coincidence you haven't been in touch, or else she's fixed up with somebody to come in regularly and feed Fidel Castro, here. The food couldn't have been sitting out for long or it would have at least begun to dry up. Either way, she hasn't scarpered, Inspector."

Lasko looked slightly pained. "You can arrange to have somebody feed your animal indefinitely, Mr. Plant."

Melrose shook his head. "No. People don't do that; she'd have taken it to a shelter or given it away. All I'm talking about is it looks like a clear intent to return. And look at the rest of the house." They were in the living room now. "Book open and facedown on chair, newspaper, cup and saucer there beside the chair. It has the look of someone who might have left on the spur—"

"Which is what I'm talking about, isn't it?"

"—to take care of some business or something and possibly been detained. What about that pub you were telling me about that she's thinking of buying up from the brewery?"

Lasko was sifting through mail and circulars lying on a table. "Naturally, I checked there. No one's seen her for two days."

"What I meant was, perhaps she's gone somewhere on business related to it. Up to London, something like that."

"Uh-huh."

Lasko didn't believe it, clearly. He was busy now with the open drawer of a delicate secretaire by the french windows, running his hands through the papers there. It made Melrose feel uncomfortable. And he also thought it a futile search. "What do you think you'll find, Inspector?"

Lasko shrugged. "Beats me." He closed the drawer, turned his eyes toward the ceiling. "I'll think I'll have a look upstairs." He left.

Melrose stood in the center of the living room and simply looked around, finding it cozy, pleasant, perhaps a bit overcrowded with the antiques brought from her former house in Hertford. What had been its name? He remembered passing it on the Littlebourne road, a big place screened by a high wall set well back from everything.

On the gateleg table by which he stood and which (he imagined) served as a makeshift dining-room table, sat a small bisque figurine. He picked it up, turned it in his hands. What did it remind him of? Jury's description of the courtyard of that house—

Stonington. That was it. Still holding the figure, he sat down and looked at it. And he tried to remember what Jenny Kennington looked like, but he couldn't. He was shocked, literally shocked, when he started counting back, measuring off subsequent events in the years that had followed the murders in Littlebourne, that it had been ten years ago. Was it possible?

No, he could not remember her face, but what he could remember was her figure standing back away from everyone on the other side of that grave site. Still and solemn. Detached and rather elegant. And the other thing he remembered: thinking her hands were empty, and then being sure that they weren't. He had stood there on the bank, looking back towards the little cemetery, watching as whatever she'd been holding in her hand had been shoved in her coat pocket. And he knew that it was only out of gratitude (or more) for Richard Jury that the damned thing she'd pocketed hadn't gone into the grave.

Melrose sighed and sat down in the one comfortable armchair. He did not consider himself as particularly brilliant at ferreting out clues; still, he noted the cold, half-drunk cup of coffee on the table beside him, noted the newspaper on the chair's matching ottoman, neatly folded to reveal the crossword. He picked this up, slid down in the chair and looked at the one penciled-in entry. Well, half an entry, as she hadn't finished putting in the rest of the word, which he thought must be

SKULK

The clue was "Not a fox-hunt, but foxes hunting"; that was a misleading clue for "skulk of foxes," he thought. But only the S, K, and U had been penciled in the little squares. She knew it, that was fairly clear. Why had she left it? It, and the rest of the crossword?

He looked over the top of the newspaper, frowning. The phone? The doorbell? Given the order of the rest of the house, the cold cup, the bitten biscuit suggested she'd left in quite a hurry. Leaving a half-finished coffee, a half-finished word. Odd.

Lasko came stomping down the stairs as Melrose had been about to open the newspaper. He said, peering at Melrose, comfortably ensconced in the armchair: "Don't knock yourself out; life's too short. Let's get a drink. You've earned it."

Melrose ignored the sarcasm and got up, forgetting the newspaper.

The cat reappeared, like a well-trained butler, to watch them make their exit.

2

THE DIRTY DUCK had been open for an hour, and had a goodish pre-theatre crowd gathered in both the pub side and the dining room (which side sailed under another name, the Black Swan). Melrose had invited Sam Lasko to dine with him, but Lasko said he'd only got time for a pint before he had to get back to headquarters. The pint had been half-consumed from a standing position, before Lasko said he wanted to call in to see if anything had come up.

Melrose took over a table vacated by a couple and glanced over the theatre advert they'd left behind. The Royal Shakespeare Company was doing one of the *Henrys* and Melrose had no desire to see it. He was in the mood for revenge tragedy. He noted that the little theatre coyly named the Other Place was doing *The Duchess of Malfi*, but not that night. Drat. He could have used a spot of that, or *The Changeling*, or *The White Devil*, or even *The Revenger's Tragedy*, hammy as it was. Last time he'd been in Stratford-upon-Avon he'd twice tried to see the RSC's *Hamlet* and twice been dragged out of it before the good stuff, such as Ophelia's going mad and drowning. Ophelia.

That brought back the Tate Gallery and the Pre-Raphaelites, the Millais portrait of the poor misbegotten girl, and then his mind's eye travelled straight around the gallery—Chatterton. Burne-Jones. Rossetti. He closed his eyes and clamped his head between his hands, gripping his hair and even pulling on it slightly, caught his reflection in a mirrored advertisement for malt whisky, decided he looked demented, and sat up straight.

Still, his mind swam with images. He wondered if a case had ever been solved by free association. Why not? Right now, something was floating gently just out of his mental periphery, something sailing there like an offshore bird, black wing darting. . . .

The voice of Sam Lasko broke into his reflections as the inspector resat himself with a heavy sigh and picked up his pint. "Your pal called you."

"I have so many."

"Sergeant Wiggins. What's he in hospital for?"

"I'm not sure, precisely."

"How'd he find you here?" Lasko had brought back a fresh lager, another bottle of Old Peculier. He drank from his pint, thumb tightly clamped on the top of the handle.

Melrose shrugged, wishing the black-winged bird would fly into his field of vision. He frowned, thinking of it. "Oh. My butler probably told him." He regretted the words almost before they were out of his mouth.

Lasko grunted and leered at him. Butlers (his expression suggested) might have been wandering halls and crypts of stately homes and crumbling castles, but Lasko had never befriended anyone who actually *owned* one.

"Ruthven's practically one of the family. Been around since before I was born—" How stupid. Why was he being defensive? Because Lasko was sitting there glaring at Melrose in the way of a serf at a feudal baron. This really annoyed Melrose. A butler did not a baron make, for God's sake. "Look: remember me? We worked on that American tour-group murder. I'm just plain old me; stop giving me that workingman's leer, that revolutionary glare as if you were going to have me trampled to death by the cast of *Les Miz*."

Sammy Lasko merely grunted again. Then he said, "You got a bunch of titles. Or am I a monkey's?"

"*Had* a bunch, Inspector. *Had*. Stop draping me in purple and ermine. You might well be a monkey's."

"You know this Jennifer Kennington's got one."

"A monkey?"

"A *title*. Lady Kennington. Probably married it—the title. Nice woman, she is. . . ." Lasko seemed to be contemplating Jenny Kennington's "niceness."

Glad to be off his titles and onto hers, Melrose asked, "Jury didn't tell me what was going on. Why do you want her?"

"She's a witness."

"That's vague enough. So are we all, to something or other."

"So what is it with Jury and this lady?"

"I don't know."

"He seems to think she couldn't possibly have done a flit. What's she like, then?"

"I don't know," said Melrose again. "Never met the lady."

Lasko was taken aback. "Then why's he send *you?* At least *I've* talked to her." But his hurt silence relaxed.

"Because, my dear Inspector, I'm an idler; I have time to waste on pub lunches and crossword puzzles. You're a policeman; you don't." Mention of the crossword puzzle called up the folded newspaper on the chair. He frowned. Why *had* she stopped in the middle of pencilling in a word? "But you haven't answered my question. What's this all about?"

"Just another case," said Lasko, mysteriously.

"You mean you aren't going to tell me?"

"No."

"I've been told to try and find Lady Kennington and you aren't going to tell me *why?*"

"No." Feudalism long forgotten, Lasko pulled rank. "Mr. Plant, it's official business, isn't it? I can't go discussing it with the public, now can I?" He whipped out a smile as if he were a waiter snapping a napkin onto a lap.

"Well, good God, I'm not exactly the *public*. And I'm doing you a favor. Trying to, at least."

Lasko smiled. "Him. You're doing *him* a favor."

"I know professional jealousy when I see it. Sure you don't want to have dinner with me? Food's good here; I've eaten it before."

"Thanks very much, I appreciate it, but I better get back." Lasko reached for money, but Melrose waved him off. "You're my guest. Oh . . . incidentally, I was wondering . . . I don't expect we might just have another look round that house?"

"I don't expect so, no, sir."

Exasperated, Melrose said, "I merely want to check and see if that news—" Melrose shut up. For if there was something to be found, if that newspaper offered up some clue that might lead him to Jenny

Kennington, would he want Lasko to know right away? "Oh, very well. I'm going back to my hotel, then. Uh, is there a newsagent's still open?—it's after six," he added, checking his watch.

"Right down there, round the corner. Or if that's not open, W. H. Smith's might still be." Lasko gulped the last of his pint. "Thanks for the drink, Mr. Plant. Mind you call your pal."

Melrose gave his departing back a sour smile.

3

MELROSE CALLED his pal.

Back in his pleasantly Tudorish suite at the Shakespeare Hotel, and with his two local and one regional newspaper, Melrose put in a call to the Fulham Road Hospital. It was nearly seven-thirty and he had not yet had his dinner, but he felt a little sorry for Wiggins, knocked up there in a hospital bed, and he felt obliged to return his call. He would just chat briefly and then have a bath.

As the call was put through the various switchboards, he hummed to himself and mentally reviewed the restaurants he thought were possibilities. He had stopped at several points throughout his return walk to check menus, and had also studied the one outside of the Shakespeare's dining room. *Blinis*, to begin, and then either the *queues de boeuf* or perhaps the *langoustines crème glacée* and a bottle of Châteauneuf du Pape or a Pouilly-Fumé. His mouth watered; he was starving; perhaps he wouldn't bother with a bath.

"Sergeant Wiggins!" He feigned a bit more enthusiasm than he actually felt. After all, he'd seen him only yesterday. "How are you coming along?" He asked this routinely as he shook open one of the newspapers and searched through the pages. No crossword.

"The treatment here is really quite wonderful, Mr. Plant. I'd no idea being in hospital could be such a relaxing experience. It's hot and cold running nurses, it is—" Wiggins came close to giggling—"at my beck and call. Tea whenever I fancy, properly done, too. Pot and china cup, none of your polyethylene cups. And this one nurse, Lillywhite, her name is, is ever so accommodating."

Melrose, who was lying full-length on his comfortable queen-sized bed, opened the other paper, and turned the pages. No crossword. His eyelids were growing heavy as the sergeant rattled on about the hospital "amenities." The third newspaper revealed a crossword puzzle, true, but it was clearly not the one Jenny Kennington had been work-ing on. He sighed and tossed it aside and listened to Wiggins go on about the "cuisine." This brought back oxtails and wine, perhaps that delicious-sounding iced nougat for dessert. He shut his eyes, but briefly, snapping fully awake at Wiggins's puzzling reference to the rondels.

"What about them? What sort of clue?"

"This Helen Hawes was one of the tapisters. And she died while she was studying the rondels, as I understand it. If you're on your way to Exeter, I'd give those cushions a serious look, I would."

What was he talking about? Melrose was afraid he knew. "Sergeant Wiggins, you're not seriously suggesting something was *embroidered* into one of the cushions?"

"A threat of some sort. Stranger things have happened."

No, they haven't. The hand not holding the receiver made a crablike crawl across his scalp, massaging his hair up into licks.

"And whatever documents you've come up with, I'd appreciate seeing." His tone was slightly condescending.

"Don't know what you're talking about." Melrose switched the receiver to his other ear. "I saw you just yesterday, remember; I showed you the only 'documents' I've seen. I told you everything I know."

Was that a patronizing sniff that came down the wire? "Mr. Plant, there's always things that go missing—"

"Damned right. And they've gone."

"I was thinking you might just fax me whatever you've come up with since. I've a few ideas—"

"Nothing since."

"*Nothing*, Mr. Plant?"

Wiggins said this ever so gently, the insinuation clear: without Superintendent Jury (and, by extension, Sergeant Wiggins) to shore him up, Melrose Plant might as well skip off with his hoop and stick, for all the good he was doing.

Melrose held the thin receiver away from his ear, above him, as if it were a Slim-line human face, and stuck his tongue out at it. When he returned it to his ear he heard:

". . . mander Macalvie. I've already got a call into Exeter HQ for him. I'm sure he'll fax me the documents his end, and if you could do the same *your* end—that is, when you've got something—it would be a big help. Now, as I said, I've some theories, based on reading I've been doing. They might have been drugged."

What? What in hell was the man talking about? Melrose switched the receiver again, rolled over onto his side. "Sergeant Wiggins, I don't know what you're talking about."

"You haven't been doing your research, is why," said Wiggins, in a tone of remonstrance better suited to third form. Pages and papers riffled and rattled. "First of all, there's plenty of poisonous plants in the American Southwest. . . ."

"For heaven's sake, Sergeant, if they'd been poisoned, the police would know it, wouldn't they?"

One could almost see the satisfied little crimping of the sergeant's lips. "If you'd my experience of poisons, sir, you'd know that it's not that easy to detect. For one thing, you have to *know* what you're looking for. *Now,* if these two Englishwomen had come across a peyotist—"

"A what?"

"Peyotist. It's a religion, really, of the native American Indians. Peyote is used in their rituals."

Melrose yawned. "Is Carlos Castaneda in this story?" He closed his eyes.

Wiggins ignored this and started in—grindingly "in"—telling Melrose all about peyote and other hallucinogenic drugs. "See, I've had this Nurse Lillywhite getting reading material for me. It's incredible how kind and helpful these nurses here are. Lillywhite's run out to Dillon's for me several times, and once even went all the way to Tottenham Court Road to get some obscure book at Foyle's—"

Thank you, Nurse Lillywhite. Your next check will not be in the mail. Melrose's stomach rumbled as he pulled one of the pillows from underneath his head and put it over his face, wondering if anyone had ever managed to suffocate himself.

The sergeant droned on, finishing with an account of poisonous plants and turning to other matters. "Now this turquoise stone. You might be ignoring something important there—"

Melrose only wanted to ignore everything except the oxtails and *blinis* as he blew hot breath back on his nose.

"You've heard of the Ojibwa—"

Pause. "Tu whu?"

Pause. "Are you all right, Mr. Plant? Not coming down with this virus going round, I hope?" Wiggins lost interest in Plant's health, and went on. "The Ojibwa actually believe that stones have the ability to respond—that's putting it much too simplistically. Let's just say, some stones are animated. Not all stones, of course . . ."

Perhaps if he rolled over on his stomach. The receiver slipped away as he now pushed his face down into the pillows and total blackness. He would lose consciousness either way, what did it matter, but he did give a passing thought to how the Ojibwa knew *which* stones were animated. Not the ones within listening distance of Wiggins's hospital bed, he bet.

The peroration of the sergeant, desperate sounding, staticky, came from the receiver as Melrose decided against the iced nougat in favor of a rhubarb coulis. When the sound stopped altogether, he rolled over again, yanked up the receiver, and said, "Fascinating, Sergeant Wiggins."

"Thank you. You've no idea how much I appreciate your bringing me this Josephine Tey mystery—"

Oh, *that* had been a brilliant idea, thank you very much! Melrose checked his watch. Wiggins had been going on for a goodish twenty or thirty minutes, nonstop.

"—and it's amazing what a person can do even bunged up in hospital. Well, her detective solved the case." There was a small commotion somewhere in the room, female laughter, comings and goings, to-ings and fro-ings.

"This is something! I've just received more flowers, Mr. Plant! I'd no idea I was so popular." And then a brief, weighted silence. Wiggins added mournfully, "I expect you haven't had time, yourself. To stop by a florist, I mean. Never mind." His sigh was grandly forgiving.

Wishing he had a few dozen peyote buttons to toss around, Melrose said he would be sure to send some, *tout de suite*, said he had to ring off, said goodbye, slammed down the receiver.

FURNISH THE DOCUMENTS! FIND JENNY! SEND FLOWERS!

4

HAVING NOW fully enjoyed his *langoustines crème glacée* topped off with the iced nougat (with Armagnac!), every bit as delicious as its name, and having put one of the bread rolls in his pocket, Melrose was taking a walk before retiring, a rare after-dinner ramble. The after-dinner pursuits at Ardry End were more along the lines of port and a book by the fire, with his dog, Mindy, asleep (or possibly dead, he was never sure which) at his feet.

After dinner at Ardry End—wait just a tick, now. . . . He paused and studied the paving stones. The French for after dinner—? *Après diner?* This had a definite ring to it! "*Après Diner* at Ardry End." Could he turn this into a book, a series of anecdotes about country life, along the lines of *A Year in Provence?* Why, Mr. Momaday was certainly a match for any of those Provençal eccentrics; after all, Melrose must have talent, too, what with all of these writers—Polly, Ellen, Joanna—treating him as if he were Maxwell Perkins—

Oh, do *shut up!* cried his other, sensible, sterner self, glaring over the top of gold-rimmed spectacles. *Bad as Sergeant Wiggins,* his other self muttered.

Melrose sighed and walked on, past W. H. Smith's, past Boots (were there a Smith's and a Boots on Venus, he wondered?) and on down the High Street. He abandoned his nonfiction writing career, but *not* his fiction, not *Gin Lane.* And, of course, all of this talk with Polly, all of this thinking about writing, brought to mind Ellen Taylor and that trilogy of *Windows, Doors,* and the untitled third. It brought to mind his promise to help her draw a bead on that absurd woman who was stealing Ellen's stuff. Melrose chuckled. His plan was brilliant! Ellen would love it. But he had to work out some of the details first.

Strange how his feet had carried him smack-up to the stone steps of the Dirty Duck. Save that for later. He crossed the road and found the path that led round beside the theatre and on into the graceful, grassy expanse of trees flanked by the River Avon.

It was a lovely night, but misty, and the ghostly columns of the little brass-rubbing center rose before him like blanched bones. He struck out from the gravelled path across the grass to the river, where he stood on the bank and looked out at the sinuous light the moon cast on the gently moving Avon. All was silent. How silent the nights could be, even in London, in pockets such as that part of Bethnal Green through which he'd taken his short walk after the meal with Bea. What had she said . . . ? That the fondling and kissing in the Tate had been merely a put-on, that Gabe liked to see other people's reactions. And Bea had had her eyes open, sitting there, out of boredom. If that were the case, though, had Gabe also let *his* eyes flutter open?

Checking reactions of the gallery-goers? And *his* eyes were looking across at Frances Hamilton. Well, it was a small thing but worth asking about.

Melrose looked down at the undulating, marshy grasses serving as a sort of soggy mattress for a circle of sleeping, bobbing ducks, several with their heads beneath their wings. He took the bread roll from his pocket and began tearing it up. A platoon of other ducks—the Avon Night Patrol—rowed over in military formation upon seeing this bit of action. Out of seeming nowhere, as if floating on air, an illusion caused by the mist across the river, came two swans, one black, one white, moving in for a share of the spoils.

Melrose tossed out crumbs as he wondered if Jury had yet received his fax. Ten o'clock here. . . . That would make it five over there, wouldn't it? No. There was another time change between the coasts—one hour? Two? Three? Where was New Mexico? Probably somewhere around California, in that area. Melrose ran a couple of blanked-out maps of the United States through his mind but could only fill in Baltimore, which was near New York City. And California. He knew where that was, naturally. With his hand full of unshed crumbs (which the swans were busily demanding) he tried to fix New Mexico on his mental map. In the manner of a blindfolded child trying to pin the tail on a donkey, he made a mental stab. THERE!

Where had that homeless chap been from? Baton Rouge, that was it. Where was it? Baton Rouge, what an exquisite name. . . . It was Jury's fault, of course, this blank map. If Jury had had him come along, he'd know where the damned place was.

He chucked the remaining breadcrumbs across the river's surface and dusted his hands. The bossy swans made mince of the ducks' efforts to capture this treat. Bullies, thought Melrose, who decided to stop feeling sorry for himself. Jury was probably right: Melrose would be of more help going back over the ground that Jury had already trod, talking to the same people and forming his own impressions. Viewpoints were important. He continued to stand on the cold, damp riverbank and consider those impressions.

But all he could think of was Miss Fludd.

And Turner's black dog.

He heard, in the distance off to his left, muted voices—the audience leaving the theatre, fanning out across the car park, the pavements, the several pathways to their numerous destinations. Flooding the Dirty Duck, undoubtedly, so he'd just as well skip that and go on back to the hotel.

One route was to walk along Ryland Street and then to cut over, and he did so. As he passed Jenny Kennington's little house, he stopped and inspected its windows. Dark.

The abysmal pressure of time seemed to weigh on him. He turned up his coat collar against the foggy night and wondered again about New Mexico, about the sun going down, or the sun coming up.

THIRTY-THREE

Movie sun.

What would they have done, Jury wondered, looking down towards the road, if the light hadn't cooperated? For it certainly was doing so. Far away, but seeming close, were the Sangre de Cristos where light spread in a wash of watercolors across the sky, turning the underneath side of the clouds to gold.

He had this fanciful thought while standing on the wide stone steps of the Rancho del Reposo lodge, watching the progress of the film crew in the distance. Voices, tiny and unintelligible, carried weakly through the cold air as if blown back from the narrow highway down there where several of them were waving their arms or using bullhorns to reroute traffic. This consisted of sending the occasional car from the narrow paved road into the oblivion of an even narrower dirt road. But the drivers didn't seem to mind; most of them had pulled over and up on a shoulder to rubberneck the film folk.

The Rancho del Reposo was, in the words of those old film westerns, a "spread." It was a rich (though not necessarily tasteful) mixture of architectures—Moorish, western, Spanish, the glassily American. Red pantiled roofs, adobe walls inset with hand-painted Spanish tiles, the glass excrescence of what could have been an arboretum off to one side but which appeared to be a dining room or else an informal cafe. It was linked to the main structure by a portico lined with cacti and desert grasses. The spread of the ranch's many buildings—low, discreet adobe casitas sheltered by piñons and juniper—stretched away for acres from the main building. All of it looked incredibly pricey. Inside, several fires burned brightly, Saltillo tiles shone beneath long, colorful rugs, guests sat about having coffee, most of them with camera equipment or walkie-talkies or other film-making paraphernalia hanging from leather straps or wound somehow about their persons.

The two women behind the desk just inside the entrance were what Jury had come to think of as Santa Fe cheerful; in addition to the goodwill they exuded for the sake of the Rancho del Reposo's PR, was also that extra something, that dollop of aren't-we-all-lucky-to-live-here? air.

Jury returned the smile of the hearty receptionist and asked (by way of breaking the ice), "What's going on down on the road? Filming something, are they?" He looked through a wide glass door out to a patio, where more people were sitting at tables than he would have expected outside in February. Still, it was warm in the sunlight.

"Oh, yes. We're used to it, aren't we, Patsy?" This was directed to the other woman, a rather heavy, horsy type, who smiled and nodded and went back to sorting registration cards. "There's usually some film or TV company around. It's the scenery, you see."

Jury wondered if perhaps she thought he'd missed it. "I've noticed." He was pulling out his police identification.

"You're registering, Mr.—?" Her well-tended eyebrows rose in a question.

"Jury. It's Superintendent Jury, actually. Scotland Yard CID." *Here* was something new! He was rather pleased when the woman looked startled; he held up the warrant card so that both of them could see it, flashy as a press pass. The first woman seemed to be primping her hair as she looked, as if the little square of plastic were a pocket mirror. "I'm making some inquiries," he explained.

The second woman, Patsy, was a bit quicker off the mark than the first. "Angela Hope. You're here about Angela Hope, aren't you?"

"Did you know her, then?"

Patsy shook her head. "Not really. I mean, yes, I'd seen her. In that shop she had on Canyon Road. Didn't really know her, though."

"I was here, actually, about these two women. They stayed, we think, at the La Fonda. At least for a day or two." Jury lined up the two photos of Fanny Hamilton and Nell Hawes. "It's possible, though, one or the other might have stopped somewhere else, too." The Rancho del Reposo would have been way beyond Nell Hawes's means, but not Frances Hamilton's. "Do you recognize either of them?"

Patsy tapped the photo of Fanny Hamilton. "This one, yes. She stayed here. You remember her, Em? American but with an English accent?"

Em squinted at the photos. Needed glasses, probably, and probably too conscious of her looks to wear them all the time. She slipped a pair out of a cowhide case and put them on. Then she nodded. "Yes. She was here—let's see—October? November? Yes, it was before Thanksgiving. Had one of the casitas. Don't recall offhand which. But I can get that for you—" She turned around to the shelves where Patsy had been dealing with the registration cards.

Jury asked Patsy, "Did she have any visitors you remember?"

"Oh, well, that's a tall order. My memory's good, but not that good. Let me think . . ." She seemed sincerely to be doing so, her eye straying again to the snapshots. "Wait a minute—yes! It was this other woman who came here; they had lunch or dinner together. I remember because they both sounded English."

Em held up a large white card, waved it like a handkerchief. "I've got it here. Mrs. Frances Hamilton, Belgravia, London SW1." She placed it before Jury.

"You remember this other lady, Em? The two of them dined here."

"Um. No, I don't think I was on duty." She shrugged.

Jury was writing on the back of one of his cards. "If you should remember anything about either of them, would you get in touch with me? I'm staying at the La Fonda." Em took the card and nodded. Jury thanked them, turned away, turned back. "Could you give me the hotel's phone and fax numbers? Probably you've more than one of each."

Patsy plucked one of the hotel's cards from a holder, turned it, and wrote a couple of numbers on the back. "The main number's printed here—" she indicated the face of the card—"with the fax number. I put the others on the back."

Again, Jury thanked them, gave the card a look. Not the number in the address book, but he hadn't thought it would be. "I wonder, if they had a meal here, could I talk to your dining-room staff. Perhaps I can find the person who might have served them."

Patsy looked again at one of the slips stapled to the card. "It was a Friday night, so it could have been . . . let's see, table thirteen, that'd be either Johnny or Sally. I think they're both here if you want to check with Chris. She's the hostess." Patsy nodded toward a wide arch across the tiled hallway.

Chris—who was extremely attractive, probably a needful thing in a dining-room hostess—was bent slightly over the lectern-like post that held her reservations book. The bottom of her face was bathed in the light from the small lamp that arched over her book. At Jury's request, she seemed fairly thrilled. "Sally Weeks? She's here, somewhere." Chris peered into the soft, dark depths of the dining room and finally pointed toward a girl at the far side wiping off a table. "That's Sally, there. Yes, she might have been working that Friday night. I mean, that's her schedule, unless she was sick or something."

Sally Weeks was on the thin side and quite young. Brown hair, brown eyes, brown uniform—like a dry leaf. But this desiccated, autumnal look was quickly dispelled by the energy of her expression. She had a boyish torso and Jury thought that might be the reason she held the small tray close over her chest, arms crossed on the tray's back, hiding her own flatness in this relative sea of actressy bosoms.

Since the lunch service hadn't yet started, and the dining room was empty, she said it was all right for her to sit down (in the smoking section, for she was dying for a cigarette). And as Jury lit it for her, she said that that was one of the reasons she remembered them—the two women—because they were the only smokers, the only ones sitting in the smoking section here.

"But mostly," she added, thoughtfully, "it's because they'd been travelling around, and *not* with a tour group, and *not* with a man. It was because they really seemed to be enjoying themselves." She made a comment about there being more smokers in England and asked Jury if he didn't smoke. He told her he was trying to quit.

Immediately, she stubbed out what was left of her cigarette. "I'm really sorry, you should have said." Jury was startled by such consideration. Now she was looking around the room. "You want to sit somewhere else?" It was as if the whole area might be contaminated for him.

He laughed. "No, Sally, this is fine. Go on with what you were saying."

"Well, it's not often you see two ladies, almost elderly—I think they were in their sixties, at least—travelling around on the loose that way. If you'd been working here as long as I've been, you'd know what I mean."

Jury couldn't imagine she'd been working anyplace for very long. She didn't look much over seventeen. But he didn't say so. "Tell me what you mean about enjoying the travelling."

Sally rubbed at her temples in an old lady's gesture of trolling for memories. "Well, they really wanted to *see* things."

"Isn't that why most people travel?"

"Oh, no. For most people it's just a way of—doing something together. I don't mean *being* together, I get the impression a lot of them couldn't care less. I don't mean they really like each other. Families—well, it's the same thing. 'We're a family; we must be, we're travelling out here together.' "

Jury smiled. "Fine distinctions you're making. Did you overhear anything they said about their plans?"

"Well, they were talking to me sometimes, actually. They were talking about Mesa Verde, that was one place, and I told them it was worth seeing."

"It is; I just got back from there."

"It's *really* kind of mystical. Not like Sedona. So I told them not to bother with Sedona. I was serving their soup. Pumpkin."

Jury was silent. He didn't want to disturb that deep look of concentration. Finally, he asked, "Why did you tell them that?"

Her answer was indirect. "I told them to go to Utah instead. Maybe to Canyonlands. Utah has all of that red rock, more than Sedona does, certainly, and it doesn't have people. You can drive and drive for miles and not see anyone, not a person, not a car. I'm pretty sick of Sedona." She topped this declaration with an emphatic nod and a look at Jury of shared sympathy: he must be pretty sick of Sedona, too.

He smiled. "Never been there." Jury gathered up his coat.

"Don't go—" She might have been directing this to Jury as well as speaking of Sedona. "It's just an ordinary town that's really built up because everybody keeps telling everybody else how spiritual and mystical it is. A real New Age place, you know. Crystals, rocks, vortexes. A vortex is supposed to be a place in earth where there's a lot of concentrated energy."

As he rose to leave, Jury was thinking that Sally herself was better than any vortex, the way the brown eyes beamed.

He walked out through the glass doors and looked around for an empty table, didn't see one. He did, however, see Malcolm Corey, remembered that Corey had told him he was "on call" today. Corey signed to him with a little wave and pointed to a chair beside him. "I'm just waiting for them to call me."

Jury sat down. "Nice to see you. Have you done your bit yet?"

" 'Bit' is the word. Mine is one line. I've been waiting in this fucking makeup for two hours now. Probably, they'll call me back tomorrow. How do I look?" Preening, he turned his face toward Jury.

Actually, except for the slight rouging of the lips, it wasn't all that easy to tell he was wearing makeup since he was ordinarily that polished oak color anyway. "Marvellous," said Jury.

"I'm waiting for a friend. My agent," he explained. "Supposed to meet me here. Benny Betts. Know him?" Malcolm craned his neck, scoping out the room.

"Don't think so. What's the film they're shooting, then?"

"It's called *The Sun in the Morning*. Terrible title." Malcolm Corey yawned and shrugged. Then he wiggled his fingers at someone across the room, a woman dressed in frills and sequins that looked out of place with the rough clothes of the others. "It's one of those 'revisionist' Westerns. Copying Clint, of course. Ever since Clint—ah! Here he is!" He nodded toward a man who was coming their way.

Even as he walked toward their table, Benny Betts was talking on a cordless telephone and carrying a second one on a leather thong slung over his shoulder like a camera. He wore a suit so fine and so loose it looked fitted by the wind; a dusty blue shirt with a roll collar that, oddly enough, went with the expensive suit. No tie, of course. Shoes with a mirror polish.

Benny Betts punched off the phone and punched into his client— "Mac, how goes it?"—and his client's friend, thrusting out his hand and gripping Jury's in a handshake that was surprising in its strength. Even more surprising was the feel of a callused palm. If he'd expected anything it would have been a hand slightly moist and almost downy in its softness. He swiveled into a chair, said to Jury, "You represented?"

Jury nodded and reached once more for his wallet. "By the CID." He smiled.

"That like ICM?"

"Not unless it's criminal investigation." He shoved his ID toward Betts.

Benny narrowed his eyes as if trying to comprehend. Then widened them. "Jesus! You're a cop?"

"So I've been told. Some might dispute it."

Malcolm Corey laughed. "Too bad, Ben; you can't sign him." To Jury, he said, "Benny misses nothing, *nothing*. I love him."

"Love me, you may well. But you're not positioned right, not for a package. I'm looking at cable options *sans cesse*, excuse me—" He plucked up the receiver of one of the phones before it had barely registered a ring. "Betts. . . . Yes. Put him—*Bobby, Bobby, Bobby!* You heard. . . . I'm talking *Wizard*, Bobby. A remake—. . . What the fuck do you *mean*, like redoing *Casablanca?* Hell, I've already got *'Blanca* packaged. I figure Alec and Isabella; nice touch, the daughter, you know. So what do—. . . Sacred?" Benny pinched the bridge of his nose, made phony weeping noises. "Sacred. This is *Hollywood* you're talking about, Bobby, not Lourdes or the Luray Caverns, so what—" For a few jumpy moments, Benny listened and sighed, then cut into what he clearly thought unenlightened comments with, "Bobby, Bobby, what do I do with you? . . . Okay! Okay! I'm not pushing, why should I? Even Woody's interested. He's great with this *noir* stuff. . . . *Noir*, that's what I'm saying. Downbeat, definitely downbeat version. No yellow brick, no emeralds. So think about it, all right; but I won't wait until you get the shit off your camera lens—. . . All right, all *right*. . . . Yeah. . . . Um. . . . Bye." Benny plunked down the phone, picked it up again and punched in numbers. "Can you believe that guy?" he asked earnestly, looking from Jury to Malcolm. He shivered, clamped the phone to his ear, asked for Jim. "Jim, Jim, Jim, long time. . . . Yes, I told you I'd get back to you. So what I've got here, definite, is Neil doing the script, Sean and Miranda are begging for it. . . . Uh-huh. Three weeks he'll be done, that's a promise. . . . Neil. . . . Yes. . . . Read it?" Benny laughed soundlessly. "You don't need to *read* it, fella, . . . Three weeks, I told you. Done, *fini*, and we'll have it on the table. *And* I'm considering Vanessa for the mother. . . . Of course there's a mother. This is Ireland we're talking about; there's always a mother. . . . No, I can't *promise* her; she's not one of mine. Personal favor to you. . . . Jim, look, if I run I stumble. . . . Breathe blue, will you? . . . You don't want much, do you? . . . I've got to have a total lock before I approach—look, these people turn down scripts like you swat flies, you know—" Benny sighed, leaned back, seemed to be gazing off at the Sangre de Cristos, shaking his head. "Jim, this package is beauty personified; it's like—" He squinted his eyes, as if reaching for a metaphor; then he shrugged, gave up and returned to the literal. "I can't wait forever. Mamet's talking about a collabor—...okay. Great....Great....Fantastic....Absolutely....Tomorrow....Bye." Benny picked up the portable phone again, dialed, and there was more patter with somebody's secretary.

Jury looked round the patio, which had been for some time now in a state of flux, movie folk moving off, coming out through the big glass doors as if they were being cued. Or, at least, Jury presumed them to be film people, given they were either holding walkie-talkies or travelling with long wires looped about them or else in costume. He thought the clothes were costumes, clothes suggestive of the old West, a lot of grimy jeans, muddy boots, neckerchiefs, mustaches, mutton-chop whiskers. Most of the women were wearing long worsted skirts, dull browns and grays, but with the occasional flash of a satin gown in ripe colors . . . such as the one rustling by the table right now of warm apricot and brilliant blue shot through with silver, which was adorning a blond woman so flawlessly beautiful that Jury stopped breathing for a few heartbeats just to hold on to the vision. No one else seemed to be paying attention to her. Was beauty really so common out here that no one else would even bother to look up? Now through the glass doors walked a redhead in velvet burgundy, the equal in looks of the statuesque blonde, followed shortly by a brunette in lavender taffeta. These dance-hall headliners (for that seemed to be what they were costumed as) gathered back by one of the stone pillars like a huge bouquet. And no one noticed.

A waitress brought over one of the house extensions, trailing a cord behind her, and set it before Benny Betts. He signed off the portable and snatched up the other one. "Neil, Neil, Neil! You hate me. You hate me, don't lie. But you won't when I tell you this: I've got a definite from Jim to produce and Sean and Miranda for the leads. A definite. But they won't do it unless you do the script. David wants it but of course I said no, you could hear weeping all the way to Killarney, right? . . . Of course, you're overcommitted, you always are, why the hell do you think these people are thrashing around trying to work with— . . . Uh-huh . . . Uh-huh . . . That's right. And Vanessa for the mother. . . . How do I know there's going to be a mother?" Benny clamped the receiver to his chest and looked quickly from Malcolm to Jury: "Get that?" Back to the phone: "Neil, this is Ireland; there's always a mother. . . . Uh-huh. So how long do you think? Uh-huh . . . Uh-huh. . . . Three months? A tad long, *mon cher*. Not that everyone won't wait, of course. It's just that Sean has another commitment—. . . Two months? . . . Uh-huh. Think you could pare that down to, ooooh, let's say six weeks? . . . You'll try." Benny gave Jury a broad wink. "You're my fave, Neil, as per always. . . . Okay. . . . Right. . . . Later."

His eyes shut, face turned up in that light-worshipping way, Malcolm Corey said, smiling, "I love you, Benny, but you have no ideals. None whatever."

"What's to idealize? That shit down there?" His eyes were on the crew moving in unison along the distant road. Then, back to the telephone: "Belinda, my sacred one, where is he? Uh-huh. Lunch? Sal's? When back?" Benny checked his Rolex, shook it, as if in so doing he could move lunch along. "Okay, just tell him I'll call back."

In the silence that befell them, the air still hummed. Jury asked, "You wouldn't be interested in police work, would you?"

Benny Betts, swivelling his head, apparently looking for action, replied, "God knows I wish I could get *something* challenging." He clamped Malcolm on the shoulder, said, "Okay, Mac. Now. We've got to get repositioned and cable is *it*. That, or a series. And we've got to reimage, okay?"

"I say shit to TV, Ben."

"Who doesn't? That's a reason? I'm working on it. Exploring cable options, like I said."

"What about that other business?"

"The deal will happen when it happens. You know me. I wait. I bide my time."

"I'm *not* doing sitcom, Benny, that's all. You may not believe it—" here Corey smiled to show he didn't really believe that Ben didn't believe it—"But I consider myself an *ac*-tor." He made the word sound like Benny's French. "An *art*-ist."

"Well, I suggest you get your artistic ass into this series I've got lined up if you want to do the Clint flick. You're part of the Tooley package, and I told him if he wants Clare Tooley, he takes this incandescent new talent I've just found. And he really wants Clare Tooley."

"And has Clare Tooley *agreed* to do this part?"

"Yes, but she doesn't know it yet." Benny was tattooing numbers again.

A gentle laugh from Malcolm Corey. "You're so louche, Benny."

"Yeah? Well, I'm rich and louche which is more than can be said *pour vous*." He repunched his number, got Belinda again, who connected him. "Stevie, Stevie! Where the hell—? . . . You can't lunch at Sal's anymore, not after that last— . . . Yeah. . . . Yeah. . . . Uh-huh. . . . I've got a project on a silver platter for—what? . . . *Wizard*? Where'd you hear—? . . . No, no, no. Not a *remake*, for God's sake. Is nothing sacred? A prequel. . . . Right. Maybe when she's eight, six, even. I've got an amazing new talent, no names, now." Benny waggled his finger. "You think I want her snatched out from under me? Before the hurricane . . . Tornado? Okay, before the tornado, before the big wind fucks with Kansas. . . . Right. Delve into character shaping, a *pièce noire*— . . . Whaddaya mean, the dog? The fucking dog's not even born yet, Steve. . . . So? . . . Well, a puppy then, it could be. Am I a scriptwriter? I'm not saying— . . . Wait, wait, man! I didn't call you to talk about this; this one's wrapped. You want a piece, down on your knees, *mon cher*." Benny chuckled. "It's the 'Blanca deal, you remember. I've got a natural for the Bogey part—new face, awesome talent. For Ingrid's, well, Isabella wants it, of course. But I was thinking Melanie. . . . I know she can't do accents, but who's talking accents? Besides, I've got a real ac-tor for the Louis role." Here, he pointed at Corey and winked. "Where am I? Santa Fe. . . . Santa—you know, it's that suburb of L.A. . . . I don't know; wait a sec." He cradled the phone again, asked Corey, "What's the name of this dog they're shooting?"

"The Sun in the Morning."

Benny frowned. "Ponderous. Who thought that up?" He repeated this to Steve. "Well, get back to me, then. But don't wait too long or the Woodsman'll get it. He's been after me for weeks now." Then, exasperated, Benny searched the cold heavens above him, shaking his head. "And who's talking *Algiers*? . . . Yeah. So that's where it is, I know that's where it is, but since when did where it is become where it's got to be? Jesus, Stevie, you been hitting the books again? You've turned literal. You've got to have vision in this game. *Le vis-ion*."

Malcolm looked at Benny in sheer amazement, mouthed the word *vision*. Looked a question at Jury, pointed to Betts, again mouthed the word *vision*. Rolled his eyes, shut them again. "Name me one time you ever had any 'vision,' Benny."

Benny pushed in the aerial, said, "To get Merchant without Ivory." He flashed a grin. "Or vice-versa." Then he sat back, drumming his fingers on the table, mouth moving slightly as if he were making phone calls in his mind.

"This film we're shooting." Malcolm's voice changed slightly, into a parody of a lilt. "Your girlfriend's in it."

Benny looked at Malcolm as if the man were speaking in an unknown tongue. He continued drumming his fingers.

"She's right over there." Here Malcolm turned and looked off in the direction of the three beautiful women, one of whom was rearranging the bouquet by peeling away from it. "Ah! Here she comes!" In a pretense of a whisper, Malcolm said to Jury, "Benny here once had a relationship with her."

Benny, back on the portable telephone, said, "I don't have 'relationships.' I leave that to the rest of the world. I hate that fucking word. Jock! Man, where you been?"

It was the redhead with the milky skin who was now hovering over their table. A beauty mark near the corner of her mouth, a beauty mark on her breast. She didn't need either. The beautiful blonde swayed by once again; Benny looked through her, didn't register her presence. He went back to thumbing his address book.

Looking, looking for something (Jury thought), *anything*. Jury smiled.

Two more calls through someone's secretary. Sean wasn't there; Miranda was. No one would do it without Miranda. Sean insisted, so did Neil. For the sister, right. It was an undone deal without her, better believe it.

Malcolm believed it.

Jury believed it.

Miranda must have believed it.

THIRTY-FOUR

It was almost like Sunny appearing out of nowhere.

When Mary Dark Hope opened the door of the adobe house, Superintendent Jury was sitting there, near the kiva fireplace, accepting a cup of coffee from Rosella, who was fussing about as she always did. And he stood up.

This astonished Mary—that a man would rise when she entered a room. It was as if she were important, certainly as if she were a woman. It was such an elegant gesture. And he was smiling too, as if he was really happy to see her.

"Hello," she said. It was all that her surprise would permit. She wanted to say more, something casual, something clever, but all she could do with her open mouth was to swallow air, which was painful and caused her to cough. She cleared her throat (perhaps a little too dramatically, in order to cover her speechlessness), and Rosella, always alert to possible illness, like any nervous caretaker, quickly went over to Mary and felt her forehead.

Mary really wanted to swat the hand away from her face, but that wouldn't have been cool, and she greatly wanted to be cool. Her expression changed to one of long suffering, patiently compliant. And her look suggested that Rosella treated everyone with this nursey propriety, as if everyone were her child—the superintendent too, if he blew his nose or hiccupped.

"I'm all *right*, Rosella." The "right" came out as a small wail.

"You sit out there in the February cold with that crazy coyote you call 'dog'?"

Mary gave the housekeeper the same patient smile one might bestow on a fractious child.

"Don't look at me that way, miss. A coyote. I know when I see."
Like Mary, she pronounced it as two syllables, "ky-yote."

Mary sat down, feigning exhaustion both physical and emotional. "Gaa-awd," she said, stretching the single syllable into two.
"Have you ever seen a coyote as tame as Sunny? Of course not."

Rosella's tone was scoffing. "You train him up from a pup and he
pays attention to you, not me, not no one else." To Jury, she said,
"What she and him do out there in the middle of the desert, I don't
know. Look at him—"

Both Mary and Jury looked. The dog—or ky-yote—in question
was lying stretched out peacefully before the fire. It whistled slightly,
woofed, made doglike noises.

"—I never see a dog with such bandy legs. Like sticks, like a
chicken."

Mary looked benightedly at Jury. "Rosella thinks Sunny's *heyoka*.
That he tricks people, or makes them act in a strange way."

Again, Rosella snorted. "You don't even know what that means.
You never learned legends. You got no respect."

Feigning kindness, Mary said, "Rosella's Zuñi. Or a little bit."

Rosella crushed her hand against her chest. "No little, miss,
most, nearly one hundred percent. You don't know the difference
between Navajo and Zuñi, you never learned legends." Rosella stood,
hands on hips, near the kiva, whose flames threw mysterious shadows
across her flattish face. She was dressed in colorful and flowing garments. She seemed to favor purple, which didn't suit her at all, making her olive skin look muddy. Her long, dark braids were sometimes
curled like earmuffs, sometimes lying down her back, as they were
today.

"Let me tell you, miss, the next time I go back to Zuñi Pueblo, I
might stay. You're so big and can take care of yourself you don't need
anybody, is that it?" Rosella, either forgetful that Jury was a policeman, or not caring, said (as one adult to another), "I came to Santa Fe
to teach at the Institute—"

Mary interrupted. "She means the American Indian Art one."

"I know what I mean," she snapped. To Jury she said, "I came
here to teach and then my hands got so bad I couldn't work the silver
anymore. I taught Angela, and Angela was very, very good, could
have been the best if she wasn't such a dreamy type." Rosella went
over to a small table, pulled out a box that when opened displayed

truly lovely and intricate pieces. "You see this—" she pointed to a necklace. "This is needlepoint turquoise, very difficult to do." There were also a bracelet and brooch of the same design. She lifted another necklace from its felt background, a thick braid of tiny carved animals and birds. "A fetish necklace. My people make very fine ones." Then from the bottom of the box she pulled out a large brooch with a single turquoise stone and said, "This is no good, it's chalk that's treated with plastic. See—it gets that hard surface." Carefully, she put the felt-lined box away.

"I see you brought out the crystals." Mary picked up a nugget of rose quartz and studied it. "What's this one mean?"

"For you, nothing. You only believe what you see and feel in this world. So, nothing." Rosella slid the remaining half-dozen bits of stone into a leather pouch as if to save them from contamination. "Your sister coulda been killed by bad thoughts, evil thoughts. You know?"

Mary sighed, in the manner of one who's heard it all before. Heard it and heard it. She slumped down in her chair, closed her eyes. It was fairly clear that she thought she had told Jury everything of importance, certainly more than he'd learn from a bunch of crystals.

Jury had come to the conclusion that the housekeeper's view of Angela Hope was decidedly myopic. He wondered if the older sister had been quite so full of the milk of human kindness, or if the "saintliness" Rosella ascribed to Angela was any more than a rootless and vague religiosity. He thought she was overestimating the one sister and underestimating the other.

Jury reckoned more on the description of Malcolm Corey and Nils Anders than he did on the one of Dolly Schell and the Bartholomew woman, the opinion of Dolly, at least, probably fueled by jealousy. Rosella had agreed with Malcolm Corey's statement that Angela Hope was the sort of person health food–herbalist gurus catered for. Except the housekeeper's interpretation of Angela's tendency toward these things was evidence, not of her gullibility, but of her spirituality. As far as the housekeeper was concerned, her addictive smoking was Angela's only weakness. Jury believed in human weakness, thought of it often as saving grace. Lord knows, he could sympathize with Angela on *that* score. What a war of nerves. When he felt he couldn't last even five more minutes without a smoke, he thought of Des, sitting on her high stool in the kiosk in Heathrow. Somehow, he felt he would be letting her down if he had to tell her he'd failed. Still, the picture he was patching together of Angela Hope was of a charming but self-indulgent woman who would turn, like a weathervane, in any wind. His picture of the younger one was exactly the opposite. She would be as steady as a compass pointing true north.

Mary sat there now in her funereal black, looking not so much in mourning as she looked like she needed a six-shooter.

Rosella had reverted to the subject of Sunny's pedigree. In a scoffing tone that must have been her usual way of talking to Mary, she said, "He's one lazy coyote, that's what he is."

"No lazier than Angela," said Mary from the depths of the chair she'd dug into.

Jury thought it was more a comment than a criticism, but Rosella turned on Mary the full force of her temper. "You can't be speaking of your sister in that way! My God! She's dead!" She fell to weeping.

It was, Jury felt, genuine grief. He moved from his chair and offered her his handkerchief, which she groped for and pressed to her face like a flannel, trying to choke back sobs.

Mary's pale face was drained even more of color. But he thought Rosella had misread Mary—her way of speaking about her dead sister made him wonder if Mary believed on some deeper level that Angela was *not* dead. It was possible that on a deeper level of her mind, she simply didn't believe it.

Jury might have said: "I'm sorry; I shouldn't be forcing you to talk about her, making you remember." But he didn't think so. The more weeping, the better, and the more public, the better. The ones who worried Jury were the ones who held themselves in check. As Mary was doing.

As Rosella helplessly fingered a cigarette box studded roughly with colored stones, her hand trembled. More reminiscent of Angela, perhaps, than a picture would be. "She don't have to worry now about what smoking does to you." And she fell to weeping again, rubbing at her eyes with the heel of her palm. "I tried to tell her, you know, to do what that ad says: Just Do It."

Mary sailed her paper missile or whatever it was toward Sunny. She said, "I'd rather redo it. Let somebody else go first."

Rosella looked round again. "Bosh, oh bosh, Miss Know-it-all."

"I don't know *any* of it. That's my point."

Jury wondered if Mary, seeing her housekeeper's distress, was being cantankerous simply to offer Rosella a way to change anguish to anger. That would be rather subtle for an ordinary thirteen-year-old. But what made him think that Mary Dark Hope was "ordinary"?

Jury got up. "I've got to be going." He patted Rosella's shoulder and gestured for her to keep the handkerchief. "I'll get it from you later. Mary—"

Mary was up and at the door. He said goodbye to Rosella and they walked out and toward his car. She asked him where he was going.

"Dinner with Dr. Anders." He looked at his watch. "I'm late." Still he stood there, leaning against the driver's door of his hired car.

She ran her hand over it. "You got a Le Baron."

Jury turned and looked at the car as if he'd never seen it before. Probably, he hadn't, except as a red blur on wheels. "That's what they gave me."

"It's a convertible." A little disgust, there, as if he weren't properly appreciative of the world's goods. "You don't have the top down."

"It's February."

She shrugged.

He wanted a cigarette. He wanted *something*. He felt her reluctance to see him go as they stood there in the blue night. He looked up. Why had he never seen stars like that in an English sky? A whole crowd, some touching, or appearing to, as if there weren't sky enough to hold all of those stars.

Mary Dark Hope was gazing upward, too. "Star rocks is what the Navajo call them." They both stood gazing out. "Rosella calls me *heyoka* sometimes, too. That's someone who acts just the opposite of what normal people do. I consider that a compliment." She ran her hand across the Le Baron's hood. "Did you find out what you needed to, what you were looking for?"

Jury shook his head. "No."

"Maybe you should go on a Vision Quest. I wouldn't mind." She sighed.

Jury smiled at her. "If I did, or if you did?"

"Both. We could go maybe together."

There was a silence. Jury broke it by saying, "I'm going to have to go back to England in the next couple of days. I think I've talked to the people your sister knew best."

"Dolly Schell?"

"Yes, of course. Your cousin."

Mary was silent for a moment, looking off into the distance. "She didn't get along with Angie. She didn't like her."

"That's what she said."

"She said that?"

Jury nodded.

She shrugged deeper into her down jacket. "That was clever of her."

Then she walked away.

THIRTY-FIVE

"What did she mean by that?" asked Jury.

Nils Anders looked across the top of his bourbon and smiled. "I told you she wasn't much on details."

Nils had been holding on to a table for them, by the time Jury arrived at the restaurant. Holding on for dear life it would have to be, judging by the crowd both sitting and standing. It was a favorite spot, a place where you couldn't get a table without a reservation, but the tourists weren't aware of that.

"She said it and just—walked away." Jury sipped his whisky, dying for a cigarette. Thank the Lord Anders was a nonsmoker and they were sitting in the No Smoking section.

"Well, it sounds as if Mary doesn't much care for Cuz, doesn't it?"

"How about you?"

Anders looked puzzled. "Do *I* care for Cousin Dolly?" He shrugged. "She's all right, I guess." Nils reached in the breadbasket for a piece of corn-and-chili bread.

"Mary hasn't said anything to you about Dolly Schell?"

"Anything like what?" Nils shook his head, buttered his bread. "Mary is very close-mouthed."

"How did Angela feel about Dolly?"

"I'm not sure. I don't think we ever talked about her. Dolores, I mean. 'Dolly' doesn't seem to suit her." He smiled slightly, broke off another chunk of bread. "I wish the food would get here."

"I second that." Nils Anders (thought Jury) was perhaps not the best person to ask about "feelings." Too rational. Or too involved with his theorems and axioms about light and space. The waiter arrived with their heavily laden plates. Maybe it was the air out here that made him so hungry. Whatever it was, Jury picked up his fork the moment the coral-colored plate was set before him and dug into the *fajita*. He noticed that Anders was contemplating his food instead of eating it.

"You don't take it seriously, then," he said to Anders.

"Take what seriously?"

Jury shook his head, changed the subject to the Colorado trip. "I'm sure she mourns her sister, but she doesn't demonstrate it much. She's a very self-contained girl."

After a moment of neatening the pile of black beans with his fork, Anders said, "You know, there might have been some trouble there."

"Trouble? Between Angela and Mary?"

Anders took a few more seconds rearranging the expertly positioned portions on his plate—pumpkin flan, tamale, fried spinach. "Ambivalence at best. Jealousy at worst."

Jury shrugged. "I expect it's quite natural for a kid to envy her older sister."

"I'm not talking about Mary. I mean Angela."

Surprise cut Jury's laugh short. "You mean Angela was jealous of *Mary?*"

The answer was oblique. "The thing about Mary is, she's so down-to-earth, so close-to-the-ground, I think she's growing out of it sometimes—"

Jury remembered his own feeling about Mary's rootedness and smiled. "I know what you mean."

"She loves the Southwest, the desert, the red rocks, the—*stuff*. But she thinks everything else is a sham. Santa Fe, or what it's become; this restaurant we're sitting in—" he motioned with the fork—"the hype, the galleries, the fêtes. There's something uncannily sophisticated, if that's the word I want, about Mary. There's something—" he paused, pushed his corn husk back a micro-measurement—"about the way she burns away all of the extraneous matter. Like this corn husk, if it were surrounding some point, some person . . . Mary would just rip it off. Anyway, she's not a walking Chamber of Commerce for Santa Fe, as are most of the people you'll meet—"

"All of the people," Jury interrupted, smiling, remembering his early-morning walk.

"Right. And Sedona—the place Angela really loved—well, that's far worse as far as Mary's concerned. 'Why would certain parts of the earth be more powerful than others?' We were arguing about 'vortexes' one day. The three of us were talking about Sedona and about stone circles—Avebury, Stonehenge, the ley lines. Mary reads a lot; I wouldn't be surprised if she didn't read more than Angela herself. But if someone she cared about was really interested in a subject, Mary would go and read a book about it so she could join in the conversation. Christ, she must drive her teachers crazy, what little she sees of them. Plays hooky a lot, is my guess." Anders tilted his head, regarding the new relationship he'd made between the corn husk and the pumpkin flan. "Anyway, this one day in the shop, we were all drinking chamomile tea or something equally revolting, when Angela brought up Avebury and ley lines. It wasn't long before her trip." Anders paused, looked sad, picked up his wineglass and held it. "Angela talking about ley lines. Mary said, 'You might as well believe in UFOs.' Angela said that was different. It ticked Angela off, listening to her."

"A woman getting angry with a thirteen-year-old because of the kid's beliefs? That's a little irrational."

"Some thirteen-year-old!"

The nervousness in Nils Anders's laugh made Jury look up quickly, but Anders was looking down again at his plate.

Deep into his own thoughts, Nils said, "I wish she were ten years older." He avoided Jury's eyes.

Jury could tell the man was deeply distressed by this admission, and said, "So do I, so what?" Anders then looked over at him, surprised. Jury went on: "I just spent—how long? Seven or eight hours with this kid and it felt more like seven or eight years. There's something extremely complex and even disturbing about her. I know exactly what you mean by 'burning away extraneous stuff.' Maybe it's from having grown up with no parents and being thrown back on her own resources; maybe it's from sitting in the desert, thinking; maybe it's from watching a lot of phonies do a lot of phony things. I don't know. But Mary Dark Hope does *not* strike one—certainly not me—as your typical pubescent kid."

Anders's look was a little less strained. He gave a brief laugh. "I was beginning to feel like a pederast."

"What we feel is one thing; what we do is another." Jury looked out over the packed dining room, and reflected for a few moments. He went on, "You know, a few weeks ago I was in Baltimore. It happened to be around the date of Edgar Poe's birthday. Now, if we were living back in his day in the nineteenth century no one would really think twice about a relationship between a thirteen-year-old girl and a grown man. But today? There'd be an uproar about child abuse. Very sensitive area, as it should be. What would have happened in this decade to E. A. Poe and Virginia? They'd never have had a chance. Poe would have been locked away." Jury added, with a force of sadness that took him by surprise, "and 'Annabel Lee' would never have been written."

Anders was still pushing his food, surely cold by now, around his plate.

"Nils," Jury said, "why don't you eat that, instead of trying to penetrate the mystery of the relationship between the spinach and the corn husk."

Anders smiled wanly and scooped up some beans, leaving Jury to think, uncomfortably, about his own fleeting reaction, quickly repressed, to Mary Dark Hope as they sat drinking cappuccino yesterday. Hoping to relieve some of Anders's obvious guilt, he said again, "Sexually disturbing, no doubt about it."

Behind Jury, a woman's voice said, "Anyone I know? Or are you talking about the tortillas?"

The voice made Anders look up, turned Jury around.

"Hello, Clare," said Nils, not very enthusiastically.

It was one of the dance-hall actresses that Jury had seen several hours before. She stood there smiling, the smile glimmering like the green silk dress she was wearing—smile, teeth, dress, hair—all with a sheen that caused a number of diners to turn and stare. Jury imagined she was used to being stared at.

Jury was introduced again and said hello. Clare glimmered at both of them yet again, then tossed the drift of dark red hair clear of her shoulder in a gesture Jury had always disliked. So coy, so clearly meant to display breasts and neckline. Then she moved off through the webbing of tables towards an escort who was stuck waiting for her.

"Definitely *not* jailbait," said Jury, his eyes following her before turning them back to his companion.

Nils Anders was poking at the cold corn husk.

He hadn't noticed.

THIRTY-SIX

Melrose had been in the company of Divisional Commander Macalvie several times before: in Brighton; on Dartmoor; at the Hammersmith Odeon. And he found Macalvie's company—like the sea air, the slanting moor rains, the thunderous applause—bracing, to say the least.

Certainly, it must be for the person now in his office, a woman, from the sound of it.

As if reading his thoughts, Macalvie's secretary cocked her head towards the inner office. "Inspector Thwaite. She'll be out in a minute." Under her breath, she added, somewhat mysteriously, "She usually is."

Thwaite. Melrose thought he recalled Jury's having talked about her . . . yes, Gilly Thwaite. One of the few people on the Devon and Cornwall Constabulary Macalvie respects. Feels affection for. Love, possibly.

Well, the course of it was certainly not running smooth, then, for the female voice rising in arpeggiated imitation of a diva was in the throes of something other than aria.

". . . her bloody ske—" And the voice took another dive.

Far more pleasant than Sam Lasko's secretary, the woman with whom Melrose shared the tiny outer office just smiled and shook her head as if any visitor to Exeter headquarters knew what Macalvie and/or this woman with whom he was closeted were like. She rolled her eyes.

Macalvie appeared to be talking about bones, a skeleton.

"Vertebrae match . . . X-ray twenty years ago. . . . It's her!"

"No, it isn't."

"Yes, it bloody *is*. Perfect ma—"

". . . do you explain *this*?"

Melrose heard a clink, a clatter, tiny, but distinct. Jingle of coins on hard surface, it sounded like. The aria ended, and now there was a cut-off wail, like a snatch of music he'd once heard on an old blues-jazz record, then a brief staccato exchange, followed by another aborted wail . . . this one seemingly of outrage. The woman who stalked out, paler (Melrose guessed) than when she'd walked (or stalked) in, was more intelligent-looking than she was pretty; but had an intensity and a vitality (even at this apparent low ebb in her crime-scene career) that more than made up for physical beauty. Yet, Melrose adjusted even that judgment as she passed before him, for she had a very graceful carriage and a headful of bobbish dark curls that softened the unflattering horn-rimmed glasses; she wore a bright coral lipstick, which made Melrose irrationally happy, seeing she hadn't permitted her femininity to be deflowered (so to speak) by the Devon and Cornwall Constabulary, of which Brian Macalvie was divisional commander and chief superintendent—either or both.

As Inspector Thwaite made her exit, the secretary nodded and smiled at Melrose, inclined her head toward the door, and said he could go in.

Brian Macalvie smiled broadly and extended his hand. They had always got on extremely well, which surprised Melrose, for Macalvie was not the sort of policeman who took easily to amateurs. Well, he didn't really take easily to professionals either, so Melrose's amateur standing had nothing to do with it. Macalvie was still wearing his coat; Melrose recalled that he had always worn his coat—and it looked familiar, down to the little tear in the elbow—as if Macalvie had just come in or were just on his way out. All of his life, coming in, going out. No one could match Macalvie for intensity, not even Inspector Thwaite. Copper hair, neon-blue eyes, Macalvie seemed to exist within a magnetic field.

Right now, Macalvie was sticking a cigarette in the corner of his mouth and patting down his pockets for a light as if he were frisking himself for a gun; finally, he snatched a little box of matches out from under a batch of papers before he recalled himself to social niceties and offered Melrose the pack.

"No thanks." Melrose was looking at the several coins that had been shoved aside in the process, wondering what clue they'd offered in Gilly Thwaite's case. He was also eyeing the overflowing ashtray, big as a luncheon plate. Probably, it *was* a plate. "Cut down, have you?"

Macalvie looked at the plate too. "Those? Those are Jury's."

"Jury stopped smoking."

Macalvie smiled cynically and rolled his eyes to suggest "a lot you know," then, apparently deciding Jury hadn't actually been in the office long enough to cause such a butt buildup, added another smoker to the pile. "And a lot are Gilly Thwaite's. She just left."

"No, they're not."

In the midst of bringing round the pot to fill two cups with muddy-looking coffee, Macalvie's brows shot up in question. "Who says?"

"I says. She wears lipstick."

"Ha! Aren't *we* the little sleuth?"

" 'Little' is the definitive word. If that coffee's for me, no thanks. I passed some roadworks chaps filling potholes who could use it for filler."

"Yeah, it is pretty revolting." Macalvie peered into the pot and returned it to the burner behind him. Then he was washing the papers all over his desk, found what he wanted, shied it over to Melrose. "Jury sent this."

The stapled photocopied pages fluttered onto Melrose's side of the desk. He picked them up and read through the notes Jury had sent, detailed sketches of the people he'd seen and talked to, what they'd said, what they hadn't. After a while, Melrose removed his glasses and said, "Mary Dark Hope. She sounds interesting."

"The kid sister. But it wasn't the sister who identified the body, according to my nemesis, DCI Rush. It was the cousin." Macalvie frowned, as if the thought troubled him. "Mary Hope's thirteen; Rush—or could be the cousin—decided it would be too traumatic for the kid to undertake the trip and make the identification." Macalvie nodded towards the photocopied report. "Though it sure as hell doesn't sound as if this particular thirteen-year-old is easily traumatized."

Melrose read; Macalvie thought.

"Coyote Village turns out to be part of the Anasazi ruins in—" Melrose looked at the notes again—"in Mesa Verde."

Macalvie unbuttoned the single button of the corduroy jacket he was wearing beneath his mackintosh. His concession to settling in for a while. He said, "That makes it a dead cert that *one* of them—Frances Hamilton or Helen Hawes, or both—talked with Angela Hope."

"Why so?"

"Because this particular ruin isn't on the must-see list. Its designation is really a number—no, not the number in the address book," he added when Plant looked hopeful—"so for anyone to write it down, to make a note of it, well, the person would have to hear it from someone. The Hope sisters went there quite often. Why Nell Hawes would write it down—" Macalvie shrugged, upended his palms.

"Do you know Hawes was the one who wrote it in?"

"Handwriting analysis shows that the Coyote Village entry and the number were written by a different hand from the one that made the neat, pencilled entries. If it was Hamilton's address book, then it's probable she was the one to make those. It's a little more difficult to tell whether two different people wrote in the number and the name. It was Nell Hawes who brought it back here. So it's clear it was temporarily in her possession. So Hamilton might have handed it to her at some point to make at least one of those entries."

"Does it make any difference, really, which of them wrote down the information?"

"I won't know that, I expect, until I know what the number means."

"What about Angela Hope?"

Macalvie lifted his eyebrows in question.

"She might have written it, you know, the way people will if they're giving you an address, or directions, or pointing out something."

"This is all rather tenuous."

"You're just like your pal."

Which pal was this, now?

"Jury kept using that same word when he was here. 'Tenuous.' 'The relationship between these three women is *pret-ty* ten-u-ous, Macalvie.'"

Melrose smiled. Seldom had he known the divisional commander to waste time in self-congratulation, but right now he was looking smug.

But the expression was fleeting, gone in an instant, as Macalvie asked, "You find anything in London?"

"I haven't come up with much. Well, I haven't come up with anything, at least nothing definitive, except—" Melrose paused and frowned.

"I love the 'except's. So go on."

"Only impressions. Do you think Frances Hamilton might have died from a different cause than the other two women?" He waited for Macalvie to disagree. He didn't. "She might really have died of natural causes, I mean, not precipitated by any outside agency. When I was talking to Lady Cray, you know, the friend with whom the Hamilton woman lived, there was another picture that emerged, different from my original impression that Frances was a shallow, silly woman. Even Lady Cray claimed she'd done Fanny Hamilton an injustice by giving the superintendent this impression. I think Hamilton might have been a woman of very strong feelings and without an outlet for them, without a confidante. She had no family except for her nephew in America, and to him she was devoted. She really loved Philip Calvert. She went to the States, went to the cabin where he was killed, talked to the police there in Pennsylvania. Jury told me that in the police report there was, of course, a description and photos—that sort of thing of the body *in situ*—and though I imagine she'd never have been shown any photos, still she would have heard just how and where he'd died. If Fanny Hamilton wasn't strong, if she had a bad heart—" Melrose sighed—"I'd have thought it could have killed her. That painting of the boy Chatterton, stretched out on his narrow bed. How could that not have brought to mind the image of Philip, stretched out on his own in that cabin?

"On that day that she visited the Tate, she stayed for some time. Beatrice Slocum said she saw Ms. Hamilton after she—Beatrice—left the Clore Gallery: that's where they keep the Turners. Bea especially likes the Turners. It's the light. But I expect light is crucial for all paintings, isn't it?" Imprinted on Melrose's eyes was the spectral diffusion of that golden, misty light in Turner's paintings of Venice, so that when he transferred his gaze to the gray rectangle of office window, he almost expected to see it, that spectral gold. "Art," he went on, "is not always balm for the soul. It can be, perhaps, like an overdose. Of poignance, not poison."

Melrose was suddenly self-conscious. Macalvie hadn't moved, but had just sat there watching him through half-closed eyes. "You don't believe me?"

"I believe you all right. I just don't think you're talking about Frances Hamilton."

Melrose said nothing and Macalvie just went on looking at him, so that finally, either unnerved or embarrassed, he returned his gaze to the window at Macalvie's back and the sky that had changed in hue from pale gray to pewter. He sat there looking at this sky, wondering if even crimes, like problems, are solved (although "solved" was probably the wrong word) because they come within the compass of one's own individual life. Because ultimately there was nothing there that was unfamiliar or unknown. Perhaps that was what he had felt following, more or less, in Fanny Hamilton's footsteps, walking through the exhibits at the Tate. The Turners, the Pre-Raphaelites. Chatterton. He could not explain it though, to Macalvie, since he could not explain it to himself.

What surprised him, when he came out of this slight reverie of sky gazing, was that Macalvie was sitting in exactly the same position, and still looking at him. Macalvie was the most energetic of men (witness that unshed coat!) whose impatience was legendary. Yet, Melrose could hear Jury talking about him, about the way Macalvie could stand immobile, taking in a crime scene, so long that it drove his team to distraction, including Gilly Thwaite, who was actually the crime-scene expert. So "impatience" was not the right word either, or was appropriate only to describe him when he was dealing with incompetents and fools—too often for people's comfort, Melrose imagined. It made him smile.

The smile apparently released Macalvie too from whatever he himself had been observing and he was fanning out some nine or ten snapshots, turning them towards Melrose. "He sent these, too. Jury did. Snaps he took inside the Silver Heron, Angela Hope's shop."

Melrose looked at each of them, carefully. Half of them were close-ups of silverwork—finished or partially finished pieces: bracelets, pendants—resting on what appeared to be her worktable; or close-ups of display cases which housed turquoise and silver. There were close-up shots of three pieces that looked much like Lady Cray's turquoise block. Hardly any doubt who had done that piece of work. Two more of shelves in the shop and one of two armchairs with a table between them that would have appeared inviting to custumers.

"No Rolodex on the customers, he says; apparently, Angela wasn't into keeping mailing lists to promote her wares. Well, we know approximately when they might have got together. But it would be nice to know precisely. It's pretty certain about Mrs. Hamilton and Angela Hope having met. I'd like to be certain about Nell Hawes, though. Look at this."

Macalvie tossed Melrose several pages of a technical report that looked like the results of an electrocardiogram: jagged lines, lines of varying lengths running down the pages. Macalvie told him it was a chromograph of Angela Hope's blood.

"I managed to wrest it from the Wiltshire police report. Jury must have moved DCI Rush to take another look at the pathology reports. What this gives you is what turned up and how much. But not everything turns up; that's the trouble with poisons and drugs. Pathologist says what killed Angela could have been valvular heart disease. According to this cousin, Dolores Schell, she had rheumatic fever when she was a kid."

Melrose studied the pages. "But you don't think it started up of its own volition."

"No." Macalvie took his feet from the desk, stood up. "Come on, let's drive over to the lab."

WHITE ROOM after white room debouching off a foam-green hallway was filled both with the detritus of crime and with the forensic experts examining it. Macalvie walked ahead of him, hesitating at one door after another, occasionally mumbling some phrase or tossing back a word—"serology," "electrophoresis," "spectrometry"—as if Melrose knew all about the forensic sciences. One room was crowded with what looked like thousands of color-coded files and even more thousands of microfiche films; another room appeared to be given over to analyses of paint, for nearly every surface was covered with charts, chips, samples, except for the windows, and Melrose had the feeling that if the technicians in there ran out of space, light would go too. All the surfaces—floors, walls, countertops—were brilliantly clean, and as his cook, Martha, was fond of saying, "You could of et off the floor." The personnel in the rooms they passed were manning microscopes, computers, and what looked like meat grinders. Melrose had no names to put to the tools of their trade; he thought most of them could have found a home in either a Mercedes body shop or a Brillat-Savarin kitchen. They stopped at one door and he followed Macalvie inside.

Melrose looked around at the gleaming equipment, at a couple of technicians wearing what resembled goggles for a scuba dive, at several huge computer monitors, and at the expert with whom

Macalvie was conferring. He assumed he was expert since Macalvie was actually listening. Melrose heard only the odd phrase—"swabbing out the mouth," "vomitus sample"—as he studied a collection of petri jars.

Macalvie walked over to Melrose, said, "Give Sloane another twenty-four hours, he'll know. He's already discounted God knows how many substances that fit the symptoms. At least what symptoms were noticed."

Melrose listened to Dr. Sloane talk to Macalvie about serum and urine analysis and the impossibility of oral ingestion in this case, as the comprehensive analysis had eliminated at least a hundred possibilities, such as barbiturates, phenothiazines, tricyclics; and the gastric juices eliminated acute oral ingestion.

"So she didn't swallow lye."

The weak joke didn't amuse Dr. Sloane. "It was all in my report. We knew this five days ago. We knew this within several hours of receiving the samples."

"TL chromography isn't sensitive enough to detect certain drugs. Cocaine, for example. Drugs of abuse," said Macalvie.

"This wasn't a question of drug abuse. More likely a therapeutic drug, but even there, we've turned up nothing. We didn't stop with that particular screening, at any rate. Gas chromatography, again, though, this is large-scale screening—Mr. Macalvie, did you read my report?"

"Every word."

"Then why are you asking these questions?"

Macalvie scratched his neck, frowning. "Things go missing."

"Well, *obviously* something's gone missing here. Precisely what agent killed the woman. Not necessarily a drug. There are also insecticides." Dr. Sloane turned away. "Read the report."

"Thanks," said Macalvie.

They retraced their steps down the hall. "Angela Hope," said Melrose, "I understand. But why are you so sure Nell Hawes was poisoned?"

"Because all three of them died."

Melrose frowned. Was a question being begged here?

As they rounded the corner to the lift, Melrose was thinking how eerie it was, the world of this lab, a world in which there were no enigmas. He wasn't sure he liked it. All of these people could not only strip you naked but could see, in the very garments shed, your history.

2

MELROSE COULDN'T help himself.

While Macalvie was talking to the women in the quire, Melrose was inspecting the long length of embroidered cushions for messages. He tried to stop doing it; he couldn't.

What amazing handiwork were these rondels! The Blue Coat Schoolboy would be hiding no secrets, as there was also a statue of the schoolboy not far from the cathedral, in Princesshay. Most of the embroidered words were straightforward enough, certainly, names and dates and historical detail about men like Bishop Baldwin, church history and local history, kingships and credos and, running brilliantly through the length of the cushioning, the Te Deum. It was quite remarkable. But what about

> THE WELLS RAN DRY
> THEY USED WINE WHICH RAN OUT . . . ?

Could that be a cleverly coded message? Oh, for heaven's sake! The whole thing was nearly spoiled for him because of Wiggins and Josephine Tey. He should have shown up at the hospital with Elizabeth Onions. *There* was an antidote for a fevered imagination!

He stopped for some moments to look down at the tiny figure of Saint Cuthbert, his gaze fixed on the drops of blood rendered in scarlet thread. Melrose studied this bit of red embroidery for some time, finally hearing in his mind's ear, not the voices of the angels, but the voice of Ellen Taylor speaking of her character Maxim: *"Who says it's blood?"* He winced; it was driving him crazy. Maxim, who had apparently been lying in a pool of his own blood at the end of *Windows*, now just as apparently had been resurrected in the second novel, *Doors*. "Apparently" must surely be the operative term here.

Maxim Redux, revived. Maxim engaged in one of his opaque and sophistical arguments with Sweetie, the heroine, protagonist, probably the alter ego. He pulled the manuscript pages from his inside pocket, rolled off the rubber band and smoothed out the pages. He read: *"I paint your portrait and who or what do you become?"*

Oh, hell's bells, he remembered this damnable argument. Maxim and Sweetie were sitting at the dining-room table, in that very dining room where he had been *apparently* lying in his own blood at the end of *Windows*. . . .

Melrose stopped by the black basalt effigy of some bishop or other, pondering Maxim's and Sweetie's situation. He moved up the nave and sat down on one of the chairs to turn his face up to the vaulted ceiling. Melrose loved ceilings. The colored bosses, the stone ribs. There was the Minstrel Gallery too, where angels held their harps and trumpets and cymbals.

Now Macalvie was sitting on the chair beside him. "What's that?" he asked, looking down at the manuscript.

"Oh, some pages of a manuscript a friend of mine sent to me. Weird story." He told Macalvie about the end of *Windows*, where Maxim had been lying in a pool of blood, and then in the second book he appeared to be sending notes to Sweetie. Maxim up to his old obfuscating tricks. Melrose wanted to be gone from here, wanted to be back downing a pint at the Jack and Hammer, or sitting at his own dining table before one of Martha's roast beef dinners. But then his mind's eye travelled farther down the table and saw his aunt gibbering away. Melrose decided Maxim might not be such bad company after all.

To Macalvie, he said, "It's something to do with the difference between appearance and reality."

"Most things are." Macalvie was leaning forward, elbows on knees.

Melrose glared at him and changed the subject. "Any luck with the embroiderers?"

"No. But who knows when one of them might remember something helpful?" Macalvie folded his arms hard against his chest as if warding off spiritual rebirth. "Rush knows sod all, is my guess. How I would have loved to have a crack at that cousin who identified the body. Jury's been gone over forty-eight hours." Impatiently, he said this.

Melrose asked him why he hadn't gone to Santa Fe himself. "You've always wanted to see the States."

"Too much of a caseload. Anyway, he's better at getting things out of people than I am."

Melrose was surprised that Macalvie would say this. He was also surprised that Macalvie was sitting still. Not just sitting either, but leaning forward, elbows on knees, palms fastened together in an attitude that in anyone else would have looked prayerful. But Macalvie wasn't praying; he was thinking. Fingertips pinched his lower lip as he stared ahead, perhaps at the giant rood screen, or the high altar, or Nothing.

Then he said, "It's that cousin worries me."

Melrose frowned. "How so?"

"She got over here in one quick hurry, didn't she?"

"Police had to have some family member identify the body as soon as possible, didn't they?"

"She was here within twenty-four hours. Less, really. So she must have caught that Albuquerque flight in record time to make her New York flight connection. All I mean is: that's bloody quick."

"It does seem rather overeager. What do you make of it?"

"Nothing. Yet."

They sat in silence for a few moments. Then Melrose asked, "If you're sure they knew one another—I mean, the Hope woman and Helen Hawes—is it possible that Angela Hope got in the way? Could she have been killed by—well—accident?"

"Accident" wasn't normally a word in the Macalvie lexicon, not in a murder investigation. He just looked around at Melrose, over his shoulder. "The point is, they knew one another. So the deaths are related. Whether only one was the target, whether all three were the targets, maybe one of them or all of them knew something or had something someone wanted or didn't want them to be in possession of. The point is, you pull at one thread, you bring two other threads with it. At the moment, that's what matters."

Melrose turned this over for a moment. "You sound a lot like Maxim."

Again, Macalvie was getting up. "So let's go, Sweetie. I need a drink."

<h1 style="text-align:center">3</h1>

CONTENTEDLY BREATHING along with his recently uncorked bottle of Châteauneuf du Pape, Melrose tucked into his smoked salmon, provided by the kitchens of the Royal Clarence Hotel. He once again envisioned Lady Kennington's little parlor. He asked himself: why did the "regional" newspaper folded near the armchair have to be the *Stratford* region? My God, of course! Lady Kennington had lived for a number of years near Hertford, in a village much too small to have a paper of its own, so why might that newspaper not be a Hertford paper, or perhaps a local paper printed in the market town of Horndean, which was even closer?

Melrose tossed down his napkin, and on his way back to his room and its telephone, told the maître d' to hold off on his entree and to decant the wine into a carafe so it could get a proper breath.

His old friend Polly lived in that same village, Littlebourne.

His old friend Polly mumbled a dark "Hello," said she didn't care if it was only eight-thirty, she'd promised herself an early night and had just fallen asleep when he had had the nerve to *call*. She then ignored his question about newspapers and asked Melrose if he'd finished reading her manuscript.

Why, he wondered, was he the editorial sounding board for writers? Why would they put any credence whatever in what he might have to say? Was he missing something? No, he had not finished and that was *not* what he was calling about. He wedged Richard Jury's name into her whining questions as to why hadn't he, and she immediately came round.

"Oh. Is it one of his cases?"

Melrose could almost picture the eyelashes fluttering over her lavender eyes. "Yes. All I want to know is, have you got a recent local paper lying about?"

"You mean the *Hertford Blare* or the *Horndean Blab?*"

"Polly, I don't know *what* I mean. You live there; I don't."

Melrose thinking of his wine patiently allowed her to go on at some length about his many (unkept) promises about visiting Littlebourne and how she had alerted its inhabitants of his coming, and how embarrassing it had been—

"Polly, would you please get the paper. Not the most recent, but the one that came out several days ago."

"I have it. It's a weekly."

Her efficiency startled him. "Look and see if it has a crossword—"

"It does; I always try to do them. The *Times* ones are too hard for me." Crinklings and rattles came down the wire. "Okay, what about it?"

"What's two across?" he asked.

" 'Shout.' S-H-O-U-T."

" 'Shout'?" Melrose considered. "Are you sure?"

"Well, I am about the T because five down is definitely 'tired.' Which is what I feel."

"Polly, what's the clue?" Silence. "Polly?"

"Huh? Sorry, I was just thinking maybe I'm wrong, maybe it isn't 'tired.' Could be 'trial.'"

"I *mean*, the clue for two across. Read it."

"'Not a fox-hunt, but foxes hunting.'"

That was it! "Yes. Clearly a 'shout' of foxes."

"What?"

"Nothing. Now, Polly, what's on that page? Besides the crossword?"

"Nothing much. Just a bunch of adverts. It's the—" she paused— "the Properties page. You know, sales, lettings, that sort of thing."

Melrose frowned. That didn't sound very promising. "Read it, will you?"

"The whole *page*? But it's just lists of properties."

"Read whatever's within, say, an inch around the crossword."

Polly Praed sighed heavily, put upon once more by Melrose Plant. "There's the church fête—oh, I was supposed to bake a cake— they've got that in with the estate sales; then here's that cottage next the Bold Blue Boy, wasn't that for sale before when you were here years ago? Weren't you going to buy it?"

"Certainly not. Go on."

She read off at least a dozen descriptions of properties, the usual glowing reports of vistas and views and amenities concocted by estate agents. Melrose sighed. He asked her directly, "Polly, do you remember Lady Kennington?"

"Of course I do. She's here."

The receiver nearly slid from Melrose's hand. *"What?"*

"Staying at the Bold Blue Boy—Oh! Is *that* what you're talking about? Well, why didn't you say so, instead of making me read all those dumb adverts? It's way up here at the top. The Kennington estate, Stonington. It's back on the market again. I expect that's what she's here about. She's always loved—wait a minute! Are *you* the one?"

Confused, Melrose asked, "Am I the one what?"

"The one who's trying to buy it out from under her? It's the reason she came here in such a hurry, because of this ruthless bast—"

"Of course not, don't be ridiculous."

"You were going to buy it once, remember?"

"I was not. That was merely a ruse, a cover. Listen, Polly, I can't thank you enough. You're a marvel!"

There was a brief silence as she coughed and reconsidered the Plant ruthlessness. "Well . . . uh . . . what about Lady Kennington? Did you want me to talk to her, or—?"

"No. No, I don't think so. It might be better if you didn't mention I was asking after her."

"Why?" She was suspicious. Jenny Kennington was, after all, available and undoubtedly attractive.

"It's something to do with—" Smoothly, Melrose went on: "I might actually have to come to Littlebourne myself."

That pleased her! That is, he inferred it pleased her, for she wasn't about to say so, despite her earlier protests about his broken promises. Casually, she asked him when. "Bring my manuscript with you and we can discuss it over drinks."

"Goodnight, Polly."

Feeling exultant, Melrose headed back to the dining room and his dinner. Talk about a bit of sleuthing! He paused, saw he was near the desk, and asked the receptionist if he could send a fax. Of course, she said.

From his wallet Melrose drew the little scrap of paper on which were the phone and fax numbers of the hotel in Santa Fe and wrote that in at the top of the sheet of Royal Clarence Hotel stationery, debated his message, and then, smiling, decided to allow himself some literary leeway. He had always been rather fond of that line in the John Fowles novel where the poor devil of a protagonist receives a telegram from the detective after years and years of searching for his ladylove.

Chuckling darkly, he wrote (with a considerable flourish)—

She is Found!

PLANT

And if Richard Jury wanted to know *where* in hell she was found, he could damned well come home and find her himself.

Melrose marched victoriously back to his decanted Châteauneuf du Pape and his exquisite-sounding meal.

You deserve it!

THIRTY-SEVEN

At the Welcome Break, Melrose broke.

These motorway cafes offered less by way of a relaxing "break" than they did of a devastated, trampled entrenchment, emptied in the wake of a city's teeming population in its hasty retreat from bombs or lethal gas. This retreat was made largely by motorcycle, from what Melrose could tell. He paused outside the restaurant complex to count twenty-eight of these shiny black monsters, ranged along one end of the car park, with several of their black-garbed monkish owners straddling the leather seats, smoking. Melrose was struck by a wave of nostalgic longing for John Wayne heading up a posse, and not one horse with a hole in its muffler. The posse of motorcycles began revving up, and soon the cortege was passing him as he moved through the door.

He quickly purchased and drank his cup of coffee, untempted by the plastic-wrapped buns and pies and puddings symmetrically arranged beneath a steel shelf displaying granite scones and dry rolls. Melrose wished there were Happy Eaters serving motorways; he shared Sergeant Wiggins's penchant for the bright orange restaurants, their bubble-wrapped atmosphere, their jolly waitresses, and their beans on toast. He deposited his cup and quickly left the restaurant.

On his way to the door this time, his eye was drawn to a machine such as he'd never seen before: its sign told him that he could print up cards of his own design. He was fascinated by the instructions. Two sizes of card were available, and a dozen different print types. But this was wonderful! For only three pounds he could get twenty-five personal cards. Didn't he need replacements for his old cards bearing the family crest and his title? Not really. Melrose hardly ever needed cards; he met new people at the rate of about one every two years (except when he was travelling to places like Baltimore; but the people he'd met there—the cabbie, the homeless—he didn't think were interested in calling cards). Still, it would be great fun to replace his elegant, outdated cards with some cheap and flimsy new ones, new ones also advertising, perhaps, the number of a facsimile machine—wasn't Trueblood getting one? The real source of delight here was that Agatha would go bonkers seeing she was now related not to a line of earls and viscounts who dropped heavy, cream-colored and engraved cards onto silver salvers, but to a line of ne'er-do-wells reduced to poorly inked, machine-printed cards so flimsy and thin you could read the *Times* through them.

Melrose shoved coins in the slot and debated the selection of typefaces. Then he was struck by an absolutely singular idea, for he realized he could put on these cards *anything he wanted!* On the larger of the two cards, he could actually print up to six different lines.

Happily flexing his fingers, he began to stab at letters, pausing only briefly to think (for the machine allowed little time for thought) and realizing he could make up as many different cards as he had coins to feed in. But he decided that the first attempt was wholly satisfactory and he collected his twenty-five square cards and made for the car park.

2

THIS TIME Melrose made sure he had his floral tribute in hand before heading towards Sergeant Wiggins's room. Though his arrangement was not precisely "floral," as the large, shallow pottery dish contained a selection of herbs and one or two nasty-looking rootlike things for which he had invented incredible curative powers.

He was sure the sergeant would appreciate this, and the sergeant did: "It makes up for me not being allowed to have my own medications in here." Sergeant Wiggins was wont to think of his own vials and bottles as medicines, things contrived by the hands of beamish doctors for him and him alone, too rich and exotic for the general run of suffering mortals. He inspected the bowl of herbs, sighed contentedly, and asked Melrose about one he said he'd never seen before.

Melrose had never seen *any* of them before today, and this one, pink and barbish-looking, he thought was probably cactus, or maybe simply dead, but he recalled something he'd read in a sporting magazine, *The Field*, possibly, and answered with authority. "Burdock. It's absolutely marvelous for cleaning out the kidneys." Yes, he had read that somewhere, for he recalled how strange it was that sporting folk were concerned with cleaning out the kidneys.

"Is it really? I've heard of that," said Wiggins. "Never tried any, though."

Melrose pulled up a chair and made himself comfortable (if that was possible in a hospital), and noticed the bookmark in *The Daughter of Time*. Wiggins was close to the end.

"Well, you deserve it, Sergeant Wiggins, all of the thought you've put into this case. It certainly stumps me."

As if it were a breviary, Wiggins picked up *The Daughter of Time* and pressed it to his chest. At least, thought Melrose, not to his lips. "Quite nasty for him, wasn't it, all the while being condemned by history and being thought to have murdered his nephews in the Tower." He was speaking of Richard III, the subject of Tey's mystery novel. Sadly, Wiggins looked at Melrose. "And him with that hump."

Quite naturally, Wiggins would drag the hump to center stage, physical disabilities being much closer to his heart than political intrigue. Melrose replied, "Yes, well, I wouldn't take Tey's version for gospel were I you. Richard was probably guilty as hell. I hear you're getting out of here soon."

Most people would have responded with a brusque "Can't be too soon for me, mate!" Sergeant Wiggins, however, looked unhappy.

And Wiggins wasn't alone, apparently, in his sadness. There was the private nurse Melrose had retained and who had given him this information out in the corridor. Nurse Lillywhite was a jolly, amiable nurse, and would have been exceptionally pretty had her eyes, leaf-green and exotically tilted, been aligned on the same course. As it was, one of the eyes drifted off-center, slightly skewed, so that it looked to be following its own line of inquiry or searching out someone more interesting than Melrose.

Nurse Lillywhite had stood by the nurses' station, weighed down by books, saying, "He'll be leaving in two or three days' time." Nurse Lillywhite was saddened by the prospect. "Honestly, he's been no trouble at all, ever so nice he's been, not like some that keeps me running my legs off, go here, go there, go everywhere; fetch me this, fetch me that . . ." Her voice trailed off as she hefted the several books up on her hip. They suggested her favorite patient was himself pretty heavily into the fetch-and-carry trade. Melrose said something to this effect.

She was surprised. "Oh, but this is so *interesting*, this research Mr. Wiggins has been doing." Sotto voce and with a quick look round she said, "He's working on a case—not that he's told me anything about police business, I do assure you," she was quick to add. "But I think it's simply splendid how he can lie there with nothing but the four walls and the telly to stare at and do all of these deductions in his mind." They were continuing down the hall together. "Now, I'll tell you what: he don't need these ones right now, seeing he's got a visitor, so you just go on in and I'll nip round later with a pot of tea."

"That would be very kind of you. You've done a wonderful job, taking care of him." Melrose had already written the check for the nurse and was now attempting to foist it on her. She recoiled slightly, as if not wanting to put her relationship with the interesting sergeant on a financial footing. "Miss Lillywhite, you've more than earned it." Melrose folded the check and tucked it into the pocket of her uniform. Amid her profuse thanks he bowed and walked away down the corridor.

"TWO OR THREE days," said Wiggins, in answer to Melrose's comment. He was not eager to leave.

Books were in abundance here, too; a stack of them sat on Wiggins's bedside table. "I met your nurse in the corridor. Looks like she has another order of books for you."

Wiggins looked quite happy. "Lillywhite's been really helpful. Gone over to Dillon's on her lunch break, or round to the library. There's a lot of research involved here, Mr. Plant."

Melrose couldn't imagine *any* research involved here.

Voice at whisper level, Wiggins asked, "Did you do as I suggested, Mr. Plant? Did you study those rondels carefully?"

"I did. But I saw nothing that could be taken as a message, no matter how abstruse."

"If there had been," whispered Wiggins, "I expect the cushion would have been removed by now."

Melrose rubbed at his forehead. The whole notion of embroidered messages made his head ache. Then Wiggins wanted to know if anything had come from "Stateside" (as he put it). Had the superintendent sent any information? Melrose capsulized Macalvie's report from Richard Jury, not wanting to give Wiggins too many fresh fields.

Wiggins reflected on this, his expression painfully studious, then said, "So the Hope woman had a mystical turn of mind."

Wanting to skirt mysticism at all costs, Melrose said, "Oh, I don't think a few visits to Mesa Verde and a handful of crystals constitute mysticism."

"Well, you wouldn't, Mr. Plant, you being a skeptic."

Melrose frowned. Was he? He had always thought of himself as rather gullible, too prone to believe nearly anything told him.

"The point is that Angela Hope was 'spiritual'—if you prefer that word—according to Mr. Jury's report. She often went to Mesa Verde, and, of course, there's that Indian housekeeper. No, I see Angela Hope as a person who could have been very much interested in Indian lore."

Indian lore. Oh, dear. "I don't really think—"

But Wiggins didn't care what he thought; already, he was pulling a book out of his bedside stack and thumbing through it. "You know the American Indians believed in putting hexes on people? This is called *Black Elk Speaks*—" and here he held the book cover-forward so that Melrose could see for himself. "Let me just read this bit here—"

Melrose really did not want to hear Black Elk speaking. But he allowed Wiggins to drone on, as he scanned the room and observed that most of the vases held now badly wilted bouquets and made a mental note to send some more. Whose name hadn't he used? Who was left as a likely . . . ah! Vivian! She was thoughtful enough to send some, and she had met Sergeant Wiggins a couple of years ago. Roses, Vivian would send. The book's snapping shut brought him out of his rosy reverie and he nodded. "Well, that's very interesting. But don't you think it's a bit, well, *contrived* as a method for murder? Putting a hex on somebody?"

"Nothing contrived about it, not if you're Indian."

"But that would mean *three* hexes, Wiggins. What about Nell Hawes and Frances Hamilton?"

Wiggins had replaced Black Elk and sorted through the pile on the floor for another book, which he was now thumbing through. "What do you know about the Anasazi, Mr. Plant?"

"Enough to get by," Melrose answered, looking round at the door, hoping Nurse Lillywhite would get her skates on and bring that tea.

3

HAVING DONE his part to succor the sick, he left the hospital and walked down the Fulham Road and across to the Old Brompton Road, pausing for a moment to look into a shop window displaying the latest in shapeless fashion. Why was it that women wanted to walk around in frocks that looked like great big pockets into which they'd been stuffed? The mannequin would have looked the same standing on her head as on her feet.

Inside the Victoria and Albert museum, Melrose received his little metal tag in return for his money and made for the rooms that housed the museum's paintings.

Standing before Constable's painting of Stonehenge, he felt a little disappointed. The canvas was certainly large enough for its subject, the painting struck him as almost banal, saved largely by its sky. He knew Constable was famous for his skies, that he would go (as the artist said) "skying." Here there were gray slabs of sky, like shattered rock. Yet the stones themselves looked as if a stiff wind might overturn them. They looked wet with new sunlight, listing, some of them fallen. There was something too watery, too filmy about the prospect, as if light were dissolving the stones. Fragile, smoky, spectral—and with the broad pastel sweep of a rainbow—it wasn't the image of Stonehenge Melrose had carried round in his mind all of these years. It struck him as romantic, almost sentimental, a noble ruin which could easily be assimilated by this landscape. Melrose had always felt one of the great appeals of Stonehenge was that it could not easily be absorbed by its surroundings; it did not blend. It was dark, gaunt, impenetrable—ironic, even. Hardly sentimental.

Nevertheless, Constable's rendition, rainbow and all, was certainly beautiful. Melrose stepped closer. Down in the corner Constable had painted a rabbit. He wanted to laugh.

Melrose walked aimlessly for a few moments in air that had the coldness of marble. Finally, he strayed into the exhibition of fashion design—a collection of women's wear of past decades and centuries. That outfit (Melrose thought), a plain but beautifully cut pale green wool, would look good on Vivian. This one, on Miss Fludd. She was intruding upon his thoughts again, and he didn't even know her.

This mannequin in lemon yellow, he imagined setting out for afternoon tea at the Ritz or Brown's Hotel; that one, wearing midnight blue velvet and clutching an evening bag of seed pearls, he saw in the foyer of the Royal Albert Hall for the opening of *Swan Lake*. (Melrose had seen only one ballet in his entire life, that one.) She would be attending the ballet with her friend, the mannequin in peach silk, making a foursome, probably. In the next display was a mannequin dressed for an afternoon at Lord's or Wembley, or better still, for Newcastle races where (in company with her friends in gray linen and pale blue cotton) she would enjoy a picnic hamper from Fortnum's. Melrose could see them all clustered around the pulled-down rear door of their Range Rover.

(And this suggested to Melrose that Vivian, instead of sending flowers to Wiggins, would send a hamper from Fortnum's.)

God. Was he going crazy standing around these androgynous, glass-enclosed mannequins, devising little worlds? More important was his stance amongst real women. Vivian, Ellen, Polly, Miss Fludd. He had the tenderest feelings for all of them, really, but had little idea how they felt about him. To Vivian Rivington he must be pure old slippers (and there was that damned Italian Count Dracula to whom she was affianced); to Polly Praed and Ellen Taylor, he appeared to be a think tank, one extra editor to bolster their egos; and to Miss Fludd, he was, quite clearly, Nothing.

Yes, they were all wonderful in their way, and yet . . . and yet. Perhaps more important, why did all of these women elude him in some way? How had he missed out, surrounded by so many flesh-and-blood women, so much that he was standing here amongst wooden ones? He was embarrassed to admit, even to himself, that he clung to the adolescent belief in love at first sight; he believed in hearts leaping, stomachs plunging, speech faltering, and time stopping. Reason dashed upon rocks where the Lorelei sung. And the more he tried to wrench away, scrape away this adolescent attitude, the more it clung, limpet-wise, to his heart.

How was it that passion had passed him by? Was he blind to his own feelings? Perhaps because he was overly susceptible, he armed himself against those feelings with port and Old Peculier and his own hearth. Now as he looked from the lady in lemon yellow to the one in amber silk, their hands raised in static attitudes of meeting or parting, Melrose could find nothing warm or hospitable, nothing to tempt him away from his fireplace.

He sighed, lingering before the sportily dressed lady in black, a raffish cap stuck on her curls, who seemed out of place beside her somber sisters. He was reminded of Ellen Taylor. But then he looked into the empty eyes of the mannequins and felt the enormous indifference of his surroundings.

THIRTY-EIGHT

Recalling how the Cripps kiddies climbed like slugs all over his Bentley several years back, Melrose found a parking space up the block from the house, near Perkins—Choice Meats and Game butcher shop. And it was out of this shop that the youthful perpetrators of East End blight were filing, yelling at the top of their lungs as they proceeded down Catchcoach Street with a couple of white-wrapped packets and, no doubt, their protection money.

After locking his car, Melrose looked past the suckling pig (wondering whoever would buy that around here) behind the shop's plate glass and into the dim interior. The kiddies had probably come merely on the innocuous errand of buying mince for their tea. However, "innocuous" and "Cripps" being a contradiction in terms, Melrose entered the shop, tinkling the tiny bell above the door, and looked around. Should he go back and inspect the meat locker? Assuming there was one? In Catchcoach Street, cows and hogs might have appeared in the bloom of health at the back door, only to meet Mr. Perkins's cleaver and go bubble-wrapped out the front. Melrose shuddered: it was the influence of Cripps effluvia that brought such bloodthirsty visions to mind.

But Mr. Perkins finally appeared out of the rear of his shop, and in a relatively fresh apron, his cheeks as pink as the porker in the window. He asked Melrose how he could be of service.

"Ah," said Melrose, who hadn't given any thought to his ostensible reason for being here. "I, uh, was thinking of taking something for dinner to a family along the street here. The Crippses, do you know them?"

"Whoever don't?" Mr. Perkins laughed. "Them kids was just in 'ere raising a ruckus, trying t'swipe that there brown sauce." He nodded towards a shelf lined with bottles of steak sauce, vinegar, mustard.

"I was wondering, well, perhaps you might tell me what they like. Lamb? A joint of something?" He hoped Perkins wouldn't head for the suckling pig.

"Streaky bacon!" he announced, clearly proud he was on such intimate terms with his customers. "Yeah, Ash Cripps likes 'is bit a streaky bacon, druther eat that than filet any day."

Though Melrose himself thought that rather a lowly offering, he told Mr. Perkins All right, wrap up a couple of pounds.

Ash Cripps's being on even more intimate terms with the nick than he was with the butcher caused Mr. Perkins to comment: " 'Course, Ash *will* get mixed up with some real bad lots."

Melrose wondered what lot, then, Ash himself was supposed to be, as he watched Mr. Perkins expertly wielding the knife; it was clear he was on good terms with the slab of bacon. " 'Im and Eddie Debens's gone into the car business. Anyone'd get 'isself in with Eddie's gotta be, you know . . ." Here, the butcher made circles round his temple with forefinger.

"Not very reliable, I take it? Where's their business, then?"

Mr. Perkins removed the bacon strips from the scale and plopped them down on white paper. "Oh, they ain't got no place of business. They just use whatever's out there." Here he gestured toward the street.

Open-mouthed, Melrose took his bundle of bacon, finally saying, "Are you telling me that Ash Cripps and this so-called business partner—?"

"Eddie Debens, that's the one."

"—that they simply *take* cars off the street and sell them?"

"*Sell*'m off the street they do. Don't ask me 'ow it works. All I know is, one a them Pakis was shoutin' blue murder when he come 'ome one night and found 'is Vauxhall gone." Then he said, sotto voce, "See, that's the ones they do it to, mostly. The Pakis and them other colored. Neighborhood's really gone down since they started buyin' in." Mr. Perkins sniffed. "That'll be four pounds ten pence, thank you."

Melrose put a five-pound note in his hand, accepted his change, said "You're welcome" to Mr. Perkins's "Ta very much," and left the shop, wondering as he looked down the street at the peeling front doors, the bald front yards, the curbside refuse, the rusted-out tricycles and chains—how the neighborhood could *go* very far down.

As he drew near the Cripps house, he saw the kiddies were engaged in playing some sort of game that would no doubt end with one or more fatalities. If they played it right. Melrose paused on the pavement to observe three of them, the older boy and two of the younger girls, busily tying Piddlin' Pete to a starved tree. It was so wispy that it bent backwards from the weight of the body. Piddlin' Pete was (naturally) heaving with sobs, since no game could be called officially a Cripps game unless there was plenty of weeping and wailing. Screaming, preferably. Two other children, one boy and one girl who might have been Crippses—it was hard to say—were gathering up bits of debris. The taller girl shoved a bundle of laundry or a blanket at Pete, insisting that he take it. Laundry? Melrose grew anxious. Or was that the infant being pressed into service? The boy was moving toward the mingy tree and appeared to be scattering the sticks and paper at its base. Melrose decided this was in danger of being lit, and since no one inside the house was paying attention to the screams and yells, the task fell to him.

"I *say!*"

They all turned toward him, mouths open, eyelashless eyes wide. Seeing who it was, they gave up their game (even Piddlin' Pete stopped yelling) and rushed Melrose, who was busily searching his pockets for coins and swatting their dirty, sticky fingers away. He held on to the coins and grabbed the baby away from Piddlin' Pete who looked about to drop it in the excitement. Then he told them to release Petey before they saw a single coin.

Petey, ecstatic with freedom, yanked down his short trousers and celebrated his release in the only way he knew how.

Melrose passed out the coins, pounds and fifty-pence pieces, and they all raced toward the front door, shouting in their various voices: "Elroy's here! Mam, Elroy's back!" so that White Ellie could barely shout her greeting to Melrose through this melee. "Shut yer mouths! 'Is name ain't Elroy, it's Melrose, ye stupid gits," she yelled, giving the ones she could collar as they raced past her a sound smack on the bottom, after which she greeted Melrose like a prodigal son. " 'E's a duke or earl, one a them, anyways, and you don't call 'im by 'is given name, anyways! 'E's Mr. Plant!"

Melrose started to hand over the infant in its swaddling clothes, but White Ellie told him to hang on a bit whilst she straightened the carriage. "Ta very much," she said, as if it were an oversight like a pint of milk she'd forgotten to pull in from the front stoop. When she reached into the carriage to pull the blankets about, a ginger cat sprang out with a baby's bonnet swinging from its mangy neck. "Gloria! You been at this cat again?" she yelled.

Neither Gloria nor the others paid any attention to this query, but merely broke the circle in order to collapse in front of the telly, which Bea Slocum was watching flanked by a short, chunky man on one side and a younger man on the other, whom Melrose presumed to be Gabe Merchant. He was sitting—or lying—on his spine and had the disoriented look of a drug user. He would have to compete with the telly again. There must have been a commercial break, for Melrose caught a glimpse of a huge can of cola. The audience was no longer watching.

White Ellie yelled to Gloria again, who yelled back "Uh-huh" and the rest all giggled and formed another circle, skipping around to the beat of "Uh-huh uh-huh uh-huh uh-huh."

"You come give this 'ere carriage a wash!" called their mother, who moved more quickly than Melrose would have imagined possible and smacked one girl (presumably Gloria) on the bottom. "I'll uh-huh all your little arses, see if I don't!"

But, of course, they took it as one more Crippsian game, this running from Ellie's stinging hand, doubled over with giggles.

The chunky fellow, Ash Cripps, introduced the fellow sitting on one side of Bea as "Gabriel," and the chunky man as "me business partner, Edgar Debens."

Mr. Debens rose and came smartly over to pump Melrose's hand and to push a card toward him reading, DEBENS USED AUTOS, "NOT AS OLD AS YOU THINK."

Freeing one arm from the baby bundle on which he had deposited the bacon, Melrose shook Eddie's hand and gave his gift of bacon to Ellie. She was ecstatic, announcing to one and all they'd have bacon for their tea.

This brought on another chorus of hallelujah as the kiddies bounced back up, formed their goblin ring, and skipped in a circle, chanting "Streakybacon, streakybacon, streakybacon!" Melrose found it almost laudable that the kiddies could work up piles of enthusiasm for whatever was available (be it Elroy, streaky bacon, or whatever);

they took their entertainment where they found it, and would applaud if their house were burning down around their ears. Ash Cripps thanked Melrose profusely, took the white package, and said he was going to the kitchen to start a fry-up.

White Ellie made no move to relieve Melrose of his burden, for she had been and still was engaged in some sort of argument with Eddie Debens. In her high, nasal voice, she began in the middle of whatever anecdote she was relating. "So I tells 'im, he wants 'is little bit a stray, 'e can bleedin' well pack up. Up t'pub 'e was, with 'er round the corner—"

Melrose had no idea what she was talking about. Nor did she make a further move to accommodate the infant that Melrose continued bouncing lightly in his arms. She continued her argument with Eddie. Argument, Melrose knew, was merely the form of discourse amongst the parent Crippses, just as bringing that lamp over there down on the head of Piddlin' Pete was the form of discourse amongst the Cripps kiddies.

Their father commanded the older boy to stop and they all fell down on the floor again, laughing.

"Idjits," said White Ellie.

Finally, Melrose sat down with the baby in a broken springed chair, covered with an ancient quilt, to talk—if possible—to Beatrice and Gabe. When he mentioned Frances Hamilton (who he had to identify for Gabe as the lady in Tate), Gabe frowned and said, "Why you asking questions? You ain't police."

"Brilliant," said Bea, sending Melrose an empathetic little smile as she rested her head on Gabe's shoulder.

"You're quite right, I'm not. I'm an anomaly, of no particular creed or purpose."

That was too steep for Gabe. He narrowed his eyes and asked, "You mean, a private detective, like?"

"Brilliant." Bea said it again.

A smell of frying bacon wafted into the room and the kiddies all jumped up and filed out.

"A friend of the police superintendent you spoke to. Jury. You and Bea are the only people we know of who noticed Mrs. Hamilton. Did you recall anything at all about her?"

"Yeah, well I told him what I know. Which was nuffin'. Hey, Elephant, ain't you got nuffin' to drink except tea?" He yelled across the room to White Ellie, and started to get up.

Bea pulled him down. "Only answer the bloody question, will ya?"

"I *told* ya." Grudgingly, he resat himself.

Melrose jigged the baby a few times and said, "You told Beatrice that you saw this Mrs. Hamilton in the Tate's portrait exhibit that day."

"So she was lookin' at the bleedin' *pictures*, wasn't she? It's a bleedin' *picture* gallery."

Behind Melrose, one or other of the kiddies was wreaking havoc on another of them, and Bea yelled at them: "Be quiet, you lot!"

The movement of the baby in Melrose's arms was no more substantial than that of a moth. The odor of frying bacon began to penetrate into the parlor here; Melrose asked Bea if there was a fish-and-chips place anywhere in the vicinity.

"Up on the Circular Road, yeah," she said.

He shifted in the rocking chair, settling Robespierre securely in the crook of one arm and pulling out his money clip with the other hand. He called the kiddies over, made them line up smartly, and dispensed five-pound notes. They gave Melrose about the same astonished look they might have given Father Christmas. Even Robespierre's blue eyes widened.

Said Melrose, "All right, be sure you buy fish and chips for *everyone*, that's six of us as well as you six. Understand?"

Ecstatic over the anticipated double treat of streaky bacon *and* fish and chips, they all chorused "Uh-huh uh-huh," which was going to be the only response elicited, since they'd discovered how funny it was.

"Get going, you lot!" said Gabe.

They got going. Led by Gloria, they threw their arms in the air like high divers on a springboard, but the footwork was reminiscent of a Hitler Youth rally. They filed in a line out the front door, chanting,

> Uh-*huh*
> El-*roy*
> Uh-*huh*
> El-*roy*

with Piddlin' Pete bringing up the rear. Just as his bald bottom disappeared through the front door, Ellie came in from the kitchen, grabbed his pants, and yelled "Yer strides, Petey, yer strides!"

Robespierre opened his eyes, fixed them on Melrose, and thrust his fist in his mouth.

To thwart sudden sickness (Melrose wondered); to hold back a scream? No, apparently the fist merely did duty as something to chew on. The eyes riveted on Melrose (if such a vacant blue stare can "rivet"), and then closed again.

"About this Mrs. Hamilton, Gabe. Why is it that you remember her?"

Gabe's brow furrowed. "Why? I dunno, do I. Anyway, what's all this in aid of? Why's everybody so interested in this lady?"

"Because there were two more deaths in similar circumstances." Not literally true, but he had to get Gabe to fix his attention somehow. "These three people, all women, seemed to have known one another. All three of them might have been murdered."

Gabe looked at him, surprised, and Robespierre opened his eyes to fix Melrose with another scarifying blue look.

Melrose rocked and asked again. "So is there anything at all, even something that didn't seem significant, you can remember?"

Gabe chewed his thumb, seemed to be honestly trying to recollect.

Beatrice raised her head and said to him, "You told me she looked chalky, white like you might get if you're gonna be sick."

"Yeah. Yeah, I guess I did. She was just standin' there lookin' sick-white and pickin' at something."

Melrose stared at him. "What do you mean?"

"Well, like a bit a stickin' plaster." He held up one hand so that Melrose could inspect the bandage around his finger. Gauze and sticking plaster.

"On her hand?"

"Nah. On her arm, like."

Melrose thought of his talk with Lady Cray. "Mrs. Hamilton had a heart condition. She treated it with nitroglycerin patches. But that she would have worn on her chest."

"How would I know, I never seen one of them things. Wasn't lookin' down her bosom." He leered.

Beatrice had sat up. "Well, my God, you think she got too much of the stuff and it made her really sick or something?"

"It's possible. Unlikely, though, I should think." *Some Harley Street specialist,* Andrew's fiancée had said about Frances Hamilton's doctor. Jury should have a talk with the physician; he wouldn't be likely to give information to Melrose. He sat there in the rocking chair, creaking back and forth, back and forth, noisily. But it didn't disturb his thoughts; he was lost in them. He was thinking about "J.M.W.," recalling what Diane had told him about Turner's black dog. "The dog was just an afterthought." Melrose frowned. An afterthought, an accident, an addition completely unplanned.

What if the death of one of them—*only* one of them—had been planned and the other deaths were accidental? Part of the whole picture, yes, but not part of the original plan. Not coincidence, but accident, an unlucky confluence of events. Frances Hamilton and Helen Hawes meeting accidentally in Santa Fe; both of them coming across Angela Hope, another accidental meeting. One of them had been meant to die and he chose Angela Hope as the target; Nell Hawes and Fanny Hamilton had died (metaphorically speaking) from the terrorist's stray bullet. The deaths of Nell and Fanny were only afterthoughts.

"Make a good mum, you would." Gabe grinned for the first time that afternoon.

THIRTY-NINE

Rosella believed that Mary came out here to the middle of this desert in order to commune with nature or to meditate. That was a laugh. The last thing nature wanted was to commune with the world of men, especially during the tourist season. Mary could think better out here where the flat land stretched away as far as the eye could see.

She sat on a smooth rock by a clump of rice grass, looking out over the arroyo. Sunny lay beside her with his head on his paws, his eyes darting between the massed rocks and the piñon bushes, tracking mice or ground squirrels. She let people think that Sunny was part silver-gray German shepherd and part something else. She was vague about the something else, hoping that would explain Sunny's extremely long legs. Sunny was a coyote. She had found him when he was a pup and could hardly believe her eyes when he squirmed out from a den in the hillside. What had happened to his family? Coyotes never abandoned their children. Unlike humans, who would do it in a heartbeat. Many knew that coyotes couldn't be tamed altogether, that deep down was the raw spirit that could exert itself. "*Attani*" was what Rosella called it: danger.

She remembered passing a sheep ranch once where there must have been a hundred coyote hides looped all along the fence. An old Navajo had told her once that if you skin a coyote, you release a powerful spirit. And she believed it. There was something about Sunny that was magical. The way he could disappear and then as suddenly reappear. He'd be there, then he wouldn't. Always he came back to her but she couldn't for the life of her explain how he managed this trick. Rosella said "that coyote" was a magician in his past life. Ghost dog, Angela had called him. Rosella called him *Trickster*.

What would become of Sunny if she had to go and live with foster parents?

That social worker. How could anyone take *anyone* seriously with a name like "Bibbi"? What sort of grown-up would allow herself to be hampered by a childhood nickname like that? Babyhood nickname, even. But the social worker (whose name was really Barbara) seemed to think it was cute. Now it appeared that Mary Dark Hope's own future depended on somebody who called herself Bibbi and asked questions like "What do you want to be when you grow up?"

Alive. That's what she wanted to be; that's what she'd told the social worker. As far as Mary was concerned, she'd been born grown-up. She was the one who had to call up the electric company when the lights went out. Rosella would go around wringing her hands and praying; Angie would just get out candles and sit in the dark meditating.

She wouldn't do it, that's all. She wouldn't go live with total strangers.

Mary Dark Hope put her head in her hands.

Now she came here more often and stayed longer since Angela's death. When the news had first been told her, she must have gone into a sort of fugue state, a state of nonfeeling.

Sometimes she saw her, saw Angela; she saw Angela walking toward her. Sometimes she would be called from sleep, and Angela would appear as if a distance away. And then would walk toward her, coming closer and closer, but never within touching distance. Angela was always wearing the same loose bluish-greenish dress that tie-dyeing had made look watery and always there would be that ankle bracelet she wore giving off the faint tinkle of bells. At other times Mary would see her out here, walking toward her from a distance, shimmering through the electric heat.

Mary had never told anyone this, first because no one would believe it, except Rosella, and she'd believe it in the wrong way. Rosella was still crying—sad that Angela's body was lying on a slab in another country, when she should have been buried the day after she died. Also, Angela's "wind spirit," her *pinane*, was to inhabit her home for four days following her death. Rosella felt wretched and Mary (who didn't believe a word of it) had tried to cheer her up by saying that her sister's *pinane* could easily make the flight from England to the U.S. in a lot shorter time than a 747. Rosella was not comforted by this remark. Second because she didn't believe it herself—which was another reason for not telling Rosella. It was a making of her own imagination, she knew. A wish. A trick. But Rosella would start with her herbs and roots and sacred incense, would start brewing and burning and go down on her knees before her own private little chapel.

No, Mary didn't want to give Rosella any visions to chew over.

The arroyo was flanked by a grove of low pines which Sunny was now cautiously penetrating. For what, she didn't know; she had seen no movement over there. Imagine what it would be like to have the attention span of a dog or a cat. Especially a cat. Cats could hold perfectly still for eons and focus on something a person had no awareness of.

And then she thought: they were like that, the scientists at the Santa Fe Institute. They could focus on a concept for hours at a time, like cats. Mary loved the idea of a place that existed purely, and only, for thought, for people to think. Smart people went there to think. This amazed her because so much of the world was simply thoughtless. Imagine getting your living by sitting around all day thinking, like Dr. Anders.

Mary cupped her chin in her hands and thought about Dr. Anders. And Angela. She supposed he must be—must have been—in love with Angela, the way he hung around in the shop. Angie had certainly been in love with him. Mary could see that. *That* didn't surprise her. But *his* returning the feeling did, because Angela was never much of a thinker. She *appeared* to be, what with all of her meditating and reading and Sedona trips. All of this Earth's-center stuff was about as meaningful as walking around with a dowsing rod looking for water. Though dowsers, she had to admit, served some practical purpose, since they sometimes found what they were looking for. Angie was not even that practical, though. Angie was not really very self-reliant; she waited for things to come her way, rather than going in search of them.

Mary stopped this critical line of thinking, feeling ashamed. She wanted, vaguely, to atone for it, and decided she would make a prayerstick, just a rude one, and gathered two of the twigs from the ground. She should have willow sticks, but there weren't any. Then she searched around for a feather, found only a buzzard's, and decided it would have to do. It would be a really shabby prayer-stick, but since (according to Rosella) women weren't supposed to make them anyway, only men were, she supposed it wouldn't have any power, and went ahead and and made a cross. The cross was held down with a small stone. Since she herself did not believe in the power of prayer, she would let the prayer stick do the work for her, that is, if there were any power in it at all.

All of Angela's mysticism—the aura balancers, the channelers—passed right by Mary like smoke. But what the Indians believed, that was different. Like them, Mary Dark Hope looked at nature from a materialistic standpoint. Whatever was spirit was connected to the material world. The Zuñi were practical in their offerings—clothes and food. It was easier to believe in supplying something basic and needful than in Angela's praying to a dolled-up version of Our Lady of Guadalupe. Mary pulled a sandwich bag from her pocket, it contained some of Rosella's jeweled cornmeal, meal mixed with bits of turquoise and coral. Mary didn't know what to do with it, but she liked looking at it.

She stretched backwards over the rock, keeping her feet on the ground and her head arched back and touching earth on the other end. She liked to feel the blood rush to her head; she liked to see the world upside down. What would she look like to someone passing by (as if anyone would, out here)? An acrobat? A dancer? None of which she wanted to be. Or would she look like someone having convulsions or a fit? No, she didn't think so. She stretched her arms out and back so that the palms of her hands were flat on the land. This she imagined was the pose of a gymnast. She hoped Sunny wouldn't think something was wrong and lumber over and start licking her face. He didn't. She could hear Sunny away somewhere scratching and digging and wondered what treasure he had found; Sunny was always burying things and then digging them up.

It reminded her of Angie, going off on some dig when she was taking that anthropology class. No, archaeology. Anthropology was something else. Anthropology, archaeology. They both sounded boring to Mary. Though she liked this particular rock. It was almost comfortable. And wrenching her body around like this kept her mind free of painful thoughts and images. The rock supported the small of her back. She lifted her arms and settled them across her tilted-back chest. Almost comfortable. Well, as comfortable as a rock could be. But she was fond of this rock; she considered it hers. Whenever she and Sunny came out here, she always ended up on this rock. She liked its changeable grays, its ripples, its indentations, the microscopic river—that is, she thought of the crevice that circled the rock as a tiny riverbed, after she had watched rain run into it, narrow as a needle at some points, widening out near the bottom. And she would have loved to think she herself had worn this seat smooth on top, which was perfect for sitting; but, of course, she hadn't. Weather had worn it away.

Then she started in thinking about rocks. Rocks, trees, the piñon bushes. Was there some sort of intelligence connected to them? And would Dr. Anders call this a "deep" problem? He had explained the various kinds of problems. The first was a problem that any fellow scientist trained in the field could solve; the second kind was the sort that made you famous and won awards; but a "deep" problem was the sort that confounded even a brilliant scientist and took a long, long time to solve. It went deep into the universe.

Dr. Anders was the one person in Santa Fe who treated Mary herself like an intelligent human being. He did not talk down to her, not even when he was talking about his theories, his work. And *that* was really hard to understand. Too complex. Well, that was the whole idea. Complexity. They were all sitting over there at the Institute on Canyon Road thinking about Complexity and Chaos. The edge of chaos. She had read the copy of the book he'd given Angela. Read it twice, but could understand only a few sentences here and there. *That's more than most people do,* Dr. Anders had said with a laugh. But Angela had read only the first few pages before giving up on it. "Too cerebral," she'd said. Mary had been surprised by this: it was, after all, Dr. Anders's *work.* Shouldn't she try to understand it? She went back to wondering why he was in love with Angie. Especially since he seemed well acquainted with Angie's faults and didn't mind letting her know. When Mary had told him her sister had a reputation for being "too dreamy," Dr. Anders had laughed and said, "Too lazy, you mean." Mary was surprised he'd seen this. Not reading his book was really sheer laziness on Angie's part.

He was always around: in the shop on Canyon Road, at their house sometimes for dinner. Which Mary didn't mind at all. She hoped, though, that he wasn't being nice to her just to get in good with Angela. But she didn't think so. He was too sincere. He was too *real.* He was sort of like Sunny over there, waiting with incredible patience for something to appear out of those rocks, those trees. Other people she knew—Malcolm Corey, for instance—seemed to be wispy, like smoke you could drive your fist through.

There was something about Malcolm Corey that was more sad than silly, she supposed. He really desperately wanted to be a movie star or at least a second lead. But he got only these tiny, walk-on parts that never amounted to anything. And he was a terrible painter on top of it. In a way she had to admire him for at least trying to do something else when it was obvious he'd never make it in the movies, even if the "something else" was no more practical. Anyone who could hold a paintbrush seemed to wind up in Santa Fe. If you stood in the middle of the square and threw a stone in any direction, you'd hit another gallery. Yet, she could understand why painters came here. As much as Mary deplored all of its commercialism, Santa Fe and the desert around it had a fundamental beauty that no matter of glitzy galleries, and carved coyotes, and too much turquoise jewelry could ruin. She loved the long stretches of umber desert, the dark mountains surrounding it, the magnificent sunsets, the light like shaved glass. Sometimes she thought if she flicked her finger at the air, the light would ring like crystal.

She had no desire to be an artist. What she herself wanted to do, finally, was work at the Santa Fe Institute. Only, you had to be some kind of genius to get into it. Her grades in school were As, but she didn't think that qualified her as a genius. They were As because she'd figured out long ago it was as easy to get good grades as bad ones. It was as easy to hand in your English paper on time as it was to hand it in late. You had to hand it in sometime, didn't you? It was easier because then people let you alone. No principal after you, no teacher on your back, no family railing at you to do better.

Mary swung herself into a sitting position and saw Sunny was gone again. But where?

She worked at Schell's Pharmacy two days a week, minimum wage, sometimes at the soda fountain, sometimes delivering prescriptions at the end of the day on her bike. It was boring and she disliked Dolly Schell, and was quite aware Dolly felt the same way about her. No love lost, probably just because she was Angela's sister and she hated Angela. Insofar as Mary could figure, she always had, for as long as Mary had known Dolly, yet Angela was unaware of this.

Dolly Schell was now her only relative. Would Bibbi try and hand her over to Dolly Schell just because she was the only "family" that Mary had? Good Lord. And why had Dolly even offered to go to England? It was really she herself who should have gone. To be told by the police a person is too young to identify a dead sister seemed the ultimate insult. She had managed to sit on her rage when Dolly told her she, Dolly, was going. Heathrow Airport and from there to Salisbury. Mary was good at hiding her feelings. And she had to admit Dolly had offered to let her come along. Knowing she'd refuse.

Angrily, she swung herself up and put her cool hands on her hot face. In a minute, she felt better and whistled for Sunny, a whistle that she knew would have no effect unless he was agreeable to doing whatever it meant. She looked around again. Ghost dog.

Thinking about the Scotland Yard detective made her feel much better. Like Dr. Anders, he treated her as if she had some intelligence; he took her seriously. Angie dead was awful enough. But Angie *murdered?*

Mary watched the sun go down. Such glorious sunsets were one thing she loved about this part of the country. On the far horizon, the sky glowed, flamed in orangeish red, dyed the horizon in shades of pink and lavender.

And in another part of the world, the sun was coming up. Did the people who'd built places such as Stonehenge think the sun was God? A God who again and again abandoned them, and for Whom, to make Him reappear, they performed a ritual sacrifice, and because they did, God reappeared? So it would go on and on, in a sort of circle, no one ever really understanding.

Such a place of myth and mystery would appeal to her sister: Angie seemed to want to think that's what life was—mystery and sacrifice. If you can afford such beliefs, Mary thought, shaking her head, her mouth tightening grimly in an old-maidish way. She would have liked to be worshipful, but it was too hard. As far as she was concerned, life was really handing in your English essays on time and delivering prescriptions on your bike for hardly any pay. Just request God to help with *that* stuff and you'd hear one huge abiding silence.

She was ashamed again; such hard thoughts seemed a betrayal of her sister. Mary pulled up her legs and rested her chin on her knees. The thing that she really couldn't explain, and wanted to, to somebody, was her lack of feeling; it was numbness, mostly. She had felt numb when the police sergeant had told her about Angie and gone on feeling numb for the last week. She was not using her "grief time" from school properly. It was like when her parents died, except she'd been only five then, and that was different. And although she'd never said this to anyone, she was happy for them. Imagine a husband and wife dying together like that, going down in the flames of their own jet plane, never having to grow old and watching the other one die, leaving you alone. Their deaths had been like them. Dramatic and dazzling. Sylvestra. Often she wished she'd been named Sylvestra; it was a name a goddess could own.

Mary Dark Hope wheeled backwards on the rock as she had done before, placing her palms on the earth, letting the tears run backwards. Out of nowhere, Sunny reappeared, magically before her. Mary raised one hand and rubbed his muzzle and wished she hadn't grown up so hard-hearted about things.

It was as if, on the way to somewhere, she had ignored a warning, and looked back and turned to stone.

FORTY

When Jury walked through the door of Rancho del Reposo with a dusting of snow on his coat, the same two clerks sorting through what looked like the same registration cards looked up and smiled; the drinks room was warmed, just as it had been before, by a fire huge as hell throwing shadowy beckoning fingers across the tile floor.

He looked for Malcolm Corey as he stood in the doorway of the atrium-like coffee lounge where the sun, reflecting off the glass walls, threw confetti-like light across the faces of the customers. He could have sworn these were the same people he'd seen two days previously. He didn't see Malcolm Corey, but over there beneath the assortment of kachinas was Benny Betts playing tag with two telephones. No, three, Jury saw as he squeezed past tables and between chairs. One of the hotel phones had been delivered to Benny's table.

Chatter buzzed around Jury, with the occasional sting of a high-pitched laugh. Benny Betts motioned him to sit as he pointed a finger at the phone and winked and smiled as if Jury were in on the deal, too. Benny also waved the receiver that was not at his ear towards a silver coffee pot and a straw basket of bread and muffins, inviting Jury to eat and drink.

Jury sat down, pulled over a clean cup, poured, as he watched Benny Betts's animated face. He was the very emblem of West Coast cool. Blue eyes, teeth white as a collar of roiling surf, well-tanned. A California dream.

Which was just what Benny Betts trafficked in and was selling (did he ever buy?) over his portable phone. At any rate, he was at the end of it, for he was saying a Betts goodbye (ending on a question or a promise).

"Yo! Richard Jury, Superintendent Flatfoot!" Benny shot out his hand.

Jury smiled. "I'm surprised you're still here, but I'm also glad. You knew Angela Hope."

Benny Betts cocked an eyebrow, looked at Jury out of innocent eyes. "Who?"

"Come on, Mr. Betts, you know who."

"Benny, please. Why so formal?" Benny flashed a whitecap smile.

"Because I expect it's safer. Otherwise, I'd find myself with an agent and a walk-on part in a remake of *The Bill*." Jury split a muffin. Why was he always eating these days? "Where's Malcolm Corey today?"

Betts pointed toward the outside, out toward the white distance where the road and the miniature figures were becoming blanketed in snow. "He's down there. I got him a couple lines in the picture. He's delirious."

"I can imagine. You must be a marketing genius."

"Pretty much. How come you're surprised I'm still here?"

"Because you strike me as a person who doesn't light for very long."

Benny shrugged, poured some more coffee. "Makes no difference where I am. Here, there, everywhere. It's all the same."

Jury ate his muffin. Carrot. He thought of Betty Ball's bakery. "Coming from you that sounds rather fatalistic. As if things were pretty much out of our control."

Benny smiled, clasped his hands behind his head, in the way (Jury thought) he must have looked in his mahogany-paneled office in his executive swivel chair.

"They are."

Jury looked up over his muffin. "This from the man who wants to remake *The Wizard of Oz*? I'm astonished."

"Dorothy got a crummy deal. And the ending was a total cheat."

" 'Crummy deal'? Meaning?"

"Well, she went through hell to find this wizard, so when she does, she discovers he's a fake." Benny brushed some crumbs from his designer jacket. "But it's the greatest kidjep picture of all time. Classic."

Jury frowned. "Kid *what*?"

"Kidjep, kidjep. You know, 'kid-in-jeopardy.' You got a kidjep situation, you got prime box office. Guaranteed." Benny drew a huge dollar sign in air.

"Does that make Toto a dogjep?"

"Yak yak." Benny eyed the phones, willing them to ring. Then he turned back to Jury. "You don't mind me saying, you look kind of down."

Jury smiled. "I don't mind you saying. I am."

"How come?"

Jury poured himself coffee, said, "I'm leaving tomorrow and I don't seem to have found any answers. Angela Hope—"

Benny Betts interrupted, frowning. "Answers? You been living in a fool's paradise, Richard Jury?"

Jury laughed. "Unfortunately, I do the kind of work that more or less calls for answers."

"You mean you're looking for a *real* one?"

"Well, I'm sure as hell not looking for an *unreal* one." Jury sipped his coffee.

Benny shoved his own cup aside to make room for his arms, which he folded on the table. He leaned towards Jury. "Did you learn about life at a fairy's knee?"

"Probably."

"Because, if you don't mind my saying it, you are just too much into rationality."

"Well, in my line of country, you deal in facts. In reality."

Benny's laugh caused a number of tables to turn and smile in return. "That's rich, Rich." He became suddenly sober. "All you can expect is virtual reality. You want a so-called solution? Hell, I can give you one. Or a dozen. The most you can do in this life is put a package together. Makes no difference what it is, take X from here, Y from here, Z from there—" his fingers flew up and out, pull, pull, pull— "and then you mush 'em together. Makes no difference whatever what the three things are. It's the package that's box office."

"X, Y, Z have to be related."

Benny looked like he was going to spit. "It don't make a fuck whether they're related or not. If somebody said 'kidjep-wizard-emerald' to you, would you think they were related?"

Jury frowned over this failure of logic. "Wait a minute. You can't use that because it's *a priori*, it's already a *fait accompli*."

"Christ, he knows French, too," Benny said to his audience of empty chairs.

"I'm talking about facts, Benny—"

"Facts?"

"To you, a dirty word; I'm a policeman, for God's sake—"

Benny shook his head at the chairs, as if the chairs empathized. "The worst kind, guys."

"It's not a *fantasy* that three women are dead—"

Benny nodded his head.

"It's not a *fantasy* that they may have been murdered—"

Nod. Nod. Nod.

"And it's not a *fantasy* that Angela Hope's body was found in Wiltshire at Sarum—"

Nod. Nod. Nod. A quick little snap of Benny's fingers, then a banner drawn in air and "By God, I can see it. Can't you see it? Sarum. Sunrise, maybe sunset. The colors, oranges bleeding into reds. Get it? Like blood, maybe paints dripping through the credits? I see Michelle—no—I see Melanie . . . hate that little shit, but she'd look great dead . . . the body on a stone slab in the middle. . . ." He grabbed Jury's arm. "We scroll back maybe a few dozen centuries—what year was it built anyway?" Benny's hand stopped scrolling and reached—

Was he *really* going for that phone? Jury put his hand on the wrist. He wasn't going to be drawn into a Bettsian fantasy. "NO—" Jury looked round, ashamed he'd raised his voice. He whispered "No" again. Benny smiled with the most irritating benignity that Jury had ever seen. "Facts may be elusive, but they're still facts. Evidence. Hard evidence. If that's the pot of gold at the end of the rainbow."

Benny gave him a sad little head shake, checked his Rolex, and started bundling the portable telephones into their holders like babies in bassinets. "Well, you ain't gonna find no pot of gold at the end of the rainbow, Rich. Trust me."

Jury smiled. "So what *is* at the end of a rainbow?" He expected an answer of grating cynicism as Benny shouldered the leather straps.

But all he said was, "What makes you think it's got an end?"

FORTY-ONE

It wasn't until he was brushing his teeth the next morning that Jury realized he'd probably been conned by Benny Betts. His head over the sink, Jury laughed so hard he nearly choked on Tom's of Maine Natural Toothpaste. Benny never did answer the question about his relationship with Angela Hope.

Chump, he said to his reflection. Then he scrubbed his face dry with a towel, went out for a walk.

Something had woken him at dawn and he had risen and dressed. Now, he walked through the sleeping hotel to the elevators and took one to the roof. He wanted to see the sunrise. It came up out of the Sangre de Cristos first as light, then as color, pale and shimmering like beaten gold, then rose, blue—so beautiful it really did look as if a film choreographer were doing magic with his camera. No wonder the film folk loved Santa Fe. Snow on the mountains, in the crevices of the foothills, clear across the desert floor. It was not, certainly, a London dawn.

What makes you think it has an end? He remembered these words of Benny Betts and somehow took comfort in them.

He walked around the plaza, nothing open yet, and drank in the light. The light had a clarity that was almost brittle. If only the mind were lit by such a light. Perhaps for someone like Nils Anders, it was. He was disappointed, returning to Exeter emptyhanded. But he had faxed a report to Macalvie every day, setting down who he saw, what was said, in as much detail as Jury could possibly remember. Unedited, no opinions given. Opinions could wait. So let Macalvie theorize. He'd even stayed an extra day when he was itching to be back in Stratford-upon-Avon. And that blasted fax from Plant: *She is Found!* Found where?

Ill humor made him feel slightly less impotent. (Blaming one's problems on others usually did.) And he shouldn't be angry with Melrose Plant, who had found her when not even the Stratford police seemed able to do it.

Jury whistled and crossed the Paseo de Peralta, admitting to himself that he must be, simply, jealous.

She is Found! But not by him.

2

AROUND THE small shopping center, the sodium vapor lights were extinguished and the interior lights of Schell's Pharmacy were just being switched on. On the glass door, the Closed sign had not yet been turned to Open. Jury waited. But Dolly Schell didn't see him before she was turning the big bunch of keys and the sign, and when she did, she opened her mouth, stepped back, eyes wide.

"Sorry. I didn't mean to scare you," said Jury, opening the door.

Dolly turned the sign and smiled. "It's just that it's so early. Come on in."

"I was up at dawn, wanted to see the sunrise. Some sunrise." He said this as he followed her through the store.

"Looks artificial almost, too pretty to be true." She stopped to adjust some plastic bottles of stuff and then went on down the aisle. Jury followed, noticing as he did all of the hair-care products. Ye gods, judging from this lot, a woman could spend half a day washing her hair. He picked up a canister of mousse and had the childish desire to write in white foam across the plate-glass window. He returned that to its large mousse family—how many brands were there of the stuff?—and studied a white plastic cylinder that said "sculpting gel." What the hell was that? He wondered if it was something you get in London and whether Fiona had it. Never mind, she could always use more. As he passed the makeup display, he thought of Carole-anne. That would only be lily gilding, so why bother? Anyway, he had already bought Carole-anne some earrings, little cascades of silver coyotes.

At the end of the aisle were more coyotes, some cloth, some tin wind-up toys. Jury tossed one up a little, judging its weight. Then he took purchases to Dolly Schell.

"I'll have these. Presents." He smiled as she took them from him. "And some Dramamine too, I think. Got a bit sick on the flight from New York."

"A lot of people say that. It has something to do with the air mass over the mountains." She took some Dramamine from the display behind her and dropped that in the bag. The drawer of the old-fashioned register popped out when she hit some keys. "You're leaving?" He nodded and she frowned, looking disappointed. "When's your flight?"

"This afternoon. Around three. That's to New York. I have to wait—oh, I don't know, with the time difference, perhaps a couple of hours for the London flight. Middle of the damned night, those flights."

Dolly returned his change and asked, "Did you get what you wanted? I mean about Angela?"

"No. Perhaps there's nothing to get." He shrugged. "Doesn't seem to be anyone, not anyone I talked to, who can think why anyone around here would wish her harm."

Dolly Schell looked up at him, an ironic smile on her mouth. "Except me?"

Jury thought for a moment. "Did you really dislike her that much? Enough to kill her?"

Now Dolly grew quiet. "I can't say absolutely no."

That was clever. Mary's voice spoke in his head. "How about Mary?"

"Mary? What about her?"

"She works for you sometimes."

Dolly frowned. "She delivers prescriptions if people want deliveries." She put her hand on a small pile of white envelopes lying by the cash register. "These should have gone out yesterday afternoon. She didn't show up. Rather annoying. I guess I'll have to get somebody else. Mary's not the most dependable person."

"Don't blame her; blame me. I was out at their house, talking to the housekeeper. Mary came in and I talked to her too. Had dinner with Dr. Anders—"

Dolly's face grew softer.

"Nils is very fond of her," said Jury absently as he collected his purchases.

"Angela? Probably."

"No, Mary. I doubt he was really all that fond of Angela." Too late to call the words back. He had spoken—albeit with perfect innocence—without thinking.

She looked at him quizzically. "Mary?"

"I only meant . . ." Jury was stumped. He didn't know how to cover up his blunder.

But when she spoke next, it was with a smile: "Is Nils really very fond of anyone?"

Jury said, clumsily, "It was pleasant, our talk. It did tell me a good deal."

Again, she gave him an ironic smile.

3

"OUT TO HELL-AND-GONE," Rosella had said, impatiently, as, inside the Casita de Hope, she pointed towards a window facing west. *"Her and that damned coyote of hers walk out there whenever my back's turned."*

Jury saw her now in Hell-and-gone. He'd been walking for perhaps ten minutes when he came out of a small cactus forest to see Mary Dark Hope a hundred feet away, sitting on a rock. He did not see Sunny.

Her legs were pulled up, her chin on her knees. She turned her head towards Jury. "Hello." Mary pushed her hair back from her face with a gesture that in a woman would have seemed flirtatious, but on Mary seemed nothing more than a wish to get her hair out of her face. "How'd you find here?"

" 'Here'?" He smiled. "I found 'here' by following Rosella's directions."

"Really? I didn't think she knew."

Jury sat beside her on the boulder, its top worn smooth by weather and much sitting. "She doesn't. It's just that you usually walk in this general direction." Jury looked towards the mountains, purple in the distance; the sky was a hard, clear blue. "You come here a lot."

"Yes. I like to watch the sunset."

He nodded. Then he said, "I talked to Dolly Schell again." He looked at her. "After that comment you made last evening."

"Uh-huh."

"You thought it was 'clever' of her to admit to something I'd be sure to find out anyway."

Apparently taking the question as rhetorical, she just kept staring straight ahead.

"It sounds pretty improbable. Even if she'd found a way to murder Angela, it's improbable that the two British tourists would be involved."

"Sherlock Holmes."

"What?"

"He said if you eliminate the impossible, then if what's left over is improbable, it makes no difference, you go with it."

"Well, Sherlock had a better mind than I have."

There was a silence, and then she asked, "When will they send—Angie home?" Her voice tripped up on the "Angie."

Painful question. "Just as soon as they determine the cause of death."

"It's taking them long enough."

"It's difficult, not knowing the—possibilities."

Mary turned to look at him through her crystal-spring-colored eyes. "That's sort of like saying, 'If they knew, they'd know.' "

Jury smiled. "Sounds like it, I expect. But it's three times as hard because of the other two women whose deaths might be related. Did the three of them meet in England? It's possible. Did the three perhaps dine together? Could they have ingested something that worked in quite different ways on each of them? They could all have died by accident." Two of them, perhaps. Fanny Hamilton had died back in January.

"And they could all have been murdered." Mary shied a flat stone at a cactus.

"That's even harder to demonstrate. But one of the reasons this is taking so long is that it's become a three-way investigation."

She picked up another flat stone. "I haven't figured out why she'd kill them too, the Englishwomen."

Perhaps her feeling about Dolly Schell could serve as some sort of channel for grief. It was easier if you could get angry. Imagine a future managed by a social worker. The knowledge that Dolly Schell was her only relation must have made the knowledge of her diminished family particularly awful.

She scratched with a stick in the dirt. "You're leaving, aren't you?" Her voice was sad.

"In a few hours."

"Will you be back?"

"We'll see each other again."

"How do you know?"

"I know."

They sat side by side, looking off across the godforsaken landscape. Jury lost any sense of time, so that he wondered how long they'd been there when he heard several short, distinct barks that soared upwards in such a desolate howl the hairs on his neck stood up.

"That Sunny?"

Mary Dark Hope nodded. "I guess it is."

"Somehow, that just doesn't sound like a German shepherd."

For a moment she was silent. Then she said, "I didn't say he was *all* German shepherd."

FORTY-TWO

After seven hours, and no sleep, Jury made sure he was in the first clutch of passengers off the BA flight and into Terminal 3, where passport control would make life a hell for travellers not holding EEC passports. Heathrow was in the throes of its usual travails and uproars: planes delayed, passengers stranded, kids squalling—and always, the lines of people looking anxious as if theirs was the last flight to heaven. Cancelled.

The plane had landed at six a.m.; it was now six-forty, and Jury wanted nothing more than to get to Islington, call Plant, call Macalvie, drop into bed. But first he had his bargain to keep.

He saw her sitting on a high stool behind the register and staring out over the terminal. What a bloody boring job that must be, he thought, as he muscled his way through a swamp of Japanese travellers, feeling not a whit guilty for being twice as big as they were. He could see from the expression on the face of the interpreter that they were making her life miserable already.

Finally, he reached the counter. "Hello, Des," said Jury, as he set down his suitcase.

Perhaps because she'd been called back from some interior landscape, she regarded him vacantly at first, but then gave a little start of pleasure. "It's *you!*"

"Me. Back from the jaws of nicotine hell. I felt pretty self-righteous sitting in the no-smoking zone, I can tell you. Five days and not one fag. I thought it'd kill me."

"Me, too. But I held out. Even so, I couldn't think of anything but a smoke. And *then* having to work this *counter* and being always having to look at the bloody things—"

As if taking a cue, a customer materialized at that moment, forcing her to look at the bloody things. He put down a ten-pound note and asked for two packets of Marlboros, one of which he jammed in his briefcase. The pack in his hand he tamped a half-dozen times on the counter, then zipped off the line of gold cellophane, then tore at the tin foil, then extracted one of the cigarettes, and finally stuffed it in his mouth. He brought out his Zippo and lit up. He inhaled, and then said, "Damn those smokeless flights." He said this sheepishly, as if he were wedded to this ritual and only after its completion was he permitted to acknowledge the presence of others.

"I know how you feel," said Jury. "We're trying to stop, too." He nodded at Des.

"Stop? God, how I wish I could. I've tried everything, every bloody thing: I've tried nicotine-free cigarettes—they taste like empty air; those holders that keep reducing the amount of nicotine; gum, pills, group therapy; nicotine patches; *individual therapy*, that costs an arm and a leg; you name it, I've done it. Nothing works."

Watching him inhale again, Jury was certain that not a centimeter of lung was missing its nicotine bath.

The stranger said, "So how'd you do it?"

Jury laughed. "Well, I haven't really 'done' it, you know. I just managed to stay off them for five days, well, seven counting the days before I left. And so has Des."

Ruefully, the man looked at the cigarette between his fingers and shook his head sadly, "Five days, bloody hell, I can't last for even five *hours*. No willpower. None."

"Oh, I don't think it's willpower."

He seemed astonished. "You don't? Then what?"

The fellow looked so terribly serious about all of this. Here were two people who had undertaken some sort of vision quest, or had faced the Minotaur, or had run the rapids and lived to tell about it. It was as if his two soul mates here were offering him some sort of Sanctuary. They might have been priests and he the penitent.

Jury said, "I think you have to try something or find something that's more important to you than smoking. Make a pact with someone else who's trying to quit. Your wife, a friend, anyone. You've got to make the goal attainable, too, like telling yourself it's only for two days, three."

"Like AA, kind of. 'One day at a time.' That kind of thing."

"That kind of thing, yes."

The man checked his watch, thrust out his hand. "Thanks. It's a relief to find that the three of us have something in common, right?"

The three of us. Something shifted in Jury's mind; he saw himself back in the Silver Heron. Then Des was waving as their newfound friend dashed to security control.

Des said, "That's right, what he said. I got a friend in AA. It's funny how much it makes a bond between people, trying to stop drinking. I expect it's the same with smoking." Des smiled. "I owe you a kiss." Keeping her end of the bargain, she leaned over the counter, threw her arms around him, and gave him one slightly clumsy, quite long kiss.

"And I owe you a bracelet." He moved to the counter on the other side of the register.

"It's gone. It's sold," said Des, sadly.

"*What?*"

She nodded. "Yesterday. Some woman bought it." She sighed. "But that's all right."

No, it isn't, thought Jury, surprised by the force of his anger. That bracelet represented something—a prize, a victory. Now, the two of them looked into the case where a satin-covered wheel turned ceaselessly, jerking to a stop and starting again.

"I don't know why I fancied it so much. I mean, it wasn't really any prettier than these ones." She reached in and pointed to a row of silver bracelets.

"The point is you *did* fancy it. That's what matters." He looked at her. "And you didn't even go for your smokes, even when that happened?" She shook her head and looked quite resolute and proud. "That's bloody marvellous." He bent down to open his suitcase, found the earrings intended for Carole-anne, and said, "Look, it's not your bracelet, but I picked these up in Santa Fe, they're very Southwest. I got them in case—" Jury shrugged, not wanting to make this into a total lie. Carole-anne would kill him, of course, coming back without a present for her.

It fairly took Des's breath away, she was so thrilled. She lifted one of the earrings out. The tiny coyote-cluster moved in the air like a minuscule wind chime. "Oh, these are lovely, just lovely. Better than that bracelet, honestly. Oh, it's so nice to know somebody's actually thinking of you, you know what I mean?" She had her old earrings out and the new ones on within half a minute. "Thanks. Really, thanks."

"You're very welcome, Des." Jury picked up his case. "I'd better be going. We'll see each other again, I'm sure."

Now, she looked serious. "You think so?"

"I know so."

It was the same thing he'd said to Mary Dark Hope.

FORTY-THREE

"Nicotine."

Jury had fumbled the receiver off the hook and wondered if he was still asleep, lost in a nightmare vision of Islington engulfed in one of its old yellow fogs, back in the days when London was called the Smoke. And the source of this smoke in the dream was not chimney pots, but Silk Cuts and Players. Here was his unconscious, sending him a message. Or a warning. Probably his brain was shattered by deprivation. And now the dream merged with reality as smoothly as the jagged edge of two pieces of torn paper rejoining. If the first thing he had done was reach for the receiver, the second thing was to bring his free hand around to the nightstand, searching for his pack of Players. Nothing. Denial making his nerve ends scream, Jury fell back against the pillow. The only call he wanted was from that Surgeon General who'd started it all, announcing he'd been wrong, and the link between Nicotine, Emphysema, and Death had now been completely discounted. But when Jury recalled that poor chap in the terminal, hopelessly addicted, bedeviled by it. And all three of them—

"You there?"

Forget the Surgeon General. It was Macalvie.

"I figured you took the red-eye flight, so I let you sleep. You still asleep?"

"Talking in it."

"Come on, Jury, it's nearly noon."

Jury lifted his watch close enough to see in the dim light. He might have landed by six a.m., but he hadn't got to bed until nearly nine. "I do not call ten-thirty 'nearly noon,' Macalvie."

"Whatever. You hear what I said? Nicotine poisoning. My girl—"

(Meaning Angela Hope)

"—died of nicotine poisoning. Nell Hawes, possibly. And your lady—"

(Meaning Frances Hamilton)

Jury said, "The three of them," as if he were speaking out of a dream. And then he understood why his thoughts had been called back to Santa Fe, to Angela Hope's workspace.

"That's right, all three. Or, at least two. I've been trying to get a court order to exhume the body. You don't kill yourself smoking, Jury. At least not that way. Did you know a cigar has anywhere from ten to forty milligrams of the stuff? I'm glad I don't smoke cigars."

"Like an alcoholic saying, 'I'm glad I only drink beer.' "

Macalvie ignored this blow to his rationalizations. "Those snaps you took. I'm looking at one of them now. Angela was definitely a heavy smoker, judging from the scars, the burn marks on the work-table."

Jury sat up. "That's what they had in common. According to her nephew's fiancée, Frances Hamilton couldn't stop for love nor money, had to hide her heart condition to keep Lady Cray from bullying her. Nell Hawes—" Jury heard a muffled rap on his door. "Listen, there's someone at the door. Can you hold on?"

"No." Macalvie wouldn't hold on for God. "When can you get here?"

"By late afternoon. I've got to collect Wiggins from hospital."

Macalvie made a noise. "Hell, I forgot to send him flowers or something. Get him a present for me, will you? A respirator, some-thing he'd enjoy? No one ever told me what he was *in* for."

"Just a Wiggins complaint," said Jury vaguely. "You know how he is."

"Tell him he doesn't want to lie around too much. It weakens you."

"Is that a hint—?" But the divisional commander had hung up.

At the door stood Mrs. Wassermann, beaming over a covered bowl. "Porridge. I know how much you like it."

Jury smiled and took the bowl; he'd never liked it, not even when he was a kid. He thanked her and told her he'd stop by and see her on his way out.

He set the bowl by the telephone and put in a call to Ardry End. No, Ruthven said, His Lordship was not there; he was in London.

Jury felt hopeful. "In London where, Ruthven?"

"I couldn't really say, sir. I do know he intended to stop by the hospital. But I haven't heard from since late yesterday."

Hope fled. Jury thanked him and hung up.

She is Found! Where, damn it?

2

IF THERE were ever two entities that fit like a hand and a glove, they were Sergeant Wiggins and his wheelchair.

"It's just hospital regulations," Wiggins had said in a loud whisper when Jury had entered his hospital room. "I'm perfectly fine, right as rain. But they're afraid somebody'll have an accident and sue the hospital."

Now he was introducing Jury to Nurse Lillywhite, who, he said, was as much responsible for his recuperation as anyone.

Lillywhite's already shining face beamed all the more at Jury, partly from Wiggins's praise, partly because of Jury himself. He was helping her load up the books—Lord, he had never known Wiggins was such a reader—and rearranging the bouquets so that they'd only have to carry three vases. Wiggins insisted on taking his flowers. And there were certainly a lot of flowers. Jury was chiding himself for not sending any, when Wiggins thanked him for the lilies and carnations. He had no idea what Wiggins was talking about, and thought perhaps the sergeant was giving him a gentle reminder that Jury, of all people, had forgotten. But then he decided, no, Wiggins used irony as often as he used gin. Never.

Then Jury thought he knew how Wiggins had come by all of these bouquets. For instance, Vivian Rivington's roses. She didn't even know Wiggins was in hospital. Marshall Trueblood, ditto. Neither of them knew Wiggins anyway, beyond a brief period more than ten years ago. And this elaborate arrangement of orchids and dahlias from Fiona was far too much for her mingy salary. A little African violet plant from the cat Cyril. Jury smiled. Nothing from Racer. But then Racer would as soon send poison parsley as a bunch of carnations.

They started down the corridor, Jury pushing the wheelchair, Wiggins with the sack of books perched on his lap, Lillywhite bringing up the rear with the vases of flowers and a sneezing fit. Probably allergic.

"I didn't know you were such a vociferous reader, Sergeant."

"Well, you see, most of these are in aid of the investigation. Mr. Plant brought me this one—" and he held up *The Daughter of Time*— "as the situation—it's about a detective inspector flat on his back in hospital—applied to yours truly."

"Did yours truly have any success?"

"As you may or may not know it was me pretty much ruled out that telephone number as a telephone—oh, goodbye, Mr. Innes—" here, a frail old person came to his door to bid the sergeant farewell— "which was, I daresay, a modicum of help."

"Absolutely." Though, as far as Jury knew, Macalvie hadn't pinned that number down.

"Anyway, getting the facts through Mr. Plant allowed me to add my tuppence to the whole affair—goodbye, Mr. MacDougall. See you again, but hopefully not under these circumstances, ha ha—" Another hand was shaken, this one belonging to a grizzled Scot who looked as if he could whip the living daylights out of any disease God had on offer. "But, of course, this Josephine Tey had the advantage over me, didn't she, seeing as how *her* perp was already dead—that's Richard the Third, you know—and masses of stuff written about him; whereas, *I* only got my information as told me by Mr. Plant—goodbye, goodbye, Miss Grissip, Mrs. Nutting, see you again, I hope—"

And it was like this all down the corridor, patients popping out of their doorways, sad, even weeping to see Sergeant Wiggins being wheeled off. How the devil, Jury wondered, had all of these patients become so *attached* to Wiggins in five days' time? Jury shook his head, listening to Wiggins rattle on about Indian curses, Hovenweep, the Navajo and Hopi Indians. They had come finally to the lifts, leaving behind them their own Trail of Tears, and Wiggins still at it. When Lillywhite sneezed again, Jury insisted on taking the flowers from her, leaving her to push the chair, which she'd probably rather do, anyway. He put two of the vases on Wiggins's lap.

"—that the Hope woman, who was, if you remember, interested in archaeology or anthropology, just might have come across something truly valuable on one of those digs—one of those black-and-white pots the Anasazi were famous for—" The lift doors opened and then closed behind the three.

Jury said, "But how do you work the other two into it? Strikes me as a bit of a reach. At any rate, Divisional Commander Macalvie rang me this morning. Looks like nicotine poisoning, according to the lab at Exeter HQ."

Wiggins nearly flew out of his chair in his excitement, as he was trundled out of the lift. "Good Lord, sir . . ." and he rooted in the sack of books until he found the one he wanted. "Ed McBain! I only just finished reading this one last night." Wiggins held up a paperback, waved it back and forth. "*Kiss*, this one is. That's what Ed McBain uses. I keep telling you he's a snappy writer. Nicotine is lethal in its pure form. One way is you can take the tobacco from cigarettes and extract the stuff, so it's possible for anyone to do it. Another way is by turning it to liquid form and introducing it into the victim's food or drink—"

As they passed through the automatic glass doors onto the pavement, Jury asked, "So how does Mr. McBain administer it?"

Nurse Lillywhite went off to fetch a cab from the rank.

"Well, I don't think I should say. I mean, you might want to read it sometime."

Jury shut his eyes, gritted his teeth, but said, "I'm not going to read it, Wiggins; I don't much care for detective stories. So how—?"

"You ought to do more reading, sir, if you don't mind me saying. Too much telly rots the brain."

"I'm sure you have a cure for brain rot in this shaving kit." As Wiggins had held up the book, Jury held up the kit, waved it around. "So how—?"

But Wiggins was adamant. "I don't want to give it away."

If he hadn't been burdened with an entire arboretum of flowers, Jury thought, he just might hit him, wheelchair or no wheelchair.

Fortunately, the cab and Nurse Lillywhite returned. There was a tearful goodbye between the two and Jury went off to one side, making himself scarce during this re-enactment of A *Farewell to Arms*. He didn't know which he wanted more: a cigarette, or a word from Plant about that infuriating message. If in London, where in London? As if the answer might be hidden in Wiggins's shaving kit, he unzipped it. He had to admit a certain fascination with the sergeant's nostrums. Never knew what you'd find. He'd smuggled in a couple of his own prescription medicines, and those vials were probably the most ordinary-looking of the lot. The others held odd-looking dusty bits of stuff that grew in some garden Jury never wanted to visit. He frowned over the prescription drugs, too. What the hell was . . . ?

And then he saw the number: 431455. Jury looked unseeingly towards the Fulham Road. What if it was a prescription number? What if—? He was pulled from these speculations by the voice of Nurse Lillywhite, who was waving him over to a cab.

Wiggins was in the cab, flowers and books and sundries stowed in the trunk. Jury got in and as the cab pulled away, Wiggins waving enthusiastically out of the back window to Lillywhite, growing smaller in the distance, a white blur.

Jury said, "No more wires and water, Wiggins. Okay?"

Wiggins turned to his passenger window and refused to answer.

FORTY-FOUR

It was astonishing how little an English village changed over the years. Except for Theo Wrenn Browne and his bookshop, or Mr. Jenks and his estate agency, Long Piddleton hadn't changed by a hair in all of the years Melrose had lived there, all of his life, really.

Neither had Littlebourne, he was pleased to see as he stood smoking beside his Bentley, watching an early evening mist across Littlebourne Green rise, shift, and resettle. It was a different season from the one he had last seen here, and the green, around which the main street ran, was not green now, but patched with white that sparkled in the light of the black lamps lining the street and throwing arcs of pale gold light across the dark pavement. But he could see in the dark that the business establishments occupied the same spots he remembered—the garage, the post office, stores. And earlier, had that figure coming out of the post office actually been Miles Bodenheim, busy, as always, in unsettling village life? On this side of the green, the pub, a candy shop, an estate agency. He crossed the road and stopped to look at Polly Praed's cottage. It sat near the granite cross that marked the intersection of the wider Hertford road. Its whitewashed stone walls were covered by a tracery of vines, the little garden in front as ill kept as always, tall grasses struggling with untrimmed hedges.

Melrose stopped in the middle of the green to relight his cigar before proceeding on his way. The windows of Polly Praed's cottage were warm lozenges of light, and as he was repocketing his lighter, the lacy curtains separated in one of the ground-floor windows, and Polly appeared, hands cupping her face, as people do when the light is behind them and, for some godforsaken reason, seem to think they can't be seen because of the dark beyond them. She looked to left and right, left and right, straining to see, and then disappeared, and the curtains came together again. Melrose was fascinated, and waited. Now, the same action was repeated at another of the ground-floor windows. Curtains parted, face appearing, looking right, left, and then vanishing behind the curtains again. Melrose stood leaning on his furled umbrella, waiting. Ah, there she was again, only this time at a window on the floor above, searching, searching.

Obviously for him. It was now fifteen minutes past seven. He had told her *probably* seven, but that he might be later, as he wasn't sure of the roads. Looked like snow. But Polly would have stopped listening, not attending to any details, certainly not to probabilities. And would make no allowances. Melrose crossed the road on the other side of the green, went up her short walk, and raised the brass knocker. No answer. He knocked again. He watched the second hand of his back-lit wristwatch sweep around a full minute. Still no answer. With his umbrella, he reached past the porch to tap on the windowpane.

Finally, the door opened and she looked out. "Oh, it's you," was her enthusiastic greeting.

"Well, hello, Polly."

"Hello." She manufactured a yawn. "Come on in."

Even before Melrose was fully into the hall, she was turning her back, walking away, and he shot his umbrella straight out, managing to connect the curved handle into the neckline of her dress, and tug.

"What—?" She stumbled backwards, far enough that he could reach her, and he embraced her and—since her back was still turned—brought his mouth down on her neck.

Polly made a disapproving noise and rubbed at her shoulder. "What are you *doing?*"

"Giving you a kiss. Haven't seen you in four years."

She walked right away from him and into her living room, straightening her dress as if he had done much more than kiss her on the cheek. "Well, don't."

Polly was quite attractive, but she didn't know how to dress. She was wearing one of those colors that she seemed to favor. An entire vegetable-color spectrum would have to be invented for her. That pumpkin-brown jumper! That aubergine-green skirt! What a combination, if you wanted to make your skin look like candle tallow and your hair mud brown. Still, nothing could distract from her marvellous eyes that, depending on the light, ran the gamut from lavender to deep purple. Amethyst eyes.

Why was it, Melrose wondered, as he sat down in the vaguely offered chair, that women went into an alcoholic-like denial to let him know they didn't care a fingersnap for him, and, at the same time, went to so much trouble to get him there in the first place? This did not happen to Richard Jury. Polly was tongue-tied around Richard Jury. But tongue-tiedness didn't necessarily mean "love," did it?

She was anything but tongue-tied around Melrose. Nor shy. Nor retiring. She frowned and demanded, "Where are you staying, anyway?" She looked round at him from the copper-inlaid sink which served as a drinks table.

"The Bold Blue Boy." It was the only place he *could* stay, as she well knew.

She handed him a whisky and water, held out a plate of mouse-morsels of cheese, and sat down on the sofa across from him. "So what's all this about Lady Kennington?"

"Richard Jury asked me to look for her."

"He can't find her himself? Has he got dim, or something?"

"It's actually the Stratford police looking for her—"

Polly became breathlessly expectant. "My God! What's she done?"

"Nothing, I'm sorry to have to tell you. Nothing except witness something."

" 'Something'? What 'something'?

"I don't know the details. Jury's off in the U.S. on some case and I simply got a message by way of his policeman friend in Stratford-upon-Avon." Melrose would have been happy to make up a story about a mass murderer, but since he knew one of the principals, he thought that would be ill advised. "Really, Polly, I don't know anything about it." He switched the subject. "It's wonderful to see you; it's been a long time."

"Do you think you could manage not to talk about time passing?" she asked crossly.

He laughed. "Don't worry; you have many, many writing years ahead of you."

"Well, I don't have many, many writing *days* before my absolutely final, penultimate deadline for my book."

"Is that why you're in such a bad mood?" Polly was a writer of many deadlines. There were the ignorable deadlines, the not-to-be-taken-too-seriously deadlines; the deadlines-before-the-deadlines deadlines, and finally, the no-kidding-around deadlines. She set these various dates, she'd told him, to fool herself. Melrose never remembered this working. "I've a friend in Baltimore who chains herself to her desk, if that's any help."

"But that's wonderful!" That it was "she" meant nothing over against the "she" being a writer. Polly would happily forgo jealousy for the pleasure of talking about writing and writers. She leaned forward, careless of her drink. "But how does she do it? I mean, we *all* could chain ourselves to our desks, but the trouble there is, you could just unlock yourself and get out." As usual, she took it quite seriously.

"She put the key where she couldn't get at it."

Polly frowned a frown of deep thought. "But—"

Melrose explained just what Ellen did.

"God!" Polly fell back against the sofa. "I expect I'm lucky compared to that!"

She didn't ask whether Ellen Taylor's work was any good. It was agony, not quality, that interested her. Polly loved to talk about writing. It occurred to Melrose that it was almost a sensual thing, and certainly passionate. It was a turn-on. So he told her he himself was writing a mystery.

The fountain of enthusiasm dried up pretty quickly. *"You?"*

"Why not? I certainly spend enough of my time reading your rumpled drafts." Probably, that's what made her scoff. If he turned his hand to the trade, he wouldn't be available for editing. He sighed. "What does the absolutely final deadline apply to? What book?"

"Remember *Death of a Doge?*"

"Actually, I've been trying to forget it."

"Well, *ta* very *much!* Anyway, this is the sequel."

"Pardon me?" If there was one book that did not cry out for a sequel, it was *Death of a Doge*. "Don't you remember what an awful time you had writing that book?"

"Yes, but I liked Aubrey."

Melrose didn't. Was he once more to have to follow the travails of Aubrey Adderly in his escape through the misty byways of Venice? "I thought Aubrey was snuffed out there."

"No, you're thinking about somebody else."

"If this book was the one I remember, I'm thinking about *everybody* else." Polly had no problem bumping off a dozen people in as many pages. "Polly, you've got too much Venetian competition. Why don't you choose another setting? Portsmouth or Bury St. Edmunds, for instance."

"Oh, don't be dim. Those places are never used."

"That's my point. Indeed, what about *here*? Are you still killing off the Bodenheims?"

Another topic she delighted in. "I just did in Julia for the eighteenth time."

Julia Bodenheim was the daughter, not only a snob, but a snob on horseback.

"Whilst she was riding to hounds, her mount threw her off the other side of a hedge and half of the field of horses jumped it and trampled her to death. Bloodcurdling." She uttered a satisfied sigh. For years, she'd been killing off the Bodenheims, one after another.

"Do you know, I saw Miles Bodenheim coming out of the post office." Melrose sank farther into the comfortable armchair. Polly might not have known clothes, but she certainly knew furniture. Her little cottage was beautifully done up. "I can't believe it's been ten years. Ten years." He studied the ceiling molding. "The place is caught in a time warp."

"No, it isn't."

Argument, to Polly, meant contradiction. She passed him the cheese and crackers.

"No? Well, I'd swear Bodenheim had that same smarmy look on his face, the one he always got when he'd succeeded in making life hell for someone. In this case, the postmistress—what's her name?"

"Pennystevens." If they weren't to talk about her books, she'd leaf through that magazine.

"Miss Pennyfeathers. Now, she looked ready to retire when I saw her ten years ago. But here she is. Here *they are*. Lord knows, Bodenheim looks the same right down to the egg on his waistcoat."

"You're being sentimental. You probably like A. E. Housman— 'What are those blue, remembered hills.' That stuff."

"You're certainly attached to your Venetian stuff, aren't you?"

She yawned by way of answer.

"Well, I expect I'd better be going. You're tired."

Ah, the yawn had backfired, had it? "No! No, you don't have to . . ." she ended up whining.

"I'll see you tomorrow, Polly. Perhaps we could have lunch."

Her expression was thoughtful, suspicious. "Did you see her?"

"Lady Kennington, you mean? No, she wasn't at the pub."

"Yes, she is. I saw her."

"I mean, she's gone out somewhere."

Polly studied the air. "Probably to that house she used to own. Skulking around the grounds, probably."

In Polly's darkling world, people didn't simply look and walk; they peered and skulked.

Melrose did not want to say that Stonington was where he was heading. "I think I'd like to take a walk round the village. See if I'm not right. See if it's not just the same."

"You can't go home again."

One of the sappier entries in the cliché sweepstakes, he thought. "Yes, you can. Goodnight, Polly."

2

MELROSE HAD NEVER been on the other side of the stone wall, but he remembered the wall itself and the small brass plate fitted into the stone with the name Stonington engraved on it.

He had looked before through its iron gates, remembered the grounds as being overgrown and unpruned in summer; February's leafless trees allowed for a better view of the house itself, which was huge. He inspected the stone posts for some sort of call box or electronic thing by which to gain admittance, saw nothing, then saw that the gate was neither locked nor chained and swung when he pushed it.

Up the gravel drive he walked, a drive that needed some seeing to, he thought, avoiding the potholes. He wondered how long it had stood vacant, for it had all of the appearance of a place not lived in for a very long time. It was the most hushed and deserted landscape he could remember. Birds should have found a bird paradise here, what with the overgrown privets, the untended herbaceous borders, but he heard no birds. He was probably still under the influence of Baltimore and Edgar Allan Poe, for he found he enjoyed finding sere landscapes, abandoned buildings he could think of as Poe-esque.

Melrose walked up the wide steps and when he got to the top cupped his face in his hands to look inside, as Polly had done earlier that evening to spy out his arrival.

What would he find?

How bloody ridiculous. He would find Lady Kennington, that's what. The bored, hence gossipy, secretary in the estate agent's office had told him Lady Kennington was most likely at the house, for she spent a lot of time there, looking at things, probably taking measurements, and did he know that once she owned it? Oh, yes, she had, and her husband, Lord Kennington, up and died on her, and she just stayed on as long as she could, well, I'd never, not alone I wouldn't, not after those grisly murders, and did he know about that? That woman found in the—

Yes, Melrose knew, he said, and thanked her and left.

THE STATUE at the center of the courtyard must have served as a still point about which the household moved. It fascinated him that it could be seen from every room, upstairs and down-, for the rooms on the ground floor gave out on this courtyard, and those on the first each had a little balcony.

He observed this through the tall windows of a large, empty room, after observing the figure of a woman—not the statue, but near it, standing, and sometimes stooping in the garden around it. And what was she doing? Weeding? At night? Presumably, for when she stood up, her gloved hand was full of black, stemlike things. It amused him the way she seemed to be surveying the impossibly overgrown garden that surrounded the statue. Still, she bent down again to continue this thankless job. If she didn't officially own the place, Melrose thought, she very much belonged to it. Like that statue, really. A permanent fixture.

Now, he was unsure what to do, that is, how to make his appearance without scaring the hell out of her. Tap on the windowpane? No, that would be even more frightening in an empty house. And her back was to him, so if he came from this direction, she wouldn't able to see him coming. He walked through this room to another, to step through the french window there so that she could see him approaching.

And she did. She rose from whatever fruitless task she was performing, looked at him for a long moment, her head cocked to one side, and smiled and said, finally:

"*I* remember *you*." She said it as if some question of identity, long plaguing her, had finally been answered; as if some destiny had finally been fulfilled.

Or that was the way Melrose wanted to hear it. "We never really met."

"No, but you were at—the funeral." For a moment, her eyes looked away.

"That's right. Ten years ago. I'm amazed you can remember."

"That long." She shook her head. "Time plays such tricks. You'd never think this house had been lived in, would you? But it was rented for several years. Now it's up for sale." And then, quickly, she asked, "You're not—?"

He smiled at the anxiety in her tone. "No, I'm not a prospective buyer, Lady Kennington."

"Oh, don't call me that." She smiled that glittery smile. "I never did like all that 'Lady' business. And now my husband's dead, I don't feel . . . Just Jenny. But, if you haven't come to view the place, then, why—?"

"I've been looking for you," said Melrose.

That was the understatement of the century.

FORTY-FIVE

"Prescription number," said Jury.

He was in Exeter headquarters, it was after the dinner hour, and the third person in Macalvie's office, a Dr. Sloane, looked as if he'd rather be anywhere else, including down in an open grave silting earth—*anywhere* but sitting in an office with a couple of coppers.

Macalvie creaked back in his swivel chair. He smiled. "I knew it'd be worth it, going to New Mexico."

Jury fiddled with the photocopied page of the address book. "Give Wiggins the credit. It was his prescription."

"I called your friend Lady Cray and asked her to check the medicine cabinets. What she found were some of those nitroglycerin patches."

"Heart condition, I know."

Macalvie nodded. "Strong stuff. Nothing to fool around with. Ms. Hamilton was taking a hell of a risk, bad smoking habit combined with that kind of medication. After I talked to you, I rang Frances Hamilton's doctor. He'd written a prescription before she went to the States, precisely with the length of this trip in mind. He didn't want her to run out. When she came back here, she got the prescription refilled. In other words, she didn't need to see a doctor in the States."

"So the prescription—assuming that's what the number meant— wasn't for her, even though it was written in her address book."

Dr. Sloane, with an exaggerated look at his watch, said, "I need to go back to the lab, Superintendent."

Macalvie made some insincere gesture of apology, said, "Tell him what you told me."

Sloane sighed. "It's all in the—"

"Report. I know. It's just that you tell it so much better."

Dr. Sloane didn't change his expression, but Jury smiled. Dr. Sloane was clearly a Macalvite, one of those very few whom Macalvie admired. Dr. Sloane let his watch fall backward on his wrist and said: "A toxic dose of nicotine produces tachycardia, mental confusion, convulsions, amongst other symptoms, such as violent nausea. In the case of this victim—" Sloane gestured toward the wash of papers on Macalvie's desk, among them, photographs of the body of Angela Hope—"it would explain one puzzling thing: how she could have fallen into that enclosure at Old Sarum. The Wiltshire police were right; she couldn't have simply slipped. But in the state she'd have been in from nicotine poisoning, the last of her worries would have been slipping and falling. It's unfortunate no one *saw* her and that I didn't have presenting symptoms, but I can see her in my mind's eye, certainly. I can easily believe the mental confusion and convulsions could force her in, if not actually catapult her into that pit. She wouldn't have been grabbing at grass, she'd have been grabbing her own body—"

"You're certain, then, it *was* a toxic dose of nicotine?" As soon as he said it, Jury could have cut out his tongue.

The pause was a mere heartbeat, but it was trenchant with implications of "Stop wasting my time" and "Haven't you been listening?" Since Sloane had the same reactions to Macalvie, Jury didn't take it personally. Sloane pulled out a sheet of paper and handed it across to Jury, who looked at its spiky lines and percentages and drug names with a fair amount of incomprehension.

"Results of a gas chromatogram that give you what's found in extracted blood. The level of nicotine that shows up here isn't surprising, since the victim was a heavy smoker."

At that moment, like the assistant in a magician's act, Macalvie pulled out an opened carton of Marlboro cigarettes and slapped it on his desk.

Jury looked from Sloane to Macalvie, said, "Sorry, I don't get it. I'm a heavy smoker—*was* a heavy smoker—" he smiled serenely— "too, but I'm not going into convulsions. I hope."

"Let's hope not," said Sloane, in his reassuring way. "I was interrupted." Here a look at Macalvie possibly as toxic as a nicotine overdose. "If you could dispense with the pyrotechnics, Superintendent? At least until I'm out of here?"

Macalvie grinned. It was hard to put him down when he was getting going.

Sloane continued. "A lethal dose of nicotine for humans ranges from about thirty to sixty milligrams. One pack of cigarettes contains around 300 milligrams." With this, Dr. Sloane let a lingering glance fall on Macalvie's overflowing ashtray, raised his eyes from that to Macalvie, and gave the superintendent a withering smile. "Most is burned off or metabolized, of course. Nevertheless—"

"Cigars are worse," said Macalvie.

Oh, you fool, Sloane's deprecating smile said. He turned to Jury and went on. "Death can occur within a few minutes, in this case, myocardial infarction resulting from valvular heart disease, probably owing to the earlier rheumatic fever."

"Within minutes? But why did it happen at Old Sarum, then?"

Sloane answered, "*Can* occur within minutes. But it might be as much as four hours, a more likely time frame—" he shrugged—"one hour. It all depends on the dose and the victim."

Macalvie nodded. "When Plant talked to the North London boyo—Gabriel Merchant—he mentioned something that he hadn't talked about before, a detail that wouldn't have registered to him as important. When he saw her in that exhibit, she was 'picking at something.' Like a sticking plaster—"

"The nitroglycerin patch?" Jury frowned. "I thought we were talking about nicotine—"

Macalvie held up his hand. "The printed directions for this stuff tell you to *remove* it immediately if symptoms occur, for one thing. She looked pretty bad, according to what this Gabe told Plant, white, or maybe green—anyway, sick. She left the portrait exhibit in a hurry. Next she shows up, not long after, in the Pre-Raphaelite room. Still looking sick. Sick to death, you might say." Macalvie leaned halfway across his desk, the blue eyes and copper hair incendiary. "Jury. If you were going to stop smoking—"

"If?"

"—and you'd tried just about everything—"

Details clicked in Jury's mind with the precision of a combination for busting a safe: *"I've tried every bloody thing—pills . . . patches . . . therapy . . ."*

"—and nothing worked, wouldn't you try a doctor for nicotine—"

"Patches," said Jury.

Dr. Sloane crossed his arms before his chest as if the February sleet were falling in his office. "What was making the lady sick was nicotine. Administered transdermally."

"Nicotine patches need a prescription. At least in the United States, they do. You don't get them over the counter. Surely, no doctor would have prescribed a *nicotine* system for a woman who was already dosing herself with *nitroglycerin*—" Jury stopped.

"Now here we've got another woman who can't stop smoking, but who hated doctors—"

"Angela Hope, you mean."

Macalvie went on: "—and those patches can only be obtained through a doctor."

"Unless, of course—"

Macalvie nodded, smiling.

"—you happen to have a pharmacist in the family."

The three sat there, silent, looking at one another. Even Dr. Sloane seemed to be enjoying things now. He said, "A pharmacist could easily inject a toxic dose of nicotine through the paper covering with a very sharp needle. Administered through the skin, one of the most toxic poisons I can think of. And even if the victim *removes* the patch, it's imperative that all of the contaminant be flushed off because if it isn't, the skin continues the absorption process. Nothing to fool around with, gentlemen." Dr. Sloane rose. "I'll leave the less technical aspect of this to Commander Macalvie." A chilly smile, here.

"Gee, thanks. Words of one syllable I can handle. Just."

Dr. Sloane walked out of the room.

Finally, Jury said. "She was right."

"Who was right?"

"Mary Dark Hope."

"The kid sister. Let's hope she doesn't advertise it. At least not around Dolores Schell. And here I have to make one of my brilliant imaginative leaps: the nicotine patches passed through the hands of Nell and, I'm certainly assuming, Frances Hamilton. Speculation, but could we assume it was in the address book because Angela Hope asked one or both of them to pick up the prescription? Did they simply take a couple to 'try out'? More likely Angela gave them some." Then he picked up the carton of cigarettes, waggled it a few times.

"Found in Angela's room at the Red Lion. Dolores Schell was being helpful, gathered up Angela's stuff, thought maybe police had missed something. Oh, they had. Cigarettes. You look like you don't understand, Jury."

"I don't. What was a woman who was using nicotine patches doing with a carton of cigarettes?"

"That's the point, she wasn't. The cigarettes were a prop furnished by Dolly. Dolly stashed them in Angela's room in case nicotine turned up in a routine analysis. If there hadn't been any cigarettes and Angela was known to be a heavy smoker, Rush might have wondered. But Dolly worked it out: if she 'found' a carton of cigarettes, then nicotine in the system would hardly be surprising. Even if Angela hadn't pulled off the damned patch, police would still assume she'd been smoking while doctoring herself with these patches. That's a very dangerous thing to do and would satisfactorily explain cardiac arrest." Macalvie leaned back, stared at the ceiling. "What's Dolores Schell's motive?"

"She told me she disliked Angela. Although I'm sure she downplayed the extent of her hatred and jealousy. The reason she told me herself was that she thought I'd probably find out anyway, from someone else, and it wouldn't look good. Over the years Dolly had had to watch Angela Hope 'seduce' everyone away from her, including her own father."

Macalvie was looking at one of the reports Jury had sent. "Including also this Dr. Nils Anders?"

"Absolutely. When she saw Nils Anders spending so much time in company with the Hope sisters, it was too much. She'd known him long before Angela. I guess it was just too much. Nils Anders—" Jury broke off, leaned over, and pulled one of the phones toward him. "What happens when Dolly Schell finds out she's killed the wrong sister?"

"So what it looks like is one hell of a bent pharmacist, agreed?"

Jury dialed. "What it looks like is a kidjep."

Macalvie frowned. "A *what?*"

FORTY-SIX

Mary Dark Hope was going to find it even if it killed her.

That number: she knew she'd seen it somewhere. She couldn't recall it precisely, except for the first three digits, which she remembered because it was an Española number; nearly all of the numbers there began with 753. So that meant seven digits all told, and that was a help. The only thing she could think of, and where she might have seen it, was on one of the prescriptions she'd delivered. Or otherwise seen, perhaps out there on the counter where Dolly Schell would place them for customers who had yet to appear.

So that she wouldn't have to turn on any lights, she was using a pen flashlight, held between her teeth. That way she could keep her hands free to search the file cards. If it was such a dim memory, it must have been a prescription filled and delivered some time ago. She gave up on the cards and opened the big prescription book, the one in which she'd seen Dolly write the numbers in. Names, dates, addresses. Mary had her penlight poised over the "Controlled Substances" book. It was the last record left, after the file cards and the "Pres. Entry" book. She doubted she'd find anything there. As she ran her finger slowly down the list of numbers, she heard a muted sound from near the front of the pharmacy. Sunny. Where was Sunny? She looked around the tiny room, past the shelves. Gone again. She should train him—make him answer to commands, to sit and stay. Ha ha. She thought about Coyote. Coyote meant a lot of different things to different tribes. There was a warning: Never look Coyote straight in the eye. That was a pretty useless warning. How would you ever get close enough to a coyote to do it?

Sunny? Mary cocked her head, stopped her finger, listened hard. A slight whistling, sucking sound near the front again. She went back to the record, moving her finger down the neat line of entries. Dolly's handwriting was meticulous, very neat and small. But, then, Dolly was a meticulous person. Everything in the pharmacy was carefully placed, from the rows of shampoos, conditioners, and hair mousses, down to the kachina display, its tall tier inviting catastrophe. People were always just missing running into it, or jostling it and bringing it down. It was odd that Dolly had set it up. Or was that the reason? Was it a subtle way of controlling people?

Actually, the "Controlled Substances" record was rather interesting. Here was arsenic handed out to Mrs. Rudolph Seese. Mary knew her. Somebody had better keep an eye out for Mr. Seese, though. Percaset and Percodan seemed to have been prescribed in large quantities, along with Valium, for an awful lot of people. And Prozac must be propping up half the city. Were all of these drugs the reason that the citizens of Santa Fe were always in such high spirits? She went on, her eye travelling down the page, the bright point of light from the flashlight illuminating it.

Finally, she finished the last record and shook her head. The number wasn't here. Nothing had even the first two digits—75—as part of the prescription number. There were some 78s, 79s, and 71s. No 75s, though. Mary closed the book and stared at it, disappointed. Then she was wrong and it must not be a prescription. Did Dolly make up prescriptions for people in Española? Once in a while, yes . . .

She jumped when the telephone shrilled. In the dark it seemed all that much louder. Someone was very insistent, for it rang and went on ringing. At least, it had brought Sunny out of hiding, or returned him to visibility. Probably, Sunny had taken the tiny explosion of sound to mean Mary was in danger. She reached down her stool to rub him behind the ears. Some coyote.

The number. Mary squinched her eyes shut to reason this out. For she was still sure it had to do with a prescription. Yet, it wasn't here. So she had to go back to thinking it couldn't be a prescription number. Or else . . . Dolly hadn't *wanted* to write it into the record book.

Mary sat in the pharmacist's cubicle and looked out over the counter into a darkness in which ghostly shapes of shelving were just visible. She knew all of those shelves; she'd certainly had to mess with them often enough. Dolly Schell was obsessed with neatness: that worn-out adage of "everything in its place" was something Dolly carried to ludicrous extremes. How many times had Mary been told to review the shelves and rearrange shampoos and hair-color kits, face creams and makeup products? "You know what people do; they just pick something up, carry it somewhere else, put it down." So Mary had to walk up and down the aisles or pluck articles from glass-topped counters and transport them back to their hair-product or makeup families. Clairol. Neutrogena. White Rain. Mary could recite this litany as if she were a worshiper telling her beads. She could find them in the dark, she'd become so familiar with the products.

It might be silly and sentimental, but Mary thought of them as "families." The Revlon family of products; the Clairol family; the Prell family—very small was the Prell family. When she returned something like the economy-sized bottle of Almay shampoo to the other bottles around it, she could imagine the family applauding: Glad to see you back.

Okay, it was really silly and sentimental, but at least it was some sort of pleasant game that took the annoyance out of the chore of neatening up these shelves. And took a little of the sting out of Dolly Schell's shrill voice. Cousin Dolly Schell, Mary now reminded herself with a shudder.

The family Hope. The family Hope was down to one, herself. She refused to include Dolly in this diminished circle.

Right now, had it not been for her determination to find this prescription, Mary thought she'd fly to pieces. Perhaps she would. She put her head down on her crossed arms and then suddenly sat up. Sunny had disappeared again.

And now the noise she heard was definitely the door sucking open or shut, and she bet on open. Sunny wouldn't shove himself out the door, that was for certain. She squinted her eyes, looked toward the front (for it was from up there that she'd heard the sound), looked into heaped shadows. The room was abysmally dark. And even though she couldn't make out the face, Mary would recognize the taut figure of her cousin anywhere.

Mary was scared. She could not stay in this cubicle, behind this sliding glass like a fish in a fishbowl. Bending down a little, she made her silent way over to and out of the low-beamed door, and now was behind the counter where the cash register sat and in front of which were shelves of aspirin, bromides, headache powders, cold pills and capsules. Back here she'd be an easy target too.

When she heard the first explosion, followed by a tracery of light, it was clear to her that Dolly hadn't just stopped to check on things. The bullet had torn the air just over her head and shattered the plate glass of the cubicle behind her. First she was frozen in her crouch, but then she moved under the hinged door of the countertop and to one of the shelves and wedged herself carefully in between the end of the shelf and the kachina display. She was around the corner from the hair-care products. It wasn't much of a hiding place; of course, she could be seen with the lights on, but it gave her a little more security than being out in the open. And if there was anything to Rosella's philosophy, she was protected by all of the gods represented in the kachina dolls. Mary didn't want to bet on them, though.

Suddenly, there was a thunderous crash and glass breaking. The gun fired again towards the rear counter. What had caused the crash? Didn't Dolly know her own pharmacy well enough to avoid bumping into the displays?

Another crash, another display over. Or this one might have been the rack of paperbacks, for there was the metallic *thump*, but no sound of breakage. And another shot aimed towards the front of the store.

Sunny! That had to be Sunny, deliberately upsetting whatever he could get near, drawing the bullets to the front of the store. Was Dolly Schell firing a revolver, or an automatic?

How many shots did she get with it? How many shots in a barrel or a clip? Six in a barrel, Mary thought. But an automatic? God. Now she wished she'd paid more attention to that dumb Nancy Drew.

Quickly, she spun around, took one step, and grabbed one of the Neutrogena family's plastic economy-sized bottles of liquid soap, then as quickly spun back. Three shots, she had heard. But Dolly could easily have brought another clip with her, though that was doubtful; surely, she would have thought one shot would do, maybe two.

One was enough, thought Mary, unscrewing the cap of the plastic bottle. And Dolly was crazy, but she wasn't stupid. She must have figured out by this time that she was shooting blind and that the noises were only distract—

No, she hadn't. In the two or three seconds allowed by the fourth shot, Mary wheeled back to the aisle and emptied the bottle on the floor for two or three feet, in a quick, zigzag pattern. At the same time, she grabbed another canister from the second shelf up—hair products—and wheeled back to her original position behind the kachina display.

Sunny. Sunny. Mary Dark Hope held the canister ready and prayed. This was going to have to be—what was the word?—orchestrated. She felt her hearing to be supercharged, ears that in this heightened state of nerves would be able, literally, to hear a pin drop. She heard the muffled sounds of someone approaching. Up the aisle.

Sunny. Mary felt as taut as a bowstring. The temptation was strong just to stand here behind these teetering dolls and hope she wouldn't be seen, and they wouldn't fall. That was stupid; of course, she'd be seen. Now there was the heaviest silence she could imagine. Like being in a cavern. But she could *feel* the person coming closer.

Then a long cry and the shelves swaying with the weight of someone trying to use them for support. Swayed too much to one side and finally fell with a thunderous crash, but fell away from Dolly, not on her. Mary darted out once again, took aim and pushed the nozzle of the canister of hair mousse, and shot it right into Dolly's face, the huge whipped egg of it messing up her eyes enough to keep her from taking aim. At the same time, Sunny lunged, knocked the half-kneeling figure of Dolly back down on the soapy tile, kept her down with his paws on her chest. His tail straight out, ears up, Sunny snapped his teeth; his gaping mouth was a hairsbreadth from her face. It was one of the scariest sights and sounds Mary had ever witnessed coming from either dog or coyote. Dolly still had the gun in her thrown-back hand, but to raise it and fire would have taken one second longer than it would have taken Sunny's teeth to rip her neck open.

Through the windows beginning to lighten, Mary could see it all. She looked all around the room. Gray light filtered through the plate glass windows, and a band of dull gold stretched beyond them over the low roofs of the houses and lit the yellow leaves of the cottonwoods. Now she could see clearly, bathed in pale light, the wreckage, the killer, the Coyote.

"Land of Enchantment," said Mary Dark Hope.

FORTY-SEVEN

"I don't think she put much faith in the rescue mission," Nils Anders was saying.

Jury had just finished talking to the Santa Fe police. Jack Oñate had told him what had happened.

"I don't think she puts much faith in anything," said Jury, the telephone cradled between his shoulder and jaw. His hands were busy trying to wrench free a bit of silk material caught in Carole-anne's zipper. Wasn't she old enough to dress herself?

Carole-anne looked over her shoulder, down at Jury who was sitting in his easy chair. " 'She' who?"

"Hold still," said Jury.

From his end of the line, in Santa Fe, Nils Anders said, "What?"

"Not you." Jury laughed. "I'm helping a neighbor dress. Why do women wear dresses with zippers down the damned back?"

Carole-anne said, "To give butterfingers like you a way to be useful."

Nice back, though, Jury had to admit. No sign of a bra strap. He guessed what was holding Carole-anne up was pure faith in her own ascendancy.

Nils Anders continued his account of what had happened that morning. "They took Dolly Schell into custody, pretty much ranting and raving."

"Did she rant about Angela Hope?"

"Oh, yes, but not by way of confessing to anything. Not that it makes any difference; trying to kill Mary—" he cleared his throat— "that's enough to hang her."

"You still lynch people out there in the West?"

"You know what I mean."

Finally, the zipper came unstuck and he pulled it up Carole-anne's back. He was almost sorry to see the back move away from him over to the sofa where she was now rooting through a sponge bag.

Nils continued to talk. Jury leaned back to listen. He knew everything Nils was telling him, but he also knew Nils needed to tell it. He watched Carole-anne dabbing bright polish on her nails, her forehead puckered in concentration.

"I can't remember ever encouraging her to think that . . ." Nils Anders paused, searching for some self-effacing way of putting the fact Dolly Schell had been obsessively in love with him. ". . . to believe I thought of her—I never encouraged her to think I felt anything other than friendship." He paused again. "I can't believe I was the cause of this."

"You weren't." Jury hoped his tone wasn't too harsh. "Her plan was too elaborate to attribute it to frustrated love, Nils. You weren't the cause; you were the catalyst. Jealousy of Angela Hope had been building up over half of Dolly Schell's life."

Another silence as Nils thought this over.

"But Mary's okay, isn't she?"

Nils laughed. "More okay than I, that's for sure. When I walked in there and saw the mess—Sunny had blood on his paws—I was terrified. I'm still terrified. I should stick to my axioms and theories, shouldn't I?"

"No. You're the one person Mary Dark Hope respects. The only one, as far as I know. You're obligated to her for that." Jury didn't know why he'd said this. The notion of "obligation" had come out of nowhere. It was something like the sense of responsibility the savior feels for the person he's saved.

There was a long silence and Jury waited. Nils Anders probably treated a phone call much as he would an in-the-flesh visit: something to be punctuated by silences. Jury could visualize him in his swivel chair staring out at the rope of lights framing the window across Canyon Road. Then he watched Carole-anne raise her hands, fingers splayed, to scrutinize her painted nails.

"Not the only one she respects," Nils finally answered. "There's you. Mary said she wished you hadn't left. Mary never expresses feelings like that."

"Tell her I'll call her."

"I will, but you better do it."

Jury smiled at Anders's tone. It was rigorous, instructive. "I will."

As they wound up the conversation, Jury saw that Carole-anne had flopped on the couch, apparently having appeased the gods of beauty. Dress zipped and nails polished, she was now released from beauty's demands, as if beauty were a chore, like washing up, that she was done with for a time and could return to being just Carole-anne, high heels flicked off, stretched out, a magazine held above her face.

He got up, stretched, walked to the window, and watched the rain streak the glass. Despite the depressing little lecture Dr. Sloane gave Macalvie, he was still dying for a cigarette. Where in hell was Plant? Should he try Ruthven again? Lasko? He'd rung each of them a half-dozen times already. He turned and started pacing. God, but a cigarette would help. Then he thought of Des, surrounded by them, yet, she hadn't fallen prey to them. And did anyone appreciate he'd given the damned things up? No. He stopped and said, "Notice anything different about me?" His tone was full of challenge.

Carole-anne tilted her head back to look at him upside down, her red-gold hair cascading to the carpet. "About you? No." That closed the matter and she lifted her head back to the cushioned arm of the sofa and kept on with her magazine. Jury was not permitted to change.

It made him smile a bit, but then he grew irritated again. He was not to be congratulated nor sympathized with. What's more, Carole-anne was one of those smokers who could actually take it or leave it. How dare she be able to smoke one day and then not for days, not for weeks even? "So where are *you* going?"

"The Nine-One-Nine. Me and Stone's going."

The Nine-One-Nine was Stan Keeler's gig. It was always jammed; it was the only club, the only place, where a person could see Stan Keeler. Jury glared at Carole-anne—not that she noticed. He wasn't sure he approved of this whole business. Approved? Who was he to approve or disapprove of Carole-anne's male friends? He was about to say something when there was a knock on the door. More of a thump, really.

Her eyes still glued to the fashion mag, Carole-anne said, "That's Stone."

Jury looked from the door to the recumbent Carole-anne, who was making no quick moves to get up.

Flicking back a page of the magazine, she said, "Well, you going to let him in?"

"*I'm* to let him in? Is this how I end up? Doorman to a dog?"

She said only, "He's early."

Jury rolled his eyes and yanked open his door. Stone sat there. "You're early," said Jury. Stone was not above giving Jury a few friendly tail swishes. "Come in anyway."

Stone entered, stopped, sniffed at some odor that eluded Jury, and then sat down and gazed at Carole-anne.

"We don't leave till nine. It's only quarter to."

Stone lay down, crossed his paws, rested his muzzle on them.

Jury sighed, shook his head, and pulled over the phone.

Carole-anne's interest was piqued enough to draw her eyes from the magazine and around to look at Jury. "You making another call?" She frowned.

With an elaborate show of looking round the flat, he said, "Yes, I do believe these are my digs. Right. I'm sure of it. And this is my very own phone." He patted it fondly.

"Ha ha," said Carole-anne, returning to her magazine. "Can't a person even ask? Aren't we the grumpy one, though." Then she checked her minuscule wristwatch, slid her legs around, rooted for her shoes with her toes. "Back in a tick. Forgot my perfume. Stay, Stone, and cheer up the grump."

Jury grunted and as she left, Stone moved over to Jury's chair and lay down. Cheering up the grump, he supposed as he dialed the Stratford number. One more call to Lasko couldn't hurt. Lasko practically lived at the station.

It seemed to hurt Lasko, though, who heaved a great sigh when he heard Jury's voice. "Nothing, Richard. I've heard not one thing."

Jury sat forward, reached down, and scrubbed around Stone's ears. "Look, Sammy, it doesn't make sense. Why would he send me that damned fax and then disappear?"

Stone made a few woofy noises and stretched out beneath Jury's hand.

"He was in Stratford two days ago."

"Then he went to Exeter," said Lasko.

"So he was in Exeter two days ago and sent the fax—"

"You're still right. You were right before."

"—and then he left Exeter and then went—*where*? Not back to Northants. Bear with me—"

"I'm bearing. I've borne."

"We're missing something—"

"Dinner, that's what I'm missing, I don't know about you. It's bloody nine o'clock, Richard, and I'm starved."

"You and Plant were at Lady Kennington's."

Sammy Lasko sighed. "Uh-huh."

"Look, he must have seen something."

"Well, if he did he didn't share the sight with yours truly."

"What was he doing?"

"Doing?"

"He must have been doing something while you were conducting your illegal search of the premises."

"Very funny. Mr. Plant was sitting. Reading the paper or doing the crossword."

"No."

"No? All right, if you say so. You weren't there, of course—"

"What paper?"

"Hell, I don't know what paper. He asked me if it was a Stratford paper."

Jury sat forward, interested. "Why would he ask that?"

"How do I know. He's your friend, not mine."

"It's a funny question."

"Hysterical."

"Was it?"

Lasko must have turned from the phone. Jury heard paper rattling. "Was what what?"

Jury sighed. "Pay attention. A local paper?"

"How in hell should I—no, it wasn't—oh, and later he asked me where he could buy a paper."

"Maybe he saw something. In the paper."

"I'm sitting here eating some of Clarrisa's leftover crisps. I'm starving, I told you. If I hear anything, I'll ring immediately."

Jury was left with a dial tone. He hung up. Well, he could hardly blame Sam Lasko.

Depressed, he reached down and gave Stone another rub. His mind's eye travelled the length and breadth of Jenny's house. Plant must have seen something.

He heard Carole-anne's spiky heels thrumming down the stairs; in another moment she reappeared, scented up. Or down.

"Time to go, Stone. Ta, Super."

The dog was fully alert and up and shaking off whatever lethargy he'd fallen victim to at Jury's hands.

"Have a good time. You and Stone."

He was a handsome dog. Incredibly agile and clever. He wondered why Stan Keeler had named him that. Drugs probably. Stone.

Jury jerked up in his chair.

Stonington.

Good Lord, *Stonington*.

FORTY-EIGHT

Out of simple politeness—or perhaps it was payment for information—Jury had attempted one of those desultory, ragged exchanges with the publican of the Bold Blue Boy, but had quickly become frustrated by Mr. Ribblesby's inclination to turn even the simplest conversational gambit into argument. Even Jury's comment about the weather—it had begun snowing in the night—had been taken under advisement by Mr. Ribblesby.

"Oh, I don't think it's getting worse; no, I think it's slowing. Yes, definitely slowing."

Jury had merely commented on the increase in the snowfall and the size of the flakes. They fell straight down and looked quite fat to Jury.

But Mr. Ribblesby shook his head as he squinted towards the pub's leaded glass windows (through which it was difficult to see anything undistorted by the wavery old panes), and slowly turned the tea towel in a pint glass as he shook his head. Solemnly.

But Jury, having secured his information about Jenny Kennington, was slow to irritation. Indeed, he had secured his half-pint of bitter not because he wanted it (for it would only increase his desire for a cigarette) but by way of payment for the information. Indeed he had offered to buy Mr. Ribblesby a drink, too, but Mr. Ribblesby "never touched the stuff, no," and had given Jury's glass of bitter a sad little shake of the head. Drink at this early hour?

Jury sat quietly, however, with what Mr. Ribblesby appeared to see as his raving alcoholism, content in the knowledge that at last he'd found Jenny. Now he felt quite sanguine. Or would do, if only he could call up in the publican a drop of consanguinity. Empathetic silence. But Mr. Ribblesby kept turning his tea towel in the glass and challenging Jury's innocuous comment about the snow. He countered by saying it was the kind of snow that didn't pack. It wouldn't stick. No, what there was would be melted by mid-afternoon, Jury could take his word for it. And Mr. Ribblesby continued to talk about snowfalls as Jury waited patiently for him to take a breather so that he could put his next question.

Finally, during a flake-by-flake account of the Great Snowfall of 1949, Jury broke in and put it anyway: "Lady Kennington, did she mention where she was going? Did she happen to mention Stonington?"

Perhaps he shouldn't have asked this as two questions. Mr. Ribblesby had difficulty enough handling one. It now took him several moments of deliberation to answer. "No."

It never failed that people who would hold you hostage for hours bending your ear about something you *didn't* want to know shut up like clams when it came to what you *did*.

Jury shrugged into his topcoat. "Well, I'll be off, Mr. Ribblesby." He tossed a few pound coins on the bar and turned to leave.

"She left with the gentleman."

Jury turned—whirled—back. "What?"

"Gentleman that booked a room—let's see . . ." Cautiously, he drew the guest register to him. But didn't open it. Mr. Ribblesby would prefer debating empty air than landing upon proof. "Now this was according to the wife, understand. I mean it's her what booked him in." He frowned, his tone doubtful, and the wife's room transaction suspect. "She's the one saw him." He opened the book and ran his finger down a page, turned the page and did the same. And then another. And another.

Why he didn't begin with the last several entries, Jury didn't know. The Bold Blue Boy could hardly have catered for the number of guests suggested by these slowly turning pages. Well, Jury wasn't going to wait for Ribblesby to learn the braille system. "Was this gentleman tall and aristocratic-looking? Blond hair, extremely green eyes? About my height?"

Mr. Ribblesby put his fingers to his lips and with an air of concentration looked Jury over closely as if measures of tallness were highly debatable. And then, instead of a mere "Yes" that would have settled the matter, Mr. Ribblesby had to embroider on the description. "But 'quite a handsome gentleman,' was Mrs. Ribblesby's words."

But. Bad enough to hear Plant thus described; worse that Mr. Ribblesby appeared to be using Jury as a yardstick in the looks department. Jury wanted to hit him. Actually, he would probably come back and kill him. If he didn't kill Melrose Plant first. His fingers, with minds of their own, groped in his coat pocket for a missing packet of Players. Hell. He settled for asking if this chap's name was Plant, and when he had arrived.

The fingers went to the mouth again, tips tapping on the upper lip again. "Now that would be on . . . let's see . . . night before last, I'd say. Or was that her came then? No. No, she's been here—" he was counting on his fingers—"at least four nights. They're our only guests."

How cozy. "And they left, this morning, together, you said? Do you mean they checked out?"

"Oh, no. Just went for a little spin in that Bentley of his. Or was it a Rolls? But it don't signify, really. Both the same, almost. I do believe it was one of them Silver Shadows."

"Ghost. Silver Ghost." Jury smiled (a little stiffly) and walked out the heavily beamed door onto the pavement, where the snow, as per Ribblesby's prediction, was stopping. He stood on the pavement and stared at nothing. Why didn't he simply get in his car and drive to Stonington? That must be where she was. They were, he corrected himself.

Then Littlebourne Green came into soft focus, and after a moment or two of blinking, he realized he was looking across the green at Polly Praed's small white cottage with the yellow shutters. Melrose Plant wouldn't come to Littlebourne without seeing Polly; perhaps he was not at Stonington, but there—

"Inspector! Ho, there!"

Jury knew that voice. He shut his eyes against a God who had no mercy and opened them to see the fast-approaching figure of the Honorable Miles Bodenheim. Sir Miles.

"Knew that was you!" hollered Sir Miles, he being as close to an aristocrat as Littlebourne had. He thumped Jury on the shoulder and grabbed his hand to pump, and declared, "This all but makes up for the torture of a wasted morning with the Pennystevens person."

Mrs. Pennystevens was the elderly postmistress whose life by now surely should have been snuffed by the obstreperous demands of Miles Bodenheim. Didn't any of these people ever die? Miles Bodenheim must have been in his seventies when Jury had first encountered him, and Mrs. Pennystevens—well, God knows how old she was. Perhaps it was the perverse presence of Miles, with his constant bickering and arguing and generally making her life hell over a tuppenny stamp, that held her to earth and life as if by magnetic force.

"Ten years," said Jury, to himself more than Miles. He had first seen Jenny Kennington ten years ago. How could that be? All of those years—

"Ah, yes, another decade gone. Getting on, aren't you, Inspector, yes, I can see that, bit of the old tattle-tale gray encroaching on the sides." He laughed, absolutely giddy at this opportunity to take someone down a peg.

Defensively, Jury covered the side of his head with his hand. Not only was he uglier than Plant, he was grayer. He didn't remember seeing any gray hair. "But you, you haven't changed at all, Sir Miles." Jury wasn't being diplomatic. Miles Bodenheim had looked embalmed ten years ago, and he looked embalmed now. Tight-skinned, rosy-cheeked. Gray hair plastered to his scalp and a mustache so well trimmed and oiled it looked fake.

"Never guess who I saw! Right here, where you're standing now."

Jury didn't bother saying yes, he could perfectly well guess.

"That crazy friend of yours, that Plant chap! Right here he stood." Miles Bodenheim tapped his walking stick thrice on the ground as if to invoke whatever spirit world Melrose Plant had sprung from. "Never could understand why you two were so matey. Bit of a chump, I always thought him."

Bit of an earl, you mean. Bit of a marquess, bit of a viscount. That's why you couldn't stand him. "He's been knighted," said Jury, staring right into Miles's oyster-colored eyes to watch him react to yet another honor heaped upon Plant's golden head.

"*Knight*—"

Why was he telling this lie? It was one thing to want to slug Melrose Plant for keeping Jenny's whereabouts from him, but it was altogether another to listen to the biggest bore in Littlebourne criticize him. "Distinguished service to Her Majesty—" Let's see: what did Her Majesty go around knighting people for? Most anything, really.

As Miles, looking decidedly less cheery than before, tried to think of a rejoinder to this (no doubt spurious) knighthood, Jury's eye was attracted by a figure crossing Littlebourne Green. Here came

Polly Praed like a gathering of leaves, dressed in her usual unflattering autumnal colors of pumpkin brown and dark green and russet.

Her expression was set and her eye was clamped on Miles Bodenheim (whom Jury knew she loathed). But then she saw who Sir Miles was standing there talking to. She stopped dead halfway across the road, opened her mouth, shut it, proceeded on her way and up to the pavement.

Jury couldn't help but smile at her discomfort upon seeing him. "I'm awfully glad to see you, Polly."

Miles Bodenheim, making hearty noises in his bid for attention, might as well have been a tree for all Polly noticed him. She said to Jury, "Melrose was here. He still might be. He came looking for Lady Kennington—"

"Kennington!" Sir Miles blustered, astonished that something had happened of which he had no knowledge.

"You remember her, don't you?" she said to Jury. "But . . . obviously! He said it was *you* that was trying to find her." Now her tone took on a mildly hectoring quality. "I can't understand why everyone comes to *me* to find out things—"

"Nor can I," said Miles. "You keep yourself bunged up in that tiny place of yours day in, day out. As for Lady Kennington—!"

Polly still had her eyes on Jury, and they had turned a much darker shade of violet. A stormy color that made Jury think of a thunderous sky over the last violet light across the mountains. Knowing Polly, it was thunder all right. "She's at Stonington," Polly snapped.

"Stonington! What on earth is the woman doing at *Stonington?* Good Lord, she's not thinking of letting—well, she can't be thinking of buying. Poor as a churchmouse now Lord Kennington's gone. Sylvia always says, 'Proud persons are soonest brought down.' Certainly true in her case. What can you expect, the woman's got no talent, no profession—" Miles thrashed a hedge with his walking stick.

"You could ask Freddie Mainwaring, he's still estate agent for it. She must've been to see him. Do you want to go to the Magic Muffin? I was just on my way—"

Jury opened his mouth to refuse, gently, but Miles Bodenheim answered for him. "Ho ho! Miss Pettigrew's probably got nothing but aubergine today, awful things. But I have a few minutes to spare, might as well spare them there as anywhere!"

"I'm in a bit of a hurry, Polly."

Disappointment seemed to weigh her down. But she perked up a little as she asked, "What'd she do? Melrose said police wanted her for something."

"What?" Miles walked back the few steps he had walked off (assuming everyone was following him to the Magic Muffin), eyes round. "The Kennington woman? Police after her? I'm not surprised, nor will Sylvia be. Now, Superintendent, how do you account for that?" He was pleased as punch.

"I don't." Jury gave Polly a salute and walked off towards his car.

2

NO BENTLEY, no Silver Ghost stood without or within the high, gray walls of Stonington.

Indeed, no sign of life whatever, no cat, mole, mouse. Nothing.

Jury walked up the wide steps and lifted a heavy door knocker in the shape of a fish, copper once, greenish-gray now, oxidized by the weather. The pressure caused the door, unlocked, to open a fraction, and he placed his hand against it, shoved it farther. He was being careful, he thought, as if he might walk in on something.

But the door ushered him into greater silence, a wider emptiness, almost, than he'd met in the drive and the grounds. He stopped in the entrance hall, bigger than most rooms, black-and-white checkered marble underfoot, green marble commodes against both walls, white marble sculpture of a woman by the curving staircase. It was an abominable reproduction of what had been an abominable original, graceless and unlovely, of a figure with arm extended that Jenny (who hated it) had used to drape her coat over. Her hat she had removed from her head to the head of the statue. At least I get some use of it, she'd said. There was no coat there now, nor hat, either.

But there were voices, faint in some distance Jury couldn't get the direction of. He walked into the first room off the marble hall, a small study with a french door, open an inch or two, and it was through this opening the voices came. He could not see their owners. He walked into the next room. The rooms all around the house were interlocking, joined each to each by a doorway, and one could move from one to another, always with the courtyard in view. The architect must have planned this, a home resembling a convent.

This room was enormous, a dining room, he thought. He remembered all those years ago standing in it with Jenny (and it had been just as empty of furnishing then as now, for she was moving away). She and Melrose Plant were outside now in the courtyard, talking. Or looking at the house; she was pointing to the first floor, to something up there. He laughed.

Had Jury seen them from the study, where he could have walked through the french windows to the courtyard, probably he would have done so. But there was no such door here in the dining room, so he proceeded to the room beyond, a drawing room. Here he stopped and watched them again, from this slightly different vantage point. And then he went on, into the long gallery. This ran the entire length of the east side of the house, and was empty of portraits. He could see rectangles of the deep red wall covering faded around where they had hung. Along the length of the gallery were three french doors, and he could have exited through any of them.

But he didn't. He stood there watching Melrose and Jenny, still talking, still absorbed. Neither noticed him, or any reflection of him.

Jury continued walking thus, through one room after another, not knowing what the various rooms were, for none had furnishings to identify them, except for the big library, with its floor-to-ceiling shelves, its huge fireplace. Finally, he had circuited the entire house and was in the last room, a little place off the marble entrance hall. He stopped here and saw now Jenny's back, Melrose Plant's face. The face looked happy. Jury had no idea why he had done this, why he had engaged in this voyeuristic performance, and felt a little ashamed. And then not ashamed, because he was, after all, in full view of his audience of two. Or was he himself the audience, an audience of one?

He stepped through the glass door here, out onto the walk that ran around the courtyard.

Oddly, it was Jenny who sensed his presence, even though her back was to him, and they must have been thirty or forty feet away. Plant didn't even see him. She turned.

"Richard!"

For a moment he was cheered; she all but sang out his name; she all but clapped with a sort of childlike delight. He did not know he'd been so irrationally annoyed until he ceased to be. Then Plant called out, too, and waved.

Jury walked up to them, and he could not help the rising anger. At both of them. He glared at Plant. " 'She is found,' is she?"

Jenny looked from one to the other, uncomprehending.

And Plant looked sheepish. Unfortunately, Plant looking sheepish, with that tilted smile on his face, was also Plant looking charming. "Sorry about that," he said, with an appealing shrug.

Nothing else. He didn't ask about the case, about the trip, about Macalvie, about Wiggins. About sod all. Jury said, icily, "Sam Lasko—of the Stratford-upon-Avon police department, if you recall—"

Her hands flew to her face. "Oh, God. We should have rung him immediately." She was looking at Melrose.

We should have, should we?

Melrose said, "I did. This morning. I told him you were here. I thought I told you I told him . . ."

And then Jury studied the sky as they had a tiny little argument about who told who what. He thought of the night before, his conversation—if you could call it that—with Sammy Lasko. And his worry. "Well, no need to worry." He tried on a little heartiness, but it rang so false, he returned to grumpiness. "You shouldn't have left, Jenny." She looked at him, seriously troubled. It was impossible to tell the source of the trouble, though. Then, trying to regain a bit of distance, he said, "I'll be off, then. My desk is piled high, what with being gone for five days."

"But you must stay, Richard," she said.

Melrose agreed, and with unmistakable sincerity. "We're just going off to have some lunch. There's a place between here and Horndean—"

Jury shook his head, managed a smile. "Back to London. A policeman's life, as my guvnor likes to say, is full of grief."

His guvnor, for once, was right.

3

RAGGED, torn, tattered, and bearing little resemblance to its original self, the stuffed coyote was once again being hauled into Racer's office by the cat Cyril.

The abuse was not, however, being meted out by Cyril (who, according to Fiona, loved the coyote), but by Chief Superintendent Racer. Again, according to Fiona.

"Said he was going to rip it to shreds and tear its heart out—the coyote's, pre-*sum*-ably—if he found it in his office again. Tried throwing it away, but unless you throw it out the window, I told him, you know Cyril'll just get it out of the wastebasket." Fiona whisked an emery board across her nails.

Jury listened to it rasping, wondered if he was going to spend half of his life watching women refurbish themselves. Between Fiona and Carole-anne, it seemed likely.

Fiona held up her filed fingernails and went on. "It's that little Velcro tab on the back: can't think what it's for, can you? Anyway, he—" she gave an unenthusiastic nod in the direction of Racer's office— "come back from his club yesterday all in an uproar. Said he'd been the laughingstock when his friends asked him why he was wearing a coyote on the back of his coat." She blew on her nails. "Can you imagine? So I says to him, Well, whyn't you toss it in the dustbin along the pavement, or something? 'Oh, no. *Oh, no,*' he says, with ever such a mean smile. So you just know he's got something evil in mind." Fiona sighed.

Jury watched Cyril through the open door. He'd jumped up on Racer's desk, coyote still firmly in mouth, and seemed debating a problem. He set the coyote on the fax machine and looked from one to the other. "Maybe Racer's got something evil in mind, but Cyril's got something eviler." Jury smiled at her and left.

"I'M TAKING IT easy first day back, of course," said Wiggins, stirring a powdered something into his glass of beef tea. "Not wanting to relapse." He smiled weakly.

Jury was sitting before his decidedly un-stacked-up desk with his feet on an open file drawer. "True. You don't want to activate some dormant electrical charge."

Wiggins finished stirring, tapped the spoon gently against his cup, and sat back, sipping with a satisfied sigh. "I'll say this, sir. The way you and Mr. Macalvie worked all that out was quite brilliant. Quite."

"No brilliance at my end," said Jury. Gloomily, he sat.

Wiggins frowned. "Shouldn't wear your overcoat inside. Just inviting a chill, you are, when you go out."

"Which is now." Jury rose slowly. Ever since he'd driven back from Littlebourne, he'd felt slow, lumbrous.

"You just got here not a half-hour ago. Where're you going now, sir?"

"Nowhere."

FORTY-NINE

"Nowhere" turned out to be Salisbury and Old Sarum.

His car did not drive him (for that's how Jury felt, as if he'd punched in cruise control) to Northamptonshire or Stratford-upon-Avon (she wouldn't be there anyway, would she?), or any other vaguely formulated destination, such as police HQ in Exeter, where he might be expected to go.

So it was night when Jury finally pulled into the empty car park at Old Sarum, and for a few moments sat there wondering how he could have driven for a couple of boring motorway hours to a place that, number one, was closed; number two, he couldn't see anyway, as it was eight o'clock and dark. A total and depressing winter dark.

As he got out of the car and slammed the door he saw that there was, after all, one other car down there at the end. Probably a couple of kids, touching each other up, which made him think of Bea and Gabe, and that made him think of his own lost youth, a loss occurring, he estimated, about one hundred years ago. He crossed the wooden bridge.

Jury stood on the ridge of the hill looking down into formless black depths—the Bishop's Palace if his memory served him right. He did not know how long he had stood there, looking blindly around, when he heard something off to his left.

A voice. He squinted. A tiny light. A voice smoking a cigarette, some dark amorphous form trudging toward him, the devil, no doubt, risen out of the ancient stone. Oh, for God's sake, he told himself, disgusted with his self-dramatization. The voice (which actually belonged to an ordinary human being) and the red coal end of the cigarette drew closer.

"You police?"

"No." The denial came quite spontaneously to Jury's lips. He wondered why. "You security?"

They could see each other clearly enough now. They were both smiling. Sheepishly, perhaps. A lark hanging about when the place was closed to visitors.

"Thing is," said the other man, "they just took away their Crime Scene—Do Not Cross tape. The coppers, I mean." His breath came frosty cold as he dropped the cigarette to the ground.

Jury watched the cataract of silver sparks before it was ground out underheel. "Something happened, did it?"

"Dead lady. American. I was the one found her, to tell the truth." He tried to keep the satisfaction out of his voice, but couldn't. "Down there." Here he pointed off toward the stone ruin of the Bishop's Palace. "See, I work for the Trust couple of days a week. So I was here. Only one here, as a matter of fact. Down there she was, in one of the latrines. Garderobes, they used to call 'em. Fancy name for privy. Let's sit down a bit. Over there's a bench."

They walked a few feet, sat down. Trevor Hastings introduced himself; so did Richard Jury. Glad to make each other's acquaintance.

And then in the way of sealing a pact, rather like some antiquated ritual of secret handshakes or pricking thumbs and drawing blood, Trev offered Jury his pack of cigarettes.

Jury looked at the glimmering white pack—what were they, Marlboros? Silk Cuts? As if it made a difference. It could have been a pack of corn husks, and he'd still feel like reaching for them. "I stopped, Trevor. Thanks just the same."

"Stopped? Good lad. I been trying to do that for years."

Jury smiled. "I've only been stopped for a week, so don't give me too much credit."

"I ration 'em." He lit up.

"To what? One every three minutes?"

Trev laughed and that made him cough. "Sound like the wife, you do. I get out of the house just to have a quiet smoke, sometimes, not have 'er nattering on. You married?"

"No."

Trev grunted. "How'd you stop, then?"

"Well, I more or less made a pact with a friend. Girl I know who works a cigarette and magazine kiosk at Heathrow."

Trev grunted. "Helluva job if you're trying to stop."

"Yes. I expect if Desdemona can stay off them, well, I can."

"Desdemona, huh? Shakespeare. *Othello?*"

Jury nodded.

"Me and the wife, we saw that, must've been ten, twelve years ago. Went up to Stratford-upon-Avon—"

Jury sighed. You thought you'd got away from something, but it just came at you round another corner.

"—and that's what was playing. They got this Royal Theatre or something there."

"Royal Shakespeare Theatre. The RSC. Royal Shakespeare Company, they're called."

"That's it. It all comes back. It's this king, what a yob he was, kills his wife—that's Desdemona, right?—because he thinks she's been messing around. Stupid twit takes the word of—what's his name?"

"Iago."

"That's the fella. Iago. Bit of a wide lad, him. So all he has to do is flash this hankie in front of the king's face and tell him he found it in you-know-who's bed and Bob's-your-uncle, that's the end of Desdemona. If the coppers looked at evidence the way that yobbo did, we'd all of us be in the nick. She never had a chance, did Desdemona. Jealousy, that's what. 'Beware the green-eyed monster,' and so on." Trevor sighed, and the end of his cigarette glowed red as he dragged in. "Just goes to show."

The two of them sat in the dark, both pulling their collars up against the cold, both wishing it were sunup or sunset, a sight that might make the sitting here worth it, maybe Nature sympathizing for a change, saying, *You put up with a lot, you yobs, but look at this, now. Flash!*

Jury was smiling. "Just goes to show."

A NOTE ABOUT THE AUTHOR

Martha Grimes was born in Pittsburgh, Pennsylvania, grew up in Garrett County, Maryland, and now lives in Washington, D.C., and Santa Fe, New Mexico.

A NOTE ON THE TYPE

The text of this book has been set in Goudy Old Style, one of the more than one hundred typefaces designed by Frederic William Goudy (1865-1947). Although Goudy began his career as a bookkeeper, he was so inspired by the appearance of several newly published books from the Kelmscott Press that he devoted the remainder of his life to typography in an attempt to bring a better understanding of the movement led by William Morris to the printers of the United States.

Produced in 1914, Goudy Old Style reflects the absorption of a generation of designers with things "ancient." Its smooth, even color combined with its generous curves and ample cut marks it as one of Goudy's finest achievements.

Composed by North Market Street Graphics,
Lancaster, Pennsylvania

Printed and bound by R. R. Donnelley & Sons,
Harrisonburg, Virginia

Designed by Cassandra J. Pappas